THE NEVERBORN THIEF

A NOVEL

ANDREW NAJBERG

Published by Crystal Cove Press

Website: www.crystalcovepress.com

Crystal Cove Press is the young adult imprint of Crystal Lake Publishing.

Sign up to their newsletter today!

Dedicated to Gillian and Elliott

WHAT HAPPENED THAT NIGHT

To the eyes of one practiced at acting like an adult, nothing unordinary loomed in Connor's room. That observer would notice a pile of dirty clothes that never quite reached the hamper, a cluttered bookshelf which also featured an old video game console as a decoration, and the arms of several action figures jutting willy-nilly from underneath a lid that barely covered the box's contents. An unpaired sock hung from a dresser drawer; its partner lay balled up on the far side of the room. Old school papers on the desk were badly crinkled and bent like they'd been shoved into a backpack by the fistful.

In other words, it gave every appearance of a normal thirteen-year-old's room.

Of course, those who practiced acting as adults often missed things. Every little kid who woke in the dark to see what lived within the shadows under their desks and bureaus and behind their closet door learned the difficulty in convincing a practiced adult of the truth. Adults assigned importance to bills, responsibility, chores, a balanced diet, minimizing screen time, and getting places on time. They discarded what they deem unimportant or unlikely, brushing it into the dustpans of their minds. Connor's mother did this all the time.

When the shadows began to converge and coalesce into something altogether new and foreign to the boy's room, Connor, like a good kid practiced at being a proper teen, dreamed of a pizza night and fast food tacos, about playing video games and going to the movies—without a parent sitting three to five rows higher watching the back of their head in the dark. His blanket rose and fell, his nose occasionally whistled. Once in the midst of a rather gluttonous dream, his lips smacked as he imagined biting into a fistful of Christmas Tree cakes.

The shadows flowed from the room's corners, from inside boxes and under lampshades. They bulged and swelled, formed the shape of a tall, featureless figure whose head brushed the cord hanging from the ceiling fan. A cool breeze, not from the single vent under the window, swirled and rustled the crumpled papers on the desk. At the same time, a most peculiar sensation invaded the young teen's dream, intruding the way an alarm intrudes into the dream before one wakes to it.

Something Connor wouldn't want to lose was being pulled out, torn from deep inside him.

The pitch-black head slowly pivoted from side to side. The spots where one could only imagine eyes nested scanned the room until they fell on the sleeping child. A snarling smile spread across the shadow's face. Legs pulled free from the shadows from which they had grown and trekked the dark figure in a slow circle around the bed. Arms emerged, black hands spread into clenching fingers that reached out and slid underneath the bedsheets, probing at Connor's back, his neck, under his knees.

It was then that Connor woke to a feeling of intrusion. Like his insides were coated in thin, cold plastic slowly being peeled off and pulled out through his belly. His heart felt nestled in a frozen fog. His muscles were ice. He opened his eyes to the tall, black form hunched over him. Clouded with sleep, his eyes could not discern a single feature of the figure other than its looming height. The thing practically brushed the popcorn ceiling.

The scream erupted from Connor's mouth, mindless at first, then shaped into words.

The figure reared up with a snarl and leapt into the darkness in the corner by Connor's dresser. Connor lurched upright, the sheets falling as he twisted to follow the fleeing shape. The creature disappeared, or, perhaps more accurately, dissolved into the surrounding shadows. As it did, something black and bulky, nearly the size of Connor, writhed in its hands. It almost seemed to reach for Connor at the last second before it was altogether gone.

Connor hyperventilated and stared into the now-empty corner, trying to wrap his head around the fact that something had been there and now was not. This was in part due to the boy's age. Like any kid his age, he wanted to believe he already had the teen figured out, but what had happened did not mesh with his understanding of reality. Little did he know he would have struggled were he already as smart and learned as most practiced adults. Those practiced at being adults know how few words exist for what isn't there, and they know how poorly equipped they are to process the idea. However, if they had any familiarity with the profound feeling of absence welling in Connor's soul, they would have understood entirely when Connor covered his face in his hands and pulled his knees to his chest.

As a single hard sob shook his shoulders, footsteps thumped down the hall. The door flung open, and his mother entered in her rumpled pink bathrobe. As the practiced adult in the household, though she knew full well that practice did not always mean confidence, she saw immediately that the best course of action was to sit on the edge of the bed, lean forward, and wrap her arms around her son. Connor clenched harder, partially wanting to pretend he was asleep because he didn't want to admit he'd gotten so scared, but also because doing so almost made him feel like if he clenched hard enough, he would be able to hold onto whatever had left him. It was a feeling he knew too well. It was much the way he'd felt the night he learned his dad had died.

The way his body constricted a bit more, of course, only caused his mother to squeeze him a little tighter. Despite her embrace, that profound absence dulled any sense of comfort the hug brought. He didn't feel like he was being squeezed by Mom. Something was wrong. Her warmth didn't feel warm. Her squeezes only felt tight. Something had been stolen out of him. What it was, he didn't know, but the thought pained him.

"It's okay, sweetie," his mother whispered into his ear. "Just a bad dream."

"No," Connor said. Part of him wanted to agree it was a bad dream, but the coldness inside him was nothing he'd ever felt, and his voice came out firm with certainty. "No, someone was in my room."

His mother sat straighter and brushed his hair back with her hand.

"You just dreamed someone was. Hard to tell the difference between being awake and a dream when you're asleep."

"He was right beside the bed, leaning over me."

His mother leaned forward and kissed him on the forehead. He pulled away, something any practicing thirteen-year-old boy would probably do, but not only because he wanted to be tough. Her lips felt cold and clammy, like the skin of a fish without scales. Then she stood.

"And where did he go?" she said. She walked over to the window, parted the curtains, and gave it a tug. It didn't budge.

"Window's locked."

Frustration stirred in Connor. His mother was treating him like a little kid. This didn't call for the nightmare routine like when he'd been seven.

"Mom," he insisted.

She crouched to look under the bed.

"Nothing down here but toys."

"Mom, stop," he snapped.

She walked to the closet and said, "See, the closet is empty," even before she opened it.

Connor opened his mouth to object again, but, for a split second, when she reached for the knob, Connor was certain the hulking black thing was waiting behind the closet door. The words died on his tongue as the knob twisted.

His clothes hung in tidy rows along the narrow closet's twin bars—shirts on the right, pants on the left, just as always. Above them, shoeboxes, scuffed board games, and bins of forgotten toys rested in quiet disuse. Everything looked exactly as it should. And yet, something was wrong. If the air didn't feel too still, too heavy, Connor might've convinced himself it had all just been a dream.

His mother sat on the bed's edge and rested her hand on his forearm. Her skin felt like a doctor's latex glove.

"Maybe it wasn't a nightmare," she said. "Maybe it was what's called a night terror."

Connor wanted to tell her she was wrong, but the words "night terror" did stand out. He'd had a friend on his soccer team a couple of years back named Tommy who said he'd had night terrors. Tommy had said he'd wake up sometimes thinking a monstrous demon was in his room sucking the life out of him and that he couldn't move a muscle. It made sense. Certainly more sense than there being some sort of shadow person who disappeared into the corner.

His practice at being a teen kicked in, and he nodded, feeling a fool even though the feeling of absence still festered all throughout him. As Connor tried to convince himself the coldness was the lingering of a particularly awful dream, his mom brushed his hair off his forehead and crossed to the door. She paused at the switch and said, "Sleep well, dear." Then, she hit the lights.

Only moonlight lit the room once the door closed and his mother's footsteps retreated to her bedroom.

Connor pulled the blanket up over his shoulders, trying to prevent his eyes darting from shadow to shadow as if the shadow-thing would re-emerge any second. A strange tiredness swelled. He was sleepy. It was the middle of the night after all, but it was more like his mind receded from the world around him.

Dark as it was, the room grew dimmer.

A whisper came from the corner, from the gap between his desk and the wall where the moonlight never reached.

"She's gone."

"About blooming time," a second, louder voice said. "I thought she'd never leave."

Then, the darkness between the desk and the wall bulged the way a bag bulges when something too large is shoved into it. The shadow expanded like an inflating balloon until it suddenly pulled free from the darkness. Connor gasped and mouthed the words, "What the—?" His whole body burst into a cold sweat as a huge shadow person, round and bulbous in the middle, emerged into his bedroom and appeared to adjust some sort of belt. A second figure grew from the corner, tall and skinny as a rail. This one shook its foot, breaking from the passive shadows like they were gum it had stepped in.

Connor squinted at the intruders. When a regular person stands in darkness, you can still make out the faint color of their skin and clothes. These shadow-people were darker than darkness, and Connor couldn't see their features at all—no lines or contours, just outlines. How could they exist? Connor's mouth opened and closed again. Even a full-blown adult wouldn't have known what to say. Connor was still practicing being a teen, so the only thing that came to mind was words he was discouraged from saying.

"So, then, what happened?" the skinny one asked, planting its hands on its hips. The voice was crisp and polite, and Connor thought it sounded like a woman. Indeed, it sounded much like Ms. Harminger, last year's math teacher. He opened his mouth to call his mom again, but an image of these shadow-people clapping their shadowy hands over his mouth stopped him short.

"What, you a mute?" the bigger one said, this one distinctly male with a low-bellied voice and an English accent. "A right problem, that would be."

The skinny one placed one shadow hand on the bed, reaching forward with the other toward Connor's face. Connor flinched, expecting some sort of attack. The impulse to slap the hand away surged, but he restrained himself because he didn't know what these beings were capable of if they could simply appear in the room at will. Fortunately, the hand merely tilted Connor's head from side to side, though the boy couldn't feel the fingers on his skin.

"Doesn't seem hurt," the skinny one said.

"Seems useless to me," the fat one said. "Lot of good he'll do us."

The thin one pressed two fingers to Connor's wrist.

"Pulse is fast. Think the poor Flicker is scared."

"Hate these calls," the fat one said. "Flicker teens are the worst. Terrified of their own shadows, let alone us. Not that they'd admit it."

"Give him a second to calm down," the skinny one said. "We came out of his walls. As I hear it, they're scared by books where that kind of thing happens."

Connor's arm fell back to the bed, and the thin shadow straightened. Both shadows crossed their arms and stared at him. He took a deep breath and swallowed hard. After a moment that felt like he was chewing the air, he said, "Who are you?"

The fat shadow snuffled.

"Who are we?" He slapped the thinner shadow on the arm. "Little Flicker doesn't know who we are."

The thin shadow didn't join the laughter, but she nodded. She crouched, the shift making her seem less threatening.

"I am Sergeant Dandrich, and this is Officer Bell," she said. "We're Shadow Police."

Connor would have felt incredulous, but nothing about the situation was credulous. In fact, he wondered if he'd blown a blood vessel in his brain and was hallucinating. However, since that also meant he would be dead, he figured he would have to run with it either way. On the other hand, since he'd obviously heard of the regular police, the gist of who they were was obvious. Were they here because the shadow woke him?

He asked, "Why are you here?"

The fat one, Officer Bell, chortled, and Connor feared the noise would bring his mother. Part of Connor wanted that, and part of him wondered how his mother would react if she came into the room to find the two shadows standing over his bed. Perhaps more importantly, how would these two shadows react? Would they hurt her?

"Why are we here?" Officer Bell bellowed. "Gone through the trouble of crossing the boundary, and the little Flicker acts like he doesn't even know he's been robbed."

"I've been robbed," Connor interjected. He meant it as a question, but it came out more like a statement.

"Now we get to the matter," the thin one said.

"Bet you he was jerking us around," Officer Bell said, leaning forward over the edge of the bed. "You jerking us around, boy? Think it's funny to waste our time?"

"No, I—I would never—".

The thin shadow pulled Officer Bell back by the arm.

"The boy's obviously confused," Dandrich said.

"Then you deal with him," Officer Bell huffed. He became interested in the room itself, craning his head about, peering towards the corners, the closet, and the bottom of the bed. He picked up an old teddy bear from one of Connor's shelves and examined it as if he'd never seen a stuffed animal before.

Meanwhile, the thin shadow stepped over to the desk, a child-sized desk, one Connor had outgrown but his mother hadn't been able to replace. In fact, most of the things in his room were ones he'd outgrown, but his mother hadn't replaced them. Heat rose to his cheeks. No one but his mother had been in his room for quite some time. Why hadn't he gotten rid of all this stuff?

The thin shadow plucked the little wooden chair in one hand and carried it over to the bedside. She sat down on it, but because it was so low, her knees bent upward and her legs splayed out.

"You're going to wake my mother," Connor said.

"Pshhhhh," said Officer Bell.

Sergeant Dandrich said, "Casters don't notice us unless we want them to. Now, let's get to the bottom of this. Tell me what happened."

Connor swallowed again, mouth paper dry. His voice barely sounded like his own as he said, "Well, I don't really know. I was sound asleep, and then I started dreaming about…at least it seemed like a dream—"

"We don't need to know about your dream," Officer Bell interrupted.

Connor blushed as he said, "Well, I woke up because I felt like something was being stolen from me."

The thin shadow nodded, and Connor thought he could make out a tight-lipped frown within the otherwise uniform darkness of her face. Were there eyes too? A nose and nostrils? The more intently he looked at her, the more certain he was that he could make out all the normal features.

"Go on," the sergeant said.

"I saw something standing over me and pulling at me. This cold, awful feeling filled my whole body" Unconsciously, he drew his knees to his chest and shivered as he talked. "When it saw I was awake, it hissed and disappeared."

"I see," the sergeant said. "Get a good look at the thief? Man or woman? Size? Color?"

"Color?" Connor said. "Aren't all shadows the same?"

"Bah," Officer Bell roared. His voice brimmed with offense as he said, "All shadows the same? Do the sergeant and I look alike? Do I look the same as the shadow under your bed? The shadows in your closet? Are shadows in the moonlight the same as those cast by the sun?"

"No," Connor stammered. "I suppose not. But it was just a shadow."

"Just a shadow?" Bell said. "No such thing as 'just a shadow,' let alone just a shadow thief. How do you think we're supposed to find him without a single distinguishing feature? Load of help this one is. Bet he can't even describe his shadow."

"It looks like me," Connor muttered, voice shrinking.

The laughter from Bell this time was decidedly nasty, and Connor realized he was terrified of the officer. Both of them really, but Bell especially as he stepped forward and leaned sharply into Connor's face. "I oughta teach you what's what."

The anger in the sergeant's voice as she snapped "Enough!" at Officer Bell brought Connor back into focus.

"I didn't see him long," Connor said, his heart pounding. He didn't like feeling so scared. He wanted to be stronger, but his mind was struggling to keep up with everything. "It was a glimpse. I don't know much about shadows."

"It's okay," the sergeant said, placing a hand on Connor's. He knew she squeezed because he felt his fingers press together. "We're used to this. Officer Bell needs to learn patience when it comes to Flickers."

Connor clenched his jaw and tried to keep fear out of his voice as he asked, "Flickers?"

"People who reflect light rather than dark," the sergeant said. "Officer Bell forgets how different the Shadowed look to those used to bright things."

The sergeant stood and turned to Officer Bell.

"You find anything useful?" she asked. "Or you been huffing and puffing the whole time?"

Still holding the bear, Officer Bell stiffened. "No trace that a shadow's been messing with any of the things about here. Thief wasn't interested in the room's shadows, only the boy."

The sergeant leaned forward, reaching past Connor to the darkness above the bed sheets and pillow. Gingerly, she lifted something and examined it. It took Connor a moment to realize she was holding a piece of his shadow.

"Looks like he only got half," the sergeant said. "The left side."

"Half my shadow?" Connor asked.

"That's the good news," the sergeant said. "And the bad."

"What do you mean?" How could something steal half his shadow? Wasn't it a part of him? When neither officer answered, Connor asked again, "But what does that mean?"

"*Paperwork*," Officer Bell grumbled.

The sergeant waved a dismissive hand at Officer Bell. "It's good news, because if he'd gotten the whole thing, there'd be almost nothing to do about it. The bad news is we have little time to find the missing half, and we have little to go on."

"What happens if you don't find it?" Connor asked.

Sergeant Dandrich sat on the edge of Connor's bed. "Half a shadow can't survive by itself. What is left will slowly slip away through the tear until there is nothing."

"What happens then?" Connor asked.

"You don't want to know," the sergeant said. "And it's not our job to explain. We need to get to work if there's any hope of catching the thief in time."

"But I'm scared," Connor said. "Can the thief come back? What if they come back?

Sergeant Dandrich reached, and Connor felt his hair smooth against the side of his head. It would have been comforting if he could feel the touch. "They won't risk it. They'll know we've been here. They'll lay low or target someone who hasn't been flagged. We'll send someone to speak to you in daylight when your shadow is a little stronger."

The form of her shadow waivered, then was gone like a cloud of breath. Officer Bell turned to Connor. A strange smile spread across his face. The officer held up the teddy bear and asked, "Do you need this?"

Was the bear evidence? Had the thief touched it or something? Something about the officer's demeanor said otherwise. He seemed embarrassed to be asking. Unsure what to say, Connor said, "Do you?"

"Well, no," Officer Bell said, stammering a bit. "Not specifically, just took to mind maybe you'd outgrown... never mind."

Officer Bell tossed the bear onto the floor and disappeared. Connor found himself again sitting alone in the darkness of his room, full of fear and confusion. As he tried to process everything, his head swam. He found himself lying down and falling into a black sleep.

THE SALESMAN AND HIS BOY

Connor's head hurt as he rolled from his back to his side. His muscles and joints ached, and his stomach rumbled with nausea. He flopped an arm across his clammy forehead to shield his throbbing eyes from the morning light. A nasty taste filled his mouth, like he'd eaten garlicky fish before bed and hadn't brushed his teeth. He smacked his teeth with a grimace.

When his mom entered to wake him, she immediately knew he was sick. She'd barely stepped into his room when she sighed. "Guess someone's not going to school today." His mom sat on the side of his bed, placed a hand to his forehead, and muttered, "Definitely a fever."

After asking how he felt, his mom left to make his breakfast. Lying back down, Connor wondered if the prior night had been some fever dream. If Connor hadn't felt miserable, he'd have laughed at himself. Shadow thieves and Shadow Police? By the time his mother returned carrying a tray with fold-out legs, the memory of the nightmare already faded. He focused on the blueberry muffin, bowl of cereal, and glass of orange juice. It was his favorite part about being sick. Normally, he got up and fixed his breakfast by grabbing a pop tart or a bowl of cereal, but virtually all people are united in their love for breakfast in bed, followed by a lazy day. Once, he'd even pretended to be sick and poured fake throw up into the toilet so he could get exactly that.

After eating, Connor pulled on a pair of jeans, socks, and a T-shirt before shuffling to the bathroom to brush his teeth and wash his face. As he stepped up to the mirror, his reflection made him pause. His entire face struck him as looking heavy except for his eyes, which looked a little hollow. Sweat matted his unkempt and curly dark hair. He hadn't realized he'd been perspiring. Sometimes he wondered how his mother knew he was sick, but not this morning.

Freshened up, he made his way to the couch where he intended to station himself for the morning. As he curled up in the corner with the best view of the TV under a throw blanket, he heard his mother on the phone in the kitchen explain to the school he was sick. He couldn't see her, but he pictured her tethered to the wall by the coils of the phone cord. The parents of all the kids at school and even most of the kids themselves used smartphones, while his mother didn't even own a portable. It embarrassed him that he couldn't even talk in his room whenever he got a call.

Connor turned on the TV and surfed through the streaming app on the player in search of the right show while his mother whisked to his room to retrieve his tray and straighten his bed. He had found nothing by the time a knock came from the front door.

Strange, Connor thought. It wasn't even eight o'clock.

The knock came louder. His mother probably couldn't hear from his room. Humphing about someone interrupting his sick lounging, Connor wrapped his blanket around his shoulders and trudged to the foyer. There, he peeked through the little window beside the door. A man in a beige suit and hat stood with a suitcase beside his feet. On the other side of him stood a boy who looked a year or two younger than Connor.

Connor hesitated. Should he unlock the door or fetch his mom? The man might have the wrong house, and he had a kid with him.

What if he needed help? It wouldn't be right to turn away someone with a kid. Connor bit his lip and turned the bolt.

"Godly morning to you, young man," the man said with a tip of his hat. "Is this the Brighton residence? Is your mother home?"

"It is," Connor said. "And she is."

"Well then, fantastic," the man said, his voice jovial like he meant it really was fantastic. Connor couldn't help feeling uncomfortable with his excitement. It was too early to be so excited. Since his father's death, they'd not had many visitors other than in the weeks following the funeral, and they'd all been sad and somber or formal and business-like.

It was then that Connor took a good look at the boy. He wore beige pants matching the man's, but instead of a jacket and tie, he wore a white dress shirt buttoned all the way to the top. Connor tugged at his collar. He hated formal shirts. The boy didn't look at Connor or at the man but gazed straight ahead as if looking through the house rather than inside it. His face was as pale as if he'd never gotten sun. Odd since Connor guessed the man to be some sort of door-to-door salesman. As a light breeze blew by, the boy's hair didn't seem to move.

The man clasped his hands behind his back, rocked on his heels, and said, "If you would get her, please, I'd be much obliged."

Connor started, realizing he'd just been standing there. He nodded, figuring himself out of it from being sick, dropped the blanket in a heap by the shoes, and wandered back to his room. A moment later, Connor returned with his mother in her pink robe. The man still stood in the open doorway, which Connor hadn't thought to close. What if the man had darted in and stolen something? Connor knew he needed to think of such things. His mother always scolded him for not thinking ahead.

When his mother stepped to the door, still tying her bathrobe around herself, the man said, "My name is Mr. James Mathis, and this is my son."

The boy raised his head to look Connor's mother in the face, but he neither smiled nor nodded. Instead, he let his gaze fall back to where it had been. What a strange kid, Connor thought.

After introducing herself, his mother asked, "What can I do for you?"

"It's not what you can do for me," Mr. Mathis said, a strong southern accent entering his voice, "but what I can do for you? Are you familiar with the word of our Lord and Savior, Jesus Christ? Because I have a whole suitcase full of it for only $19.99 each in beautiful, gold embossed hardcover.”

Connor's mother shook her head and reached for the door to close it as she said she wasn't interested. The man reached out with the flat of his palm and prevented the door from closing.

“Oh, but I think you might be,” Mr. Mathis said. “I'm not just any door-to-door Bible thumper. You were referred to me by a Miss Claire Underwood.”

Connor knew the name. It was his friend Tommy's mom. He and Tommy used to play soccer in the backyard.

“I'm sorry, but I'm not religious,” his mother said.

“I understand, ma'am,” the man said. “But Miss Underwood said you are still recovering from a personal loss that has left you in a difficult situation.”

A bit of irritation fluttered on his mother's face.

“Well, I'm not sure how that's any of yours or her—”

“Business,” the man interrupted with a perfunctory nod. “Yes, and normally, I'd agree.”

Mr. Mathis lifted his suitcase and patted it on the side twice.

“But this isn't only full of Bibles and the love of the Lord,” he said. “No, indeed. My organization also offers a wide variety of special assistance programs for people in situations like yours. Help folks get back on their feet and running. They're free of charge, and you wouldn't have to join a church or speak a word about God. If you could give me a few minutes of your time ...”

His mother pursed her lips, tugging at the sleeves of her robe.

“It's awfully early, and my son is sick...” she started.

“Won't be a problem at all,” Mr. Mathis said. “I'm sure my son can keep your boy entertained while we talk. I can't guarantee you'll accept our aid, but I guarantee our programs can make your life a whole lot easier with no obligation from you.”

Connor looked at the pale boy, but the boy showed no response. Connor suspected the boy would do little entertaining.

“But Mom,” Connor said. “What if I get him sick?”

The strangest look passed over his mother’s face. It was as if she heard his words and consciously chose not to at the same time.

"He'll be fine," Mr. Mathis said. "He's got a robust immune system."

The wholesale acceptance on his mom's face dumbfounded Connor as she said, "No doubt—it's a bit silly to worry about such small things."

And then, she motioned the visitors into the foyer. Connor wanted to protest, but he didn't know if it would do any good. As the man took off his hat and laid it on the table by the door, Connor's mom asked him to show the boy his room.

"Couldn't we watch TV?" Connor asked. "Or play video games?"

His mom shook her head sharply. "I'm sure you'll sit on the couch all day once I leave for work. Which is fine because you're not feeling well, but it can wait for a little while."

"But Mom—"

"Now, Connor," his mom said sharply.

Connor pressed his lips together, confused by how determined his mom was. With a sigh, he pointed the kid toward the hall. He didn't feel up to it, but he resolved to try to be a good host.

When the pale boy—he still hadn't given his name, and his father hadn't called him anything other than "my son"—entered Connor's room, he immediately sat cross-legged on the rug in the middle of the room with his back to the window. He folded his hands over his stomach and stared at the floor as if looking for something. A strange, hungry look came upon the boy's face. Connor sensed something was missing from the room, but he couldn't quite put his finger on it. The boy's silence, however, made Connor nervous. He figured he was going to have to be the one to talk.

Trying to act nonchalant, Connor said, "Well, this is my room."

"It is?" the boy said, not lifting his eyes.

"Yeah?" Connor asked, a bit surprised by the boy's lack of attention. Making another attempt, he pointed to his shelves. "Got a few nerf guns, a deck of cards. Some action figures. A couple boxes of Legos. More in the closet."

The boy didn't look up.

"I've got some posters," Connor said, half-heartedly gesturing to the fantasy and sci-fi posters up on nearly every wall. "I think they're pretty cool."

"Looks like a room," the boy said, with hardly a glance around.

"Yeah, but it's mine," Connor said.

"Does it being yours alter its importance?"

Connor opened his mouth to answer, but then closed it because he wasn't sure he understood the question.

"Do you like board games? I have a few. They were mostly my dad's, but they can be fun. Life, Monopoly, Battleship, and Sorry."

The boy's forehead creased like he was trying to remember something. He shrugged.

"Really? You don't know Monopoly?" Connor said. He couldn't imagine someone never playing Monopoly.

"I don't play games," the boy said.

"Why not?"

"I don't play."

Connor faltered again. Did the kid mean he was too old to play? He certainly looked younger—and though Connor sometimes pretended he was too cool to play, he still enjoyed playing—especially games. When Connor was eleven, he hadn't thought that way at all. It seemed like the boy would play all the time with his dad bringing him to different houses and sending him off to play with the kids who lived there. Maybe he was having a bad day?

"Are you… depressed or something?" Connor asked.

"No," the boy said, still staring at the carpet. "I used to feel sad, but not anymore."

"Okay, so we can sit here and do nothing, but we don't have to be bored," Connor said.

The strange boy considered this a moment.

"Ever had a really big dream you tried really hard to remember, but the more you tried the more you forgot?"

Connor didn't know how to answer. Everyone forgot their dreams, sometimes even when they try really hard to remember them. That was how dreams were. Moreover, he wasn't feeling great, so he really didn't have this kind of conversation in him. If he'd been up to it, he'd be in school.

"Well," Connor said. "How about we play one of the games anyway, to pass the time? Life's pretty chill, and it's kind of funny to dump eight kids into a station wagon. Plus, practically the only rule is 'spin to move'."

"Okay," the boy said, but he didn't seem interested. In fact, he sounded as if he wouldn't be interested in anything Connor said. Still, Connor reached under his bed and fumbled out the white game box. The pale boy squinted at the box as Connor pulled off the lid.

Connor set up the game board between them, holding up the pieces, money, and cards, explaining each as he went. As he explained the insurance and the betting strip, he realized maybe there were more rules than he'd really thought, but it was too late to stop now. The boy seemed to listen but gave no sign as to whether or not he understood. Finally, Connor pointed to the spinner and said, "You go first."

The boy stared at the spinner as if it were a UFO, something Connor admitted it did resemble.

"What's the point?" the boy asked.

"To see how many spaces you move, duh," Connor said, regretting being mean as the last word left his mouth.

"But what's the point of the game?" the boy asked.

"To get more money than me," Connor said.

"But I don't want more money than you," the boy said.

"That's the point of the game," Connor said. "To win at Life."

"That's not how you win at life," the boy said.

Yet again, Connor was at a loss. Of course, that was how you won at Life. Not only was it in the rules of the game, but his mother was constantly preoccupied with money, talking to herself about the bills and the mortgages when she thought Connor wasn't listening. Most of the problems they had would be solved if they had a little more money.

Connor considered the fact the boy's father was a bible salesman. His mother was not religious, at least not since the accident, but Connor's grandfather had taken them both to church every Sunday when he was alive. Connor remembered long sermons about the dangers of money and what the priest called "*material possessions.*" Maybe this boy believed the same. Some kids in school didn't drink cola or iced tea.

"Are you religious?" Connor asked.

"I don't think I'm able to be," the boy said.

Connor placed his hands on his hips and said, "Well, what do you want to do?"

"I can't," the boy said.

"You can't what?" Connor asked. "What the heck do you want to do?"

"I want to get my shadow back," the boy said.

Connor froze. His whole body turned cold. Like the night before, he felt as if nothing in the world could warm him. He realized what the boy was looking for as he stared intently at the floor. The boy had no shadow. This boy was who the Shadow Police had sent.

Connor softened his voice as he asked, "Why can't you get your shadow back?"

A tear ran out of the boy's eyes as he blinked, shining on his pale skin.

"Because it's gone," the boy said. "It's gone forever."

"But—" Connor started, before the boy cut him off.

"It's gone!" he snapped, his face snarling. Then, the emotionless expression returned. "It's gone. I was too late, and so they asked me to bring my father here so I could talk to you about how to find yours before it's gone, too."

Connor jumped to his feet, restless.

"Who are you?" Connor asked.

"I'm Shadowless," the boy said. "I had a name once. My father calls me by it occasionally, but I can't hear him when he does. I think he's learned that I don't notice. So, he calls me 'son,' though it doesn't mean much to me anymore, either. Soon, I don't think I'll hear him talk to me at all."

"That's terrible," Connor said. His mother was sad and worried all the time, but she was an adult. Connor couldn't help but feel it was just how adults were, even though he knew it wasn't completely true. It pained Connor to see a kid so miserable.

"It's okay," the boy said. "I have no choice but to accept it. But you—"

"Is the same thing going to happen to me, too?"

"Not if you find the rest of your shadow," the boy said.

"But what can I do?" Connor said. "I hardly thought about my shadow before last night."

A grimness fell over the shadowless boy and the room seemed to grow a little darker as he said, "You must go to the Shadowlands and find the thief."

"The Shadowlands?" Connor asked. "How long do I have?"

"The Shadowlands are where shadows without bodies live," the boy said. "And how long is different for everybody. It could be days. It could be weeks. I had three days."

"But how do I get to the Shadowlands?" Connor asked. "My mother rides the bus, and I don't even have a bike."

The boy laughed softly, but it was like no laugh Connor had ever heard. The laugh seemed thin, like something he thought he heard but only imagined, and there was no humor in it.

"You can go right now," the boy said. "From this room. Getting there's easy if your shadow is damaged."

Connor straightened his shoulders and lifted his head high. He wanted to be like the characters in the movies he'd seen who went on dangerous adventures with little more than their hat and a confident chuckle.

"What do I have to do?" Connor said.

"Go into your closet and close the door," the boy said.

Connor rolled his eyes. "Really?"

"Do it," the boy said.

With a shrug, Connor strode into the closet, and closed the door. Surrounded by darkness, his clothes pressing in on both sides, the dangling chain of the exposed bulb brushing against his face, Connor said, "Okay, now what?"

"Reach up and unscrew the light," the boy said, his voice muffled by the door. "Then close your eyes and pull the chain like you're turning the light on."

Connor snickered.

"You've got to be joking," Connor said.

"I don't joke," the boy said.

"If it's so easy, why don't people do it all the time?" Connor asked.

"Most people have a whole shadow," the boy said. "Someone from the World of Light must be incomplete to cross the boundary from light to dark."

Connor looked up at the bulb. No way it would work. Still, his room had been invaded by shadows emerging from the walls, so who knew what on earth was actually possible. No matter what, the boy knew about shadow people and the theft, so it was worth a try. He reached for the light bulb, standing tiptoe on one of his toy boxes to close his fingers around it. After a couple of fumbling attempts, the bulb came loose in the palm of his hand. Trying not to laugh, Connor closed his eyes and gave the chain a swift jerk.

THE IRON DESERT

When Connor opened his eyes and lowered himself to the floor, nothing had changed.. He still stood in the dark closet, his hanging pants brushing against his left arm, his shirts against his right. He hadn't expected to teleport to a booming shadow metropolis, nor to find purple-glowing forests teeming with talking mushrooms from a dark fairy tale. The truth was, he didn't know what he had expected—if he expected anything at all. Perhaps a whooshing sound and a strong wind like being swept up by a tornado. Or, maybe a blurring effect, like in the movies.

Instead, he stood in the same spot, surrounded by the familiar smell of laundry detergent and dryer sheets. It was every bit as cramped as ever. Connor even spread the clothes on the hanger bar, checking to make sure the walls were still there. He had read The Lion, the Witch, and the Wardrobe in school after all.

What he found were walls, plaster walls to be exact, one with the same jagged crack from top to bottom that had been there as long as he remembered. Maybe the crack would widen to a fissure and some sort of purple light would beam out, followed by scaly and spiny tentacles?

That did not happen.

Connor ran a sheepish hand through his hair. The pale boy had fooled him, and he'd let it happen like an idiot. Obviously, he was sick and not thinking straight. He wasn't that easy to fool. Pulling the cord on an unscrewed bulb in a closet to travel to the Shadowlands? Connor couldn't believe he fell for it. Every boy knew how to play Monopoly and Life. Every boy remembered his name… though he did know about the Shadowlands. If the theft had been some sort of fever dream, how would the boy know it? Maybe, Connor thought, he had been talking to himself and didn't realize it. Either way, he would teach that kid a lesson about playing tricks on the sick.

There was certainly no reason to keep standing in his closet. He reached for the knob.

When he opened his door, he gasped.

Before him stood a great, broad desert covered in reddish-brown sand. The sky was the deep brown of brackish water, except high up near a great red, smoldering coal half lost behind the mucky clouds. On the other side of the sky hovered the moon, a pale pearl giving about the same light as a giant ping-pong ball. All along the horizon rose black mountains. Whether they were black or poorly lit, Connor could not tell.

A harsh wind blew streaks of sand into dust devils dancing into the darkness over clusters of black stone. Farther ahead, two lanterns on stout poles a few feet apart flickered a flame the color of a lit jack-o'-lantern. Between the lantern poles ran a road paved with black stones, and on the far side, a sign faced away from Connor.

Connor stepped out of the closet. The ground under his feet didn't give the way a sandy beach would. Rather, his foot sank about half an inch before clanking against metal. Crouching, Connor scooped a bit of the sand into his palm and discovered it wasn't sand, but flakes of rust. A round cluster of the black stone also rested a couple of feet away. He leaned closer. Its surface was contoured with little bulges and crevices reminiscent of pictures he'd seen of coral—or a brain.

Connor reached out to touch the stone, but froze right before his fingers touched it. Little black specks skittering around in and out of the groves like fleas.

Connor brushed the rust off his palms and turned around. His closet still stood there with the door open, but the rest of his house was gone. Instead of the familiar walls of his bedroom on either side, there stood a rickety shack with a boxed, wooden roof and cracked stone walls. Beyond, the same empty desert stretched out, broken only by more of the black coral rocks and an occasional distant pillar resembling the Egyptian obelisks he'd learned about on a school trip to the museum. Where on Earth was he? Was he still on Earth? Connor ducked back into his closet and closed it. Heart pounding, he jerked the light chain and flung the door back open.

The metal desert was still there. Had he done something wrong? He still held the lightbulb, so he screwed the bulb back in, closed the door, and pulled the chain.

When he opened the door, nothing had changed.

Connor hadn't asked the boy how to get back. It had all sounded so stupid, who would have thought to ask? His mother always nagged him to think before acting. Why couldn't he have listened this one time?

Faint voices arose outside. Connor pressed himself against the hanging shirts. Someone was coming. Were they dangerous? Could they tell him how to get home? Should he hide? Dropping to all fours, Connor crept to the door and peeked towards the road. The voices grew louder, and he made out two shapes approaching.

The two figures were shadow people as indistinct as the Shadow Police had been in his bedroom. As they stepped into the little bubble of light the lanterns provided, the illumination didn't reveal their features. They were both somewhat short, and neither were fat nor skinny, but none of the cues he might use to judge people were discernible. He couldn't see a sweet smile or rosy cheeks or kindly lined eyes. He couldn't even make out their voices well enough to guess their tone. They could have been talking about eating children as easily as about gardening.

This place was strange and dangerous, Connor thought. His parents had taught him things that had once sounded like rules of life: eat a nutritious breakfast, brush your teeth, and don't talk to strangers.

Things that seemed like they made sense every day. Here, was there such a thing as breakfast? Where would cereal come from if the ground was metal and rust? What if the shadow people ate metal and rust or those strange coral rocks? He couldn't even tell if these shadow people had teeth to brush. With no one else around, nothing stopped them from kidnapping him or beating him up.

At the same time, if he didn't talk to strangers, he had no way to figure out how to get home or to find his shadow. He'd get nothing without taking risks—and he couldn't hide in his closet scared. So, as the two figures passed beneath the lanterns, Connor leaned out of the closet and said in a timid but polite voice, "Excuse me."

Neither figure paid the slightest notice.

Connor scrambled to his feet and took several steps out of the doorway.

"Excuse me," he said again, a little louder this time.

Again, they ignored him.

This time, Connor felt a little offended, so he clapped his hands sharply and snapped, "Hey!"

One shadow seemed to look his way. Its voice was low and gravelly, almost like a growl, as it said, "What's it to ya?"

Connor cocked his head, a bit confused. Wasn't that something people said when asked a question they didn't care to be bothered with? He hadn't asked a question at all. Still, Connor didn't want to waste the opportunity. "Can you help me?" he said.

"Pssht," said the first shadow, still walking. The other reached out and took the arm of the first, and both of them stopped. Connor felt momentary relief.

"Hey," the second shadow said. "It's a flicker."

The first shadow laughed a nasal laugh and slapped the other shadow on the back. "Well, then by all means," it growled, stepping towards Connor. "You got some questions, Half-Caster?" There was venom in both shadows' tones. They did not think him being a 'half-caster' or a 'flicker' was a good thing. The two shadows strode towards Connor, and he stepped back towards the closet. However, he doubted the racks of clothes—or even the door—would protect him.

The shadows split as they approached. One stepped left, the other right. When they came to a stop, he had to turn from one to face the other. Up close, they wore layers of tattered clothes, practically rags. Their facial features were murky, but Connor could almost make out toothy, lipless smiles, sharp cheeks, and hollow eyes.

The boy faced towards the road, trying to keep an eye on both of them at once. Connor hoped they only seemed scary and stammered, "W-w-where am I?"

"Aww, little Flicker's scared," said the second shadow.

"Scared nothing. Sounds ignorant," said the gravelly-voiced shadow. The shadow thrust its hands out, shoving Connor towards the other. "You ignorant, Half-Caster?"

"No," Connor said. "I need to know where I am."

"Those sound the same to me," said the first shadow. "Our place ain't got no place for those who don't know theirs."

Anger welled in Connor like a hot ball of fire in his chest. He didn't understand why they were being so mean, but if he let them bully him, they'd know he was at their mercy.

"I need the rest of my shadow," Connor said.

"At least you got a body," the first said.

"Not enough for ya to cast half a shadow?" the second snapped, shoving Connor with both palms. Connor turned and tried to shove the shadow now in front of him away, but that shadow caught him by the biceps and pushed him back even harder than before, saying, "Don't you know only shadows belong in the Shadowlands?"

Connor stumbled, his arms pinwheeling. The second shadow sidestepped, and Connor's foot caught on one of the coral stones. He pitched forward, crashing chest-first in a billow of rust. The impact drove the air from his lungs and jolted him something awful. Connor pushed onto his back and scooted himself backward.

"Leave me alone," he said. He wanted to sound tough, but the pain from hitting the ground choked the strength from his voice.

"We'll leave you alone," one of them said, though Connor was too panicked to tell which one. "After we've taught you some respect."

Connor forced himself to his feet, turned away from his closet and the road, and took off at a full run. He curved into the empty desert expanse, chased by cackling laughter. Connor ran and ran, thinking only of escape. His feet smacked against the metal under the rust. Clouds of red flakes kicked up from each step. His eyes burned as flecks worked under his eyelids. They scratched his throat as he breathed in, flooding his mouth with the taste of metal. His vision tunneled until all he could see was what loomed directly ahead.

He had no idea how long he ran. When his body refused to move any further, he stumbled to a stop and slapped his hands down onto his knees. His chest heaved. The deep breaths burned until a fit of ragged coughs wracked him.

When his heart slowed, and the pulsing in his vision faded, he straightened. He couldn't see any sign of the black road, the lanterns, or his closet. He could hardly see anything at all. His eyes worked and it wasn't too dark, but there was little to see. It was like being underwater, where distance becomes difficult to estimate without anything to provide scale. He could still see the dim, red smolder of the sun in the sky and the black mountain ridges on the horizon. Otherwise, the surrounding desert was nearly empty, save for a couple more stone obelisks and scattered clusters of coral stone.

Though Connor knew he'd gone too far for the obelisk to be one he'd seen by his closet, they provided him a place to start. Any place had to be better than no place at all. So, he started towards the one closest to him.

His feet still hurt from the run, so he walked slowly. When rust stained his socks to the neck, Connor realized he wasn't wearing shoes. How could he have forgotten something so simple? There were a couple of old pairs in boxes on the floor of his closet. Putting them on should have been the first thing he did. He couldn't have known he'd be attacked, especially so quickly, but he needed to think things out and prepare for anything.

To keep himself calm, he fixed his eyes on the obelisk ahead. How far was it? A hundred feet? A thousand? It was so hard to tell. If it was a thousand feet tall, it could be miles away.

A deep chill settled into Connor, and his T-shirt did little to protect him. Had he felt so cold when he'd first arrived? The closet had sheltered him from the wind and might have held a little of the warmth of his house. Here, the wind gusted strong and unobstructed, jerking up rust clouds. The dim sun didn't help. Again, Connor wanted to kick himself. There were a couple of decent coats in his closet, not to mention plenty of long-sleeved shirts. Heck, he could have packed one of his old backpacks.

Connor also knew regretting his mistakes wouldn't help. He had to focus on what was ahead. He narrowed his mind to his feet and moved them one step after another. The immensity of the surrounding space dropped away, and he felt a little warmer as his circulation increased.

Before he knew it, he stood at the base of the obelisk, and though he didn't know what to do next, he silently cheered at accomplishing a small goal.

One lap down, he thought. Then, unbidden: but how many more to go?

With a puff of his lips, Connor looked up at the obelisk. It rose about thirty feet like a giant finger sticking out of the desert. Bands of engraved images alternated with bands of engraved symbols all the way up its height.

Connor reached out and traced a figure along the edges of a symbol shaped like an x with a circle around the crux. As his finger touched the worn stone, a strange vibration pulsed out of the pillar and into his arm. The edges of his mind trembled with indistinct flickers of deep purple and reds. A vague image like a half-forgotten and distant memory formed, a tall, shadowy form in crown and cloak looking down from a high perch. Below a mass of shadows cheering or shrieking—and underneath it all, a cold rhythmic voice. It was almost as if he could hear a whisper in the stone's heart, and it tugged at something deep inside him. He tried to concentrate on it, to coax his mind to isolate the phantom sound, as if it would whisper to him the secrets within the monument.

However, another strange feeling pulled his mind away. He withdrew his hand as a prickling rose underneath his skin from more than the cold. He scratched at the back of his neck as if something had landed there. He felt the same thing on his lower back.

He suddenly felt as if he weren't wearing any clothes.

Specifically, he felt like he did when he forgot to get a clean towel before his bath and had to dart across the hallway to the linen closet. Like he was being watched.

He couldn't tell where it was coming from, so he listened. The only thing he heard was wind.

He peered into the desert. The only thing he saw were ribbons of rust kicked up in the drafts.

He tried to sniff the air, but everything smelled of metal.

Almost like blood.

He grew certain he wasn't merely being watched: he was being watched by multiple somethings. Their eyes were all over him, in front and behind. They were moving around him in a circle, even if he couldn't see them. Had the two shadows followed? Were they planning to attack him here, out in the desert, far from the road and the lanterns and the closet and anyone who could help him? Everything in him wanted to run. But where? There was no shelter anywhere he could see. He instinctively backed against the obelisk.

A low growl carried on the next rush of wind. Something awful about the sound ground straight into his bones, and a fear more powerful than Connor had ever felt spread through him. The growl came straight out of his nightmares with a vicious edge. His muscles quivered. His mind filled with images of all sorts of monsters with long slashing claws and streams of drool pouring from between razor-sharp teeth, things worse than from any horror movie he'd watched while his mother was at work.

Another growl came from Connor's right, long and sustained. Connor could hear it moving in its deliberate circle, but all he could see was another cloud of rust. How close was it? How much time did he have? Where would the first blow land? Sweat poured down his forehead, and he looked left and right and turned as fast as he could. Why couldn't he see anything? There was nowhere for something to hide! He closed his eyes. His heart beat so hard it was like it was trying to claw its way up his throat. His mind conjured images from every horror movie he'd ever seen. Claws hacking. Teeth jabbing. A tentacle jerking his legs out from under him. Would there be poison? Would they lay eggs inside him? His breath came hard, trying to keep up with his heart.

A fresh wind pulled the sweat off his skin.

Something seemed to suck out of the air in its wake. His lungs felt like they refused to fill.

He sensed something gather itself to strike.

His eyes opened wide as a horrific yowl erupted. A black shape launched through the air towards him. Even as Connor opened his mouth to scream, a dark figure swinging a long stick burst between him and the attack. The blow struck the attacker out of the air. The bulky shadow of an animal tumbled across the ground, skidding to a stop on its feet. Rust exploded around it like it was a dirt bike grinding still after a jump. It crouched like a panther, poised and hissing fiercely. Connor's savior sidestepped, pivoting into a second strike as another beast leapt from the darkness. The dark figure drove the shadow back with a blurring staff.

The first creature seemed about to leap at the back of the fighter, and Connor yelled, "Behind you!"

The stranger pivoted, staff ready, but the first creature fell into a slinking retreat. The man advanced, spinning the staff in front of him, swinging the ends down in lashing strikes and thunking the metal ground. With a snarling hiss, the retreating animal turned and bolted off, disappearing into the cloud of rust its huge paws kicked up. A second yowl sounded as the other creature bolted after its companion in a cloud of its own. The sense of menace fled from the air with it.

For several moments, Connor stood dead still except for the rapid rise and fall of his chest. His heart pounded so hard his vision blurred. The man watched the vanishing shapes, his staff held out in both hands in a ready position. His fingers clenched the weapon hard.

Finally, the stranger seemed satisfied the fight was over. His whole body seemed to deflate, and he lowered the staff to his side. Then, he planted the weapon's tip and leaned heavily against it with a long sigh. After a few more seconds of peering into the desert darkness, the figure turned towards Connor.

The figure wasn't a shadow; he wore a heavy, black cloak with a hood he pulled down to reveal a mop of pepper-gray hair. Under the cloak, his clothes were simple cloth trousers and a shirt, but the rust stains saturating them made them appear tattered like the travelers from the movies about great adventurers. Was this man a great adventurer? He'd beaten back the creatures. No matter what, Connor couldn't imagine the man would be worse than the shadows outside the closet — not after he'd saved his life.

The man spoke in a clipped and hard tone, his mouth a sharp, thin line as he spoke.

"What kind of fool are you?"

"I don't know," Connor said, dropping his eyes. Maybe this man wasn't any better.

"Don't you know where you are?" the man said.

"In the Shadowlands," Connor said. "In my closet. I don't know."

The man scanned the area as if to make sure the creatures hadn't come back. When he looked back at Connor, there was sympathy in the lines of his face.

"A lucky fool is what you are," he said. "The Iron Desert isn't a place for anyone who doesn't know their what from their why."

Connor felt his face redden.

"How'd you find me?" Connor asked.

"Came down the Nightglass Road," the man said. "Looked like you got a less-than-kind welcome when you got here. I assume that rinky closet is yours?"

"My closet isn't rinky," Connor snapped, immediately regretting it. He added in a sheepish voice, "And if it is, it's all I got."

The stranger smiled slightly.

"Well, at least you've got some attitude. Need it here. Sometimes that's all you have."

Connor tried to return the smile, but his lips quivered. The man shrugged and turned to the obelisk. He touched his thumb to his lips and then to his chest and gave a half-bow before turning back to face Connor.

Connor expected the man to say something, but the man did something that filled Connor with a horror even the creatures hadn't been able to generate. He began walking away.

"Wait!"

The man looked back over his shoulder.

"What's it to you?" he said.

Again, Connor was a bit thrown by the phrase. He wondered if maybe it was simply something people around here said.

"Can you take me back to my closet?"

The man shrugged.

"You've got legs," he said, and continued on.

THE NIGHTGLASS ROAD

The man walked a long-legged pace, not sparing a glance back. Connor jogged to keep up. His arms and legs grew cold as the chill in the air saturated his clothes, and his teeth chattered. He'd never liked being cold. If the pale boy hadn't come, Connor thought, he'd still be lounging on the couch, wrapped in warm blankets. He could have shuffled to the kitchen and made himself a snack and some hot chocolate or something. His stomach rumbled at the thought, but he tried to ignore it since he didn't have any food on him. The fast they could get back to the closet the better.

Nonetheless, Connor wanted the man to stop and talk. He'd saved Connor after all, so he must be nicer than the two shadows by the road. It wasn't like getting back to the closet meant Connor would be going home, and he was still basically a kid in a place he knew almost nothing about. Could he learn whether someone was trustworthy within a question or two? It wasn't like he could bluntly ask him… or give him something like the Trolley problem.

"My name is—" he began.

"Shush!" the man hissed, freezing.

Connor's heart lurched. Had the creatures come back? The man glared at Connor.

"What did I do?" Connor asked.

"Never reveal your real name," the man said. "Name's from the Light have power here."

"S-sorry," he stammered. "I-I didn't know."

"Of course, you didn't," the man snapped. Then, his voice eased as he said, "The first thing to know about the Shadowlands is you know nothing."

Connor cocked his head. Of course, he knew things. He knew all kinds of cool stuff about space from that series of animated YouTube videos about science. He'd streamed all sorts of folk talking about music and movies. He was taking pre-algebra. Knew how to figure out how many passengers were left on a train if some got off and some got on and when two trains travelling at different speeds in opposite directions on parallel tracks would reach the same point. He could write an essay on Valley Forge without doing a lick of research. But, not wanting to be rude, he said, "Okay."

The man sighed. "The second thing you need to know is you are not welcome here."

"I know," Connor said, looking down at his feet. "I was chased into the desert right after I arrived for being a… flicker. The Shadow Police called me the same thing, and they were pretty nasty too – at least one of them was. What's it mean?"

"We come from the world of light, and we stay here a short time," the man said.

Connor thought for a moment. He hoped he would only be here a short time, but how could he find his shadow quickly?

"This place is really unfriendly."

"Ever stand outside on a bright sunny day?" the man said. "You know how good it feels for the light to bathe your skin?"

Connor nodded.

"They don't, and they're jealous. There are a lot of beautiful things in the world of Light they can't ever have." The man paused and licked his lips. He cocked his head and said, "You can call me Journeyman. I'll call you Little Bit. You're obviously new here, so I'll let you ask me three more questions."

Connor wanted to protest the name "Little Bit," but stopped himself—it wouldn't do him any good to be difficult. Journeyman actually helped him, but the impatience hanging on his manner made Connor feel he might be gone at the drop of a hat. He had to think things through if he was going to make it here. What did he need to know? Who was Journeyman and how was he in the Shadowlands if he wasn't a shadow? Had his shadow been stolen, too? Could the man find a stolen shadow? Did the man know how to get home? Question after question clamored in his mind, but he glanced back over his shoulder towards the obelisk and immediately knew the first thing he wanted to know.

"What attacked me?"

"Shadowcats," Journeyman said, and nothing more. No explanation of where they were or how to avoid them. How were they made of shadow? How'd they vanish into the clouds of rust? Would all the man's answers be so useless? Maybe the problem was the question itself. He thought about how he could rephrase the question to require a more complete answer, though he didn't want to waste a second question on the same topic.

Then, Connor noticed Journeyman shuffling his feet and glancing ahead. Could he use the man's impatience? Connor stuffed his hands into his pockets.

After a few more seconds, Journeyman groaned.

"Shadowcats are predators of the Iron Desert," the man said. "Always travel with their mates. Hunt by graves for lost or curious travelers, hide behind rust clouds the wind kicks up."

Before Connor could stop himself, he asked, "Graves?" He sucked in a breath and winced as soon as the question escaped his lips.

Journeyman said with a shrug, "It's alright. I won't count that one, but with most folk, answers will cost you. Don't expect anything to come for free here, and if it looks like something does—assume the costs are hidden. The obelisks are graves, tombs of the ancient kings of the Shadowlands. They're all over the Iron Desert."

The man pointed to a pillar off to the left and another to the right.

"There seem to be a lot of them," Connor said, careful not to make it a question. "Must be a lot of names to learn in history."

"There were a lot of kings. A few have names, most merely leave an impression in your heart when you draw near. The Shadowlands are old as time itself," Journeyman said. He then pointed to the black mountains. "You see those mountains? They're not mountains. They were once palaces and cities, all made of copper, tungsten, and iron. Far, far back, the Shadowlands were a massive empire with many kingdoms thriving with art and music and all kinds of commerce. Then, one day, a massive light appeared in the sky. In the world of Light, scientists call it the Big Bang—here, it's known as the Great Flare. In that flash, the entire Shadow Empire was reduced to ruin, its towering spires left in melted heaps. The music turned to silence except for the ever-blowing wind and the hiss of volcanic rains. In time, the iron turned to rust, and those same winds and storms spread rust over swathes of the landscape. The survivors struggled to build what they could among the ruins. The obelisks were meant to be the hearts of their new civilization, but the land beneath them never settled, and even now, huge volcanic fields choke the air, and creatures like the shadowcats stalk anyone who dares venture too long in the open. The shadows buried under the obelisks were great and terrible, and the shadowcats are drawn to the mark they left on this world. One pays homage to the kings of old at great peril."

Journeyman paused as if reliving some important memory. Then he added, "The cats are pained by light, though. The road is safe as long as the lanterns burn."

Connor felt awed to stand in such an enormous ruin. The only ruin Connor had ever seen was the Alamo—and it was squeezed between stores and restaurants, like someone had forgotten it was supposed to be important. There were other ruins in the world, even entire cities in South America from a thousand years ago, but nothing so endless and old. He wondered what the desert looked like before but needed to consider his next question.

Did he want to ask about how to find his shadow or how to get home? Perhaps he should learn more about Journeyman because he still didn't know if he could or should trust him. But could he learn whether someone was trustworthy within two questions? It wasn't like he could bluntly ask him if he was trustworthy or give him something like the Trolley problem and have him all figured out. Instead, he asked, "Can you," he started, then added, "and will you help me find my shadow?"

Journeyman frowned. He looked again toward where they were headed, his body language resuming its impatience.

"I'll take you to the Town of Gissu," Journeyman said. "I have business there, and you can ask about your shadow with my associates. I'll make sure they treat you fairly."

Connor smiled but had mixed feelings about the response. The man didn't say they would answer the questions, only that he'd be treated fairly. Was he thinking too hard about it? He couldn't risk more foolish mistakes, but from what he'd already seen, fair treatment was the best he could hope for. At least Journeyman's offer meant he wouldn't travel alone. There was comfort in that.

Journeyman cocked his head. "You look dubious."

"I don't know what dubious means," Connor said.

"It means doubtful," said Journeyman. "And if you doubt me, good. Shows you have some sense. However, I mean my offer. If you accept it, it will happen."

Connor nodded.

"Good enough," said Journeyman as he started walking again. "And what is your last question?"

Connor fell in step beside the older man. He didn't feel pressured to come up with a question. He didn't know how long the trip would take. The time would let him think of exactly the right thing.

Connor said, "I'd like to save my last question."

Journeyman gave an approving smile.

"Smart lad," he said, then fixed his gaze ahead.

Before long, Connor made out the shack that contained his closet in the blowing rust clouds, and as they grew closer, a funny type of cart parked in front of it. The cart only had two wheels, and two long poles tilted down to the ground. Connor had seen that type of cart before in a movie set in China. They were called rickshaws and were kind of like taxis. This rickshaw was heaped with boxes and sacks, and several little shadows climbed all over it.

Journeyman broke into a run and yelled, "Get!" and "Scram!"

The little shadows, clearly small children, leapt from the cart and took off running down the road, several of them carrying armfuls of objects.

Journeyman shook a fist at the running shadow children. "Thieves!"

Connor knew the man wouldn't have left his cart unguarded if he hadn't come to rescue him. And it wouldn't have been unguarded so long had Connor not stopped to force him to answer questions. It was his fault.

Journeyman kicked up a cloud of rust and swore.

"I'm really sorry," Connor said.

"Yeah?" Journeyman demanded, leaning over the cart to take stock of what was left. "Sorry won't get me my umbrellas back."

"Umbrellas..." Connor started to ask, but he trailed off. If he didn't watch himself, he'd use his last question on something stupid. He shoved his hands in his pockets.

Journeyman pressed his lips together into a grimace and took hold of the rickshaw poles. He hoisted the load with a grunt and trudged onto the road, the wobbly wheels of the cart groaning and clunking on the glossy, black cobblestone.

Running into his closet, he pulled his hanging clothes aside. To his dismay, all his shoes were missing. Apparently, the thieves had taken them, too. All the boxes had been dumped out, his outgrown clothes in little, disheveled piles. The small plastic bin full of his old toys was missing, as were the board games. Connor spat out several words his mother would have yelled at him for.

Grumbling, he poked around for socks figuring a second layer would at least cushion his feet a little more, but they were in his dresser in the bedroom. Was there anything else still in his closet he needed? Not wanting to let Journeyman get too far ahead, Connor grabbed his old green soccer jacket and threw it on. Then, he jogged up the road.

As Connor stepped behind Journeyman, he took a moment to read a sign he'd been unable to see when he first stepped out of the closet. In bold white letters, it read, "NIGHTGLASS ROAD. TOWN OF GISSU 9 MILES."

They walked in silence. Journeyman led and Connor trailed in the haze of rust kicked up by the rickshaw's churning, wooden wheels. They plodded far too slowly to pass anyone, but Journeyman periodically pulled off the road to let other shadows pass. Those who did were all grim or glum. One muttered to herself and kept twisting her scarf around her hands as she walked with a rapid gait. None of the travelers addressed the older man or boy, except a rider galloping on the shadow of a horse shouted, "Out of the way!" and one who stepped up alongside Journeyman and fell in brief step.

"Journeyman," the shadow said. Connor couldn't make his face out well, but it seemed a little portly and had a beard.

"Quick," Journeyman said with a nod. For a split second, Connor wondered what Journeyman meant, but as the man nodded back, he realized Quick was the man's name.

"The Shopkeeper's been watching out for you," Quick said.

"You can tell him I'm on my way," Journeyman said.

"Better to arrive than send messages. You're late."

"An emergency delayed my crossing," Journeyman said. "The Shopkeeper doesn't like it, what's it to him? He can get his wares from another peddler."

The man nodded and picked up his pace.

"There's going to be a price," Quick said over his shoulder.

"Has to be," Journeyman muttered.

The sound of the wind took back over as Quick diminished ahead. Connor's hair ruffled in the breeze and his scalp prickled with cold. Connor wanted to ask Journeyman about the 'price,' but Journeyman hadn't even addressed him since they'd left the closet. Connor worried he'd end up ditched if he said the wrong thing. As they trudged on, Connor wondered what people in the Shadowlands paid prices with. Even if he'd raided the few dollars from his change box, Connor wasn't even sure the Shadowlands used money.

Meanwhile, the more they walked, the more the shining black stones of the road hurt his feet. He eyed the rickshaw. Was a pair of sneakers somewhere in the now half-empty boxes? To distract himself from his aching soles, Connor tried to picture Gissu. Was it a town? A city? A little village full of farmers and chickens? What kind of name was Gissu? Journeyman had said the shadows built towering cities in the distant past, but the Iron Desert was a wasteland. The obelisks were graves, but it was like the whole place was a graveyard. Did they still build grand things? Did they build at all? With what? The brain-like coral rocks? What if Gissu was just a bunch of caves? The meanness of the shadows he'd met made more sense; hard to be happy with so little. Connor knew how unhappy it made him and his mother to scrape.

Journeyman embodied the only glimmer of hope. He had stuff, so he was a little nicer. Maybe there were others like him. The shopkeeper would likely have more than most; otherwise, he wouldn't have a shop. Here, Connor had next to nothing, so maybe he should be unhappier than most. Part of him simply wanted to ask Journeyman how to go home so he could crawl into his bed, pull the covers over his head, and pretend none of this had ever happened.

His eyes adjusted to this world's light as they walked. Though the world around him was still dark and dim, he could spot different shades of rust on the road shoulders. Across the desert, he caught the rise of rust dunes dimpling the terrain. It was easier to pick out the rise of rock formations in the darkness. As they passed between the lanterns, their glow now seemed almost warm. He could feel their light on his skin, and the feeling comforted him.

They had just passed between two lamps when Connor happened to catch Journeyman's shadow swing from behind him to in front of him. The shadow was missing an arm and a leg, and the torso was unnaturally thin. The man had half a shadow. He was like Connor. Had his shadow been stolen, too? Perhaps he was here to buy his shadow back?

Finally feeling he had something good to ask, Connor jogged up beside Journeyman but held his tongue as the man rolled his eyes at the boy's approach. Clearly, the man was still angry, or maybe wrapped up in his concerns. After all, the shadow, Quick, had pointed out that Journeyman was late for something. Connor thought of his mother. Did she secretly roll her eyes whenever he bothered her for something? She tried to hide her worry, but he'd seen her sitting at the kitchen table or in the living room with her head in her hands when she thought he wasn't looking. Sometimes he'd get angry she didn't tell him more about what was going on, but now the image felt lonely. He felt lonely too, but what was it like to lose someone you'd married and then spend every day without their help?

The thought chilled Connor. His head felt muddled, and the cold and exhaustion that had filled him after the thief stole his shadow returned despite his jacket. Maybe it had never left. Maybe he'd been too distracted and worried to notice it. Connor feared this emptiness, this inability to feel alright, might be part of being an adult.

What if the Shadowlands forced you to grow up? Connor felt older trying to be careful. He remembered overhearing his mom on the phone with her uncle, saying, "I never feel like I can get my feet firmly on the ground." His legs wobbled, and his eyes drooped with sleepiness. He wished he were still home sick on the couch. Sick people were allowed to be much more like children.

Connor lacked a watch or any knowledge of how or even if time passed in this place, so he didn't know how long they walked. It felt like hours. Every minute here could be a day in the real world, or maybe no time passed at all for his mother. Regardless, the shivering exhaustion grew. He worried his legs would stop and he'd collapse onto the side of the road. Journeyman might leave him if he did.

Right when Connor thought he couldn't take another step, Journeyman wheeled the cart off the road. Connor checked behind them, but no one approached. When he turned back, Journeyman was shuffling through a box in the rickshaw.

"Need to eat," he said. "Need to rest, too, unless you want to pull the 'shaw a while."

Immediately, Connor experienced ravenous hunger and thirst. His tongue felt like paper, coated with the metallic taste of rust. The man pulled a small cloth bundle and a leather flask from the box and looked at Connor.

"Don't suppose you have any food?" the man asked.

Connor shook his head.

The man nodded as he sat on the ground beside the cart and opened the bundle. Connor wondered what kind of food there would be. On family road trips, his dad always packed a cooler of ham and cheese sandwiches and fresh fruit like grapes, and the man carried protein bars on him everywhere he went. A ham and cheese sandwich wouldn't be so bad. Connor figured he'd give anything for some pizza or mac 'n' cheese—anything hot and melty, really, would taste amazing at this point.

His mind swam with visions of warm, greasy cheese, so when he saw only dark black shapes in the package, his heart sank. Then, the man pulled out his knife, leaned over a nearby rock—the same coral-like rock—and scraped off a bit of dust from it into his palm. He took a pinch of the dust and sprinkled it into the mouth of the flask.

"Makes the water potable," the man said. "There's something in blackwater that the iron coral kills. Otherwise, well, let's say it's not good for you."

So, it actually was coral, Connor thought, which made him realize at some point the whole Iron Desert might have been an ocean. Was that before or after the kingdoms were destroyed?

As if reading his thoughts, Journeyman closed the flask and shook it while he said, "After the Great Flare melted the iron cities, the Shadowlands warmed for more than an age. When it was all darkness, vast glaciers and mountains of ice stood everywhere. The flare melted them, too, and torrents of water swept the land leaving endless lakes and wide oceans on all but the highest land."

The flask prepared, the man took a long swig from the leather flask and passed it to Connor.

"I'm sure you know how rust forms," he said as Connor took the flask. "Once the sky cooled, the water leached through the pores in the rust and into reservoirs far beneath the surface. Almost impossible to tap for wells."

Connor tipped back the flask to his lips, half wondering whether he should trust Journeyman enough to drink it. He immediately spit out what filled his mouth. The liquid was thick and oily with a nasty taste like the worst cough syrup ever.

Journeyman chuckled.

"You expect champagne? Or milk?"

"Water maybe," Connor said.

"It is water," Journeyman said. "Water of the Shadowlands. Us

Flickers call it blackwater."

"You could have warned me."

"Where's the fun in that?"

Connor pursed his lips, but he felt better. Somehow the man joking made him feel more familiar. The boy examined the flask, trying to peer into its mouth, but it was darkness inside. So, *blackwater*, he thought, bracing for another swallow. He could barely stand the thought of tasting it again, but his thirst was too strong. When his mother gave him bad-tasting medicines, she told him shutting his eyes helped, so he did so as he took several swallows. He didn't throw it up. Barely.

When he lowered the flask, he felt strange. His mouth and throat were wet, but the terrible thirst deep in his body remained.

"It won't quench your thirst," Journeyman said. "But none of the waters you'll find in the Shadowlands will. The best you can hope is they make you more comfortable. At least we're not beyond the mountains near the Boiled Sea, the water there…is something else."

"There's no real food here," Connor said with a bit of dejection, his gaze fixed on the black lumps. "Nothing to drink."

"There is," Journeyman said. "Just rare. Brought some myself when I came, but any food you bring rots before long no matter how fresh. Any water grows stagnant and sour."

Connor was relieved Journeyman no longer seemed angry, and despite the complete lack of appetizing qualities, the thought of chewing and swallowing the shadow food set Connor's stomach churning.

Journeyman picked up a roundish object Connor thought might be the shape—or shadow—of an apple, and extended it. Connor took it. In his palm, it weighed about the same as an apple, though the skin was a little coarse and drier than an apple's waxy touch.

As Connor was about to bite into it, Journeyman said, "It'll fill your stomach, but it won't give you energy."

Connor wanted to ask why, but he closed his mouth even as it opened so as not to squander his last question.

Journeyman, noticing, cocked his head for a moment and then sighed.

"You remind me of my boy," he said. "Ask your questions."

"Thank you," Connor said.

Journeyman gave Connor a strange look.

"Thank you..." the man mused. "Don't hear that much in the Shadowlands."

"Mom's always been big on manners," Connor said. "Please and thank you, and don't curse. I don't always listen."

"When kids listen at all, it's a miracle," the man said. "What were you going to ask?"

Connor took a deep breath. Though he'd intended to ask about the food, he knew there were more pressing questions.

"Why are you in the Shadowlands? You have half a shadow. Was yours stolen too?"

Journeyman shifted, and a look flashed across his face as if he regretted offering to answer questions.

Journeyman took a swallow of blackwater and said, "I traded it."

"Traded it?" Connor asked. "Why would you? You're going to be Shadowless."

"Well," Journeyman said, "it's more like I loaned it."

"To whom? Why?"

"A shadow broker." Journeyman scooped a handful of rust and let it sift through his fingers. "He gets me in and out of the Shadowlands, provided I earn enough while I'm here to buy my way back out. Otherwise, he keeps my shadow."

"But why would you take that chance?"

"To help my son," Journeyman said. "He's very sick, and some shadows can help the sick in ways doctors can't. Once I earn enough to get back, anything extra goes toward favors."

"So, could I buy my shadow back?"

Journeyman shook his head. "The thief isn't going to hand your shadow right back if you find him."

"Why would he steal it?"

"To sell it, of course," Journeyman said.

"If he wants to sell it, why can't I buy it?"

Journeyman nodded.

"I guarantee he works for someone who collects shadows," the man said. "There would be penalties for breaking his obligation even if you somehow convinced him to do so."

Connor furrowed his brow. It was all so frustrating.

"But who would buy it?" Connor asked. "Why would someone do something like this to me? Could I get my shadow back from the thief's boss?"

"No one buys a shadow for a good reason. And if they've already done it, they've decided they're more interested in their gain than your loss," Journeyman said. "And you really wouldn't want to deal with the type who buys them."

Connor thought maybe Journeyman could be wrong. It was the closest thing he'd had so far resembling a plan. If he could find out who the thief was going to sell his shadow to, maybe he could find a way to get it back. However, he didn't want to push the matter. Instead, Connor asked, "Will the shadows make your son better?"

Journeyman frowned. "When people die, they pass through the Shadowlands on their way to wherever it is they go. Many get lost along the way, and they get trapped here. Those with a lot of sadness, anger, or fear get lost easiest. There are shadows here who delay my son from crossing into the Shadowlands, and others can help him pass through when it's time. No one can save him."

A cold chill fell over Connor, and a terrible pity filled him. The answer didn't give Connor what he'd hoped to learn, but he now felt he could trust the man. No one who risked so much to help his son could be bad; Mom always said good people acted out of altruism and empathy. It also helped Connor understand the meanness of the shadowfolk; it was easy to get angry and confused when one was lost. Confusion brought out the worst in people. His dad was usually patient and calm, but Connor remembered a time they had gotten lost on their way home from a trip out of town because the GPS took them down a blocked road when they tried to bypass an accident on the main highway. After almost an hour of wrong turns, his father had lost his temper and shouted for everyone to be quiet. It was one of the few times he'd shouted at the family.

Silence settled over them, the only sound being the wind sliding over the rust dunes around them. Connor finally remembered the shadowy apple—or whatever it was—in his hand. He took a bite. His teeth sunk straight through with little resistance. Something filled his mouth as he chewed, and something else slithered down his throat when he swallowed, but otherwise, Connor wouldn't have believed he'd eaten anything at all if there wasn't a chunk missing from the thing in his hand.

"Disappointing, isn't it?" Journeyman asked. "Lots of things here are. Myself included."

"No, you're not," Connor said. "You're the nicest person I've met here so far."

"And that should be disappointing," the man said.

Chapter 5

A FEW SQUARE FEET OF CANVAS

The temperature plummeted enough to bite Connor's skin through his soccer jacket. He rubbed his hands over his biceps as he walked, and every time his teeth chattered, the grit of rust between his molars made him wince. Even Journeyman paused periodically to blow into his hands as he plodded onward like a pack mule.

When a sharp gale tore through, the chill burned Connor's cheeks. The wind howled with an intensity one would expect from a tornado or a hurricane. His jacket sleeves fluttering and his hair rustling, Connor felt as if a giant hand pressed him between the shoulders, threatening to knock him over.

Journeyman dropped the handles of the rickshaw and stepped around it, peering back down the road with his hands shielding his eyes like a pair of imaginary binoculars. He stood still as a post for several moments, except his lips, which pressed together and worked against each other silently.

"Dang," Journeyman muttered.

Connor stepped up beside the man. He tried to shield his eyes, but the wind blasted his face all the harder. Bits of grit pelted his cheeks and neck.

"What is it?" Connor asked.

Journeyman pointed the way they'd come. Connor could barely see through his incessant blinking but grew accustomed to the discomfort. Even then, he couldn't tell what Journeyman pointed to. The road stretched to the horizon and beyond, visible only as a line of lanterns. To either side, the Iron Desert stretched, empty as ever. The sky in the distance was dark as wet tar.

"Is it a storm?" Connor asked.

"Of a sort," Journeyman said, still pointing. "The road."

Connor returned his attention to the lantern trail, and then, as another vicious gust tore through, he saw it: almost as far off as he could see, a pair of distant lanterns had extinguished.

"The lanterns..." Connor said.

And then another.

"Indeed," said Journeyman. He lurched into motion, grabbing the rickshaw poles and pivoting the rig one hundred eighty degrees so the cargo bed faced the way they were headed. He shoved the boxes off the seat, extracted a key from a chain around his neck, and unlocked the seat top, opening a hidden compartment. Within seconds, a pry bar, a small satchel, what looked like a camping lantern, and a large bundle of canvas were laid out at Journeyman's feet.

Two more pairs of lanterns vanished. Initially, Connor thought the wind doused them, but wouldn't they darken randomly and not in pairs? Someone or something had to be putting them out. The thought unsettled Connor, so he asked, "Can I help?"

"Stay out of the way," Journeyman said. The man's tone reminded Connor of when his father had said the same thing, gathering supplies after a tornado warning in the neighborhood as he gathered supplies for them to huddle with inside the coat closet.

After he locked the seat back down, Journeyman snatched the crowbar and popped a cap off one wheel of the rickshaw. Then, with practiced skill, he did the same to the other. Then, bracing the rickshaw with his hip, he pulled one of the wheels off, lowering the rickshaw's rear corner to the obsidian. He repeated this on the other side, so the rickshaw sat flat on the ground.

In the meantime, more lanterns had extinguished, the darkness growing rapidly closer. The blackness towered into the sky over Connor's head. They were in a desert, and in deserts there were sandstorms—so, in this desert, it was probably a rust storm. Connor imagined being pelted by a billowing cloud of the harsh flakes, and the first thing that came to mind was the skin stripping off his face.

Journeyman didn't even glance at what approached as he snatched the canvas bundle and undid the clasp holding it together. With a snap of his arms, the whole sheet unfurled, about ten feet on each side. He slid his fingers to one corner where he grabbed a metal ring which he fixed to a hook on the back of the rickshaw. He did the same on the other side.

Out of the satchel came a steel mallet and several silver spikes. Each clank jolted Connor's ears as Journeyman pounded spikes into the other corners of the canvas. Connor realized the man was pitching a tent.

Finally, Journeyman unscrewed part of one of the rickshaw's pulling poles, grabbed the lantern and satchel, lifted the edge of the tent, and pointed underneath.

"In," Journeyman commanded. "Now."

Connor scrambled under the canvas sheet, Journeyman crowding behind. Once under the tarp's protection, the man angled the pole into its center to prop the tent and snatched the lantern. With a flip of a black switch on its base, the lantern burst with an intense, purple light that pulsed and dimmed steadily—a strange sort of light causing all sorts of specks on Connor, Journeyman, and the tent's interior to glow an eerie green.

His face mere feet from Connor's, Journeyman flitted a relieved smile. His teeth lit up like a glow stick.

"That was close," he muttered as the storm rolled down upon the tent with a 'whump.' The whole cover jerked taut against the stakes and pole. The pole itself leaned, but the base held. The canvas edges flapped madly as the wind began to shift and swirl around them. The walls bowed and pressed against the backs and shoulders of the two refugees while the gale screamed like a wounded animal.

Connor stared at the lantern, the same type of black light he knew from the bowling alley during Rock and Bowl. The boy realized he'd not been bowling since his father had passed. It had always been something they'd done together. He remembered his father guiding him by the hand the first time he hefted the ball with his fingers in the holes. They'd talked about the different weights and what the lines and triangles on the lane meant. Where to hit the pins. The first time he let the ball roll, his father stood right behind him, guiding the back swing and then the forward. The first hit had knocked down six pins. Most of the rest were gutter balls. Tears came to Connor's eyes.

Trying to distract himself from the memory, Connor said, "I love blacklights."

"Yes," Journeyman said. "I do too. Shadows don't. With the lanterns out, shadowcats will come."

"Did they follow us?"

"Probably not. There are plenty of them prowling the desert," Journeyman said. "On the other hand, shadowcats have long memories and even longer lives to use them."

The Journeyman reached into his satchel and extracted a long knife. It had the shape of a hunting knife but seemed to be made entirely of shadow.

"There was a man whose name meant Night Blade," Journeyman continued. "Hunted all the other beasts of the Shadowlands. They said he could steal a dragonshade's egg straight from her nest and fry it at her feet without being noticed."

"Dragonshade?" Connor interrupted.

"Yes," Journeyman said. "Legends say at one time, the shadows of dragons built nests on the highest peaks of the Ditallu Mountains, though they've long passed from this world to wherever it is dragons go when they leave the world. After everything he'd killed and everything he'd stolen, Night Blade decided he wanted the pelt of a shadowcat cub. In the dead of night using every form of stealth he knew, he slipped one from under its mother's teat in their nest. He then traveled across the Shadowlands peddling his pelts and trophies in town after town. The journey took much of his life.

"One night, he set up camp in a cliffside cave overlooking the ocean. He built a fire, lit lanterns, and hung a heavy shroud over the cave mouth to hide the light. After he ate a hot meal of the meat of whatever he'd killed last, he fell asleep.

"That night, a sudden storm tore its way over the ocean and ripped the cover from the cave. The fury of the tempest blasted through the opening and doused fire and lamps alike.

"It was then the cub's mother crept down the cliffside into the cave and tore the man's body limb from limb, having tracked the man for decades by nothing but the faintest of scents he'd left in the nest the night of his crime."

Connor listened with rapt attention; his awareness of the storm almost vanishing. Journeyman spoke with a strong and clear voice, his eyes pored over the blade of his knife as if the story came from the blade itself. However, despite being spellbound, something bothered Connor.

"But if he slept in the cave alone, how does anyone know what actually happened?"

"Smart lad," Journeyman said. "Some tellers of the story say Night Blade had taken on a partner who witnessed the killing from behind a rock, others add a wanderer lost in the storm who saw the cat enter the cave mouth, but really, the story is precisely that: a story told to teach a lesson. Even if it didn't happen exactly so, it doesn't make the point of the story less true."

Connor nodded. As silence fell between them, the surging roar of the storm swelled anew. It was hard to say how long they huddled as the storm of rust-laced dust bombarded the canvas. The stronger gusts caused the canvas to pull sideways fiercely, allowing small tornadoes of rust to burst into the shelter. The corners of the cover lurched against the stakes holding them down as if the whole tent would rip loose and they'd be flung through the air like dolls. Connor suspected if it weren't for the rickshaw anchoring them, such a thing might actually happen.

It was then a new sound intruded: a low rumble like a truck engine. It approached from the rickshaw side and curved around slowly, circling the tiny shelter. A second rumble joined it from the other side. Growls.

"They're here," Journeyman said.

"Do they know we are?"

"Yes."

Sweat poured down Connor's back and from his armpits as he remembered being circled by the beasts at the obelisk. They'd hung back in the darkness behind clouds of rust. Now, the entire world was a giant cloud. How many shadowcats hid within? Connor's whole body tensed.

"Are we safe?"

Journeyman glanced at the pulsing, UV lantern.

"As long as that glows," the man said.

The response offered no comfort. Something in Journeyman's voice, a slight pause between 'that' and 'glows' told Connor there was nowhere to plug it in. His hands shook as he clasped his forearms across his chest.

"How long?" he asked.

"If the storm is short, we'll be fine," Journeyman said. "The light drains the batteries fast, and I only have one. Electricity here is rare and expensive."

"How long do the storms usually last?"

"Longer than I like."

From outside, the growls closed in tightening circles, only backing away when the wind lifted the edges of the shelter enough for a bit of purple light to escape the shelter. The urge to bolt out into the storm struck Connor even though such an act would be madness. He imagined the cats leaping onto his back, clawing at him through the canvas, their talons shredding through the cloth and his flesh like scissors through paper. Connor heard a strange whimpering mix into the growls and realized the sound came from his throat.

"Talk to me," he begged Journeyman.

"What about?"

"Tell me about your son," Connor said.

Journeyman closed his eyes. His Adam's apple bobbed with emotion. For a moment, Connor thought he'd asked for the wrong thing. Then something about the man's entire demeanor seemed to give.

"About a year younger than you I'd say," Journeyman said. "Though tall. Very, for his age. His mother... always so proud of his height. His smile melted my heart every time I see it, no matter how rare it's become. There's a little curve on the right side of his lip that makes him look like he's up to something. He's got brown hair, dark as mine before it grayed, but blue-green eyes like the Gulf of Mexico. I swear, they cast a glow over any room he's in. When he was a baby, I used to wonder what the world looked like through eyes that color. I imagined it made everything look a bit like paradise."

Tears welled in Journeyman's eyes as he spoke, and he kept looking to the upper right as if a photograph of his boy hung inside the tent.

"Now, he's so thin. So thin. Arms and legs like wires. His ribs stick out. He hardly gets out of bed, and when he does, he needs help to cross his room. His arms get me the most. Hard to believe those arms swung a baseball bat at games every weekend."

"Does he like baseball?" Connor asked. "I play soccer."

"Loved it," Journeyman said with a brief smile at one corner of his mouth. "Soccer, too, actually, but he didn't play long. He managed baseball until midway through last summer. His mother and I didn't understand at first, but he preferred baseball because he ran so much less. Soccer was too demanding. It was a symptom. If only we'd realized... we missed a lot of signs."

Journeyman trailed off, the tears now rolling down his cheeks. Connor's heart ached. He felt like he had to share something in return.

"My father's dead."

Journeyman met Connor's eyes, his eyes still swimming.

"A car accident," Connor said. "Just my mom and I now, but he used to come to all my soccer games and even my practices. Every Sunday after church, he'd take me somewhere. Sometimes the zoo, sometimes the park, bowling. It didn't matter. We found something, and it was great. Now, Mom and I rarely go anywhere. We don't have money, and she doesn't want to do the things we did as a family. I think I understand, but sometimes I hate her for it. I loved my dad so much. It's like I'm not living my life with him gone."

When Connor stopped talking, his mind was racing. What he'd said surprised himself. Some things he'd never thought before, though he knew them immediately to be true. Journeyman reached out and put a hand on Connor's shoulder, giving it a soft squeeze.

"I don't know which is worse," Journeyman said. "Having your entire world shattered in an instant, or watching your world die an inch at a time."

Connor didn't know what to say. Even if he did, he wouldn't have had the chance. A sudden, shrieking yowl erupted from outside. Journeyman cried out in response and jerked Connor towards himself. He lunged over the boy, thrusting his dagger through the canvas. The motion was so violent, for a heartbeat, Connor was certain Journeyman was about to plunge the dagger into his back.

He braced for something to crash onto the shelter. Crunched under the weight of Journeyman's torso, Connor could barely breathe. Would the shadowcat take Journeyman in its jaws and drag him out of the tent? Would they burst inside with a frenzy of claws and teeth?

A sharp tear of canvas took what little breath Connor had left away as Journeyman's weight lurched to the side. *This is it,* Connor thought. *They're going to kill us.*

He tried to steel himself against pain he knew no amount of bracing could dull.. He tried to cover his head with his arms, but they remained trapped under his companion. He willed himself to be anywhere else, his bed, his school, at church, somewhere he would be safe from the attack about to take him.

He didn't go anywhere.

No attack came.

Journeyman pulled back, withdrawing his dagger. Connor twisted his head as far as he could. The tearing hadn't been the shadowcats at all, but Journeyman jerking the knife sideways through the canvas, ripping the fabric. The edges of the rip flitted in the wind.

Then, all at once, the wind died, and the air stilled. The storm was over. The shadowcats were gone.

GISSU

Journeyman lifted the canvas and stepped out. Connor followed hesitantly, worried the shadowcats could still be waiting. The desert outside appeared as before, except a drift of rust half-buried the rickshaw. Journeyman pulled a wide brush from his pocket, pressed a red handkerchief over his nose, and set to cleaning the cart. Then, the man folded the canvas, repacked his shelter kit, and stowed it all in the cart's bench. The whole process was practiced and exact; no energy nor time wasted. When he was done, Journeyman mopped his forehead with the handkerchief.

Connor fidgeted, scratching his arms and shifting his feet, addled by the memory of Journeyman's sudden lunge with the knife. The violence of the moment had been terrifying.

So, he asked, "Why did you stab the tent?"

"The storm was about to end, and the cat knew it was about to lose advantage. Its yowl was a challenge," the man said. "I answered it."

"Have you ever killed a shadowcat?" Connor asked.

"No."

"Can you?"

"I'm no Night Blade. They're easier to drive off than kill. They're ambush predators. They don't like to fight."

Journeyman closed his mouth, took up his poles, and curved the cart onto the road to Gissu. While conversation didn't resume as they walked, the walk felt different now. The tension had vanished, and the man now looked at the boy with something like warmth. Unfortunately, as they plodded, Connor's hunger and thirst resumed. Before long, the boy felt ready to plop down on the roadside.

He was about to collapse when he discerned something faint growing on the horizon. A soft, reddish glow swelled, much like the glow of the lanterns along the road, only brighter and more concentrated. It was the light of a great many lights. He'd seen a glow like that before; it never left the sky over Dallas. His father had called it light pollution.

At first, the buildings that appeared on the horizon looked like tiny, rectangular black shadows, but Connor assumed they would grow grand and towering. His mind flooded with images of bustling streets, shadowy towers, crowded markets, shadowy shops, and stadiums. Would there be cars and police stations and people walking the shadows of poodles? For some reason, he pictured it like some 1930s street scene, except everything would be a silhouette. A shadow train would actually be really cool, maybe cool enough to make him forget how much his feet hurt, or how hunger gnawed at his belly like a splinter.

Unfortunately, it soon became clear they weren't heading towards any fantastic city but rather a smaller, walled settlement. The buildings remained small. Halfway there, it became apparent there wasn't anything over two, maybe three stories tall. Many had gaping holes in their roofs. At least one had clearly burned. What looked like it had been meant to be a water tower right at the wall appeared as if the top half of its basin had been sheared off.

The only thing that didn't disappoint Connor was the lights.: a dense ring of lanterns surrounded the town, and more hung in windows and on rooftops. It wasn't like all the signs and neon in downtown

Dallas, but it was the brightest space he'd seen since arriving in the Shadowlands. It almost felt welcoming.

A line of lanterns stretched away from the city and led out into the desert to the left, culminating in a small, tight ring around an obelisk. There, several shadows knelt, stood, and sat around the pillar. Connor couldn't quite see what they were doing, but they appeared to be pouring little glowing heaps onto the ground.

"They're spreading fresh embers around the base of the stone," Journeyman said, stepping up beside Connor. "A ritual to honor the past and hope for future prosperity."

"Like when people light candles in church and pray?" Connor asked.

"Sort of," Journeyman said. "They believe when the embers extinguish, the shadow king's spirit has eaten the light and will later return it to light their way."

"Sounds silly," Connor said.

Journeyman shrugged. "Beliefs often do to those who do not practice them. How strange does it look to someone who's never been to church to watch everyone stand and kneel, all to line up and eat a tiny piece of bread?"

"There's a sip of wine too," Connor said.

Journeyman rolled his eyes. "You know what I mean."

"Do you know who the obelisk is for?"

Journeyman nodded. "A king named Jakayn, one of the last great kings, and the one who commissioned the building of The Nightglass Road, the longest road in the Shadowlands. The town of Gissu grew here because of his tomb," he said. "And Jakayn was his real name. The rulers of old were among the few in this realm who didn't hide who they were. It was a mark of their power to say others could not take power over them."

"What happened to him?"

"One of his followers used his name against him to take the throne."

Connor frowned. "Guess he should have picked a nickname."

"Indeed." Journeyman gave the boy a smile and then gestured to the town. "Now, when we get inside don't wander off or lag behind. Stay close."

"Is it dangerous?"

"Everything here is," Journeyman said. "Especially for Flickers."

Journeyman reached into the cart. He pulled an umbrella from under the seat and passed it to Connor.

"If we get separated," he said, "trade this for help."

Connor didn't understand why the umbrella had value, but he took it, nonetheless.

"Thanks," he said.

"I'm not giving it to you," Journeyman said. "You'll owe me if you spend or lose it. I'll decide on a price later."

They started towards the town itself. Behind the lanterns ringing the outer edge stood an iron fence almost as high as the lower eaves of the surrounding buildings. The road cut a straight line toward a gate which Connor and Journeyman approached. A complicated lock with several interlocking bars, latches, and gears held the two halves of the gate shut. No sounds emitted from inside the town.

"Say nothing," Journeyman whispered. He approached a metal pole with an arched top from which a large brass bell dangled from a frayed rope. The man rang the bell three times, each clang breaking the silence.

The door of the building closest to the gate, a small shack with what appeared to be tin walls and roof, opened, and a lean shadow stepped out, muttering to himself.

"State your business," the shadow said after a yawn.

"Commerce," Journeyman said with a gesture to the rickshaw. "Shade Row."

When the lean shadow peered at the cart through the bars, Connor could see the shadow's face better than any of the shadows he'd seen so far. The shadow wasn't pure black, as Connor had assumed all shadows would be. Rather it contained faint hues of deep gray, blue, and purple. The shadow was the shadow of an older man with a serious face, prominent cheeks, and deep-set eyes whose gaze swept over the whole cart and both travelers.

"Who's he?" the gatekeeper asked.

"My companion," Journeyman said.

The gatekeeper's jaw flexed, and his eyes narrowed. What would happen if he didn't let them in? What if he let Journeyman in but not Connor? It's not like Connor was Journeyman's kid.

Then, the gatekeeper exhaled sharply through his nose.

"You know the way," he said, gesturing to the guard shack. A metallic clank rang from within the shack, and the lock on the gate came alive with mechanisms and disengaged from the gate's joint.

The doors groaned open.

Journeyman hoisted the rickshaw and trudged inside with Connor close to his side. After the cart cleared the gates, the iron doors creaked shut and locked. Suddenly, Connor felt trapped. The urge to scramble up and over the gate flooded him. Could he convince the gatekeeper to let him back out? He was just a kid, a stranger, who needed to get back to his mother. Journeyman placed a hand on Connor's shoulder and moved him along.

The dismal town, the buildings little more than shacks and shanties, failed to comfort. Some structures simply possessed three walls leaned against each other without a front or roof. Inside, shadows sat on bare floors, lay down as if asleep, or simply stood about. A couple rearranged their scant furnishings. Another appeared to be drawing even though both pen and paper appeared to be black.

The town worsened the further they went. Rubbish, sheets of metal, and iron beams were piled between shacks, some of which had collapsed. Did no one clean the streets? Where were the garbage collectors and road workers? There were Shadow Police, but what about all the other people who kept the world running? Connor's stomach sank. Surely, living like this was worse than being Shadowless.

As they pushed on toward what Connor assumed to be the town center, the streets grew crowded with shadows. Many milled about like the shadows in the shacks, but more paced about or trudged towards unknown destinations. A few broke their reveries to glare at Connor and Journeyman as they passed. A couple drew uncomfortably close, their dim faces fixed on his own, their lips drawn in half snarls. Connor wished he hadn't grown more accustomed to making out their faces. They glared at Journeyman, too, but many of them glanced at his cart and gave him a reluctant nod.

A burly shadow with a shaggy mane of hair steered directly towards Connor, bumping its hip against his as they crossed. The shadow smelled of oil and coal.

Connor let out a startled cry, but Journeyman didn't seem to notice even as another pair of shadows curved into Connor's path, splitting at the last second to brush by him on either side. One of them muttered something about the 'damn casters.' The urge to run for the gate returned as he remembered the two shadows outside his closet. How long until one of these shadows confronted him? The woozy sickness returned, and Connor's legs wobbled.

Journeyman marched towards a black arch spanning a gap in a fenced-in section of the town. As they passed underneath it, Connor saw the arch read "Shade Row" in wrought iron letters.

Connor heard calls and shouts from within. The road inside widened into a broad square. The buildings edging the square rose taller, some definitely two stories. Their shapes spoke of multiple rooms. The buildings here were better maintained, and nearly every one of them sported a colorful awning or canopy over its entrance. Underneath, some had tables crowded with shadows hawking a variety of goods. There was a lantern maker, a wheelwright, and a shop with clothes draped over its front advertising "the new colors," though all the clothes displayed looked gray to Connor. A small flea market-like stall was heaped with a wide variety of broken toys, and two shadows rummaged through them, commenting on 'the brightness of the reds and blues.' Several of the vendors showed off assorted umbrellas, and shadows haggled over their prices.

Connor's gaze returned to the awnings, their bright greens, blues, reds, and purples the first vibrant colors he'd seen in the Shadowlands. Some were solid, others striped with white or black, and still others were paisley or plaid. Under one awning, several shadows sat around a table playing what looked like a card game. A shadow slapped the table hard, and the others burst into a roaring cheer.

"You've got the luck of the thirteen," one declared, which struck Connor as odd since there was nothing lucky about the number thirteen.

At the shop beyond the game, a burly shadow wearing an apron stood over an anvil and examined a piece of glowing metal held in a pair of tongs. A fire burned in an oven built into the shop's side, and the light from both fire and object pushed against the smith's skin, making his cheeks and forehead appear sunken as if his body was repelled by the brilliance. Shadows passing his station curved away while turning their heads to watch his work.

Despite still feeling sick, Connor's spirit lifted a little. Shade Row felt alive with its awnings and din. He could almost ignore the hostile looks and how close many shadows drew.

"Don't relax," Journeyman said. "Assume everyone to be dangerous as a shadowcat."

Connor tried not to smile but couldn't help it. There were so many... people here. Surely, he'd find someone to help him. Connor adjusted the umbrella, crooked under his arm, and weighed whether he could buy something. Maybe something for his mother. Wouldn't that be something? A souvenir from the Shadowlands?

Connor froze amid the meandering shadows and stalls and calls of the vendors. His mother had no idea where he was. A pang twisted in Connor's heart. How long had he been gone? Was she beside herself with worry, her face and neck bathed in tears? Had enough time passed that she'd even noticed he was gone?

Journeyman's hand pressed between his shoulder blades.

"Keep moving," the man said.

Connor's feet didn't want to cooperate. His shoulders shook a little as a sob rose in his throat.

Journeyman dropped to one knee and said, "Are you okay?"

"My mother," Connor said. "It feels like I'll never see her again."

Journeyman nodded. "No journey into the Shadowlands comes without great sacrifice," he said.

"Is there any way I can let her know where I am?"

"No," Journeyman said. "But be thinking about an excuse for where you've been. You'll find whatever you come up with turns out convincing."

Connor opened his mouth to ask what he meant, but Journeyman rose and again nudged his hand flat on Connor's back. They trundled past a few more shops Connor hardly noticed as he fretted about his mother. What could he say that she'd possibly believe? He started entertaining thoughts about running away. So wrapped in thought, he nearly walked into the rickshaw when it came to a stop under an awning. Connor squinted at the awning, trying to figure out its color, until he realized it was actually black.

"We're here," Journeyman said.

The building before them was the largest Connor had seen in all of

Gissu, a large, black structure of welded iron posts and tin sheets. A large shadow leaned against the door frame. Connor's eyes were still adjusting to the subtle details of the surrounding shadows, but this particular shadow's broad and angular face seemed somewhat uneven. The left jaw and cheek seemed wider than the right. It smiled at Journeyman, but the smile was more of a snarl. This was not a nice shadow. For real, why did this need to be the one Journeyman had business with?

"Inside," the large shadow said. He opened both doors as wide as they would open before stepping into the shop. Journeyman dragged his rickshaw through the broad doors, Connor close at his heels. Just as Connor passed through the portal, he caught a glimpse of a tiny shadow peeking at him from around the building's corner, but it disappeared from sight the moment his eyes fell upon it.

The inside of the building was dimly lit by hanging lanterns and clearly some sort of store. Many cluttered counters, tables and shelves displayed cauldrons and urns and books fatter than any textbook Connor had ever seen. One table displayed the shadows of bones, all different sizes and shapes. Surely, they came from animals of the Shadowlands. However, among them also sat what appeared to be the form of a human rib cage. Connor shivered to look at it.

Other tables held various odds and ends, but all seemed to display, among their other wares, a great many knives, swords, and axes. Some looked like the ones Connor knew from the real world, with others made of shadow.

"You like blades?" The Shopkeeper said in Connor's ear.

Connor jumped. The Shopkeeper had stepped up behind him so close, the fabric of his clothes rustled against Connor's back as the shadow breathed. Connor actually did like blades—especially the replicas from fantasy movies they sold at the comic books store which he could never afford, not even at Christmas—but he felt like the Shopkeeper was thinking something much darker. He stepped back and turned to face the Shopkeeper, bumping his hip against one of the tables.

"No sir," he said.

The Shopkeeper straightened and snorted.

"Sir? I'm nobody's sir," he said. "And those with no interest in blades best form one quick."

"I-I don't want to hurt anything," Connor said.

"Maybe," the Shopkeeper said. "But in these parts, nearly everything wants to hurt you. Journeyman crosses the Iron Desert, so if you made even half the hike with him, I'm guessing you've already learned that firsthand."

The Shopkeeper rolled his shoulders and turned his back on Connor to amble behind the counter. He leaned underneath it and pulled out a metal box. He looked at Journeyman and then Connor and then Journeyman again.

"Always something odd about you," the Shopkeeper said with a humorless laugh. It sounded much like the one Connor had heard from the Pale Boy. "This time you've got a Flicker for a shadow."

"What's it to ya? The Iron Desert is a curious place," Journeyman said. "Never know what flotsam you'll find out there."

"What's it to ya, indeed," the Shopkeeper muttered. He gazed at Connor, his eyes strangely hungry, his fingers tracing the edge of the metal box. Connor wanted to leave the shop or at least duck under the table to avoid the glare. "You gonna keep him?"

"We gonna talk business or gloom about strays," Journeyman asked.

The Shopkeeper leaned closer. "You got a name, half-shadow?"

Connor swallowed. "Do you?" he answered. He tried to sound confident, but the words barely came.

"You can call me the Shopkeeper," the shadow said with a sneer. "And what do I have your permission to call you?"

"Little Bit," Connor said. He needed something better but had no idea what. He wondered if Journeyman might suggest something different now that they knew each other.

"Well, Little Bit," the Shopkeeper said. "What can I do for you?"

Connor hesitated, unsure whether to ask this shadow anything or even stay in the shop at all, but Journeyman answered for him.

"I promised him I'd ask you to treat him fairly as he asked you some questions," he said.

"Did you now," the Shopkeeper said with a raised eyebrow.

"Can we get on with this," Journeyman said. "I've got places to be in less time than I have."

The Shopkeeper shrugged. He then opened the box in front of him and pulled out a stack of papers. He shuffled through them until he found the one he was looking for, read it, and then put them all away, returning the box under the counter. "The little flicker can wait. You got my order?"

Journeyman's shoulders slumped, and he sighed. "About that," he said. "Bit of a problem."

The Shopkeeper crossed his thick arms across his chest and said, "Which is?"

"Cart got robbed while I was off collecting this caster," Journeyman said. "They didn't get 'em all, but I lost half the order."

"That is a problem," the Shopkeeper said. He gestured to a table along the back of the shop, nearly empty except for a few tattered umbrellas. "Short on umbrellas. You ask mighty big favors, and I don't know why I should dole them out to folk who can't keep their end of a bargain."

Journeyman's shoulders sank even further. Connor's skin prickled with guilt. What if Journeyman couldn't help his son because he'd saved a stupid kid?

The Shopkeeper rolled his huge shoulders back and smiled a terrible smile. It was terrible because the man was genuinely happy, but there was nothing kind in his happiness.

"Well," the Shopkeeper said, "let's adjourn into the back to discuss payment privately."

"Very well," Journeyman said.

The Shopkeeper stepped around the counter and wrapped a massive arm over the man's shoulder, making Journeyman seem tiny and shriveled in comparison.

As the two of them walked towards the back door, Journeyman looked over the Shopkeeper's thick arm to Connor and said, "Stay here."

Then, the Shopkeeper looked back with narrowed eyes. A mask of loathing washed down his features, and he hissed, "Don't steal anything."

They disappeared into the backroom, leaving Connor amidst the cauldrons, baubles, and blades.

Chapter 7

PROMISES

Now, normally, a young teen left unattended in a shop full of things both dangerous and dangerous-looking would be concerning. Children, teens, and even adults all across the world stick their hands in places where hands shouldn't be stuck. Curiosity combined with naiveté can be dangerous.

It helped that Connor suspected the people in the Shadowlands didn't follow many principles of supervision and safety, and the place made even the familiar seem unfamiliar. Water didn't quench thirst, food didn't sate the stomach, and umbrellas sold for high prices. Even the simplest item felt foreboding. Could the bones be crawling with shadow-borne diseases? Did he really know what those blades could do?

Most worrying of all, though, did he really know what the Shopkeeper could do? Even now, the shadow-man's oily demeanor seemed to hang in the air he'd occupied like toxic gas.

Afraid to touch anything or even move, Connor shuffled uneasily, tucking his hands into his armpits. His feet grew cold. The hard, iron floor sucked the warmth out of his soles and reminded him how sick he felt. Walking the Nightglass Road had taken so long. His body cried out in distress, and he had no way to help it. What if he starved or died of thirst? There was no fridge to rummage through. He thought longingly of the pantry at home, stocked with store-brand cookies and crackers. He doubted he'd find a McDonald's around the corner.

With nothing else to do, he swallowed his fears and poked around the shop, searching for shoes among the cauldrons and bottles and books. Maybe he could trade his umbrella for sneakers and something to eat. Connor turned the umbrella over in his hands, a sorry umbrella, dark gray with a black handle. One spoke had torn out of the fabric, and nothing happened when Connor pushed the button that should have opened it. The umbrella, the shop, Gissu itself; everything here seemed so broken.

After a while, Connor crept up to the back door and pressed his ear to it. The wood muffled the sound, but he could hear the faint, angry voice of the Shopkeeper and the occasional, brief interjections from Journeyman. Connor strained to make out the conversation, but the clearest words were swearing and insults. It felt as if he could turn the volume up a single notch, he'd have it.

Something tugged at his shirt, and he gasped.

He spun and saw the tiniest shadow before him. Less than three feet tall, it was the shadow of a little girl wearing a purple sweater and an ankle-length black skirt. Braided pigtails hung on her shoulders. She chewed her lower lip and tugged one of her braids.

"Mister," the little girl shadow said. "Mister, you've got to come."

Connor shook his head and said, "I'm waiting for someone."

"But I need you now."

"I can't. I've got to speak with the Shopkeeper."

"Oh, no," the girl said. "You know his name already."

Connor's forehead creased. "Well, he is a shopkeeper," he said.

"No matter," the little girl squeaked. "You can't speak with him. He's poison."

Connor hesitated. Certainly, there was nothing nice about the Shopkeeper, but Journeyman had promised fair treatment. Also, if the

Shopkeeper was bad, maybe he knew bad shadows like the thief.

"The Shopkeeper's gonna help me," Connor said. "Journeyman promised."

"He doesn't help anyone but himself," the little girl said. "But I need your help."

This dumbfounded Connor. He couldn't help anyone. "You've come to the absolutely wrong person," he chuckled. "I'm not sure I can even help myself right now."

"Most can't," the little girl said. "Doesn't mean they can't help others. Follow."

The little girl jogged to the exit, bouncing up and down. Was he going to stand here with an ear to a door, waiting for a clearly hostile man to suddenly become helpful? What if the man didn't answer his questions? Or if he answered them, but the answers weren't useful? For all he knew, the girl might have some answers for him, too. There didn't seem to be many people in the Shadowlands willing to help, so if she couldn't turn to him, why should he expect to be able to turn to someone else?

The little girl seemed too young to be dangerous anyway.

Connor looked at the back door. Perhaps he should tell Journeyman he was leaving? The tone of their conversation made interrupting seem a bad idea. Could he leave a note? He couldn't see any notepads, but he remembered the box of papers the Shopkeeper had pulled out.

Connor ran behind the counter. The shelf underneath was cluttered with all sorts of little boxes and jars full of strange things like faces made of leather and little animals floating in fluid. After a moment, however, he found the box. When he lifted it up into the dim light, he could see its metal surface wasn't plain—it was etched all over with small runes in interlocking spiral patterns. The runes themselves reminded Connor somewhat of the ones he'd seen on the obelisks. His palms grew sweaty as it occurred to him, he might have something dangerous in his hands.

He set the box on the countertop beside an old earthen mug with a broken handle full of pencils. Then he grabbed a pencil and opened the lid. As he pinched the corner of the top piece of paper, a tingling numbness ran up his fingers to his wrist. He lifted the small, folded sheet, and an image of a pale man with sunken eyes formed in the back of his mind, blurred as if he was seeing it through smoke. His brow was furrowed, his pupils filled with the reflection of a hospital bed.

Connor unfolded the paper. It read, "The Sad Husband. Thirty tents. Five more days with his wife."

A chill quivered through Connor's belly. He slipped the sheet to the bottom of the stack.

When he picked up the next, an old woman in an armchair replaced the grieving man, a TV droning on from somewhere out of sight. This one read, "The Spinster. Two boxes of rare books. Two more weeks to say goodbye to her children."

"What are you waiting for?" The little girl said from the doorway. "We need to hurry."

The next note showed Connor a woman who wept at her window, her fingers clenched into the sill like she wanted to rip right through it. "Lost Woman. A dozen hourglasses. Word of where to find her brother. Delinquent."

The one underneath: a man holding someone's hand as they watched a young boy cough and writhe in his sleep.

"Journeyman. Five crates, umbrellas. Safer passage for son."

The pencil fell from Connor's hand. His fingers felt oily and dirty. Each receipt described deals made with Shopkeeper by people in pain. It seemed wrong that they needed to come to a place like this for help. Connor clenched his jaw, returned the papers to the box, and shoved the box under the counter.

He wouldn't sell his help. He would help because it was right.

"Come on, hurry up," the little girl said and darted out of the shop.

He followed her into a cluttered and narrow alley with a chain-link fence at the end. The links had been cut and pulled apart. The little girl darted into the gap without a glance behind. Connor followed, but the gap was a tight fit, and the sharp edge of one of the severed links scratched his temple. He yelped.

The little girl paused briefly as Connor pressed his fingers to the wound, then darted off again. The fence opened to another alley, which led to a street. This one was every bit as dismal as those approaching Shade Row. Every building was run down, and many were on the brink of collapse. Everywhere, shadows slumped or stood about, their heads drooping. Several even lay on the side of the road and stared up into the dim sky. Was no one okay here?

The little girl led Connor down two more streets before she slowed and crept to a low, long building with metal walls rusted through in a dozen places. She glanced about as she neared a tiny door barely taller than her. As Connor caught up, she cracked the door to usher him in.

The building was one hall with an obsidian floor and a roof made of overlapped metal sheets. Partitions divided the walls into tiny cubbies, no larger than Connor's closet. Slouched shadows occupied a few of the nooks, one of which gazed absently at the pages of a book. Another sat cross-legged, taking items out of a bag and sorting them into neat rows at its feet. What looked like a mother and two children huddled beside the main entrance like statues.

The little girl led him to a cubby in the back corner. Inside, Connor found a little girl, a Flicker, curled up on her side under a scratchy wool blanket.

The little girl shadow shifted from foot to foot. "This is Mouse. She's a half-caster too. She's real sick."

Connor didn't know what to do. He knew nothing about helping sick people. He sat beside her and lay a hand on her shoulder, setting his umbrella beside him. The little girl stirred, and her eyes popped open. Her blue eyes were dull and murky.

"Who. Are. You?" she asked.

"Co—" Connor began, but he broke off. If he didn't trust Journeyman's advice, he would have nothing to go on. So, instead, he said, "I'm Little Bit."

The girl managed the slightest smile. "Pleased," she whispered, "to meet you."

"Please," the little girl shadow said. "Please help her."

"What can I do?"

"Do you have any food?" the little shadow said.

"No food," Mouse whispered. "Can't eat."

"Why not?" Connor asked.

"Trying to go home," Mouse said. "So hard to go home."

Connor squeezed Mouse's shoulder. She wasn't making sense.

"She needs food," the shadow said.

"I don't know how to get food," Connor said.

"She needs to find the rest of her shadow," the shadow said. "Then she'll feel better."

Connor snapped, "But that's what I was trying to do. The Shopkeeper was supposed to help me. Maybe he could help her, too."

"The Shopkeeper helps only himself," the shadow said. "Even if you think you'll win, you'll lose in the end."

Connor opened his mouth to say he needed to find help somewhere, but an enormous gasp from Mouse shut him up. Her breathing accelerated into shallow wheezes. Her whole body lurched straight, her back arching. A long, rattling exhale followed. Then, nothing.

Before Connor's eyes, Mouse's body grew transparent and vanished. The woolen blanket settled to the hard floor beneath her without a sound. The little girl shadow broke into heaving sobs and sank to the floor.

Connor was aghast as he stared at the limp blanket. What happened? Had Mouse died in front of him? Where did her body go? How could she vanish? Connor fixed his attention on the sobbing shadow. Had she brought him to see this?

"What the heck was I supposed to do?" Connor said.

The shadow bawled harder in response. Connor swore under his breath. She was just a little girl. He took a deep breath and tried again.

"I'd hoped if she knew she had help, she'd find the strength to keep going," the little girl shadow said.

"What happened to her?" Connor asked. "Where did she go?"

The shadow sniffled several times. She raised her head and said, "Home."

"How?"

"She starved."

Connor had never been so confused, not even when the Shadow Police first came. "Who are you?" he asked. "What happened? I don't understand."

The shadow wiped her face with her sleeve. She fingered a little opal necklace from under the collar of her sweater.

"Call me Quiet," she said. "And you don't know?"

"Know what?"

"How to get home."

Connor shook his head. Quiet sighed.

"You die," she said as if it were the most obvious thing in the world.

Connor stared at her. Die to go home? He hadn't expected to click his heels together, but what kind of horrible place was this? Quiet saw Connor's astonishment and said, "Well, not die, exactly. Casters can't die in the Shadowlands. Your mind will get too weak to hold onto this world. It doesn't want to be here. It wants the Light. It wants things… it finds good. I'm sure you've been feeling sick since you got here. Your mind is resisting this place."

Well, that's awesome, Connor thought.

"Then Mouse is okay?"

"No," Quiet said. "Her shadow is weak. Every time you return, you leave more of your shadow behind. She might already be Shadowless."

"How will we know?"

"If she comes back," Quiet said.

"Can I help her?"

"I hope so," Quiet said, "It might not be too late. You're a half-caster, and since you're not a grown-up, I assume your shadow was stolen, too. Maybe yours and Mouse's thief is the same."

"Where do I start, though?" Connor said. It was all too much. He wasn't used to taking on more than homework. He was barely a teen.

"I'll do what I can," Quiet said. "I know a lot of shadows. Some are nicer than the Shopkeeper. Some are... worse."

Quiet looked away as she spoke the last word. She sounded like his mom when she didn't want to explain something. It was clear she wouldn't say more. How strange so much in the Shadowlands revolved around which questions one should and shouldn't ask.

An odd thought struck Connor. "You don't really talk like a little girl," he said.

"I'm a lot older than you think," she said. "I've been here for decades."

"How?" Connor asked, his mouth hanging open.

"Because I can't find my mommy," Quiet whispered. "How can I get to the light without my mommy?"

Connor sat back against the wall of the cubby. The metal gave under his weight and, for a moment, Connor thought it would fall backward. He didn't know what to say. There didn't seem to be words to make any of it better.

Quiet regarded him. Her eyes didn't look like the eyes of a little girl, but more like the eyes of his grandmother.

"You sleep," Quiet said. She picked up Mouse's blanket and offered it to Connor. Connor flinched. Even knowing Mouse was still alive, he still saw it as the blanket she'd died under. "Take it. It's going to be night soon. Casters should never travel at night here. I'll be back as soon as I can."

Quiet pushed to her feet. She darted across the hall and disappeared through the little door. For several moments, Connor sat, unsure of what to do. He would need to sleep eventually, but how long before he, too, starved? He heard somewhere that a person could only go for three days without water and a week without food. Sick and exhausted as he felt, he knew he couldn't stop trying, or he'd become like the Pale Boy.

The hall seemed to be stiller with Quiet gone, and Connor became aware that the parent and children by the door were whispering in unison. He peeked around the cubby's partition and heard them say, "May the Unlucky Number guide us. May the Unlucky Number protect us. May the Unlucky Number absorb our woes, and in doing so, absolve us of our darkness so we may find our way out of shadow into light."

The family repeated the lines over and over like a prayer. Connor remembered the card player who exclaimed about the luck of the thirteen. Was that what they'd meant? What was the Unlucky Number? Should he ask?

The prayer completed, and after a moment of silence, one of the child shadows asked its mother, "Can you tell us a story?"

"What story would you like to hear?"

"Tell us about Bell," one said. Then the other said, "I want to hear Basket."

The mother shook her head at the first.

"You didn't bring back anything we can trade today," she said, "so we'll hear your sister's choice."

The rejected shadow crossed its arms and pouted. But as soon as the mother began to speak, the anger was replaced by attention. Both children froze, silent and wide-eyed, as the story began.

BASKET AND THE FLOWER PETAL

"Once," the mother began, "there was a little shadow named Basket who didn't know from where he came or to where he was going.

"He survived by collecting bits from the trash and fashioning them into other things. He would find a metal disc and a piece of twine and created a pendant, trim a piece of torn cloth into a bandanna or a handkerchief, or cut bits of colored rags into flower petals he'd stitch together into dull blossoms whenever he could find thread.

"One day, he was poking through the refuse scattered outside an arena in the city of Kiln after the crowd had left when something amazing caught his eye: it was the brightest color he'd ever seen, poking out from underneath a wad of newspaper. He had never known purple could be so bright and vibrant. His heart beat hard at a mere glimpse of it.

"He snatched it up as quickly as he could and held it in his palm. It glowed vividly, like the sun. It was shaped like a teardrop, the width of his thumb. Thin as paper, though far softer. It was a flower petal, but not the type he made from rags.

"Though he'd never seen one before in the Shadowlands, he knew this one was a real flower petal from the World of Light. How it got outside that dirty arena, he couldn't say, but it was the most spectacular thing he'd ever seen. He couldn't believe his luck. He knew if he rushed to the bazaar, it would fetch the biggest trade he'd ever made. Indeed, he knew just the trader who would offer well for such things.

"However, as he walked towards the market square gazing at the petal in his palm, he couldn't take his eyes off this thing of beauty. He kept tracing its edges with his fingers, feeling its softness, wishing some part of its loveliness would sink into his skin. He might never find something like this again. If he traded it away, he'd forget what it was like to hold something so precious. The urge grew for him to keep it, to protect it.

"By the time he'd reached the gates of the bazaar, he knew he loved this beautiful thing too much to part with it. So, he turned and hurried off home. There, he sat for three days, staring at the petal, still tracing it even as his fingers tore and frayed the edges. The first day, the color started to fade, and on the second, it was a pale imitation of its former self. The purple dulled and brownish-gray spots spread along the edges. Brittleness replaced the softness. On the third day, as he sought that softness with the gentlest touch of his index finger, the petal crumbled into dust and blew away in a draft entering through his open door.

"He had never cried harder in his life. When he'd calmed down, he spent the rest of the day imagining the beauty of the petal, trying to fix it in his memory. He pictured it again and again, thought about its tiny weight on his palm, what true softness felt like. For weeks, as he returned to collecting and fashioning scraps, the image of the petal served as his constant companion. He whispered to it at night when he had no one else to whisper to. He found himself drifting back to the arena, hoping he'd find another.

"Then, the memory too faded. Within a few weeks more, it was like the way the petal had withered in his palm. The memory of the petal barely formed at his command, and when it did, it was fleeting. He wandered the arena aimlessly for days at a time, poking into the piles of remains, staring off across the ground. He grew so tired and hungry his hands couldn't fashion trinkets, and he could barely remember how to get back home.

"Finally, he took a seat outside the arena gates and never got up again. He watched the shadows come and go through the gates as if one of them would drop another petal right in front of him. They say you can still find him outside Kiln's arena, still so long people think him made of stone."

The mother stopped speaking, and the children sat quietly for a moment before the smaller one, the one who'd chosen the story, fidgeted.

"I wish I'd find a flower petal," she said.

"What would you do with it once you found it?" the mother asked, her tone indicating the little girl had said this before.

"I'd trade it, of course," the little girl said.

"To whom?"

The little girl paused, then replied, "I'd take it to Shade Row. I'm sure someone there would want it."

The mother nodded.

"But what was wrong with keeping it in the story? What did we talk about last time?"

"It faded," the little girl said. "He couldn't keep it."

The mother nodded. "And who would buy it if they, too, wouldn't be able to keep it?"

"But the story said the boy knew he'd get a lot for it."

"And what if the boy was wrong?"

The little girl frowned. Her sibling, who Connor was pretty sure was a boy, piped in.

"The boy was wrong about everything," the little boy shadow said. "The flower petal had no value at all."

The little girl seemed about to protest but hesitated.

"Why not?" the mother asked. "I asked you to think about this last time."

"Because…" the little boy began and trailed off. He straightened his back and pressed his palms on his knees, but then his shoulders slumped. "Because it's a stupid story, and I'd rather hear about the Bell

Gemini."

The mother sighed. Connor stepped out from the cubby and walked towards the family. He hadn't been thinking about the question at all, merely listening, but something in him clicked, and he said, "Because beauty doesn't belong in the Shadowlands. Nothing from the world of light belongs in the Shadowlands."

The smile the mother gave him, as she looked up, chilled him to the core. It was really a smile. Her lips turned up and her eyes squinted just enough to show the expression was real. But her face carried in its lines a complete confidence in despair. It was the same look he'd seen on his mother's face for months after his father died whenever something made her forget her thoughts long enough to smile.

"I suppose you would know," the mother said.

Connor nodded. If there was one thing he'd already learned more than anything else in his time in the Shadowlands, it was that he didn't belong here.

Then, the mother's smile disappeared, and she said, "You should go home."

"I don't want to die."

"Well, we do," the mother said bitterly. "Why should you be any different?"

"Because I'm from the World of Light," Connor said.

The mother nodded, turning her attention to her children.

"Perhaps now you understand the point of the story," the mother said.

Connor couldn't make out their expressions, and neither of them said a word. Instead, they met his gaze and did not break off until his own stare focused on the floor. Connor found himself restless, and his mind turned back to Shade Row. He worried about his absence. Surely Journeyman and the Shopkeeper had finished their business. Would Journeyman be worried?

Connor clenched his jaw, grabbed his umbrella, opened the door and stepped back into the streets of Gissu..

As he hunched over to crawl out, he heard a "tsk!"

Connor looked back over his shoulder. Now, both the children and their mother were staring at him.

"You shouldn't leave," she said.

The light was poor, but Connor thought he could see heavy features in her face. Deep lines of worry covered her face, deeper than even those of his mother.

"Staying put didn't help Basket," Connor said.

The mother shook her head and said, "Clearly, you didn't understand the story, after all."

Connor frowned and said, "Would any good come of staying?"

"Things won't get worse," she said.

"Can they?"

The mother drew her children into her arms so they fell back against her breast.

"Yes," she said. She kissed each of her children on the top of the head. "And they will."

Connor shuddered, but defiance filled him. Maybe the mother meant well and was content to stay. She did have her children to protect. But if he did nothing, he would lose himself, and what more did he have to lose than that?

Without another word, he ducked through the door and onto the streets of Gissu.

THE RULE OF NEED

Those accustomed to making deals understand the three types of deals: good, bad, and those in between. Deal makers seek the first, avoid the second, and accept the third when it leads to more of the first or lessens the risk of the third. Dealers also know how easy it is to mistake any of the three for any of the others and how easily one can be cast as another. One thing all three types of deals have in common is how easily someone can be forced or led to consider making a deal. All it takes is for someone to open their mouth.

Unfortunately, Connor did not have this in mind when he approached the shop. As Connor turned the corner out of the alley, the Shopkeeper clasped a massive, iron padlock straight out of a dungeon onto the front door latch. The big man saw Connor and said with a sneer, "The runaway stray's returned."

"I had to help someone," Connor said.

The Shopkeeper snorted. "Someone asks me for help, I say 'what's it to ya?' and send 'em on."

"Good for you," Connor said.

"Indeed, it is," the Shopkeeper said. "Didn't get this far helping every which-way that drags itself through my door. Hope you got paid for services rendered."

Connor opened his mouth to retort, but a mental flash of the box of promises shut it back promptly. That box… it buzzed with something dark and ominous and powerful even when he pictured it, and he knew it must be vibrating in its spot beneath the counter.

Anyone who kept such dark things in a box like that was probably best not to be offended.

Instead, Connor asked, "Where's Journeyman?"

"Off and away. Other business, I'm afraid. You've got to realize a little bit like you doesn't add up against the bigger bits and bolts of this place. As he told me, he only agreed to take you this far—far more generous than I would have been. But he asked me to give you fair treatment," the Shopkeeper said with a sigh, "And I agreed. For a price."

"What price?" Connor asked, again worried he'd caused Journeyman more problems. Probably, he made it worse by running off with Quiet.

"Between me and Journeyman, all written in my little box." The Shopkeeper paused. "Which I know you went through."

Connor swallowed hard and said, "I—I didn't mean to. A note—I wanted to leave a note."

"Like what you read?" the Shopkeeper asked, still smiling awfully.

"N-n-n-no," Connor stammered. He wanted to lie and say he hadn't thought about it, but lying would do no good if he wanted fair treatment. Instead, a strange anger stirred inside, so he added, "It felt wrong, and I didn't like it."

"No one does when they know the truth behind it all," the Shopkeeper said. "You're probably too young to understand, right and wrong don't always figure into the real world, but it won't take too many bad breaks to teach you the rule of need. You'd be amazed how quickly you'll laugh at pretty little principles when you *must*. But I said

I'd deal you fair, and what kind of businessman would I be if I didn't keep my word?"

Connor felt like the Shopkeeper was contradicting himself, but obviously the shadow-man couldn't be trusted, so there was no point in arguing over little things like this. The Shopkeeper was right about one thing. Connor *must* get answers. He needed help, he was here, and this was his chance.

"So, you'll help me?" Connor asked.

"A deal's a deal, isn't it?" the Shopkeeper said. The grin spread even wider. "But there's a price. Got to be a price to be fair, wouldn't you say?"

"I thought you said the price was between you and Journeyman," Connor said.

"The price to honor his bargain," the Shopkeeper said. "You and I must settle our own."

Connor didn't like the sound of that. Not at all—but then he considered the umbrella in his arms.

"How about this?"

The Shopkeeper chuckled. "Don't need umbrellas long as I got Journeyman. Even if he doesn't always deliver everything I'm due," he said. "But don't worry, I only ask a small favor. Always things a shadow needs doing, especially a shopkeeper like me."

Connor considered this. He'd mowed lawns and washed cars for summer money. He did dishes, took out the trash, and carried in the groceries. If he needed to take a job for the day, he could. The Shopkeeper closed his hands together and cracked his knuckles.

"Make a delivery for me," the Shopkeeper said. "Carry a little bag to a customer who can't pick it up himself. Can you handle that?"

It didn't sound bad. "You'll help me if I do it?"

"I'll make the time to make sure you get your questions answered," the Shopkeeper said. "Fair is fair."

"Then tell me where to find the thief who stole my shadow," Connor said.

"Tut-tut, Little Bit," the Shopkeeper said. "Favor first. You casters are too crafty for anything else."

Connor frowned. Would it be reckless to accept the deal? Quiet promised to help him, but she was so little… He didn't really have a better lead. He let out a long, slow breath. "I'll do it."

The Shopkeeper extended his hand. "We have a deal."

Connor shook the offered hand. His fingers crunched in the Shopkeeper's tight grip, but he couldn't feel any skin on his own. The feeling was as strange as when the Shadow Police had examined him.

"Tell me where to go."

"Ah," the Shopkeeper said. "Too late today. I've never claimed to be kind, but I wouldn't send a caster through Gissu at night. I want my delivery to arrive. You have a place to toss your shadow down? I can lock you in my shop."

The thought of being locked in the store all night with the box of promises terrified Connor. It would be better to go back to the long hall and wait for Quiet.

"I have somewhere," Connor said.

The Shopkeeper raised an eyebrow but nodded. "Then be off. Come back first in the morning."

The Shopkeeper turned and walked off into Shade Row. Connor lingered a moment. Had he made a mistake coming back here? Full of misgivings, Connor wandered into the alleyway and towards the gap in the chain-link fence.

Connor approached Quiet's home as the smoldering sun met the horizon. A new type of darkness settled over Gissu. Though the daytime sunlight had been dim compared to the real world, this new darkness astonished Connor. It felt thick, like he could spread out his arms and swim in it. The streetlamps still glowed, but whole buildings were swallowed in the gloom, and everything lost its edges.

Shadows poured into the streets from the shanty houses, many locking hungry gazes upon Connor. He still struggled to make out their faces, but whenever he looked long enough, their expressions transformed into masks of hunger. He didn't know if their hostility was because he was unwelcome, or because he had to look at them so long to discern their features. Images of them collapsing onto him and eating him flashed in his mind. Perhaps if he'd come back any later, he might not have come back at all. He picked up the pace, ducking and weaving down the dimming paths.

Moments later, full of relief, he entered the long hall through the little door.

The hall was almost deserted. Even the family of shadows had departed, much to Connor's surprise given what the mother had said.

His eye fell upon the room's only apparent inhabitant: Quiet, standing beside her cubby in the dim lantern light. She glanced down at something hanging from her hands.

A pair of sneakers.

Connor hung his head. Surely, the shoes were for him, and she couldn't have had much to trade for them. She'd done something real nice. Quiet had only asked one thing of him. It was like the days his mother wanted to surprise him with something special—a dessert or a trip somewhere cool—only for him to tell her he'd gotten in trouble at school.

She extended the sneakers towards him by the laces and muttered, "For you."

They looked a little small, but it would be better than being barefoot.

"I'm sorry," Connor said. "Thought I'd get back first."

Quiet's hand fell away from the sneakers.

"You went to him, didn't you?"

Connor nodded. "I thought it would help. Journeyman promised he'd be fair—"

"You can't be so trusting," Quiet said. "Fair doesn't mean the same to us as it does to you. The Shopkeeper offered a deal, didn't he?"

Connor nodded again, feeling too lousy to speak.

"Did you accept?" Quiet asked.

"Yes," Connor blurted through a lump in his throat. "But I won't do it."

"No!" Quiet squeaked, throwing her hands in the air. "You must never break a deal here. There are penalties."

Connor bit his lip as his stomach sank.

"I didn't know," he said.

"There are a lot of things you don't know," Quiet said, shaking her head. "Including the fact that you should listen to those who do."

Connor winced like he'd been slapped. She sounded like his mother.

She traced the shadow of a foot over the obsidian floor. "Do the shoes fit?"

Connor looked at the sneakers. There wasn't any brand on them, and the left shoe's lace was broken midway up their zigzag. They'd once been white, but the leather had darkened reddish brown with rust and was scuffed and worn all over. The shoes reminded Connor of a pair he'd worn the year before, except in far, far worse shape. He sat down on the hard floor and pushed his foot into one. They were tight, but he managed to pull them on.

"They fit fine," Connor said with a small smile.

"Promise me you'll listen," Quiet said, "I'll only help you if you listen."

Connor's smile grew. "We have a deal," Connor said, then winced. "Not the bad kind. Just... a promise."

Quiet squeaked again, excited this time. She threw her arms around Connor and squeezed, her body seeming even smaller as he returned the hug. The hug felt as strange as any contact he'd had with shadows, but nonetheless made Connor feel much better.

After a moment, Quiet let go and sat cross-legged in front of Connor.

"I did find out a couple of things," she said. "I found Journeyman."

Connor felt hopeful, sitting and facing her. "Did you tell him where I was? That I was okay?"

"I don't know if you can trust him," Quiet said. "The shadows he does business with..."

"He has no choice," Connor said. "They're the only shadows able to get what he needs."

"There's a lesson in that about what he needs," Quiet said.

"But he promised—"

"What exactly did he promise?" Quiet interrupted.

"To take me to Gissu, to be sure I'd be treated fair, and... and..." Connor paused. There wasn't anything left. Sure, Connor thought they'd shared something during the rust storm, but how far out of his way could the man be expected to go? So, Connor asked, "Why are you helping me?"

"I need you to help Mouse."

Connor frowned. While it was true she needed something, it wasn't really her who needed it. What was in it for her? Why did she want to help Mouse? He asked her.

"That's between me and Mouse," she said.

The response disappointed Connor but didn't surprise him. No one in this place shared much. He held forward his umbrella.

"Take this then," he said. "At least for the shoes."

Quiet smiled. "A generous offer," she said. "But I don't need an umbrella."

Quiet told Connor what she'd learned. She'd followed Journeyman to three houses on the town's outskirts. She overheard him say he planned to stay in Gissu for two nights. She didn't know where he was going or what business he had, but Connor felt a little better knowing he'd have a chance to find him if needed. No matter what, it would be right to catch him and say thanks.

More importantly, Quiet said a young shadow named Tonic told her rumors of a shadow thief staying outside Gissu in a place called the Daggers. Tonic was willing to take them there, but they would have to leave no later than midmorning if they hoped to be back before dark. Would he finish with the Shopkeeper's errand by then? He didn't want to lose another day.

Connor tried to stand. Immediately, he felt dizzy. His stomach churned so badly he sat back down hard.

Quiet said, "Oh my goodness, I'm so sorry."

She grabbed Mouse's coarse blanket and pulled it aside, revealing a small metal pitcher, two bowls, and a canteen. She uncorked the canteen and passed it to Connor. He grimaced as he put the canteen to his lips, already guessing it contained black water. It tasted every bit as nasty as before.

Quiet then poured a thick, chunky liquid out of the pitcher into the bowls and passed one to Connor. He gazed over dark gray chunks breaking the surface of the purple liquid.

"Soup," Quiet said, tilting her bowl to her mouth.

Connor took a swallow. The taste struck him like bad potatoes and dirt, so he gulped down the mixture as fast as he could. His stomach subsided, leaving the same worn-out and uncomfortable feeling as when he ate Journeyman's food. His head hurt a bit, and a massive tiredness filled his limbs.

Quiet said, "It's time to rest."

Connor lay back on the hard floor. If he hadn't been so overwhelmingly tired, he wouldn't have expected to sleep. However, Quiet lay against him with one arm over his chest, and he was drifting away before the blanket had been pulled over them both. He was grateful for Quiet. Maybe there was still hope he'd find his shadow.

Connor stood in the Iron Desert, his back to an obelisk, the sun setting behind the mountains. A strong wind dragged clouds of powdered rust across the expanse like a clinging mist. He squinted and tried to shield his eyes from the blowing flecks as he peered for signs of shadowcats. How had he gotten himself stuck out in the desert at nightfall?

The sun disappeared, its last dim rays slipping from the sky, leaving nothing but an ocean of black hanging over the world. Regardless, Connor could still see. A dull, green pall pulsed through his immediate surroundings. It took him a moment to realize it came from the obelisk. He turned, his back immediately feeling exposed, clenched his jaw, and put a hand on the monolith.

An image flashed in his mind of a cave with rock spikes jutting from the floor and ceiling like alien teeth. The sound of single droplets plopping into puddles echoed from the stony throat. Along with it came a sound akin to humming. He took a tentative step forward. Nothing was inviting about the look of the tunnel before him, though the hum seemed to call him forward.

He took gentle steps, trying to minimize the noise he made, but it seemed every time his foot fell, it sent pebbles clattering. He couldn't actually see down the tunnel at all; there were no visible light sources. However, somehow he knew how the path was formed, the width of the floor, the height of the ceiling, and when to duck beneath an outcropping. It was almost as if he could hear the edges because of the hum.

As he pushed on, the hum fell into an unfamiliar melody, notes slow but warm, like a lullaby even as the air chilled and grew damper. His heart grew cold. He looked over his shoulder but could see nothing. Nor could he discern anything about the way back like he could the way ahead.

Ahead though, the song seemed brighter than ever, so Connor pressed on. The frequency of drips increased, the little plunks all around him now. His steps splashed softly in shallow puddles. The chilly water soaked into the bottoms of his shoes. The tunnel widened into a chamber, and at the far end, he was certain there was a window.

He stretched out his hands and pressed his palms against the glass.

A light clicked on in the ceiling of the room on the other side of the pane. It was a nursery. A closed door stood on the other end of the room. A crib and a bassinet, an armoire, and a changing table furnished it. A mobile of stars and planets hung over the crib.

The door opened, and a young, pregnant woman entered. She wore a stretchy, powder blue shirt and wide-waisted jeans. Her hair was dark brown and pulled back in a ponytail, and her eyelids were half closed. She was the source of the hum. She approached the crib, which Connor was pretty sure was empty and leaned against its rail. She let her hand fall inside the bars, and she adjusted the corners of the sheet. For a moment, the song she hummed, its gentle melody filled Connor's mind almost entirely.

The spell broke when Connor realized the water was now up to his calf and rising. The hum ceased, and the chamber filled with the sound of water rushing in. The water rose past Connor's knees. He beat on the glass. If the sound of his blows carried into the nursery, the expectant mother gave no sign.

Then, the window went dark, and the water reached Connor's waist.

He turned and tried to run back the way he came, but the resistance of the water slowed him to a churning trudge. A current swirled into the deepening pool and nearly knocked his legs from underneath him.

Panic swelled in his chest. His heart pounded and his breath came in short gasps. The water was past his navel now, and he wasn't even sure where the mouth of the tunnel he'd entered lay. He reached blindly about, trying to find the walls, to find his way, but his hand found the ceiling instead, far lower than it had seemed before he'd approached the glass. Was he going to drown? The cold bite of water submerged his shoulders. He tilted his head back to keep his mouth as high as he could. There was no doubt.

Even as the water rose, the ceiling lowered.

Water rushed into his mouth as he tried to scream. It was frigid and tasted brackish. His throat clenched against it, and he closed his eyes.

Hands pinned his shoulders down as his body thrashed about like a beached fish. His breath was frantic, and whimpers and cries rose from his throat. Connor opened his eyes and found Quiet on top of him, using all her weight to subdue him. His mind regained control of his body, and he forced his body to relax, though it trembled uncontrollably.

After a moment, Quiet slid off and pulled the blanket back over him. She knelt beside Connor and stroked his hair.

"You were having a nightmare," she said.

Connor sat up and drew his knees to his chest. He could feel the dampness of sweat down his back. His thoughts swam with the memory of the dream. The nasty taste of the water still clung to his tongue.

"I brought breakfast," Quiet said, pointing to a bundle of shadow bananas on the ground beside the pallet. Hungrier than ever, Connor thought only of eating. He devoured three of the black fruits even though they tasted like chalk and lint. It felt like he'd never eaten before in his life. If he wasn't sure Quiet needed to eat, too, he would have eaten the whole bunch. If only his mother was there to make him breakfast.

Connor dropped the black peel of his last banana. His mother. My God, Connor thought, she must be going out of her mind. The nightmare dissolved from his mind as he pictured his mother pacing frantically in the kitchen, tethered by the phone cord as she spoke with

Connor's friends' parents, neighbors, the police, and maybe even the FBI.

He tried to stand, but his knees buckled, and he braced himself on the wall. His head swam, his muscles felt weak, and his forehead was burning up. Whether or not he'd been sick before stepping into his closet, he was sick now. He swallowed hard against roiling nausea.

Quiet took Connor by the shoulders to steady him until his balance returned.

"The hunger is hard," Quiet said.

"How would you know?" Connor said. "You can't starve."

Quiet flinched, and she let go of his shoulders.

"I can't die of starvation," she said. "But I can starve. I have starved. You think you can get food here whenever you want? You think I push a cart around a grocery store? Plenty for me would be a day having what I need. You don't know shadow hunger. You don't know how you go so long without food you eat handfuls of dirt or swallow rocks to have something in your stomach. Shadows have chewed their fingers off when the hunger drives them mad enough."

Connor's face flushed, and he mumbled an apology.

"It's okay. Even Casters become shadows of themselves here," Quiet said. "But off with you. You have a deal to keep, and you need to be back quickly. Be careful. Don't trust anything the Shopkeeper says."

Faced with the prospect of carrying out his end of the bargain, Connor felt helpless. He threw his arms around Quiet in an embrace. For a strange moment, she hesitated, perhaps startled by the abruptness of his contact. Then, she gave him a squeeze and smoothed her little hand up and down his back a few times.

"One thing you'll learn about the Shadowlands," Quiet said, "is you do what you must when you must. When you think you can't, you find you can. Then, you come back home."

Connor nodded, sniffling back brimming tears. He slid from Quiet's arms and strode across the hall towards the small door. As he did, the word 'home' echoed in his head. No matter how much kindness Quiet showed him, his mother's house would always be his home. He'd get back there as fast as he could, even if he couldn't imagine how much trouble he was in for.

He ran straight for the shop, arriving right as the Shopkeeper removed the padlock. Déjà vu struck Connor.

"What's it to ya?" the Shopkeeper said as Connor approached. He thrust the doors open. "Come on inside."

Connor barely stepped through the portal before stopping as the Shopkeeper walked behind the counter where the box of promises had been. Connor shuddered, imagining his name now listed in the box. It might read something like, "Little Bit. One delivery. Answers about his stolen half shadow." Did it make him a worse person to be in that box? It bothered him that the Shopkeeper knew he'd found it. He'd seen movies where people made deals with the devil. Had he done the same?

He scratched at the insides of his arms and folded them over his stomach, forcing himself to look around the store to take his mind off the box. His eyes fell onto a table by the door heaped with the shadows of animal furs. Pelt after pelt sat stacked in a large pile.

"Like the hides?" the Shopkeeper said. "Shadowcats. Fella who calls himself Hunter brings 'em in. Special fella. Shame about his aunt. If you like, I'll give you one after our business is done."

"What's it going to cost me?" Connor asked.

The Shopkeeper chuckled. "Smart lad," he said. "But this one's on the house."

Connor doubted anything came without a price. He'd somehow be snagged into another deal if he accepted. Quiet was right. He had to be careful.

"I'll pass," Connor said.

"Suit yourself," the Shopkeeper said, hoisting a duffel by the handles from behind the counter. "Just so you know, those pelts fetch a good trade. Not too many folks got the gumption to skin 'em themselves."

Connor shook his head.

"Well, down to business," the Shopkeeper said. "Deliver this bag to a warehouse called The Bins on the edge of town. The manager's too busy to get it himself."

"That's it?" Connor asked. "I drop off this bag and you'll help me find the Shadow Thief?"

"I'll arrange the opportunity for you to get answers to your questions," the Shopkeeper said. "Whether the opportunity helps is up to you."

Connor didn't like that answer. He wished the Shopkeeper had just said, 'yes, you'll get your answers.' But what choice did he have? He wanted the job done so he could get back to Quiet.

"What do I need to do?" Connor asked.

The Shopkeeper gave him directions. The route sounded meandering, but the Shopkeeper assured Connor it simply avoided bad streets. Connor repeated the route in his head.

"How will I find the manager?" Connor asked.

"You're expected," the Shopkeeper said.

Connor didn't know what else to say and wanted to get away from the Shopkeeper as fast as possible, so he turned and left.

The streets were quiet. A slight morning haze of dust and rust hung in the air. If shadows were most active after sunset, they were least active after sunrise. Ratty sheets and moldy blankets hung over the doors and windows of almost every building. A handful of vendors stood behind their wares, most of the stalls vacant. One vendor gestured across an old doctor's bag on the table of his stall and a spread of various rusted stethoscopes, forceps, scalpels, tweezers, and needles.

"Wanna buy a listener?" the vendor asked Connor, holding up a stethoscope. "Hear straight through doors and walls, my friend. You can even hear into yourself."

Connor kept walking. Though he stood out more than ever, the stillness brought him some relief. No shadows stared at him and jostled him. Seemed less likely they'd set upon him like the shadows outside his closet. He clenched the bag handles tight. Journeyman wasn't there to keep him safe. What if the shadows stole the Shopkeeper's bag? What would he owe? The load wasn't heavy, so it wasn't something as cartoonish as guns, knives, wads of dirty cash, or gold bars. The Shopkeeper hadn't warned against looking inside. What harm could there be?

Connor set the duffel on the ground, crouched beside it, and opened the zipper. The bag was full of umbrellas. The one on top had a bright paisley pattern in purple and sky blue. Connor laughed. Maybe Quiet was wrong about the Shopkeeper. Maybe he'd been wrong not to take the shadowcat pelt. It didn't mean he could abandon caution, but he felt more confident. He zipped the bag and continued.

Like the rest of Gissu, the warehouse district was quiet. A few shadows trudged underneath heavy sacks over their shoulders, and a group of them dragged a sled heaped with crates. The area held a lot of wide, low buildings on either side of a railroad track that disappeared through a gate in the outer wall and into the desert.

The buildings were smaller and shorter than he had pictured warehouses, but the shadowfolk didn't seem to be the best builders. Although these appeared much sturdier than the shacks around Shade Row, they still looked cobbled together. Smokestacks made of a patchwork of brick and sheet metal belched thick black smoke from several roofs. Most of the walls were corrugated tin, but many buildings had sections of stonework or wood panels, or a hodgepodge of two-by-fours and old furniture. One building even had a train car as one of its rooms.

The Bins itself wouldn't have been recognizable as anything special if it hadn't been for a hand-painted sign over its entry. He approached the broad, sliding door. A tattered brown awning hung underneath the sign, and a couple of unlit lanterns were mounted at its corners. The door was pebbled metal painted a deep green streaked with rust, and it was cracked open.

The interior was dark and cluttered like the Shopkeeper's store, with boxes and bags heaped everywhere. A few lights hung from the roof and illuminated little areas of junk. One shone on a clear space in the center of the warehouse. Specks of something — dust, rust, or both — hung in the air under the lights. The whole place smelled like dirt and pennies.

Connor crept inside, hesitant because he couldn't see any shadows or people. The sign said he had the right place, but he assumed he'd be met at the door. Connor's footsteps echoed in the space. Was the place deserted?

"Hello?" Connor called out from about ten feet in.

A bright light flared directly onto Connor, accompanied by raised voices. Connor threw his free hand over his eyes.

"Don't move!" a voice snapped.

Connor squinted against the light; a spotlight mounted on a ledge beneath the roof. He couldn't believe how bright it was. It was the brightest thing he'd seen in the Shadowlands, and since his eyes had adjusted to the dimness, they watered and hurt.

"What's going on?" Connor blurted as several shadows poured from behind the boxes.

"Shadow Police," one of them barked. "You're under arrest. Drop the bag."

Connor dropped the duffel as he said, "What did I do?"

Six shadows approached Connor from all sides. Two stepped forward from the rest, both very large. One was rotund with a fat face and glasses perched on the tip of his nose. He wore an ashen gray uniform with a charcoal black, star-shaped badge pinned to his chest.

The other was the Shopkeeper.

"That's the little thief," the Shopkeeper said.

"Thief?" Connor said. "I'm not a thief!"

"What's in the bag then?" the fat shadow asked.

Connor looked down at his feet.

"Um... um... brellas," he stammered.

"A dozen of them, no doubt, unless he kept one for himself. Just like I told you, Captain Sallow," the Shopkeeper said.

Captain Sallow stepped right up to Connor and pushed him aside with one of his fat arms. The officer opened the bag and nodded. He straightened and turned to one of the others, a lanky shadow with no hair.

"Cuff him," said Captain Sallow.

"I didn't do anything! I just want to find my shadow," Connor said. He looked the Shopkeeper straight in the face. The man was smiling that awful, wicked smile. "You gave them to me," Connor said.

"I did nothing of the sort," the Shopkeeper retorted.

"We had a deal!"

Captain Sallow turned to the Shopkeeper and asked, "Did you make a deal with this Caster?"

"He asked for help with finding more thieves like him. I agreed to make sure he got the chance to ask his questions so I could have time to summon you," the Shopkeeper said. Then, he said to Connor, "While you're in jail, you'll find exactly the sort of folk who can answer questions about thieves."

Connor fell to his knees. He held his hands up to Captain Sallow. "Please," he said. "I want my shadow back." It was then Connor remembered the Shadow Police in his room. "Ask Sergeant Dandrich and Officer Bell," he said. "They were there."

"We'll check into it," Captain Sallow said. "Give me your name so I can find the report."

The Shopkeeper leaned forward. The report was probably under his real name, though neither Dandrich nor Bell had asked for it. While Connor hoped he could trust Captain Sallow, he would not say his real name in front of the Shopkeeper. He clenched his jaw.

"I thought as much," Captain Sallow said.

As Captain Sallow walked off, the Shopkeeper paused beside Connor. "Almost a pity. I'd have liked to add your name into my little box. You'd be surprised what names you would have found down at the bottom," he said, flicking his eyes to the Captain.

Connor burst into tears as a shadow officer pulled his hands behind his back. Cold metal clasped around his wrists. He fought against the tears welling in his eyes, but his heart pounded so hard it hurt his head. How could this be happening?

"My mom," Connor said as he stepped out into the dim morning. "Call my mom!"

"She ain't going to help you," the officer said grimly.

"But I didn't do anything," Connor insisted. "I'm—"

"Save it for The Judge," the shadow snapped. "You casters always think you're special."

Connor's mind went blank as they walked. The group of shadows who'd been dragging the sled of crates had stopped their work to watch and laughed when they saw Connor. He wanted to cover his face. Everything in the Shadowlands made him more miserable. Sickness and fever resurged. If it hadn't been for the constant push of the officer's hand, Connor would have sunk to the ground and might not have risen again.

THE JUDGE

The police station was not what Connor expected. He anticipated either the sturdy-looking police stations he knew or a grim, foreboding structure out of an unhappy sci-fi film. What his escorting officer stopped him in front of was little more than a standing, black door with a roof over it. The words "Shadow Police" were stenciled in white letters down either side of the frame. The shadow officer opened the door and led Connor down chiseled obsidian steps. Pictures of shadow officers wearing black medals hanging from purple ribbons lined the walls.

The stairs opened to a receiving area with a long counter broken by a rusted old turnstile. On the other side of the counter, a bald officer with a caterpillar moustache twitched his nose and opened a fat tome as Connor approached.

"Name?" the deskman said.

"Goes by 'Little Bit'," the escort said.

"Charge?"

"Theft."

"Accuser?"

"The Shopkeeper."

"As always." The deskman made notes in the book, and then said, "Send him through."

A buzzing sound went off, and the escort shuffled Connor through the turnstile without passing through himself. On the other side, Connor watched as the officer departed the station with a brief wave to the deskman.

The deskman knelt in front of Connor and unclipped a tape measure from his belt. He held the little metal tab to the floor and measured Connor's height and width. He jotted the results down in the book.

Then, he spread a large sheet of white paper on the floor beside Connor. With a pencil, the deskman made a small 'x' at one edge of the paper.

"Stand here," the deskman said, pointing to the 'x.'

Connor did so, and the deskman removed Connor's cuffs. Then, he pulled close a standing light like the kind used by the school photographer. Once turned on, the bright light threw Connor's half-shadow onto the paper. Because the light was higher than Connor and pointed downward, his shadow was fairly small, but half was clearly absent. Though he'd rarely taken much note of his shadow, Connor could now make out faint features; eyes, ears, and nose. The deskman took his pencil and traced Connor's shadow onto the paper.

When he was done, the deskman jotted notes down the edge of the silhouette too quickly for Connor to read, folded the paper, and stowed it in a drawer under the counter. The officer pushed a button on the light and the white bulb switched to a powerful blacklight. Connor expected the deskman to draw his shadow again, but the man simply stood there. After a moment, little black specks scrambled off his shadow.

"What are those?" Connor asked.

"Lice shadows," the deskman said. "UV drives 'em away."

Connor couldn't help feeling a bit disgusted at his shadow's lice. He remembered the yearly lice checks in his school and how anyone found with them basically lost all their friends. Thankfully, he didn't have friends here except maybe Quiet, but he found even the shadows of lice icky.

Finally, the deskman planted his hands on his hips and looked down at Connor. "You have someone you'd like me to contact?"

"My mommy," Connor said.

"She a caster?"

"Of course," Connor said.

"No can do," the deskman said. "Can't contact the World of Light."

Connor's shoulders deflated. Who else would he contact? Quiet? Connor suspected by the way she'd snuck into her home she didn't want to be found. The only other people who came to mind were Journeyman and Sergeant Dandrich.

"I know Sergeant Dandrich," Connor said.

"Do you now?"

"Yeah, they investigated the theft of my shadow," Connor said.

"I see," the deskman said. "Well, if you'll give me your name in the light, I'll find their report. It could help your case; theft victims often receive at least a little sympathy."

Connor hesitated.

"If I give you my name, is it kept secret?"

"Of course not," said the deskman. "All our cases are public record. The Shadow Police have nothing to hide."

Connor felt torn. Journeyman had been clear about not using real names, and everyone else seemed to agree since they all used nicknames. Even so, Connor couldn't help thinking things might be easier if he gave his to the police. How could he know which was the right choice?

Then, Connor got an idea.

"What's your real name?" Connor said.

The deskman laughed and shook his head. That settled it. Connor mirrored him and shook his head.

"It's hard out there, isn't it?" the deskman asked. "Remember, even if your shadow was stolen, it's still no excuse for breaking our laws."

An officer entered from a door at the back, strode straight to Connor, and took him by the wrist. Within seconds, Connor was half-led, half-dragged into a large room divided into workspaces by desks heaped with papers and folders, file cabinets, and small, free-standing dividers. A few potted shadow plants rested near some desks. Most of the desks were unoccupied, though a couple of shadow officers hunched over reports and case files. He hoped he would get a glimpse of Sergeant Dandrich or Officer Bell, but he saw no sign of either. Most likely, they were in some other child's bedroom, delivering bad news and scaring them.

At the far end of the room, the officer pulled Connor to a flight of stairs leading to a windowless hallway ending with a gate made of iron bars. The powerful odor of a bathroom assaulted Connor's nose. On the other side of the gate was a jail. The jail floor, walls, and ceiling were worked obsidian, and the black rock seemed to suck all the light away despite several mounted lanterns. Four cells lined either side of the hall, three of which were occupied. The rest contained only a skinny little bed and a seatless toilet each.

Connor was led into one of the middle cells beside a cell holding a tall shadow who wore some sort of shimmery pants and a shirt resembling a burlap sack with armholes cut into it. Across the aisle, the cell held a short, squat shadow who wore a tattered black T-shirt and badly worn jeans. Both looked half-starved with sunken cheeks and hollow eyes. In the far corner, a Caster lay on a narrow bed.

As he locked him in the cell, the officer informed Connor he would have to wait for The Judge.

"How long?" Connor asked.

"However long he feels like," the officer said. "No reason to hurry a sentence."

The officer left, locking the gate to the stairs behind him. Unsure what else to do, Connor took hold of the bars and stared out through them.

Time passed. With no windows or clocks, Connor had no way of knowing how long. Connor let his gaze linger unfocused between the other prisoners and the toilet. His bladder and stomach hurt. Could he use the bathroom in full view? The toilet didn't appear to have a flush handle, and it had not been well cleaned. In fact, the more he looked at the cell, the filthier it became. Boot prints lined the stretch at the bars in back-and-forth tracks of what Connor hoped was mud, and the pathetic mattress on the bed was heavily stained. Connor bounced his feet nervously on the floor and tapped his hands on his hips. He wanted to sit, but he felt so sick and dizzy he might not get back up.

"What am I going to do?" Connor wondered out loud.

The squat shadow said, "Wait."

"How long? What's going to happen?"

The squat shadow shrugged. The tall shadow sat on the floor against the bars. The Caster still hadn't moved. None of them seemed to care about him. Connor bit his lower lip and unbuckled his pants. Trying to shield himself as much as possible with his shirt, he sat on the toilet and relieved himself.

The gate at the end of the hall clanked open, and the shadow officer returned. He approached Connor's cell with a smirk. It was as if the officer had waited for that exact opportunity to come down.

"The Judge will see you now," the officer said. "You don't want to keep him waiting."

Connor looked around for toilet paper but found only a small pile of gray rags at the toilet's base. He cringed but reached for them, anyway. He yanked his pants up as the officer opened his cell. In his rush, he realized there was nowhere to wash his hands.

"Is there a sink?" Connor asked after a moment.

"Sure, there is," the officer said. "For officers. We don't waste water on your likes."

"But I didn't do anything," Connor said.

"You think we arrest people without knowing they're guilty?" the officer said, motioning Connor into the hallway. "Get a move on, or they won't be inclined to hear you at all."

As he left his cell, Connor noticed that the Caster, still lying down, had turned onto his stomach and propped his chin on his hands, watching with a vague interest. The boy was sure he heard the man mutter, "Don't expect much."

Connor said nothing as the officer led him up the stairs and through the main room of the station. One officer at a desk watched Connor with a look of contempt as he passed. Again, Connor sought even a glimpse of Sergeant Dandrich and Officer Bell. Only a couple of unfamiliar officers chatted in a doorway at the far end of the room. Connor passed a doorway marked "Courtroom" and was pulled to a stop at one marked "Judge's Chamber." The escorting officer unlocked the door with a key and swept Connor inside with one hand, closing the door without entering.

The Judge's chamber was lit by numerous wall-mounted candelabras, and it smelled like a school library. Shelves filled with fat books lined the walls. At a desk in the room's middle sat an old Caster in a long black robe, like the judge's robes Connor had seen on TV, except this one had a hood hanging down the man's back. An obese shadow stood behind him with her hands clasped together in front of her belt buckle. Two high-backed chairs faced The Judge. A Caster sat in one; a shadow in the other, though Connor could not see their faces from where he stood. A large painting of two giant scales holding a crowd of people on one side and a single person balancing them on the other hung on the wall behind the desk in a gap between bookcases. The faces on one side seemed dismayed; the face on the other appeared joyful.

The Judge hardly looked at Connor as he rubbed his papery and pale chin with a knuckle. Flakes of skin peeled off and fell like a dusting of snow on the front of the black robe. The Judge's eyes were hollow and bulbous, the irises dark as elderberries. When he parted his lips to speak, strings of thick mucus stretched between them.

"Come," The Judge said in a thin and raspy voice, squinting at Connor. "Approach the desk so these poor eyes can see the accused."

The Judge picked up a pair of round, wire-spectacles from the desk with spidery fingers and perched them on his nose as Connor stepped between the chairs. Connor saw the chairs' occupants as he did so. Connor wasn't surprised to see the Shopkeeper, but he gasped when he recognized the other as Journeyman.

"Journeyman!" Connor exclaimed. "Thank God!"

Journeyman's eyes flitted to Connor and away again. Sweat beaded on the man's brow, his hair was a mess, and dark shadows raccooned his eyes.

"Tell them I didn't do anything," Connor pleaded.

Journeyman kept his eyes on the shelves as The Judge snapped,

"Silence from the prisoner."

The Judge gazed at the others in his office for several moments, muttering to himself. He lingered the longest on the Shopkeeper, and Connor was certain he caught a glimpse of disdain on The Judge's face. The thought made him a bit hopeful.

Finally, The Judge held up his hands and said, "Officer Marbeth, the Hands of Listening, if you please."

The female officer bent down, slid open one of The Judge's desk drawers, and reached inside. When she straightened, she held a pair of hands. One hand grasped a pencil, the other a long horn-shaped object. Connor was sure the hands were made of plastic despite being extremely lifelike. She set the hands on the desk in front of The Judge and then took him by the wrists. Connor couldn't believe what happened next.

Officer Marbeth unscrewed The Judge's hands like light bulbs, twisting first one and then the other. With an audible pop, they released. She set them on the desk and screwed in the new hands. The Judge stretched both of his arms before setting the one holding the pencil on top of a notepad on the desk and bringing the one holding the horn up to his ear. The hands appeared to come to life. One tightened its grip on the horn, the other tapped the pencil eraser on the pad. The Judge stared at Connor.

Connor stared back, dumbfounded. His school once brought in a guest speaker who had both of his legs replaced with prosthetics, but Connor was pretty sure the man didn't just swap out different legs for different actions. Furthermore, the speaker's legs were made of metal and plastic. These hands looked every bit as alive as Connor's. He wasn't sure, but he thought he could even see little shifts of the joints as The Judge's fingers shifted around the pencil. The Judge rolled the wrist of the hand holding the pencil and raised his eyebrows at Connor as if to say, "Well?"

Connor did not know what to say. How did one defend himself here? Were there rules? Should he say he was innocent? That hadn't worked well so far. What did they expect of him?

After a moment, The Judge sighed. "Identify yourself for this inquiry."

Connor hesitated. Should he give his name or his nickname?

Connor was more unsure than ever. Until now, he'd trusted Journeyman, but Journeyman wasn't leaping to help. He didn't want Journeyman and the Shopkeeper to know his name. Thinking things through was hard. How did his mom expect him to do it? He gave it his best as he said, "Little Bit."

The Judge nodded and jotted the name down on his pad.

"Place of origin?"

"Um, Plano, Texas?" Connor said.

"Where you entered The Shadowlands," The Judge said in a way that called Connor an idiot at the same time.

"My closet," Connor said. "On the Nightglass Road."

"The same closet beside which Journeyman's cart was robbed?"

"Yes, sir," Connor said, forcing respect into his tone. But the question stirred an unsettling suspicion in him: this conversation would not end well.

"Very well," he said. "And how do you explain your presence in The Bins with a bag full of stolen umbrellas?"

"The Shopkeeper gave them to me!" Connor said.

"And how could he have done that when they were stolen from Journeyman on the Nightglass Road right beside your very closet?"

Connor hesitated. Maybe the shadow children who stole them worked for the Shopkeeper? Had the Shopkeeper ordered the umbrellas stolen to increase Journeyman's debt?

"I don't know," Connor said. "But I didn't know the children who stole them."

The Judge jotted something else on the notepad. Connor tried to read it, but the writing was upside down and in some kind of shorthand. The judge addressed Journeyman.

"It was this half-shadow who led you away from your rickshaw so it could be robbed?"

Journeyman dropped his eyes into his lap as he said, "Yes."

"But you interrupted the robbery in progress?"

"Yes, but only because I defeated the shadowcat ambush the boy led me into," Journeyman said.

The Judge's forehead crinkled at the mention of the shadowcats.

"So attempted murder, is it?" The Judge said. "If that be the case, this is a graver matter than I was led to believe."

Journeyman said nothing. Connor's heart pounded. He couldn't believe what he'd just heard: attempted murder. At the same time, he caught the Shopkeeper's mouth curling upward slightly. The Shopkeeper had to be forcing Journeyman to accuse him.

After a moment, The Judge said to Journeyman, "Very well. If you don't wish to escalate this with further comment on the matter, then that is your business." Then, he said to Officer Marbeth, "And where is the second witness? The accomplice?"

Officer Marbeth trotted to the back of the room and disappeared out the door. A moment later, she returned leading a small shadow by the hand. Connor's heart jolted when he saw Quiet.

Quiet walked slowly to the desk. As she passed Connor, she whispered, "I told you not to see him."

Officer Marbeth stopped Quiet beside the desk by clasping both hands on Quiet's shoulders, though Connor couldn't tell if the grip was comforting or restraining. Then, the officer rounded the side of the desk and resumed her position behind The Judge. Quiet kept her attention locked onto the desktop blotter and crossed her arms over her chest. She seemed to refuse to look at anyone in the room, but Connor felt she avoided him most of all. His head spun. Quiet and Journeyman were betraying him. What kind of place was this?

"Are you going to lie about me, too?" Connor asked Quiet.

"Silence!" The Judge barked. "Immaterial!"

Quiet cringed, her shoulders narrowing as if she wanted to collapse in on herself. Then, The Judge reached out with his pencil hand. He slipped the eraser under her chin and raised it, forcing her to look him in the face. She did not resist.

The Judge said, "Explain the nature of your testimony."

Quiet grimaced and traced her toe along the obsidian floor.

"I was one of the thieves who stole the umbrellas," Quiet said. "Two of my associates pretended to bully Little Bit so he could lead Journeyman from his cart."

Connor opened his mouth to insist he'd done nothing of the sort, but a single, vicious glance from The Judge shut it before a sound escaped.

"The Shopkeeper offered not to hold you accountable in exchange for testimony?"

Quiet nodded glumly.

"And how would you describe the overall role of this 'Little Bit' in the robbery?"

Quiet sucked a long breath between her teeth, looked straight at the Shopkeeper, and said, "It was Little Bit's idea. He planned it. He plans all of our thefts."

"Liar! How could you say that?" Connor said, so angry his vision pulsed. He was shouting, but he could hardly hear himself over the thud of his heart and the blood rushing to his head. "You stinking liar!"

The Judge half rose in his seat, his form appearing much larger and far less frail than it had. His robes billowed in the motion. The wind from the movement extinguished several of the candles.

"You will not interject again until you are asked, lest I call for the Hands of Silencing!" The Judge boomed.

The Judge set down his pencil and said to Marbeth, "Please remove her."

Connor dropped his eyes, and his gaze fell onto his shoes. It dawned on him: they weren't like a pair he'd worn the year before. They were the same pair, just worn down enough that he hadn't recognized them before. She hadn't been kind. She'd simply given him back something she'd stolen from him. Connor shot Quiet the ugliest look he could muster as she passed.

"I'm sorry," she whispered, "but I need to find my mommy."

"I hope she's dead," Connor said.

"She is," Quiet said.

And then, Quiet was gone. Connor felt a pang of regret. Even if he'd been wronged, he knew what he said had been cruel. He turned back to The Judge.

"They're lying," he pleaded.

The Judge shrugged.

"In my experience," The Judge said, "when three stand against one, it is the one who is the liar." He pointed to the painting of the scales. "When one is weighed against the many, the only joy lies in confession of guilt. Can you present any evidence or testimony contradicting the accusation?"

Connor turned to Journeyman, who fidgeted in his seat but said nothing. The shopkeeper remained unsurprisingly silent.

When Connor didn't answer, The Judge said, "I offer you this chance to make a full confession and ask for leniency."

Connor clenched his jaw. He would not lie. He wouldn't be like everyone he'd met here. Maybe they thought it was somehow fair, but it was wrong. Connor realized fair and right weren't always the same thing.

"Very well," The Judge said and held up his hands. "Give me the Hands of Judgment."

Officer Marbeth reached back into the drawer and withdrew two hands clad in black gloves. One held an iron gavel, the other a round metal disc. She removed the Hands of Listening and screwed in the Hands of Judgment.

The Judge set the metal disc on the table and struck it with the gavel. The clank made Connor wince.

"Little Bit, who stands accused of theft under the eyes of Libericia of The Thirteen," he said. "Based on this testimony and your presence at The Bins with the stolen goods in hand, I find you guilty of this theft. I will now deliberate on your sentence. You are to be returned to your cell. This matter is concluded. Justice has been served."

The Judge struck the gavel again. Connor's body heaved in fitful sobs as the door opened, and an officer entered. The officer took Connor roughly by the arm and dragged him towards the hall. Connor grabbed the doorframe as he passed through it.

"Sergeant Dandrich!" Connor cried out. "She can testify!"

The Judge pressed his lips into a flat line and said, "Sergeant Dandrich is not in good standing with this chamber."

The officer continued to drag Connor out. However, Journeyman had finally turned in his chair to look at Connor, and though he couldn't be certain, he thought he saw tears rolling down the man's cheeks.

Chapter 11

WHAT GOODNESS IS

Back in his cell, Connor threw himself onto the narrow bed and pressed his face into his arms. The betrayals drove out all other thoughts. He'd trusted Journeyman, and the man had lied to The Judge, whether he felt bad about it or not. He'd believed Quiet meant to help him, but she'd blamed him for everything. Where did she get off? Ringleader? If she hadn't barged into his life, none of this would have happened. While she had warned him to avoid the Shopkeeper, she knew the Shopkeeper meant to trick him yet kept the truth to herself. Who knows what he might have been able to do differently?

Somehow, the worst part was how The Judge seemed to accept all the lies without question. Judges were supposed to be fair. They were supposed to listen. That judge probably made up his mind before Connor even entered the chamber. Connor almost appreciated the two bullying shadows outside his closet. They hadn't hidden anything. Better to hear an awful truth than a kind lie.

Connor sat up and pulled his legs to his chest. He was cold, but there were no blankets or sheets, only a rough, gray mattress stinking of sweat and mildew. The hallway lanterns threw Connor's shadow onto the bed beside him, and it looked more incomplete than ever. He was locked in a cell with no escape awaiting some awful punishment, and he'd accomplished nothing. He had no friends or leads. If he could escape, he might find the shadow named Tonic who Quiet mentioned, but if he couldn't trust Quiet, he couldn't trust Tonic. For all he knew, the whole thing could be a lie. Probably was.

Then, Connor remembered what the Shopkeeper said in The Bins. What if someone in the jail could answer Connor's questions? Shopkeeper had obviously meant it as a mocking way to keep his end of the deal, but what if there was truth to it? Heck—if Connor could be in jail without having done anything, maybe others could be too. At this rate, it wouldn't surprise Connor to learn all the good people in The Shadowlands were in jail. Even the slightest of hope was better than none.

Connor tried to stand and walk to the cell bars, but dizziness overpowered him, and he collapsed to his knees. His forehead blazed with fever. His stomach rolled so badly, he crawled to the toilet, heaving the emptiness in his belly.

Embarrassed, Connor looked to see if the other prisoners were watching. The two shadows seemed absorbed in whatever they stared into, but the Caster in the corner was perched on his bed and staring at Connor. He smiled — neither nasty nor friendly. It seemed to say, "Yup." What if this Caster knew how to find his shadow? What if he was also looking for him?

The man scratched his square jaw. His head seemed a little too big for his body, and his skin was almost as pale as the Pale Boy's. He wore a baggy, dark beige T-shirt over black pants so Connor couldn't guess his build. A bit of the man's shadow was visible on the bed, but Connor couldn't tell if it was whole.

"Are you looking for your shadow, too?" Connor asked.

"Found it, found it," the man said in an almost sing-song voice. Then more evenly, he said, "That's why I'm here."

Connor furrowed his brow.

"What do you mean?"

"What's it to ya?" the man asked. Connor believed he was actually asking.

"I'm looking for my shadow," Connor said. "Half of it, anyway."

"Figured," the Caster said. "Saw you half-casting when they brought you in, but didn't know if yours had been stolen or if ya'd traded it. Can't trust a fella who'd trade his shadow for the types of things you'd get from the Shadowlands."

"You got that right," Connor blurted. "I trusted Journeyman and look where it got me."

The Caster stood up and walked to the edge of his cell, closing his hands around the bars.

"The thing you got to remember about folk is they'll do anything to get what they want if they think what they want is important enough. Nothing will make someone do worse things than love. Or what they think is love."

Shopkeeper's etched metal box came to mind. The faces he'd seen in his mind when he'd held it. The promises he'd read. They were all about siblings, spouses, and children. Journeyman's son was sick. Other people's loved ones were missing. Would his mother betray someone to protect him? She might. Would it really be wrong for her to do so? Could the right reason justify a wrong action? Connor's head got a bit fuzzy. He was too young for such thoughts. Those thoughts were for adults.

"What's your name?" the Caster asked.

"Little Bit," Connor said.

"Cute," the Caster said. "Used to call my sister Little Bit. Call me Mosley."

"Okay, Mosley," Connor said, needing to get to the matter at hand. For all he knew, The Judge or the officer could come down at any time and sentence him to God knows what. "What do you mean getting your shadow back put you here?"

Mosley laughed like he was in on a secret joke.

"Found my shadow," Mosley said. "But not in time; they'd sold it to the Shadower."

"The Shadower?" Connor asked.

"Some honcho growing big out East," Mosley said. "Most of the thieves work for him."

"Why does the Shadower want shadows?" Connor asked.

"Don't know," Mosley said. "Nothing good, I'm sure. But I ain't about to ask him."

"But maybe you could have traded with him for your shadow."

"I don't know much about the Shadower," Mosley said. "But I know I want as little to do with him as possible. Even the thieves are terrified of him."

Connor wanted to know more, but he could tell Mosley wouldn't share even if he knew. However, something about Mosley's story bothered him, so he asked, "You were Shadowless?"

"Yup," Mosley said. "Almost a week."

"But I thought being Shadowless means it's over," Connor said. "I met this Pale Boy…"

"Being Shadowless means you lose your ability to care, but it's not all at once. It fades."

Connor thought back to what the Pale Boy said about no longer feeling sad or playing. The boy said he'd slowly stopped hearing his name.

"Why does it matter so much if you have a shadow?" Connor asked.

"Best I've been able to figure, your shadow contains all the 'dark'—" Mosley held up his fingers in quotation marks as he said this—parts of yourself, and without your shadow, you lose those dark parts."

"Wouldn't that be a good thing, though?" Connor asked. "How could it be bad to lose your dark parts?"

"Can you have day without the night?" Mosley asked. "Be awake if you never sleep?"

Connor shrugged.

"What does it mean to be good?" Mosley asked.

"You make good choices," Connor said. "Do the right thing."

"Would there be good choices if there weren't bad?" Mosley asked. "Would it matter if you told the truth, if you didn't sometimes want to lie?"

"I don't know," Connor admitted.

Mosley sighed. "Guess it doesn't matter if you understand. You're a kid. But know this: you can't be happy if you've never been sad. When you lose your shadow, the light of yourself fades too, and then you just are. Not a care in the world, but nothing to live for, either. Doesn't happen at once though. Takes time to forget yourself. Once I lost my shadow, I felt myself slipping away – but I knew what was happening, so I returned to The Shadowlands."

"You don't need a shadow to come here?" Connor asked.

"No," Mosley said. "In fact, the Shadowless are very powerful here. For a brief time. Time I used to get my shadow back from the underling taking my shadow to the Shadower."

"Wouldn't that work on the Shadower too?" Connor asked.

"No," Mosley said. "The Shadower is... different. To be honest, I don't even know for sure what he is let alone how to beat him."

"But why arrest you for taking your shadow back? Why don't you go home?"

"Once my shadow passed from the thief to the underling, it was the rightful property of the Shadower. I became a thief myself when I stole it back. And being able to return home with a whole shadow isn't guaranteed. Not quite as easy as you've had it."

"Easy?" Connor said. "I have to die!"

"Well, not really," Mosley said. "That's one way to do it—the most efficient if your shadow's incomplete. Your body doesn't want to be here, after all. However, if you have a whole shadow and you die in the Shadowlands, you really die like you would anywhere in the World of Light. When they execute me, that's it. I'm done. There will be no light for me to find, and my shadow will be stuck in the Shadowlands forever."

Connor felt awful for Mosley. He wished he could help, but he had nothing to offer until he could help himself. He had to find a way out.

"How can I get out of here?" Connor said.

"Judging by how flushed you are, fever's going to take you back soon. All you have to do is lean into it."

"But then I'll have to start all over," Connor said. "It took me so long to get here."

Mosley shook his head.

"You'll return to the last place you slept here," Mosley said. "My advice is don't fall asleep here. Die first."

Where he last slept meant Quiet's cubby. Was that why Quiet was insistent he slept? What if Quiet was there when he returned?

"Do the Shadow Police know where?" Mosley asked.

"No," Connor said, but then he added, "I don't know. They might."

"They won't be too happy if you escape before they sentence you," Mosley said. "My advice is to run as soon as you come back. Get out of Gissu as fast and quiet as you can."

Connor nodded. His head felt so heavy. He tried to speak, but his tongue wouldn't cooperate.

"Lie down," Mosley said, the melodic quality returning to his voice. "Let your body do the work. I can't say I've died in the real world, but I've died here. It's only awful for a little bit. Lie down, lie down."

The suggestion to lie down sounded too necessary for Connor to ignore. Connor's body slumped over, and he curled into a ball on his side. His stomach churned with both nausea and unmatchable hunger. His throat burned with thirst. His thoughts fragmented.

Minutes or hours passed; he couldn't say which. Maybe even days. He tried to keep his eyes open, but his cell darkened as a pounding headache drowned all other feelings. He vaguely heard the clank of the hallway bars as his vision blacked out.

He couldn't tell if his eyes were open or closed. The mattress beneath him ebbed away.

Then came the scent of lavender fabric softener and mildew. Boxes pressing against his arm and leg, his cheek lying on something rough but yielding. Carpet maybe?

Two thick snakes slid underneath him, one under his shoulders, one under his knees. No, not snakes. Arms. He lifted through the air, his feet brushing through hanging clothes, his body drifting out of darkness and into light. The vague outline of a face wavered in and out of the field of gray.

Suddenly, a world of light poured into his eyes with stinging intensity. Tears dropped from his mother's cheeks onto him as she laid him into his bed.

The fever clouded his mind too much for him to speak. His whole body ached as he felt a blanket being pulled over his body. Nausea turned his stomach over and over. Had he collapsed in his closet and dreamed the whole thing? He tried to reach out to his mother, but his arms wouldn't work. He tried to groan, but his mouth and throat were so dry, he couldn't even swallow.

Suddenly, the bed beneath him felt like the softest thing he'd ever felt, and his body melted into it. It wasn't warm, and neither was the blanket, but the embrace of the softness caused his mind to drift again. His eyes were still open, but the world seemed removed, like when he used the vacuum cleaner attachment as a spyglass. The last things he registered were his mother's lips, just her lips, no nose or chin, and they were moving slowly, possibly singing.

The darkness returned, a different darkness from before, the darkness of sleep.

Connor stirred twice as a hand tilted his head and neck upward. A cold liquid came into his mouth in tiny drops, each drop a blessing. A hot liquid followed, and somehow, he knew to swallow. Many times, curved metal passed between his lips bearing something thin, savory, and salty. Each mouthful exploded with flavor, nearly overwhelming his senses. Several times, he sputtered and coughed, his body jolting, steeped in exhaustion. Eventually, the liquids stopped coming, and he passed back into darkness.

When Connor awoke again, his thoughts were still muddled and his body ached, the light hurt his eyes, but he squinted enough to focus on his mother. Her eyes were red and swollen, her face flushed. She broke into a huge smile as their eyes met.

"Oh, my baby," she said. "Oh, my baby."

Connor smiled weakly before he fell asleep again.

A MORNING UNLIKE EVERY OTHER MORNING

The next time Connor awoke, his mother pulled him upright; his whole body wobbling until she shoved enough pillows behind his back to support him. The blankets slid down his chest to his waist. A breakfast tray stretched over his lap. Though the pillows held him up, she turned his face side to side as his head bobbed. Somehow, he remembered how to hold his head still, and she finally released him. He tried to speak, but only managed a gasp.

His mother's face was clearer than before, eyes still swollen, concern written over every feature. Exhaustion lined her face as deeply as when his father died. How long had she been watching him, worrying? Had it been the days he'd been in the Shadowlands, or had she found him collapsed in his closet, the Pale Boy still sitting by the Game of Life? Connor struggled to believe he was home and not dreaming somewhere in the Shadowlands.

A glass of water came to his lips. He took a sip and his mouth flooded with water. The first full swallow was hard, the lump of liquid bludgeoning its way down his throat, but the second came easier.

Then, as if the water had purged some sort of blockage, the smell of eggs hit his nose. It was the most amazing thing he'd ever smelled. His mother scooped a bite of yolk with a fork and lifted it to Connor's lips. He snarfed it down voraciously. After two more bites came a glass of orange juice, and he drank the whole thing in one long chug.

His mother muttered, "Thank God, thank God, thank God."

"What happened?" Connor whispered, his voice thin and raspy.

"Later, later," his mother whispered, bringing a piece of toast to Connor's lips. The raspberry-jellied toast tasted as magnificent as the eggs. At the same time, there was something off about it. Something missing. Not that he cared. The food bit into the hunger howling from his stomach. Each swallow brought a bit more clarity.

"What time is it?" Connor asked.

"Almost night," his mother said. "How are you feeling?"

"Better," Connor said. "A lot better."

"Good, sweetheart," his mother said. "That's good."

Connor took the fork into his hand and finished the rest of his meal himself, his mind registering nothing but the food. When he finished, his mother pressed him back into the bed and said, "Go back to sleep."

Connor did not resist.

The next time Connor woke, he was alone. His mother's chair sat empty at his bedside. There was a pile of wadded-up tissues on the nightstand. His stomach dropped thinking about how much stress he'd put his mother through.

Still, he felt the strongest he'd felt since the theft. He held out hope that it had all been a dream. But as soon as he sat up, he saw the left half of his shadow was gone. So was part of the right side. He rubbed the sleep away with a balled-up fist, but still the broken shadow stretched off his torso. When he stood, his shadow was still wrong, and he felt to the core something was missing. Even the floor felt funny under his bare feet.

Quietly, he pulled on fresh underwear and socks and then a long-sleeved shirt and jeans before he crept into the hallway. How would he explain himself? He didn't know what he needed to explain because he didn't know what had happened here while he'd been in the Shadowlands. He did his best to mentally brace himself for the interrogation he knew was coming.

His mother waited at the kitchen counter in her pink bathrobe, drinking a cup of coffee with something cooking on the stove. She immediately crossed over to him, her mouth pressed in a tight line, either suppressing a smile or a frown, or both at once. Her stride was rigid and urgent, and her arms extended the moment her body moved.

She drew him into a quick hug that seemed to last forever, the type of hug that should have swept all of Connor's cares away. Unfortunately, the boy didn't feel such security. He could barely smell her, and there was something slightly sour in the scent. No doubt it was because of the theft. Nothing would be right unless he got his shadow back.

His mother let him go and knelt, placing her hands on his shoulders. Her face was heavy with concern, and though her eyes were no longer pink and puffy, they had recently streaked her cheeks with fresh tears. Her mouth opened. Now the questions would come.

"Are you feeling better?" she asked.

"Much," Connor said. He opened his mouth to say something else, though he wasn't sure what—he wanted to say many things at the same time. It might have been about the Shadowlands, or it might have been a lie. It might have been how much he loved his mother and how much he'd missed her, or it might have been about how hungry he was and how good waffles would be. Regardless of what it might have been, he didn't get a chance to say it. His mother placed her index finger over her lips, its tip nestling into the little indentation under his nose.

"Eat," his mother said.

Connor's brow furrowed. Was she at a loss for words that he was back? She stood and watched him for several moments with a strange expression on her face. There was happiness in it, but there was also a sense of confusion. Not a confusion like she had many questions, but something more vacant. Connor considered what Mosley had told him:

he'd find her easy to convince with whatever explanation he offered.

His mother shook her head slightly and went about gathering up his breakfast. She served the food at the table: over-easy eggs and toast, bacon, and pan-cooked tomatoes and mushrooms. It was his mother's favorite breakfast, and she'd told him many times it was the same breakfast her own mother used to cook for her on special mornings. Together, they ate, staring at each other through the thin steam rising off the food.

When Connor had shoveled the last bit of garlicky mushrooms into his mouth, his mother took an unusually long sip of her coffee and set her mug down on the table. She linked her fingers together in front of her plate. For a fleeting moment, her features skewed with the same confusion as before they ate. She nodded firmly, looked Connor in the eyes, and said, "Well?"

Connor sighed in regret, because he knew he would lie to his mother. And this wouldn't be a little lie like, "I didn't sneak into the cookie jar," or "I only watched cartoons while you worked."

No, this would be a big lie.

It would be a big lie for three reasons. First, the truth was too fantastic; the thieves, judges, and shadowcats seemed too straight from a book or a movie. Second, if she believed him, no doubt it would terrify her, especially since he had not found his shadow and would need to go back. What mother would allow her kid to face predators and liars while being wanted by the police to seek a thief? The third reason was simple: Connor simply couldn't worry his mother any further. He needed a simple explanation, one potentially true for any child. In the moment of silence between them, Connor remembered his conversation with Journeyman during the rust storm, and the lie came to him.

"I ran away," he said.

"But why? What did I do?" Fresh tears rolled down his mother's cheeks from both eyes, parting at the lines of her lips like they were trying to escape each other.

"It was because of the salesman and his son," Connor said, thinking quickly. "I saw the two of them together, and it reminded me of how much I miss Dad. How much I miss doing things with him. And you. The boy spends every day with his dad, and I'll never see mine again."

His mother remained still, and what Connor said next was the truth, even though he hadn't meant to say it: "You're at work every night, and when you're not, you're too sad to spend time with me. I lost Dad, too, you know?"

The last sentence hit the table between them like an anvil. His mother's hands shot up to cover her eyes, knocking her mug over in the process. The cup thunked sideways on the table, the last of her coffee flowing out onto the wood and dripping to the linoleum. The liquid, untouched by cream or sugar, so dark brown it was nearly black, reminded Connor of blackwater. The oily and rancid taste filled his mouth.

His mother tried to speak, perhaps to defend herself, but Connor knew if he didn't keep talking, the lie would unravel.

"I hid in Tommy's backyard," Connor blurted. Tommy was the only friend of his who lived within walking distance. "In the shed where his parents keep all the pool stuff. He didn't know I was there. I didn't bring any food or anything to drink, and I was already getting sick, so I got worse and worse. By the time I realized how awful I felt, I could barely walk home. I was so afraid of what you would say, I snuck in."

Connor stopped talking. His insides roiled. Not only was guilt choking him, but even as he'd spoken, he wasn't sure how he'd gotten home; for all he knew, she'd found him on the lawn. Perhaps the worst part was that Connor knew his story was hurtful enough that his mom would be so concerned she might not question the bigger picture. He wondered if he told this lie so well as the result of being in the Shadowlands and losing much of his shadow. Was he becoming a worse person? Connor hoped his mother wouldn't believe a word of it.

She started nodding.

"I knew it," she muttered through her tears, her hands still over her face. "I've been trying so hard, but I can't do enough."

Her hands fell from her face, revealing cheeks fully flushed and wide eyes.

"I'm so sorry. I don't know how to do this. I don't know how to do it all."

His mom crossed her arms on the table's edge, thrust her face onto them, and sobbed.

Connor stood, stepped forward, and threw his arms over his

mother. He felt guilty about the lies, and he felt guilty about the truths they contained. And he was only going to make things worse by going back to the Shadowlands and then lying about it all over again.

For several moments, the boy held his mother, coffee dripping, the last bits of food drying on the plates. Connor's mother's shoulders rose and fell in rhythm with her sobs.

Finally, his mother lifted her head, dried her eyes off with her napkin, and said, "We'll spend more time together. We will. We'll start next week."

Even though he needed to return to the Shadowlands as soon as possible, Connor found the promise stung him. Whenever he asked her to go somewhere or play a game, she always said next week or tomorrow. Neither seemed to come. Connor told her so.

His mother sniffled and said, "There's nothing more I can do. You've missed three days of school—so it was three days, Connor noted—and I'll be fired if I miss more work. I'm going to try to get a couple of day shifts next week. We'll talk a little this afternoon before I go to work."

A silence settled between them. His mother wiped the tears from her cheeks with the shoulders of her shirt.

"Thank God I didn't call the police," his mother said, a strange detachment entering her voice. "What a mess that would have been. Bet you I'd have lost today, too, explaining everything."

Connor was shocked by both her voice and that he'd been gone for three days.

"You didn't call the police?" he asked.

His mother shrugged and held her hands palms up off to her sides.

"I wanted to," she said. "Lord knows I must have picked up the phone a hundred times. But every time, something nagged me to hang up. I was so sure you'd be back any minute."

She chuckled.

"One time, I picked up the phone and dialed nine and one, and somehow—and I don't know how it's even possible—I forgot the next number."

Connor couldn't help but smirk.

"You forgot the number for 911?"

"I swear, I remembered it as soon as I started to walk away. But then

I told myself it had to be a sign I was overreacting, that I needed to wait a little longer. The strangest thing? For a moment, I simply couldn't think."

They laughed together, and it felt good. The humor aside, though, Connor was certain this was the effect of the shadowlands Mosley talked about. She should be more upset. Was the Shadowlands actually altering her thoughts? What if it was bad for her?

Connor's thoughts froze as he realized his mother was looking at him with a focused interest as if she were about to ask him what he was thinking about. Thankfully, she simply wiped her mouth with her napkin, brushed a few crumbs off her lap, and got up from the table.

"We'll talk more after school," she said, clearing off the plates.

"I'm going to school?" Connor asked. She'd already said so, but it hadn't sunk in yet. It seemed like the appropriate response would be her saying he'd never go anywhere again. However, if he went to school, he wouldn't be able to use his closet to get back to the Shadowlands, at least not for several more hours.

"Of course, sweetie," she said. "It's a school day, and you're not sick anymore. And to be honest, I need a bit of time to collect myself. I've been more than a bit of a mess."

Connor nodded. He forced a smile and gave her a long hug, which she returned with a sort of desperation that tore at the boy's heart.

Connor's mom drove him to school. They said little during the drive, though Connor could see his mother looking back at him in the rearview mirror. Her face showed a mix of emotions, and Connor felt the truth at the back of his tongue like some little animal fighting to climb out. At the same time, what he'd said had hurt her, and to say it was all a lie would make it crueler. If he admitted he'd told such a big lie, wouldn't it make the truth even harder to believe? As much as he wanted to pour everything out, he kept his eyes out the window as much as possible, though he hardly noticed the trees and lawns, and basketball poles streaking by. All he wanted was to get out of the car and into the school before his mother asked him something he would need to answer with a lie.

When they pulled up in front of the school under the shadow of the waving flag, Connor hoisted his backpack and slipped out of the car with a quick 'love you'.

He had hardly taken his seat in homeroom before the day felt intolerable. He tried to act normal, but when his friends asked him where he'd been, all he could say was he'd been sick. Then, he'd fall silent until they turn to someone else and talk about video games or football games or action movies. A couple of times, Connor tried to listen in, but he couldn't see anything they discussed as important. Especially not with everything weighing on his mind.

His friends aside, being so distracted bothered Connor. Normally, he liked school. He wasn't crazy about it like the more bookish kids, but he enjoyed science and history. He liked learning about the world and its wonders and was typically glad to share his thoughts on whatever the class discussed. However, he couldn't focus on ratios in math class or World War II in world history. When Miss Evers asked him for the answer to a problem, he shrugged and said he didn't know. She knew he'd been sick, so she nodded and moved on to another student. Before the start of history, a couple more of his classmates asked where he'd been, and, again, he said he'd been sick and looked away.

At lunch, Connor sat on the edge of the courtyard as everyone else hunkered down at the round tables under the canopy, laughed in twos and threes leaning against the wall, or sat cross-legged on the ground because they'd gotten outside after every seat had been taken. Tommy came over and invited Connor to join him and his friends, but he couldn't even meet Tommy's eyes, feeling terrible he'd used his friend in his lies. Tommy seemed surprised, but said, "Well, okay." He then ran off to eat his lunch-line tacos.

Instead, Connor watched a few birds picking at a slice of bread someone had thrown into the grass. They pecked up crumbs and pecked at each other. One of the pigeons fluttered its wings out of the reach of another and then hopped cautiously forward before it resumed pecking. Somehow, that all reminded Connor of the shadow children robbing Journeyman's cart. Was that how they all survived? Pecking for scraps left unattended?

Mouse's face came to mind. She was the only person in the whole Shadowlands who hadn't mistreated or deceived him, though she probably didn't have enough time. Was she now Shadowless, or had she already gone back into that dark place? Could he find her? If what Quiet said could be trusted, Mouse didn't know how to get her shadow back. Maybe together they'd have a chance.

Every minute or so, he dropped his gaze to the ground and his shadow. In the bright noon light, his shadow appeared darker and more vivid than ever, but the strength of its color only accentuated what was missing. All morning, he'd expected someone to notice how strange it looked, but he remembered what Sergeant Dandrich said about casters not paying much attention to shadows and the strange way his mom seemed too hesitant to raise too much of a ruckus looking for him. Heck, until it had been stolen, Connor had gone days at a time without so much as looking at it. Was it lonely? Did shadows have thoughts and feelings while they were still attached to their casters? Or did they only come to life in the Shadowlands?

As he thought about it, one certainty became clearer. He couldn't waste time before going back; he didn't even want to wait until he got home. Sure, he could go back to his closet after his mom left for work, but then half the day would be gone.

Then, it struck him: what if he didn't need to use his own closet?

Connor sat bolt upright. The school had lots of closets—storage closets, the janitor's closet, classroom closets, and more. Even the bathrooms had little closets where they kept toilet paper, paper towels, and plungers. Connor was clambering to his feet when a voice behind him said, "Mr. Brighton?"

Connor whirled. The voice belonged to his history teacher, Mr. Paxter, who was on lunch duty. Mr. Paxter was a tall man who always came to work in khaki pants and a white button-down shirt. About the age of Connor's mother, the teacher had sandy brown hair and brown eyes. He offered Connor a warm, friendly smile.

"Hello, Mr. Paxter," Connor said.

"Feeling better?" Mr. Paxter asked.

"Yes, sir," Connor said, antsy to slip back into the school. "Quite a bit."

"Glad to hear it," Mr. Paxter said. "You seemed distracted in class today. I was worried you might be getting sick again."

"No, I was thinking about things."

Mr. Paxter nodded. He squatted in front of Connor, hands hanging over his knees. "Everything okay at home? With your mother? I heard about your father."

"Yeah, it's fine," Connor said.

Why was Mr. Paxter asking about his mom? She hadn't gone to this year's parent-teacher night because she had to work. So, as far as Connor knew, none of his current teachers even knew his mother. Connor didn't know why he felt suspicious.

Part of Connor wanted to tell Mr. Paxter about the Shadowlands. He liked Mr. Paxter. He was straightforward, spoke clearly, and never talked down to the class. Moreover, Connor felt like he needed to tell somebody, even if it was just to test how crazy it all sounded. Likely, his story would be treated as little more than a fib at worst and, at best, a creative story. Maybe they'd take it as a sign he was disturbed and report it to the counsellor or the police.

However, something Mosley said popped into Connor's head, so he asked, "Can someone be happy if they've never been sad?"

"A tough question," Mr. Paxter said with a frown. "Advanced for someone your age."

"It's something someone told me," Connor said. "Can someone be good if they never want to do something bad?"

Mr. Paxter shrugged. "People spend their whole lives thinking about those kinds of questions," he said. "I think we understand the world through contrast. It's like World War II. In class today, I was saying we often define the war as us vs. them, Allies vs. Axis, freedom vs. fascism. However, I'm sure both sides did things they wish they could take back. At the end of the day, what really matters is that many, many people died there who did not deserve it. Things like war are never totally black and white. If it's day where you are, somewhere else it's night."

"Like what Mosley said," Connor said, then shut his mouth because he wasn't sure he should have mentioned Mosley.

"And who is Mosley?" Mr. Paxter asked, perking an eyebrow. "A friend? Of your mother's, maybe?"

Connor immediately felt uncomfortable, shuffling on his feet. Then, inspiration struck.

"I'm sorry," Connor said, "but I have to use the bathroom. May I go?"

"Of course," Mr. Paxter said.

Connor trotted over the grass towards the school door, glancing back once to see his teacher watching him. However, by the time he'd crossed the doors and looked back through the glass, Mr. Paxter had wandered off to another part of the playground.

Connor stopped in the hallway to decide where to go. The bathroom closets? No one would think twice about him going into the bathroom. But those bathrooms might have shelves behind the doors with no place to stand. And no light bulb to unscrew. The janitor's closet would probably be the best option. It was after lunch, so the janitor would be sweeping and mopping the cafeteria.

However, the janitor's closet was only a couple of doors down from the principal's office, and the school secretary could see through the plate-glass windows. He would have to walk right on by.

What if he walked by like he was going somewhere specific? No one would think he was up to something. His hands grew sweaty as he walked, and his heart beat hard as he approached the edge of the window. He wanted to stop and peak to see if the secretary was watching, but if she saw, she would be more likely to stop him. Connor smiled to himself at how well he was thinking things through.

Connor strode past the windows, glancing through only once. Fortunately, the secretary had the phone pinched between her ear and shoulder and was busy digging through one of her desk drawers. He was home free.

He jogged to the janitor's closet and took a deep breath as he pulled open the door. It was empty. Well, not empty—no one was inside. The room itself was not empty by any stretch, but cluttered and narrow. A desk sat on one side with shelves buried in bottles of cleaning solutions and boxes of rags on the other. The closet smelled of vinegar and ammonia.

A single exposed bulb hung from the ceiling, dangling from a chain like the one in his closet. Connor reached for the bulb but stopped as his hand fell more than a foot short. After a quick glance around, he dragged the janitor's wheeled chair away from the desk and stood on its cushion.

His fingers closed around the bulb.

Instantly, he jerked them away, hissing through his teeth. The bulb was so hot, the tips of his fingers hurt something awful. The chair wobbled beneath him. After balancing himself like a surfer, Connor grabbed a dirty rag off the shelf and used it to protect his fingers from the hot glass.

The room fell dark after a couple of twists. Connor closed his eyes as he took hold of the chain.

THE GOOD DEAL

The instant Connor pulled the chain, the world lurched into motion. He tumbled off the chair to a terrible splintering of wood and crash of things falling from the shelves. Something popped with a boom, like a giant balloon, and liquid sprayed his face. The chair fell over, its wheels whirring. All the breath burst from Connor's lungs as he hit the ground. Mop and broom handles clattered as Connor rolled onto his stomach on top of them. One was broken, and the sharp splinters pressed against his thigh. He pushed up onto all fours and groped through the darkness for the door.

Dim light streamed in. Connor turned to see what had happened but couldn't make sense of what he saw. The walls of the closet jutted at weird angles, and it looked like there were more than four—eight, in fact. Four were the cinderblock gray of the janitor's office, but four more were pastel yellow. The janitor's metal shelves were twisted and bent, and a rod laden with clothes jutted through them. The clothes themselves passed in and out of the metal. From the amount of pink and other soft colors, they were most likely girls' clothes.

Hands grabbed Connor under the arms and dragged him out the door. He kicked his feet and twisted his shoulders against his captors. When he tore free, Connor spilled sideways with a thud.

"Woah, there," said an unfamiliar shadow, perhaps the one who'd grabbed him. "Calm down. Not gonna hurt ya."

The shadow was tall enough to be a teenager, but not an adult. He had a narrow face with strong cheekbones and pronounced lips, and though his face looked young enough to match his height, lines around his eyes gave him a strained appearance. His hair seemed lighter than any Connor had seen in the Shadowlands. A soft gray with a tinge of purple. He wore a V-necked T-shirt with a ragged collar, and from his belt over his left hip hung three bright tassels: one blue, one red, and one yellow.

Connor was about to ask the young man who he was when Quiet and Mouse stepped into view from behind him. Quiet appeared to the left and Mouse to the right. Both girls stared at him with concern.

"What the heck happened?" Connor asked.

"You and Mouse both slept in the same place," Quiet said sheepishly.

Understanding dawned on Connor. Similarly to how his closet had appeared in the Iron Desert, the janitor's closet had appeared in Quiet's cubby. Unfortunately, so had Mouse's, and now both closets occupied the same space. Mouse looked aghast as she peered into the mess.

"My clothes," she said. "My stuff. It's all ruined."

The boy shadow frowned, pointing at the wreckage. "That's your closet?" he asked Connor.

Connor looked back into the twisted mess. "It's the janitor's closet from my school," he said.

Mouse frowned. "What happens if someone tries to open one of these closets in the real world?"

Connor shrugged and, after a moment, reached up to where the chain-link fence had cut him while he'd snuck through the alleyway. The cut was gone. Had it been there at home? Had it healed while he was sick? Had the injury vanished when he'd come back to the

Shadowlands? Maybe injuries in the Shadowlands disappeared when one returned to the World of Light. If that was the case, then it was possible the closets would appear as normal back in the real world.

Connor was about to mention this when his attention shifted to Quiet. A more powerful feeling threw everything else out of mind: betrayal. Quiet had betrayed him. She'd lied to The Judge, let him fall into the Shopkeeper's trap, and even stolen his shoes and given them back to him like they were a present. Connor strode towards the little door that led out of the hall and into Gissu. Mosley's advice had been to leave immediately, anyway.

"Wait!" Quiet shrieked. "Please wait!"

Connor froze, but he didn't turn to face her.

"I didn't want to do it," Quiet said. "But I'd made a deal. I'd made the deal before I even met you. I had no choice."

Connor spun about, raising his hands angrily.

"Sure, you did," he snapped. "You could have broken the deal."

"You don't know what happens to deal breakers."

"Not much, apparently," Connor said. "You, the Shopkeeper, and Journeyman all broke deals with me, and you seem fine."

"I did nothing of the sort," Quiet said. "And I doubt the Shopkeeper or Journeyman did. They probably lived up to the letter of what they said, even if it was in a way you don't like. I admit, I did the same thing, and I'm sorry. You don't understand how things work here. I'll still help you. Please, let me help you."

"You stole my shoes and gave them back to me," Connor said, looking down at his feet, which were clad in the Nikes his mother had given him to replace the other pair.

"And I refused to take anything for them," Quiet said. "Telling you would have broken my deal with the Shopkeeper."

"For all I know, everything you say is part of your deal," Connor said.

Quiet looked like she was about to cry. Connor's heart stirred. He wanted to believe her, but how could he? At the same time, he thought about how he'd lied to his mother. He hated to admit it, but he understood how someone could say something they hated if they felt it mattered enough.

"I promise you it isn't," Quiet said. Then, she pointed to the boy shadow. "Look. I brought Tonic. He can still take us to the Daggers."

Connor thought Tonic looked about fourteen, maybe even fifteen. He had a tough look about him, lean and ropey, like the baseball bullies who pushed around the kids who were bad at sports during gym class. The boy gazed off to the side and tapped his foot as if he wasn't paying attention to the conversation.

"How can I trust you," Connor demanded. "How can I trust any of you?"

Tonic looked Connor dead in the eyes. "You can't," he said. "You don't get guarantees here. You make do with what you've got, and you won't find anyone who is going to give you much. If you don't accept that, you don't accept the Shadowlands, and you're going to have a very hard time here."

Connor didn't want to accept it. Surely, he could find someone good, someone who would never lie. But even as he thought it, the notion seemed unrealistic. Even his mother lied, telling him she'd spend more time with him. It wasn't her fault it never worked out, but it always twisted her good intentions into lies. Would it be better for her to never make promises?

Mouse cleared her throat and raised her hand like she was in class.

"That's not true," she said. "I know you don't know me, but you can trust me. I will never betray you. I promise."

"Do promises mean anything here?" Connor asked. "Do they mean anything at all?"

Mouse stepped forward and placed one of her small hands on Connor's elbow.

"They don't mean anything to the Shadowlands," Mouse said. "They don't always mean much in the real world. But they do to me. I keep my promises."

Maybe it was because she'd had her shadow stolen, too, or maybe Connor needed to believe someone, but Mouse's promise felt different. Maybe she would break her promise, like his mother broke her promises, but at least for now, she meant it, which was better than nothing.

Then, Connor had an idea.

"What happens if you break a deal?"

Mouse's blank expression showed she didn't have a clue. Tonic's eyes flicked to the side. Quiet shuddered and looked down. She traced her toe over the obsidian floor.

"I've only known one," Quiet said, "a young shadow like Tonic who used to look out for me. He broke a deal with a merchant he'd made for his father to forget about his death for a whole month. His name was Parson. He disappeared so long that we thought he was gone forever. But when he came back, he was like a zombie. He wouldn't speak or look at you, and he only moved if you made him. He stopped eating and drinking, wasting away until we had to leave him because we didn't know what else to do."

Quiet broke off. Tonic took up the slack.

"Deal breakers disappear and come back broken," Tonic said. "Don't know how, but if you ever meet one, you'll know why you don't want to become one."

"So, Journeyman…" Connor started.

"He's different," Quiet said with a shake of her head. "According to Shadow Law, he kept his deal with you. It's about exact wording and fine distinctions. At the same time, I overheard him talking and arguing with the Shopkeeper after they left the courtroom. It sounded nasty."

Connor nodded and made his face as serious as he could. He knew what to do.

"Then let's make a deal. I won't betray you or let anything I do force me to betray you. In return, you all do the same."

Mouse agreed, and not only did she shake Connor's hand when he offered it, but also drew him into a hug. Tonic shrugged and gave a distinct, single nod.

Quiet hesitated. "I'm still in debt to the Shopkeeper," she said.

"Did betraying me help you find your mother?"

Quiet looked at her feet. Again, she drew her toe over the floor. "He said I've only paid part of the price."

Connor didn't know what to say. Could he accept that the deal with Mouse and Tonic was enough? It would be a lot harder for Quiet to do any more damage if he could trust the two of them. Still, he wanted Quiet to accept. No, he needed her to.

"The Shopkeeper would have to tell you to betray me," Connor said. "Right? Well, what if he doesn't see you?"

Quiet smiled. "I can avoid him."

"At least until I find my shadow. Until we find Mouse's shadow," Connor said. "The same goes for all of you. We'll make this deal stand until we've caught the shadow thief.

"Or thieves," Mouse said.

"Yes," Connor said. "Do we have a deal?"

"We have a deal," Quiet said.

Satisfied, Connor felt far better than he had before, like he had finally done something right in this place. For better or worse, the four of them were bound together.

THE GATE

Tonic stepped over to a little pile of cloth by the wall, picking up what appeared to be two hooded cloaks made of shadow. He handed one to Mouse and one to Connor.

"Put these on," he said. "And wear the hood up. We'll get less attention if it's not obvious there's a couple of Casters."

Connor threw his over his shoulders. The fabric was coarse, and it itched immediately.

"As we approach the gates," Tonic said, "take down your hood. Don't look like you're hiding from the guards."

Then, Tonic hoisted a backpack over his shoulder and walked to the little door. Mouse followed, but Quiet tugged Connor's hand and took him aside.

"Listen," she whispered. "While I was looking for Tonic, an officer of the Shadow Police stopped me. She was asking about you."

"What did you tell her?" Connor said, remembering Mosley's warning. Could the Shadow Police be waiting outside?

"I don't think she was looking to arrest you. She didn't say your name, but I could tell she meant you."

"What did she want?" Connor asked.

"I didn't want to ask," Quiet said. "If I asked too much, she might have suspected I knew where you were."

The fact that Quiet called the officer a 'she' made Connor wonder if she was talking about Sergeant Dandrich. Had she learned something about the thief? Could he trust her enough to seek her out? The idea seemed promising, but he couldn't just go to the station. It would need to be enough to keep an eye out for her.

Without another word, they all ducked through the low door and into Gissu. Tonic led them through the town, sticking as much as he could to alleys and narrow streets, all of which smelled like rotten apples. Every surface seemed covered in a thin coat of rust. Their path was purposeful, shifting from one pile of debris to another, stopping behind crates and barrels. When groups of shadows occupied the street ahead, Tonic backtracked and took another route without hesitation. Something about the confidence of his movement inspired confidence in Connor. As frightening as the shadows had been approaching Shade Row with Journeyman, he found himself hardly worried about them now.

The one time they hit a dead end of sorts was at the end of an alley where they paused behind a rickety, iron shack. A large group of raucous shadows paraded by on the street. There had to be at least twenty of them, and their noise was by far the most noise Connor had heard in the Shadowlands, except maybe at his arrest. They all chattered animatedly, interjecting, cutting each other off, and talking over each other. Connor caught very little of what they said. The gist was they were headed towards something exciting.

"We're going to hit the main streets now," Tonic whispered. "Cut through the Square of Justice."

"That's the plaza at the town's back gate," Quiet whispered to Connor and Mouse.

Tonic nodded. "We'll be in the open, but there's going to be a big crowd. This group is headed there. Folks 'round here don't get this riled up often. A lot of Shadow Police will be there, but enough people should be passing through the gates for us to slip through."

"What's going on?" Connor asked.

"A crowd this big heading for the Square of Justice can only mean one thing," Tonic said.

Connor looked at Tonic quizzically, but it was Quiet who answered.

"An execution," she said.

Connor wondered how a shadow could be executed, but he didn't have a chance to ask. Tonic waved them forward as the crowd vanished at the next street corner. Two blocks ahead, a huge crowd filled an open square. Shadows comprised the bulk of it, all in raucous conversation, but Connor spotted a couple of Casters among them. Unlike the shadows who mingled freely, the Casters seemed alone, motionless, and fixed on the center of the square.

At the center stood a tall, metal platform. Against the dim sky, the silhouette of a noose hung from its frame. Unlike everything else in Gissu, the gallows was not ramshackle. Every joint was smoothly angled and seamless.

Beneath the gallows, a phalanx of Shadow Police in black uniforms kept the crowd at a distance with tall metal shields. Connor looked for Sergeant Dandrich among them but did not see her. Even if he did, he knew it would be unwise to approach her with so many other shadow officers about.

Connor's group skirted the edge of the crowd. Along the edges of the square, vendors manned stalls, hawking shadow snacks and refreshments; bundles of shadow bananas and baskets of dark apples filled one display. Another sold miniature gallows, cheap items made of sticks and plastic shafts, resembling the shapes drawn while playing hangman Two shadow children argued with the vendor over the price, attempting to trade for the "toys."

As Tonic weaved through the onlookers, a tall figure mounted the gallows followed by two officers towing a bound Caster with a hood over his or her head. The tall figure was The Judge. The man had replaced his black robe with a scarlet one with white and black trim. Though he'd looked old in his office, now he beamed with energy, clearly relishing the ceremony. The man's eyes were wide and fiery, and they seemed to blaze brighter as the hooded figure was stopped underneath the noose. Captain Sallow stood at the head of the steps leading up the gallows and watched the crowd with intent, scanning eyes.

Tonic held up a stopping hand.

"We need to wait for The Judge to stop speaking," the shadow whispered. "The police will mark anyone moving during the ceremony. Face the platform."

Connor's stomach fluttered. He didn't want to stay a moment longer than necessary.

"Shadows and Casters," The Judge said. His voice boomed across the square, clamping silence upon the crowd. "You are gathered here today to witness the execution of justice. Remember that crime is punished without mercy in The Shadowlands."

The crowd roared with applause and cries of "Hear! Hear!" until The Judge silenced them with a sharp whistle.

"If you please, officers," The Judge said. "The Hands of Proclamation."

An officer knelt and opened a metal chest at his feet. He pulled out a pair of hands holding a scroll between them. As the officer unscrewed The Judge's hands, Connor thought how strange the whole thing was. Why did The Judge need so many pairs of hands? How could his hands unscrew at all?

The Hands of Proclamation in place, The Judge opened the scroll and faced the prisoner. The other officer pulled off the hood. Connor gasped.

Mosley.

"Lewis Washington Dewey," The Judge read. "AKA Moke, AKA Mosley, by the light of Libericia and the rest of The Thirteen, you have been found guilty of the crime of shadow theft and are hereby sentenced for your Caster body to be hung by the neck until dead. Your shadow will be kept in custody until such time it can be returned to its rightful owner. Those who break the Shadow Laws cast darkness upon their light. Do you have any last words?"

Mosley glared at The Judge, his jaw clenched and his lips pressed tight. Connor wanted to cry out. How was this justice? The man had done nothing but take back what someone had stolen from him. Quiet tapped Tonic on the wrist and shook her head with a hand cupped over her mouth.

"We'll wait until after the execution," Tonic whispered. "Slip out as the crowd disperses."

Connor shuddered. He wanted to leave now. How could he watch this? He was too young.

The Judge closed the scroll.

"Officer," The Judge said. "The Hands of Execution."

The officer attached hands clad in black leather gloves onto The Judge's wrist as the other officer pulled the noose around Mosley's neck and tightened the knot. The entire crowd drew a collective breath as The Judge took hold of a tall lever. Connor had seen hangings in old westerns and learned about them in history. Please let it be quick, Connor whispered.

One officer and then another stomped on the metal platform, their boots booming a steady rhythm. The rest of the Shadow Police quickly joined. The crowd began stomping their feet, the clops of their shoes joining the echo. As far as Connor could tell, the only ones who didn't join were his companions and the few, solitary Casters.

The beat started slowly, then picked up speed, pushing towards a thundering crescendo. Connor covered his ears. What he was seeing was bad enough, but something about the unison of the crowd was maddening. He wanted to scream.

The Judge heaved the lever back, and the crowd exploded in bellows and cheers. Connor closed his eyes, but the howl of the crowd seemed so much louder that he had to open them again. His gaze was fixed on Mosley's kicking and thrashing form. The man's eyes bulged wider than seemed possible. Mosley's tongue thrust from his mouth as his face turned a deep red and then a horrifying purple. His back arched, his feet bending upwards at an almost impossible angle. Then, his writhing slowed to weak twists and then to twitches. Connor didn't know how long it took for Mosley to stop completely, but when he did, hot tears poured down Connor's cheeks. Never in his life had he seen something so awful.

Then, Mosley's shadow screamed, high and wailing, full of pain and confusion. It fell from Mosley's body and grabbed hold of the dead man's calf. Pulling a black club from his belt, Captain Sallow leapt forward, and he brought the rod down on the shadow's head and shoulders with cruel, hard strokes. The shadow squealed and yelped, trying to shield itself with its arms as the baton arced and curved around them, striking from all angles. Still, the shadow fought to claw itself standing until a blow caught it square between the shoulder blades at the base of the neck with a dull thud. Shadow Mosley sprawled on his back underneath the gallows. A cacophony of jeers, shouts, and whistles exploded from the crowd as Captain Sallow rained down several more strikes, beating it again and again until its motion ceased altogether.

When the sickening whumps stopped, the crowd's energy deflated. The show was over, and they dispersed even as two officers of the Shadow Police dragged Mosley's shadow away by limp arms. As they left, the faces in the crowd beamed wide smiles and brimmed with excited chatter. Connor hated them all. How could they be so happy? Even if Mosley was the worst criminal, Connor couldn't imagine enjoying what he'd witnessed. He fought the urge to shout what monsters they all were.

Mouse tugged on his hand, which felt warm in hers, warmer than anything he'd felt since his shadow was stolen, and he clasped it tightly. The urgency of her grip reminded him how much danger they were in. Over Mouse's shoulder, Tonic and Quiet passed in and out of sight, already well ahead in the crowd.

"We're not out yet," Mouse whispered. "When we get to the gates, walk right through. Don't look at the guards."

Mouse's words reminded Connor of sneaking past the principal's office. Act natural and walk like you have a destination. Unfortunately, this was far more dangerous. Here, the police wanted Connor. Only a few of them had seen him during the arrest, but nothing would be worse than being dragged back to jail, especially since he finally had some hope.

As they approached the gate, he and Mouse pulled down their hoods as low as they could. Unlike when he arrived with Journeyman, the gates were wide open, and a steady stream of shadows funneled through. Guards stood on either side armed with shields and batons, but they paid little interest to the throng. Still, Connor and Mouse maneuvered to the center of the crowd to pass as far from both officers as possible. There was no sign of Tonic and Quiet. Hopefully, they'd already made it through.

"If they try to stop one of us," Mouse whispered, "the other should keep going. Won't be able to help each other if both of us get caught."

Connor nodded, though he didn't know if he could simply leave Mouse behind. However, he didn't dare speak now. They were close enough for the officers to hear. The crowd wasn't thick enough to hide them completely.

A shadow bumped hard into Connor from behind and sent him stumbling.

"Watch where you're going half-caster," the shadow snapped.

"You walked into me," Connor answered more sharply than he intended.

The shadow stopped and faced Connor. Three words came to Connor's mind: big, burly, and ugly. The shadow rolled up its tattered sleeves and crossed its arms over its chest.

"What's it to you?" it said.

All at once, being bullied by the two shadows surged into Connor's mind along with all the stares and jostles he'd received when he'd arrived at Gissu. His whole body trembled.

"What's it to me? You shadows think you can push me around for no other reason than you feel like it."

"This is my world," the shadow said. "Go home if you want flowers and sunshine."

First one guard's, then another guard's, eyes fell onto the pair. They stepped into the crowd, closing in. The brutish shadow caught their approach out of the corner of his eye, and he raised his chin and curled a cruel smile. Connor looked for Mouse, certain she had kept walking, but she'd broken her own plan and stayed by his side. Connor then knew without a doubt he could trust her, and, at the same time, wished she would go on.

The Shadow Police came to a stop on either side of the trio.

"We got a problem here?" one of them said.

"This half-shadow can't stay out of the way," the ugly shadow said to the officer.

Connor wanted to protest, but he knew better.

"I'm very sorry, sir, it was rude of me, and I'll be more careful," he said. Then, after a tiny pause, he added, "I don't know what came over me."

"It won't happen again," Mouse chimed in. "We were both distracted."

"Psht," said the officer who hadn't spoken. "Typical Casters, always making excuses."

"But I didn't do anything wrong," Connor blurted, knowing it was a mistake, remembering how little the protest had done for him in The Judge's chamber.

"You trying to tell me Shadow Law?" the second officer said, reaching for Connor's arm.

The blood drained from Connor's face. The shadow officer's fingers closed around his wrist as a new voice interrupted from behind.

"What seems to be the problem, officers?"

Time seemed to slow as both officers froze. Then, the first officer saluted the newcomer, and the one holding Connor gave a brief nod of deference. The mean shadow stood its ground, unfazed.

The hand on his wrist kept him from turning completely, but Connor twisted enough to see the speaker. The shadow behind him was a woman in uniform with a narrow, worn face that looked older than Connor's mom. She was thin but muscular and had short-cropped midnight blue hair streaked with gray at the corners of her temples. It took Connor a moment to realize who he was looking at because when he'd first seen her, he'd been unaccustomed to looking at shadow folk. In fact, the only reason he recognized her was her voice.

Sergeant Dandrich.

The officer gripping Connor's wrist said, "Just a couple Casters who don't know how to mind themselves. This one's giving me the 'what's it to ya.'"

Sergeant Dandrich looked down on Connor gravely, her eyes narrowed in rebuke. Connor's fear grew. Maybe she wouldn't help. Maybe she would cuff him and take him to the Shadow Station.

"Little Caster needs to be taught a lesson," the mean shadow said.

"Don't tell me my business," Sergeant Dandrich snapped.

The mean shadow bared his teeth but didn't respond otherwise. The Sergeant didn't seem to pay him further notice. Instead, she addressed the two officers.

"And I'll remind the both of you it's hard for a Caster to see other Casters die," Sergeant Dandrich said. "Guilty or not, you know how foolish they are."

The officer holding Connor's wrist eased his grip and let go. The other officer shook his head and said, "I'll never understand the World of Light. Wish the whole lot of Casters would stay there."

"Understood," Dandrich said. "Exactly as I understand it, The Judge is a Caster. You'd best be served to understand that, too."

The officer looked down at his feet. His entire face darkened. It took Connor a blink to realize the shadow officer was blushing.

"Point taken," the officer said.

Dandrich then turned to Connor and Mouse and said harshly, "Be off with you. Don't forget, the Shadowlands look after shadows first."

"Yes," Mouse said. "Certainly."

Connor wanted to talk to Sergeant Dandrich, but before he could, she was walking off. Mouse took him by the hand and pulled him through the gate. Connor tried to look back to see where Dandrich went, but she had vanished from sight. She probably couldn't speak openly in a place like this, anyway.

As they made it out of Gissu, every part of Connor buzzed. He could hardly feel grateful that Sergeant Dandrich had saved them. Would he ever go a day without being terrified by what he'd witnessed?

Walking as quickly as they dared, the gates diminished behind them. Connor wondered where they would find Tonic and Quiet. They'd taken only a few more steps down Nightglass Road before Mouse pulled Connor to the side.

"I'm sorry," Connor began, "I don't know what came over—"

But already, Mouse had thrown her arms around him and was bawling into his shoulder. Connor immediately returned the favor. As he too sobbed over Mosley's death, the awfulness of the crowd, the terrifying judge, and the altercation at the gate, one thought came to Connor again and again: he would never return to Gissu.

BLACKWOOD

The grief and horror did not leave Connor, but something inside him was exhausted. Both he and Mouse fell silent and released each other. A cool wind blew from the desert. Connor shivered, and it caused him to realize something. Though the wind itself was cool, it felt colder where Mouse's body had pressed, because she'd felt warm. In fact, all of Mouse's touches felt warm, while even his own mother's touch felt hollow. What was different about Mouse? Was it that she was a half-caster too?

"Thank goodness the officer came," Mouse said. "I thought we were toast."

Connor glanced back to the walls of Gissu and the line of lanterns lighting them. "Sergeant," he said.

"What?"

"She's a sergeant, not an officer," Connor said. "That's why the guards let us go."

"Do you know her?"

"She was one of the police who came when my shadow was stolen," Connor said. "Quiet said she was looking for me."

"They came to you?" Mouse said. "I've never talked to the Shadow Police."

Connor was surprised. He'd assumed whenever a shadow was stolen, the police came.

"They didn't send you a Pale Boy? How'd you know how to get to the Shadowlands?"

Mouse's face took on a weird, pained look, but she neither had time to explain it nor did Connor have time to ask. Someone cleared their throat.

Tonic and Quiet waited a few feet away in the glow of one of the Nightglass Road's lanterns. Quiet had her arm around Tonic's back. Tonic fingered the tassels hanging from his belt. At their feet rested a large, black bag.

"A close one," Tonic said. "Saw you get hassled by the guards."

Mouse elbowed Connor in the ribs playfully. "Yeah, we were lucky, no thanking this lug."

Connor felt his face flush. He began to apologize, but Tonic waved it off.

"It all worked out. We're gonna make mistakes. We're all kids here," Tonic said with a wink and playful poke at Quiet.

"I like not looking my age, thank you very much," Quiet answered.

Connor couldn't help thinking, from the way the two stood together, that there was something more than friendship between them. It seemed strange, both because Quiet looked so much younger than Tonic, and because she was so much older. In truth, he had no idea how old Tonic was. In fact, he had no idea how old any of the shadows were other than Quiet.

"Anyway," Tonic said softly, "we can't stay here. If we don't get moving, we'll get caught out in the dark."

"And in the wilds, that's not good for casters or shadows," Quiet added.

Behind Tonic and Quiet, the crowd on the road had thinned, and now only a handful of shadows were within sight, most disappearing into the distance. As the quartet filed in with the stragglers, Connor wondered where they were headed. Are there other towns nearby? Had all these shadows traveled to Gissu to witness the hanging? Could they really be awful and heartless?

"What's down the road?" Connor asked. "The Daggers?"

Tonic shook his head.

"There's a little town called Hollowdell," he said. "We'll head there after the Daggers, since Quiet says the Shadow Police will be looking for you in Gissu."

"Where is the Daggers then?" Connor asked.

Tonic pointed across the Iron Desert. Connor followed along. In the distance stood more mountains, a large and dense wood welling before them.

"We go through Blackwood," Tonic said. "The Daggers is on the other side at the base of the mountains."

"Are those melted palaces too?" Connor asked.

Tonic smiled. "You sure you're new here?" he asked. "But no. Those really are mountains. The Midnight Mountains. Dangerous place."

"Dangerous how?"

"Never risked them myself," Tonic said. "But rumors say some pretty nasty giants live there, and they don't welcome travelers."

"There are giants in the Shadowlands?"

"Well, I said rumors of giants," Tonic said. "Legends about all sorts of beasts, really."

"Like dragons?" Connor asked.

"Again," Tonic said, "you sure you're new here? Anyway, we won't actually get into the mountains, so we can worry about rumors and legends later."

"What do we have to worry about?"

"Shadowcats," Tonic said. "They breed in Blackwood. We should be okay if we avoid their nests, but they're territorial." He kicked the bag at his feet and a couple of poles lying beside it. "We'll be okay," he continued. "I brought some weapons I had stashed."

Connor nodded, but doubt filled him. Journeyman had said he didn't know if he could kill a shadowcat, and he clearly knew how to handle himself. Tonic seemed confident, but if he was as young as he looked, he could be too confident. Connor had made that mistake before. He'd gotten into a fight once back in elementary school with a kid who'd been picking on one of his friends. The result had been an afternoon in the nurse's office with cotton shoved up his nose and a shirt soaked with toilet water. If the path to the Daggers was dangerous, why was Tonic helping him and Mouse? He didn't seem to have anything to gain. Connor asked.

"We have a deal," Tonic answered.

"But why'd you make it? Mouse needs my help," Connor said. "And maybe Quiet feels guilty about what happened with the Shopkeeper, but what's in it for you?"

Tonic shrugged and wiped his forehead with the back of his hand. "Life in the Shadowlands is very hard," he said. "You second-guess everything and everyone. You scrutinize every word someone says. Many trap you with favors. All of them want to accumulate enough favors and opportunities to find their way into the light, which is almost impossible once your shadow gets stuck here. Our deal is the first chance I've had in a long time to trust someone other than Quiet, and that trust is worth a bit of danger."

The answer made Connor feel a little better, but only a little. He would need to keep an eye on Tonic. While they had a deal, Connor figured since Tonic had been in the Shadowlands longer, he probably better understood how things worked. He might have a different understanding of what the deal meant, like the way the Shopkeeper twisted the words of their bargain at the arrest.

Tonic, however, seemed satisfied with his explanation, because he opened the bag at his feet and pulled out the weapons. To Connor, he passed one of the long poles, a staff much like Journeyman carried. The one he took for himself had a round, metal ball at the end to add oomph. Connor weighed the staff in his hands. It felt sturdy, but he had no idea how to use it other than to swing it like a bat or try to emulate a Ninja Turtle. There was no way he could wield it like Journeyman had.

Tonic passed a shadow knife, hanging from a belt, to both Mouse and Quiet, which they strapped around their waists. Tonic caught Connor staring at Mouse's dagger.

"Anything can hit a shadowcat," Tonic said, "but only a shadow blade can kill them. I wish I had more, but they're hard to get. You and

I have more weight to put behind the staves."

Connor wondered if shadow blades could also kill shadows, but Mosley had seemed to suggest otherwise. Indeed, Connor had to imagine the beating Mosley's shadow had received would have killed anyone from the World of Light. Why were shadowcats and the shadows of people different? Connor felt the need to ask.

Tonic shrugged. "All the shadow animals, birds, and insects can be killed by weapons made of shadow. The shadows of people, whether or not they are attached to a caster, can't be. As far as I know, it's how this place is." Then, he pointed across the Iron Desert. "Shall we?"

Tonic didn't wait for a response. He set off, Quiet close in tow. Mouse glanced at Connor, eyes imploring him to follow.

A strange feeling passed over Connor as they crossed the stretch of the Iron Desert before Blackwood. He could hardly believe what he'd seen in Gissu and knew it would haunt him. At the same time, it felt far away. After all, he'd barely known Mosley, and as horrifying as the hanging had been, he had to focus on the Shadowlands and watch for the shadowcat rust clouds and obelisks that would tell them they were drawing near their haunts.

The rust thinned out as they walked, their feet clanking on increasingly bare metal. Ahead, Blackwood loomed tall. At the forest edge, the trees weren't dense but grew thick quickly. Even from a distance, the trees were barren of leaves, their tall, reaching branches silhouetted against the dim sky. The sun had risen high and had already begun its descent, indicating it was probably mid-afternoon. The rumble in Connor's stomach and his growing thirst served as affirmation.

Before long, they passed short trunks dotting the landscape. Their thick roots rose through the metal. The trunks themselves didn't look like wood, but some sort of stone. Petrified, Connor realized. He'd seen petrified wood in a museum with his father, but he'd imagined it buried deep with dinosaur bones. Was it possible in the real world for a tree to petrify while still standing? Did the Shadowlands have dinosaur bones?

What if the shadows of dinosaurs still lived here?

He trotted up to Tonic and Quiet.

"What else lives in the Shadowlands?" Connor asked. "Besides shadows and shadowcats and maybe giants?"

"Pretty much everything you'd find in the World of Light," Tonic said. "Or, at least a version of them. Where do you think we get our food and our clothes? In fact, between Blackwood and Hallowdell, there's a blackwater lake and a couple of shadow farms. We'll pass right through them on our way back from the Daggers. The lake's pretty cool, and you might see some livestock in the pastures. Maybe even a shadow horse."

"They have horses here?"

"Like I said, pretty much everything in the World of Light. In fact—" Tonic paused and squared his shoulders back with pride. "—I own my own horse."

"Wow," Connor said, eyes wide. With a skeptical chuckle, he added, "Sure would be handy right about now."

"Four of us and only one horse. Not to mention horses don't much like dense woods and the smell of shadowcats everywhere. Truth be told, it wouldn't last halfway into Blackwood before the cats took it down." Tonic's shoulders sagged. The teen sighed and unslung his pack. "I guess we should eat something before Blackwood. Won't want to be having a picnic with shadowcats about."

Tonic opened his pack and pulled out four little bundles. He passed one to each of them, taking one for himself. They held what seemed to be the shadow of a roll with what might have been cheese on top. It was hard to be certain. It was all shadow food. Connor raised his to his mouth but froze before taking a bite because Tonic appeared to censure him with a stare.

Tonic nodded and said, "May the Unlucky Number guide us. May the Unlucky Number protect us. May the Unlucky Number absorb our woes, and in doing so, absolve us of our darkness so we may find our way out of shadow into light."

When he finished, Tonic passed around a flask of shadow water. They all took a long gulp before digging into the food. It only took moments to devour, tasteless as it was.

When they were done, Connor asked, "What's all this about the

Unlucky Number and the Thirteen?"

"Have you heard of the Great Flare?" Tonic asked.

Connor nodded.

"So, you know about the ancient kingdoms?"

"A little," Connor said. "What Journeyman told me."

Tonic explained. Before the Great Flare, many kingdoms in the Shadowlands had co-existed for countless millennia. Their iron towers and fortresses sprawled all across what became the Iron Desert. They'd thrived with all manner of shadows and commerce and art. Then, a terrible shadow known as The Eater of Light set out to conquer everything. He marshaled great armies and drove out or destroyed the ancient kings. Many resisted, but they had always ruled separately, so they fought separately, each too prideful to ally with the others. One by one, they fell. By the time they realized their mistake, it was too late.

However, thirteen heroes, some shadows, some from the World of Light, all from different walks of life, banded together. There was Leon, a blacksmith's apprentice who wielded the glow of the forge and the weapons it created with might and courage. There was Solana, the maiden, an old woman who came from the World of Light to find her grandchildren and fought with the radiance of her love for her family. There was Cane, the merchant, Hydren the servant, Libericia the judge, Tauren the herdsman, Luza and Ereb, the farmer and her lover. Each had a story, thirteen in total. Alone, they were only heroes because of their will to fight, but, unified, they were immensely powerful. Together, they brought about the Great Flare and banished the Eater of Light.

"Banished?" Connor asked. "They didn't kill him?"

"I don't think the Eater can be killed. Legend says it is older than time," Tonic said. "Can you imagine the World of Light with no light at all?"

"Sure," Connor said. "There are blind people. There are shut rooms without windows."

"But the light is still there," Tonic said. "It's just blocked. I think it's the same here for the Eater of Light. They say it is the source of darkness itself."

Connor frowned. Did darkness have a source? Wasn't darkness simply where there wasn't any light? Of course, a week ago he would have thought something in the light simply had to cast a shadow, but he'd seen the Pale Boy since then. Regardless, it didn't seem the type of thing for which there was a better answer, so he asked, "How'd they do it? Make the Great Flare?"

"No one knows," Tonic answered. "Scholars all throughout the Shadowlands study their stories for clues, but the answer is most likely lost forever. Summoning the Great Flare also destroyed the Thirteen, and they were the only ones who knew. It's why they're called the Unlucky Number; their quest doomed them."

"Someone should find how," Connor said. "There has to be a way."

"But why?" Tonic asked. "Some think the power of the Great Flare would be the salvation of the Shadowlands, but what if it brought about its ruin?"

"Ruin?" Connor said. "Didn't they save the Shadowlands?"

"Did they?" Tonic asked. "Or did they destroy it? You've seen the Iron Desert and Gissu. The Shadowlands never recovered from the Flare. Some even hope to bring back The Eater of Light, believing it would bring a new era of glory."

"What do you think?" Connor asked.

Tonic shrugged. "I think they're stories to explain something far back in history in terms people can remember and understand. If people were involved, people could make sense of it. Personally, I like Leon's story. I've always wanted to be a warrior like Leon."

"Are you a blacksmith?" Connor asked.

"Don't have to be," Tonic said. "It's not the point. The point is about the light of courage. Leon was nothing special when his quest began. They say when the Eater's forces ransacked his town, they took much of the population with them, including Leon's sister. He went to the town elders and begged them to pursue, but they said they were grateful to have been left behind. Leon knew then if he didn't stand up, he couldn't expect anyone else to, so he traded everything he possessed except his hammer for a horse and set out to find the Eater."

"Is that why you wanted a horse?"

Tonic blushed. "The point is," he said, "we can't expect others to solve our problems. And if we're brave enough to take responsibility, we'll find others with the same strength."

Connor thought this sounded like the stories from the Bible he'd heard in church and the ancient myths in history class. Connor wanted to ask more questions, but Tonic said, "Speaking of courage, I think it's time we moved."

The group fell silent as they pressed on, watching for shadowcats among the trunks of the petrified trees. The deeper they progressed into the woods, the more apt the forest's name became. It wasn't that the trees were all black. As the trunks grew thicker and closer together, their branches grew denser. Despite being leaf-bare, the skeletal fingers blocked out the sunlight.

Mouse grumbled about wishing she had a torch, but Tonic insisted any lights would give them away in the darkness.

Otherwise, they walked in discomforting silence. There was a breeze, but the petrified branches didn't rustle. There were no creaking trunks, no leaves. The ground changed. Connor didn't notice when his shoes stopped clomping on metal, but the ground softened. His shoes sank into a dark muck. His steps peeled away with a soft sucking sound.

"What the heck is this stuff?" Connor asked, lifting his foot to examine the goop. The light was too dim for him to make it out beyond its darkness.

"Ash," Tonic said. "Wet ash. It gets worse the closer we get to the Shadowrun."

"That's the river running through Blackwood to the lake," Quiet whispered.

Ash? Connor scraped a bit of the muck off his shoe with his finger and smelled it. It smelled burnt, but also like wet dog.

"Oh," Connor said. "From the Great Flare?"

"You might think so, but no," Tonic said. "It's from the Daggers."

"What are the Daggers, anyway?"

"You'll see," Tonic said.

Then, he froze, dropping into a crouch. Tonic crept up to the nearest tree and peered around its trunk before ducking back. He leaned against the petrified wood and motioned for them to get down. "Shadowcat nest," he said.

Ahead, the canopy of branches grew dense. It cast a patch of pitch darkness in its shelter. At the center, two fat trees formed a gateway into its depths. Connor didn't see, however, the clouds of rust—or maybe ash—Journeyman told him to watch out for.

"Where are they?" Connor whispered.

"The female will be inside," Tonic said. "And the male is right in front of that big tree."

Connor squinted. He couldn't see anything but the black tree trunk and its twisted roots arching out of and back into the ground. Was Tonic pulling their leg? It reminded Connor of when he used to play in the woods with his friends and their foam dart guns. Someone would always try to make it more exciting by pretending they saw something ahead or behind.

Then, a slight flicker of motion appeared at the edge of a root as a long, lank thing slid over the forest floor. A tail.

Connor followed the tail into the darkness of the tree trunk and recognized the shape of a shadowcat. It sat upright with its hind legs hunched underneath and its forearms resting straight to the ground, much like a normal cat might sit at a window. Connor didn't let that fool him. He would never forget how they'd leapt at him by the obelisk. A low rumble rose from the silence, a strange grating sound like a faraway engine.

Tonic picked up on it, too.

"It's purring," he whispered. "He's telling his mate it's safe. If the purr stops, then we're in trouble. It shouldn't see us as a threat if we don't get any closer. This way. Keep quiet."

Tonic crept sideways from tree trunk to tree trunk while fixing his gaze on the shadowcat. Every time the ground sucked at his feet, Connor winced, but the purr continued. He found himself barely able to breathe, and still, each breath seemed too loud. Thankfully, it was only a matter of moments before the cat was nearly out of sight.

Mouse gave a sharp squeak before cutting it off with a clamped hand over her mouth. She wasn't looking at the shadowcat, though. She was looking ahead, past Tonic.

There, not ten feet away, two shadowcats crouched.

Quiet's body went stiff as a board. Her rapid breaths caught in her throat. She opened and closed her mouth as if to say something, but no sound came out.

"Don't move," Tonic whispered. "They're not here for us."

He was right. The shadowcats' gaze and motion were fixed dead upon the sentinel. Side by side, the two cats approached the group. Just before they passed among them, the cats divided, one going left, the other right, neither paying the four kids the slightest notice. Quiet's body trembled so badly that Connor feared she would fall over. Her eyes were wide and panicked. Don't run, Connor thought. Don't draw their attention. Judging by the way Tonic looked at her, he thought the same.

"They're going to try to take the nest," Tonic said. "Whatever you do, don't move."

The purr stopped.

A low-throated growl followed.

As still as Blackwood had seemed before, now it seemed a crime even to sweat. Connor gritted his teeth and curled his toes.

One of the two attackers let out a piercing yowl. Quiet panted. Her hands clawed at her belt until they found the handle of her knife. She drew the dagger and clenched it in both hands. Mouse seemed as petrified as the trees. Tonic gripped his staff and lowered into a defensive crouch. Connor did the same.

The yowler, now about fifteen feet to the left, yowled a second time. The one to the right darted at the guarding male, who seemed to ignore the attack. Right before the charging cat struck, the mother sprang from between the two great trees. She tackled the leaping cat in mid-air.

A frenzy of hisses and shrieks exploded as the two cats wrestled, bodies slamming into roots and trees. The guard cat kept its ground, body tensing as it stayed fixed on the other shadowcat. Then, it too leapt, and the two remaining cats met in a battle of bites and claws.

"Keep moving nice and slow," Tonic whispered. "If the attackers win, they'll invade the nest to eat the cubs. If the defenders win, they'll make sure the cubs are okay. Either way, we'll be safe..."

Tonic trailed off as new movement appeared at the mouth of the nest. Two small, shadowy shapes poked their heads out. The cubs paused when they saw the fight. Then, one charged at the tussle containing the mother. It dove headfirst into the tangled mess of flailing limbs and jaws, attacking the cat that attacked its mother. Almost instantly, the aggressor batted it to the side, the blow launching it into the air. The cub hit the ground in a roll. Its body skidded to a stop against a tree root.

Then, for reasons beyond Connor's comprehension, the other cub charged straight towards him.

"Oh, God," Tonic said.

Before anyone could react, the cub leapt onto Connor. He dropped his staff and grabbed at the furry thing struggling against him. Its paws beat at his body, but he realized it had no claws. Its mouth clamped onto his forearm. Though its jaws were strong, it had no teeth. Connor tripped over a root as he took the little creature in both hands. He crashed onto his back, holding the thrashing animal above him.

Tonic snatched the cub from Connor's grasp and shoved it into his bag, closing the zipper in one fast motion. Inside, the cub kicked against the fabric.

As Connor picked himself up, he realized the sounds of fighting had stopped. All four adult cats now fixed their gazes directly upon them. Their intentions were clear: they all wanted the cub. The mother advanced first, her body low and tense. Her feet crept forward, seeking the right purchase to launch.

"Run," Tonic said. "Just run."

Tonic slung the backpack and the cub it held over his shoulder. He snatched up his staff and took off at full speed. Quiet and Mouse burst after him. Connor took one quick look at his staff on the ground. To reach it, he would need to step towards the shadowcats. The staff was lost. As fast as he could, he took off after his friends.

The shadowcats made no sound, but Connor knew they chased, even though he didn't dare look back. He ducked around tree trunks every chance he got, trying to put a tree between him and his pursuers. Sharp pains erupted from his arms and cheeks as he ran. He'd sprinted through forests before with his friends and knew what it felt like to have branches slashing at his face and arms. This was different. The petrified fingers on the end of the limbs didn't give and bend the way branches in a real forest would have. They tore at his skin wherever they struck. He bled from several places.

Somewhere ahead, he heard the shadowcat cub screeching from within the bag. He knew Tonic was ahead of him, but he lost sight of Mouse and Quiet as they zigzagged in and out of the trees. Once, he thought he glimpsed Mouse off to his left, but Quiet disappeared against the blackness of the tree trunks.

He sensed the shadowcats were no longer behind him, but veering off to come at him from the sides. They were faster than him. He knew it. They would tear him down, and soon.

A new sound emerged ahead: running water. A river. The Shadowrun.

The trees ceased. Connor knew what he had to do. As the forest vanished around him, he leapt off the embankment without so much as a look at where he dove. For a brief second, his body flew through the air. Certainty filled him: the shadowcats would snatch him mid-flight and jerk him back. Then, the cold water shocked his senses, and he was cast about by the current. His body slammed into a large rock. He yelped even as he grabbed hold. Icy water filled his mouth and caused him to sputter. For a moment, the current suspended him as he glimpsed back at the shore. Two shadowcats paced the riverbank with rapid turns, snarling and hissing.

Connor's grip on the wet rock slipped, and the rushing water pulled him under.

THE BANK OF THE SHADOWRUN

Connor woke, half in the water, half on the mud, to a sputtering cough. He rolled onto his side and a dribble ran down his cheek to the ground beneath. When the fit subsided, he lay in a soaked heap, cold to the bone, aching all over, his mind fogged like an autumn morning. His eyes slowly took in the flow of the Shadowrun. He recalled fragmented memories of thrashing to keep his head above water, slamming against rocks, and the black froth cresting the rapids.

When his eyes fell upon the opposing shore, he lurched to his feet. A shadowcat crouched like an Egyptian statue, its gaze fixed upon him, tail swishing. How far had the current dragged him? And how far had it followed? Why was it watching him if Tonic took the cub? Connor remembered Journeyman's story about shadowcats and their grudges. How long would this beast track him? Did the shadowcat think he was the one who stole the cub? If so, would it ever give up?

The cat growled. Its body tensed as if to strike. Connor backed away from the water's edge with careful steps, lest he trip over a rock. The river was at least twenty feet wide. Could it jump that far? He wasn't sure why, but as he backpedaled, he held his hands out and said, "I'm sorry, I didn't mean to. The cub came at me."

The shadowcat's growl continued unabated, but it did nothing else.

Connor turned from the cat, hoping he was out of its reach and peered about. There could be danger from this side of the river. Were there more shadowcats in the trees, ready to claw him apart? Nothing moved among the trees on his shore. The water itself was almost pitch black. Realizing he was ravenous with hunger and thirst, Connor crept back to the water and drank several handfuls, all the while watching the cat.

He wiped his mouth and exhaled deeply. The sun had disappeared below the top of the trees. Night was approaching. On the opposite shore, there was no sign of his friends. If they'd made it across, how far away had they washed up? Other than the watching cat, he was alone.

The forest grew denser as he moved farther away from the river. He could make out no potential destinations, no features, or signs of where he should go. If he proceeded into the forest, it seemed doubtful he would find anyone. Finding a shadow in the dark forest seemed virtually impossible. He assumed Tonic had gone into the water, since he'd followed the sound of the cub almost to the bank. But what if Tonic had turned down the shore rather than had jumped in? What if Mouse and Quiet had gone off in other directions, since the shadowcats may have focused on him and Tonic?

Connor looked at the shadowcat and said, "I suppose you didn't see where they went."

The shadowcat licked its paw and combed its ear.

Connor scratched the back of his head uncertainly. The light was better at the river with fewer obstructions. *Yes,* Connor thought, *I'll search the banks.* He wasn't sure which way to go first, but he figured the current was strong, so it might be best to start downstream.

Only then did Connor notice it was snowing. He'd been so anxious and wrapped up in his thoughts, he hadn't noticed the white flakes drifting down through the gap in the trees over the river. Some flakes disappeared into the water, while others accumulated on the shore. A thin coat even dusted his clothes. Forgetting where he was for a moment, Connor held out his hands, tipped his head back, and stuck out his tongue.

As the first flakes landed in his mouth, Connor grimaced. They tasted burnt. The flakes on his palms hadn't melted like snow would, either. He smudged a flake with his index finger, and it left a black streak on his skin. Ash—from the Daggers, Connor remembered. The faint scent of rotten eggs drifted in the air. He remembered learning about a substance that smelled like rotten eggs when burned, but he couldn't recall what it was. However, if the ash came from the Daggers, maybe the smell did, too. Could he be close? The others might meet there.

Connor didn't feel right leaving the shore, so he resolved to search along it before cutting into the forest to find the Daggers. As he set out down the shore, the cat followed along, loping over the rocks and root clusters. He'd never be able to let his guard down. Even if Journeyman was wrong and the shadowcat gave up the chase, he'd never be certain. He wished he hadn't lost his staff, even though he hardly knew how to use it.

The riverbank grew thick with black and bristly grass that snapped under each step. Under the ash, the rocks shifted and wobbled, their edges sharp and jutting at all angles. A fine place to crack one's head open, Connor thought. He huffed and puffed from the effort of holding his arms out to maintain his balance. His legs burned with exertion.

His heart leapt.

Ahead, a dark shape on the shore. Mouse lay curled in a ball half in the water.

"Mouse!" he called out. She didn't move.

He forced himself not to run since breaking his ankle would do him no good. Pebbles clattered and clacked until he dropped to his knees beside her. After a quick check to make sure she was safe, he stuck his hands under Mouse's arms and dragged her out of the water, pushing back with all his strength until he could roll her onto her back.

Her head rocked, and her eyelids fluttered before she broke into a harsh cough. She vomited a stream of black water. She smiled weakly when she saw Connor's face in the gloom.

"Did we make it?" she asked.

"We did—at least the two of us."

Mouse weakly lifted her head and looked first up and down the bank and then across the river. Her eyes widened as they fell upon the shadowcat.

Connor gripped her shoulder firmly. "I don't think it can get to us," he said.

"Quiet and Tonic?"

"Haven't seen them, and I don't know how the heck I'm supposed to find a couple of shadows in a place this dark."

"They'll be okay," Mouse whispered. "If they escaped the shadowcats."

"We should go down the bank to see if they washed up."

Mouse shook her head. She eyed the now-sitting shadowcat as if to make sure it wasn't about to attack. "I need to sit here a bit. That was too much."

"How will we find them?"

"We'll meet at the Daggers," Mouse said. "I don't know how to get there, but Tonic said to follow the smell until we see the glow. I don't think we'll be able to miss it."

Connor nodded, then plopped to the ground beside Mouse. It felt strange to sit there with a shadowcat so close, and though he wasn't sure why, he felt certain it was listening to them over the rush of the river.

"Are you okay?" he said, taking her hand.

"No," she said, "but I will be."

Despite the fact it felt nice to hold Mouse's hand, Connor grew impatient after a short time. More shadowcats could find them, and he was losing time to find his shadow. The answer could be waiting at the Daggers; it could also be in leaving the Daggers. However, Mouse was probably closer to losing her shadow than he was, so if she wasn't willing to leave yet, she really must need the rest. Instead of urging her to move along, he asked who she was.

She wore a funny expression before straightening her dress with both hands and saying, "My name is Lily. Lily James. My mother is Martha James, and my father is Roger James. We live in Nashua, New Hampshire."

Connor gestured to the falling ash. "Then this must feel a lot like home. If it really were snow, at least."

"Kind of," Mouse said. "There's a creek behind my house with a huge boulder beside it. I love to sit out on the rock with my notebook and write about my day."

Connor was about to reply how nice that sounded, or how he'd never been able to keep a diary, when shock struck him. She'd told him her name. Her real name. Judging by the fact she called herself Mouse, she knew to keep it secret. She was showing how much she trusted him.

The least he could do was offer the same in return.

"I'm Connor Brighton. My mother is Elizabeth Brighton. My dad is dead, but his name was Jerry. We live in Plano, Texas."

"Brighton," Mouse snickered. "Bright-one. Good name for a Caster. Nice to meet you."

"Pleased to meet you, too," Connor said. A pause followed. Connor was not used to talking with girls, especially not a girl he'd been holding hands with. He felt his palm growing sweaty, so he slipped his hand from hers and wiped it on his pants. He racked his brain for something to say. What he came up with was "What do you think of the Shadowlands?"

Mouse smirked, and Connor wanted to kick himself for asking such a stupid question. The answer was obvious. The Shadowlands were awful.

"Well," Mouse said, "I think you know what I would say, but there are things about it I like."

"Really?" Connor asked. "Like what?"

"Well, I like the colors, and I don't mean the awnings and Tonic's ribbons. The more you look at the shadows here, the better you see them. It's like seeing the entire world for the first time." Mouse paused. "And I like The Thirteen and all the stories. I love myths. They've always been my favorite part of school, and some of the shadow myths are lovely. Hopeful."

Connor remembered the story about Basket and the Flower Petal that the mother had told her children in Quiet's refuge. That story hadn't struck him as hopeful, but he didn't say as much. Instead, he said, "I like myths, too. And history."

"Yes," Mouse said. "This place is full of history. And I think it's beautiful how they don't seem to separate myths from history. To the Shadowfolk, they're one and the same."

It felt good to listen to Mouse talk. Her voice made him feel more confident. Connor said, "I've only heard a couple of stories since I've been here. Can you tell me one?"

Mouse blushed.

"I don't know them well," she said. "Quiet and Tonic are much, much better at it."

"So what?" Connor said.

"Well," Mouse said, biting her lower lip, "my favorite is the story of Luza and Ereb."

Mouse told the story. Luza was the daughter of simple folk who lived in isolation on the family farm. They'd come from the World of Light after she and her family were killed when their house collapsed in a tornado. The storm had thrown their souls into a frenzy. They were so desperate to find each other that they lost their way to the Light. When they reunited in the Shadowlands, her parents were angry, the mother blaming the father for not taking them someplace safer, and the father blaming the mother for losing track of Luza.

They settled on a farm, knowing little else to do. They made a peaceful life in the Shadowlands for a time until the Eater of Light advanced. Their land lay within one of the first places the Eater conquered. As his armies burned and pillaged their way toward the farm, Luza's mother hid her daughter away in a secret storage room under the barn before both parents set out to meet the Eater's captains. They never returned. Luza stayed hidden under the barn for days as she felt the ground shake with the terrible thunder of the vast host of shadows marching across it.

When she emerged, the farm was in ruins. The Eater of Light saw little value in farms like hers, so they'd left the countryside empty and devastated.

Poking through the splinters of her home, Luza knew she had nowhere else to go. Barely in her teens when she'd died, she'd known no one but her family. So, she tried to rebuild the farm herself. She toiled day and night to build a small new house and plant a small crop, working every waking moment until she shook with hunger, thirst, and exhaustion. She grew thin as a skeleton, driven only by the hope her life would improve at harvest.

However, the shadows of rats came. They ate her crops on the vine and branch. At first, she attempted to reason with the rats, but the rats were unwilling to listen. She tried to appease the rats by leaving food on the edge of her fields. It worked at first, but the rats multiplied. Soon, there were so many rats, they ate the sprouts as soon as they broke the soil. Luza grew desperate.

When it seemed she had no choice but to seek a livelihood elsewhere, a visitor came to her door in the middle of the night, a young shadow named Ereb. Ereb didn't say where he came from, but he was traveling to one of the great cities to find work and had grown exhausted. Luza put him up for the night and made him a meal of everything she had left in her home.

While they ate by the dying light of her only lantern, Luza told Ereb her story. In return for her hospitality, Ereb promised to rid the farm of rats. He bade Luza to sleep and told her that in the morning her problem would be solved. Luza didn't believe him but agreed.

In the morning, she woke up to an empty house. When she ventured out into the fields after washing her face with dirty cooking water, she was astonished to find the rats were not to be seen. It wasn't until she reached the edge of her land that she discovered their bodies lining the fence. They weren't dead, but they'd been turned from shadows into creatures of light without shadows. They all stared out into the air, not even moving when she poked them with her shoe.

Luza was struck with great pity for the rats. She didn't know what Ereb did to them, but she believed their state wasn't fit for anything living. Ereb came up behind Luza and she rebuked him, saying he didn't have the right to steal their beings. Ereb was shattered. He confessed no one had ever shown him kindness like Luza's, and declared he'd solved the problem in the only way he knew how. Luza couldn't stay angry. She forced Ereb to swear he would do nothing of the kind again. Moved by Luza's compassion, Ereb vowed to follow Luza's guidance, and the two were joined for eternity, at least until the Great Flare.

"So, it's a love story," Connor said when Mouse fell silent.

"Yeah," Mouse said, dropping her gaze to her lap. "I like love stories."

They sat quietly, and Connor wasn't sure what to do. Did Mouse like him? He wondered if he should try to kiss her, but he had no idea how one went about doing such a thing without looking stupid. Besides, he was only eleven.

Connor was relieved when Mouse broke the awkwardness by saying, "So Texas? That's really far from New Hampshire."

"Yeah," Connor said. "The whole other side of the country."

"In the real world," Mouse said, "we probably never would have met."

Connor thought about this for a moment. Though he hardly knew Mouse, he did kind of like her, which was funny, because he didn't care about any of the girls he went to school with. In fact, he'd made it a practice to avoid them altogether. They always looked like they were about to tease him. Mouse didn't look at him that way at all.

"It almost makes me glad my shadow was stolen," Mouse said.

Connor looked at her. Her hair was a dirty brown, and even in the dim light, he could make out traces of blond. He wasn't sure he could agree he was happy to be in the Shadowlands, but he said, "You have a good way of looking at things."

"My mother raised me right," Mouse smiled.

"My mother is raising me alone," Connor said.

"She must be strong," Mouse said.

"I guess she is," Connor said.

They sat together side by side for several moments, smiling in silence.

Then, Mouse stood.

"Well, Connor Brighton," she said. "I think it's time we got going. We might get to the Daggers by nightfall."

THE NEVERBORN

They conversed as they wound their way among the tree trunks, pausing now and again to gaze at them when something rustled off in the darkness. Once, they huddled together in the crook of a titanic stump when they thought they had glimpsed a moving shadow. Otherwise, there were no real threats.

Mouse told Connor about her parents. Her father was a doctor, and her mother a librarian. She missed her father especially. He doted on her whenever he had the chance. As she told him about trips to the zoo and the movies, Connor couldn't help thinking about outings with his father. His mind settled on the day his father took him to a soccer field and taught him the rules, a child-sized soccer ball in hand. He'd shown Connor how to dribble, and it was one of his favorite memories.

However, the memory was strangely blurry. Before, he'd been able to remember the smell of the field, the unsteadiness of his ankles as he tried to kick the ball as he jogged. Now, he couldn't even remember if the grass had been wet or hear his father's voice as he explained the field lines. As if trying to reinforce his memories, Connor described his mother and father to Mouse and told her the story of the night his father died in a car accident.

"It was weird," Connor said. "Every morning, he put on his shoes and left for work, and he came back every evening, setting his shoes side by side inside the door. Then, one morning, he left for work and never came home again. His shoes never came back either and no one ever puts anything in his spot by the door. I still expect him to come home some days for dinner."

"I couldn't imagine life without my father."

"I miss him a lot," Connor said. "Every time I have a soccer game, I hope he'll show up. The worst part is knowing that while I'm here, my mother is alone. I was supposed to talk to her after school today. She must be going out of her mind."

"You have to explain everything when you go back," Mouse said.

"This morning, when she asked where I'd been, I told her I'd run away."

"Then the truth is even more important," Mouse said. "One thing I've learned from the Shadowlands, lies never solve problems. They bite you in the butt down the road."

"Do your parents know?"

"My shadow is almost non-existent, a smudge on the ground, even in strong light. I'm so scared of what will happen if I lose it," Mouse said. Her eyes trembled and her lips quivered. "I had to tell them, so they'd know why I forgot them if it happened."

"And they believed you?"

"I can't say for sure," Mouse said. "They didn't, but then they watched me go into my closet, and I haven't come back. So, I don't think there's a lot of question."

They walked in silence for a few moments longer, but the conversation eventually resumed and wandered back to less serious topics. Mouse talked about playing chess and reading mysteries. As he listened, Connor made sure he thought of her as Mouse rather than Lily. He felt special knowing her name, but he couldn't use it unless the two of them were alone. Even then, it was best to refrain in case someone overheard. He still didn't know what kind of power names held here, but since no one he'd met used their real name, Connor knew secrecy was right.

Ash fell through a tiny patch of sky showing through the clawing forest canopy. The sky was rich with deep maroon and purple hues of the Shadowland sunset. The surrounding darkness deepened. Mouse grew fretful, remarking frequently about needing to keep moving. The smell of rotten eggs thickened and Connor's stomach turned. Sulfur, Connor remembered. Sulfur smelled like rotten eggs.

It was then they spotted a soft, greenish-purple glow through a gap in a thick growth of trees ahead. Driven by curiosity, they steered towards it.

Mouse gasped as they entered a clearing. Trees ringed the space so densely, there seemed to be only one other way out on the far side. Thick roots buckled from the trunks into the ground like fat knees, and their sharp rises and drops made climbing over them look like a chore. A strange moss, emanating a phosphorescent green light, covered each root.

In the center of the roots lay a pool as wide as Connor's bedroom and shaped like an almost perfect oval, pulsing a royal purple. Sharp and spiky reeds about a foot long jutted along the pool's edges, curving around and crossing each other in a thick tangle. The water itself was still and reflected a small patch of darkening sky above.

"It's beautiful," Mouse whispered.

Connor nodded, but he wasn't listening. He was focused on the roots. Some rose as tall as him, and the dips between them were sharp, their bottoms filled with runoff from the pool, probably from the last rain. It would be difficult to clamber over them. The only way through the clearing seemed to be through the pool itself. Was it shallow enough to wade? He eyed the sharp reeds. What if they coated the whole bottom of the pool? He didn't want to imagine stepping on one of them.

At the same time, Connor found the light soothing and warm. It reminded him of waking up in bed wrapped in blankets. The tension left his muscles, and before he knew it, he sat slouched against the tree trunks by the glade's entrance.

He wiped sweat from his brow, wincing as the back of his palm dragged across the cuts on his forehead he'd gotten while running through the forest. When he pulled his hand away, thin smears of blood streaked it. His face burned from all the scratches. He didn't want to think about what he must look like.

Again, he looked to the pool. It would feel nice to splash the cool water over his injuries and clean off the blood, dirt, and ash covering him. After all, he was aware not only of how he must look to himself but also to Mouse. The only thing keeping him from kneeling beside the reeds and dipping his hand into the water was the glow. If it had been real, ordinary water, or even the Shadowrun, he wouldn't have hesitated.

Mouse, too, stared into the water, mesmerized.

"What do you think it is?" Connor asked.

"I dunno," Mouse said in a breathless whisper. "But it's amazing."

"Why's it glowing?" Connor asked.

Mouse broke her gaze from the pool, and the strange, almost hypnotized look fell away.

"I've read about whole lakes and bays that glow green if you touch them. Some sort of algae. Maybe this is the Shadowlands' version of the same thing?"

"Yeah, but we're not touching the water," Connor said, realizing he meant it as a warning. Something in his gut told him not to touch the pool.

Mouse nodded succinctly. "Well, the sulfur is getting really strong, so I think we're near the Daggers. Might as well rest a moment so we're ready when we get there, and I can't think of a better spot. This is the prettiest thing in this whole place."

Connor agreed. Something about the glow made him want to feel safe, even as his thoughts told him otherwise. He glanced through the trees. Already, the maroons had faded from the sky, leaving only a marbled field of blue and purple.

"What happens once it's night?" Connor asked. "Why is it bad to be out after dark?"

Mouse smirked.

"I'm new here too, you know," she said, feigning annoyance.

"Sorry," Connor said. "I'm trying to understand this place."

Mouse sighed. "The way Tonic explained it, shadows become more powerful at night. In the light, the physical shape they'd held while attached to bodies restrained them. That's why they look like people. But think about how shadows can change shape when the light is in a different place."

Connor understood. He always loved making his shadow thirty feet long.

"So, then what shape is a shadow when there is no light?" Connor said.

"Exactly!" Mouse said. "Tonic said they can change their shape in the darkness. There are limitations, but many of the shadows aren't nice. They can turn into terrible things if they get you in a dark corner. It's why shadows like umbrellas and awnings, and wide-brimmed hats are so popular. They cast shadows on the shadows and make them feel stronger. Be very careful of shadows in shadow. It's like the Shopkeeper. Out in town during the day, he's like any other shadow, but in the darkness of his shop, he can be powerful."

A frightening thought occurred to Connor.

"What about the thief?" he said. He pointed to the near-night sky.

"I wish we could wait until morning," Mouse whispered. "But I have to confront him as soon as possible."

"It's going to be dangerous," Connor said.

Mouse didn't reply.

"How are we going to beat him?" Connor asked.

Mouse held her breath for a moment. "I don't know, and there's more. The thief is different," she said. She swallowed hard and licked her lips as if deciding whether she should tell Connor something. "He's one of the Neverborn."

Neverborn? Connor had no idea what that meant and said as much.

Mouse's voice fell solemn. According to her, not all shadows were people who had died or lost their way. There were several types. Shadows like Quiet were called Lightborn. They'd begun as the shadows cast by living people who either died or let their minds fall into darkness. All the Lightborn wanted the same thing: to be reunited with their bodies in the Light. "Heaven," she said. "If that's your thing." There were also shadows like the Shopkeeper who were called Shadowborn, because they were born in the land of shadows. They had no hope of moving on because they had no body to reflect light. They thought the Shadowlands belonged to them. Still, they often had families and hoped they'd rebuild the Shadowlands to its former glory for their own sake and those of the ones they cared about.

Then, there were the Neverborn. No one knew how they had formed. Some said they were birthed from the darkness itself. Others said the Eater of Light made them. The Neverborn hated both light and darkness, and they hated love most of all because they were consumed with emptiness. They were little more than loss, chaos, and confusion at their core. Many of them became shadow thieves.

"But why steal shadows?" Connor asked.

"I've never asked one, but I'd guess envy," Mouse said. "Jealousy. They hate that Casters have bodies to cast their shadows from."

"Why me?" Connor asked. "Why you and me?"

"Because we have a lot of darkness in our lives. Your father died, and you're angry with your mother based on what you've told me. Thieves are drawn to shadows in turmoil."

"Well then, what about you?" Connor asked. "Your parents sound great. You have a happy life, you're pretty, you seem really smart..."

Mouse's face contorted, her mouth pursing, her forehead creasing.

"And I'm thankful for it all," she said. "But it doesn't mean I don't have problems. You shouldn't be so quick to judge people you know so little about."

Connor blushed. He'd thought he was complimenting her.

"Didn't mean anything by it," Connor said.

"Well, you shouldn't say things you don't mean then," Mouse said. "Not here. Not to me."

Mouse tore a handful of moss from a tree root and threw it into the pool. The moment the clump hit the water, the pool lurched into motion. The reeds along the edge shot into the air. They were connected to enormous lips that snapped together several feet above where the pool had been. The gigantic mouth quivered, and a thick, glowing syrup oozed from between the spikes. It was drool, or maybe venom.

Mouse was riveted in place, every muscle rigid.

Connor's body buzzed with alarm. The thing eased back down into the pool until it was hidden again. All except for its teeth. The thing had looked like some sort of giant Venus flytrap.

THE DAGGERS

As they left the flytrap glade, Connor's mind raced with a repeating image of the monster lunging from the pool, the snap of its jaws, and its curving teeth scraping together. How could such a thing exist? It was bizarre and alien; perhaps most importantly, it wasn't a shadow. The light from the glowing water made that clear.

"What was that thing?"

"Seriously," Mouse said. "Why do you think I'd know?"

"Because you're smarter than me?" Connor said.

Mouse kept walking. If anything, she might have quickened her pace. Why was she so upset? Her parents sounded awesome. How could that be bad? How could she not be happy? Was it because he didn't understand girls, or had something happened to her? She drew her shoulders inward, and her face wore a soured frown.

Connor tried to focus on the task at hand. He had no idea what they would do at the Daggers, especially if they found the thief. Heck, he didn't even know what the Daggers were. Would they be dangerous? He supposed they would be. So far, everywhere seemed dangerous. Even the tree roots in the fly-trap glade had been arranged to make it look like the only path through was a straight line. Had the trees somehow conspired with the carnivorous plant to plan the trap? Or were they all part of the same plant? When they got to the Daggers, what kind of traps would await? Would they march straight up to the thief and demand their shadows back?

He wished Tonic was still with them. The boy seemed to have a plan. No matter what, he'd led them out of Gissu, and though they'd stumbled on a shadowcat nest in Blackwood, it was Tonic who knew what to do. Still, why had Tonic shoved the shadowcat cub into his bag? Why not leave it? Maybe the shadowcats wouldn't have chased them. What if Tonic had decided it was all too dangerous and abandoned them? He had nothing to gain, and if he thought they were all killed by the shadowcats or drowned in the river, he wouldn't really be breaking the deal. Why was trust so hard?

To be fair, Tonic had few reasons to trust Connor. Connor hadn't even told his mother about the theft and the Shadowlands. Sure, he'd thought hiding things had been necessary, but could his mother want something for herself enough to do something that wasn't best for Connor?

No, Connor decided. His mother did so much for him, he had no reason to feel anything but gratitude. As soon as he had the chance, he would tell her everything, no matter how hard it might be.

He was so lost in those thoughts, he bumped into Mouse, who had come to a stop.

"Look," she whispered when Connor apologized, pointing through the trees.

The forest ahead was a black silhouette against a soft and flickering orange glow.

Connor and Mouse kept low, crawling over the roots. The trees thinned. Connor couldn't see the glow's source as they ducked from tree to tree, but he could tell from its flicker it had to be fire. A very large fire. A haze thickened above them as they crept, the smell of sulfur so strong it was almost choking. The snow of ash increased from a flurry to a storm. The ground beneath them crunched and shifted. The light swelled, and Connor saw through the accumulating ash obsidian pebbles covering the forest floor.

When he glanced back, he saw huge pillars of the black rock through the trees. The pillars curved and tapered at the top like dragon's teeth, and Connor understood the name of the place. Distant pings like metal striking rock carried from the forest depths to their ears.

"What is that sound?" he whispered.

"The workers," Mouse whispered back. She didn't sound angry anymore, just focused on what lay ahead. "They mine the obsidian and load it into rail carts to take to the heart of the quarry. The stone is chiseled into bricks and polished at the quarry before they're loaded into wagons to be hauled to the cities and towns. One of the first things I saw in the Shadowlands was one of those wagons."

Either how much the obsidian columns resembled teeth or the memory of the fly-trap thing might have caused Connor to ask, "Are we going to get eaten in there?"

"I hope not," Mouse said. "Filthy as we are, we'd probably taste terrible."

Connor smiled. If Mouse was joking, she wasn't angry. And Connor didn't want Mouse to be angry with him.

They slipped ahead to the next tree and then the next. When they reached the tree line, all Connor could see of the quarry was more stony teeth. They were taller than the trees of Blackwood, and he could see nothing of those who mined them. The only thing he could tell was the Daggers were vast. They stretched to the left and right along the edge of Blackwood.

"Where do we go?" Connor asked. "It looks so big."

"The heart of the quarry. Before you destroyed my closet… I mean arrived, Tonic said we needed to find the Foreman's office," Mouse said. "Apparently, bad things happen there."

"Great," Connor said. "Right where we want to go."

"If we're lucky, Tonic and Quiet will find us along the way."

Connor almost suggested it might be better to stay where they were, but he knew there was no choice but to press on. They had to find their shadows. Time was short for Mouse, especially, and this was their only lead. Connor stepped past the last tree, intending to dart for the nearest pillar.

A pulsating heat struck Connor's entire body. It was like stepping over a powerful heating vent. Sweat broke down his back and in his armpits. It poured from his brow, the salt stinging the cuts on his forehead and cheeks. He still couldn't see the workers among the obsidian teeth, but the clang of their tools grew louder. He heard an occasional voice call something out, but the echo off the rocks distorted the words.

As he reached the first pillar, Mouse crouched beside him with her back against it. "Keep behind the daggers," she said. "Tonic said the supervisors won't take kindly to us."

They darted to the next column where the stone was warm, and the air was stifling.

"What are they burning?" Connor whispered.

"You never stop asking questions, do you?" Mouse whispered back.

Then, she pointed. Connor peeked his head around the column. The glow's brightness exceeded the Shadowland sun. His gaze wandered over the black stone to a bright orange patch between two pillars. His eyes widened.

A stream of lava. Little jets of flame burst from its brilliant surface. Lines of black ash marked the flows and eddies of its current. A stone bridge arched over it down its length, and a gravel road disappeared among the columns.

"Don't get too close," Mouse whispered. "Your clothes will catch fire."

"Fantastic," Connor said. "Broiled me. Which way?"

"I don't know. We've got to go deeper, but I can't tell where the workers are."

Connor weighed their options. To the left, the columns were thinner with less cover to protect them and longer gaps in between. The right seemed denser, but the only clear path through the obsidian spikes wound close to the lava stream. He suspected he'd need to get pretty close to the lava to catch fire, but the work sounds came stronger from that direction.

A voice from behind made them both jump.

"Psst..."

As Connor turned, Tonic peeked from behind a pillar. Tonic broke a broad smile as he darted toward Connor and Mouse. The smile faltered, however, when he got a good look at Tonic. Strangely, Tonic seemed... less there. He looked thinner, and the edges of his body seemed to fight to hold their shape. Did the brightness weaken him? Connor didn't like this at all, since Tonic was the strongest among them. At the same time, maybe the thief would be weaker, as well.

"You made it," Connor whispered.

"Took a nice swim," Tonic said, brushing his hair back. "But yeah, nothing I couldn't handle. Been waiting at the edge of Blackwood since. Luckily, I saw you and Mouse cross into here. Was beginning to think you'd turned back."

Something about Tonic's confidence made Connor want to seem confident too, so he chuckled, "Takes more than a river to stop us."

Tonic nodded and asked, "You seen Quiet?"

Connor and Mouse shook their heads.

Tonic shrugged, "She'll find us at the complex."

Then, the older boy unslung his bag and held it out by the strap to Connor. It wasn't moving, but the bulk at its bottom suggested the shadowcat cub might still be in it.

"I believe this is yours," he said.

"Mine?" Connor said. "The cub? Why didn't you get rid of it?"

"You know how valuable a shadowcat cub is? It's yours because it came for you. Means it will let you tame it."

"Are you kidding me?"

"Tame shadowcats are rare," Tonic said, "but they're fiercely loyal and nasty to anyone who tries to hurt you."

Connor reached out and took the bag, still uncertain.

"You owe me, though," Tonic said with a wry smile. "It ate all our food."

Connor stared at the bag in his hands. What if the shadowcat woke and started yowling and hissing? There's no way anyone wouldn't notice. However, if the cub was as valuable as Tonic said...

"Could I trade this for our shadows?"

Tonic sucked air through his teeth. "Tough one," he said. "You risk a lot to steal a shadow, but you risk a lot to get a shadowcub. Might be worth a try."

Connor smiled at his luck. He'd been right: with Tonic back, things looked much better. At least now he had a plan. Connor slung the bag over his shoulder, gently trying not to wake the creature inside.

As if reading his mind, Tonic said, "Don't worry. Cubs sleep like the dead. Especially if they've eaten."

Connor nodded and gestured around them. "What now?"

Tonic pointed at the lava stream.

"We follow the stream," he said. "The compound is around the burning lake. All the streams lead there."

The burning lake didn't sound like a place Connor wanted to go, but then, nowhere in the Shadowlands sounded welcoming. Tonic strode in a direct line for the next column. To avoid the lava's oppressive heat, they kept their path a careful distance to the right of the stream, dodging behind one pillar and then another, working deeper into the Daggers.

After a bit, Tonic motioned for them to stop. Connor stepped up beside him behind a pillar and pressed against the smooth, glassy stone. Mouse did the same. Black soot smudged Mouse's face except for the bright whites of her eyes and her lips, making her look like a cartoon character. Connor snickered.

"Sorry," Connor whispered. "Your face."

"Look in a mirror," Mouse said.

Connor didn't have a mirror, but he looked down and noticed his hands were pitch black. His face must look the same. He tried to see if Tonic was equally filthy, but the shadow was too dark to tell.

Tonic pointed between the next two columns. Beyond, ran the metal rails of a small train track. "They run mine carts down the tracks to haul the obsidian to the complex," he whispered. "Much more likely to see workers around here."

As if on cue, two huge shadows carrying picks and black buckets crossed the gap between the daggers. They didn't look Connor's way, but his heart accelerated.

"Where there's one worker," Tonic said, "there's more. And there's bound to be a taskmaster nearby. One at a time."

Tonic ducked low and crept out of cover towards the track. Connor held his breath as the teen passed through the open space, peering left and right for any sign someone watched. No other shadows appeared by the time Tonic was pressed against the other side of the pillar opposite the tracks.

Mouse went next. Connor ran his hands over the obsidian pillars. He hadn't known Mouse long, but he cared whether she was okay. The echoes of the workers' tools pinged all over the obsidian quarry, merging into a strange clamor almost like muffled conversation. The harder he listened, the more the strange clanks and pings resembled some sort of song or chant.

"Tsss…"

Both Mouse and Tonic stared at Connor from the pillar. He needed to stay focused. When he did his schoolwork, he often found his mind wandering to movies and soccer games and drawings. He couldn't do the same here. His actions affected Mouse and Tonic, too.

Connor slipped from behind the pillar in a crouch so low, he almost crawled. He kept his attention between the two pillars and the mine track beyond. He was nearly safe when a sharp 'chink' of a tool striking obsidian rang out from the far side of the very pillar Tonic and Mouse hid behind.

Connor dropped to the ground, pressing into a depression in the rock. He wasn't completely hidden, but filthy as he was, he felt certain he was obscured enough to be overlooked if someone glanced his way. The cub stirred in the bag. A leg pushed a little knot into Connor's back. He feared it would wake. At the same moment, a loud, nasty voice called out, "What you think you're doing, you lout? You flea?"

For a second, Connor thought the voice was directed at him. He nearly leapt to his feet and took off running, except a second voice responded from beyond the pillar.

"I-I-I was only f-finding a new spot," the voice said.

"What's it to ya?" the mean voice said, growing closer. "We ain't set to chip this section 'til next week! Get on with ya!"

Immediately came the unmistakable crack of a whip followed by a shrill yelp.

"Get on with ya!"

The whip snapped again.

The worker yelped, and stones tumbled like marbles spilling on concrete. Connor glimpsed a scraggly worker jogging between the pillars before disappearing out of sight.

"Good for nothing, no good lout," the nasty voice said, softer this time.

An enormous shadow with broad shoulders and a flat, ugly face stepped into the gap between the pillars beyond Mouse and Tonic. It ground its jaw, and from one of the great hands it placed upon its hips dangled a long, barbed whip. It had to be one of the taskmasters.

Connor tried to press further into the crevasse in the stone, but the gap was too small, the ground unyielding. The shadow made a slow, complete turn, but its gaze passed right over Connor.

"Any other layabouts shirking their work?" the whipper snarled as it strode off down the mine track.

Connor let out a long and heavy breath as the taskmaster disappeared. Sweat dripped from his forehead and ran down his neck. Connor felt ashamed for being so afraid as he crept over to Mouse and Tonic.

"That was close," Mouse whispered.

"Let's hope we don't come any closer," Tonic said.

"What was that?" Connor asked.

"One of the taskmasters," Tonic said. "The last kind of trouble we want."

"And I didn't think shadows could get worse than the Shopkeeper," Connor said.

"They're not shadows," Tonic said. "They're older, from a time before light itself. They're remnants of the Eater of Light's army."

"I thought the Great Flare destroyed them all," Connor said.

"His army was too large and spread nearly everywhere. Without their general, they built places like this where they could carry on their cruelty."

"And no one stops them?"

"Who is there to stop them?"

Tonic slipped between the pillars and crossed the tracks. When Connor himself crossed the tracks, somehow it cemented in his mind there would be no going back.

Their path meandered, and their progress came in fits and stops.

Several times, they backtracked to avoid clusters of workers hammering and picking the obsidian, loading heaps of shining shards into great buckets. Whip and club taskmasters, who seemed to exercise their cruelty for the sake of being cruel, oversaw every group they found.

The increasing number of mine tracks among the towering obsidian blades also slowed their progress. Most of the tracks were unused, but twice, heaving and grunting workers trudged carts down the rails. Both times, Connor, Tonic, and Mouse pressed against pillars, trying to be invisible. Both times, Connor found himself pressed against Mouse, the warmth of her body comforting against the welling heat embracing the whole quarry.

The heat and the lava's glow intensified the deeper they went. A second lava flow joined the stream they followed from the other side. Combined, they created a wider and hotter flow. Connor wiped sweat from his brow every few steps. His hands grew so slick that they slid over the obsidian pillars he touched like they were made of ice. Sweating was exhausting because there was no water to drink. There might have been some blackwater in the bag, but he couldn't risk waking the cub. It probably wouldn't help much, anyway. Connor spat out a clump of ash. God, he was thirsty.

Tonic held up an open hand and asked for a brief rest. The lava's brightness seemed to take a heavy toll on him. His form wavered and wobbled and became transparent. Could it get bright enough to kill him? The story of the Great Flare seemed to suggest it might be possible.

"You okay?" Connor asked.

"Never better," Tonic gasped. "What's it to ya?"

"You're not going to die on us?"

"Not planning on it. But I wish I was a Caster about now."

"Yeah, then you could die of thirst," Connor said.

"And go home," Tonic said. "I've heard about air-conditioning."

While Tonic rested, Connor wished the teen hadn't mentioned air-conditioning. What he wouldn't give to plop on the couch in his nice cool living room and watch TV. Maybe eating a popsicle. A cold, delicious popsicle. With the fan on. No matter how much he used to wish for a quest like his favorite heroes, quests were better to watch. Besides him, sweat poured down Mouse's forehead and cheeks, leaving little streaks in the grime. No doubt she felt the same.

When they moved again, they didn't move long. A dozen pillars later, a third lava stream blocked their path. A single, arching obsidian bridge spanned it, and two huge groups of shadows thronged about it, one on each side. The group on the far side was hunched over, and they trudged at a crawling pace as if burdened. They dragged picks, shovels, and sledgehammers along the ground as they shuffled over the bridge. A layer of ash coated their heads and shoulders, and they all but disappeared in the intense flares of the pulsing lava.

The group on the near side was alert and fidgety. They muttered and murmured as the slow group crossed. Several paced in tight circles. Others clustered together, passing flasks. At the edge of this group, a throng of taskmasters huddled, speaking in sharp, irritated voices, watching the proceedings with impatience.

"Shift change," Tonic whispered. "Must be full night now."

Connor glanced at the sky but saw neither sun nor moon. The ash cloud hung thick over the whole quarry.

After what felt like an eternity, the departing miners finished crossing the bridge. Immediately, the taskmasters unfurled their whips and struck at the backs of the fresh workers.

"Get a move on!" they snapped.

The fresh shadows filed over in a shambling jog to escape the merciless blows. Within a matter of minutes, the path was clear.

As the three of them approached the bridge, Tonic began leaning on his staff. He panted and shuddered, and suddenly, Connor found the teen leaning against him, putting an arm over his shoulder for support as they trudged up the incline. By the time they crested the bridge, Connor felt like he was supporting the older boy's full weight, which, thankfully, was substantially diminished by the light. When they made it across, Tonic was able to stand without help again, but he seemed to be limping.

"Do you need to rest?" Mouse asked him.

"Can't," Tonic panted. "I'll be okay soon. It's the light. So intense. But we need to follow them. They'll head straight to the complex. The taskmasters will be too busy to notice us if we're lucky."

"What if we run into someone coming the other way?" Connor asked.

"I wouldn't worry. The workers don't straggle," Tonic said. "Even if one did, it'd be too tired to care about us."

They did, in fact, pass two workers as they pressed on, and Tonic proved right. The trio passed within direct view of one, and the older-looking shadow whose face held countless lines and scars didn't so much as glance at them, its eyes lost in whatever thoughts ran through its mind. Thankfully, Tonic's strength gradually returned, and Connor hoped they wouldn't get so close to the lava again.

They moved at a steady pace, keeping out of sight of the new shift, but never letting the sounds of the taskmasters grow too dim. Then, the obsidian daggers ahead ceased at a cliff.

As they approached the edge, the quarry towers rose into sight, taller and larger than anything in Gissu, with massive frames and walls made of what looked like the petrified wood of Blackwood. Long conveyors stretched from building to building, tumbling with fractured obsidian. Thick chains and giant pulleys lifted huge pallets of obsidian bricks into the air. Clusters of shadows worked enormous lever wheels that turned the cranes' giant gears, the cogs' teeth churning and grinding. A low rumble filled the air like the growl of some great beast. Voices rose and shouts echoed across the complex. About a dozen warehouses surrounded the burning lake, with shadows carrying boxes and sacks in and out through the doors.

However, Connor only paid passing attention to the complex buildings. His eyes couldn't escape the lava pool itself. Lava streams spiraled towards it from the slopes of the valley, each spanned in several places by tall, arching bridges much larger than the one Connor helped Tonic cross. The lake pulsed with waves of light, and the lava within swirled toward its center. The whirlpool reminded Connor of pictures he'd seen of black holes, only this one was on fire. Thick billows of smoke and ash rose from the pool's center into an enormous pillar stretching to the sky.

Tonic pointed to a building at the far edge of the lava pool. "The Foreman's office."

The Foreman's office differed from the other buildings. It didn't look at all like an office. To Connor, offices were boring, small buildings in strip malls or tall boxy skyscrapers in downtown Dallas. This building was a small fortress with grim obsidian walls and a single, tall tower rising out of the center with a parapet on top. An enormous figure stood at the parapet's edge with its hands on the railing, peering into the lava pool.

The Foreman, Connor knew even before Tonic said it.

"And you think we should talk to him," Connor said.

"Not sure 'should' is the right word," Tonic said. "Neither is 'him,' from what I've heard. Rumor says it's one of the few things remaining in the Shadowlands that stood directly in the presence of the Eater of Light."

Connor let his eyes wander back to the complex. Everywhere he looked, shadow miners stood between buildings. Taskmasters paced up and down, whipping any shadow who straggled. The whole place bustled.

"How the heck are we supposed to get through?" Connor whispered.

"Patiently," Tonic said. "It'll clear as crews head into the Daggers. We hide until then."

Tonic turned and crept back into the obsidian teeth. Connor and Mouse followed. It did not take long to find a depression walled in by five columns, preventing someone from seeing them unless they walked right up. However, it bothered Connor that he could not see out.

He crawled to the edge and peeked.

Nothing happened for some time. The wait ground on Connor's nerves. The heat and his thirst made his head swim, and he felt like he had in jail. Don't let me pass out, Connor thought.

Then, the first of the workers marched into sight. Connor counted them at first, but gave up when he passed a hundred, and a new group too thick to count approached. As the shadows passed by, Connor was astonished at how many suffered this horrible work. Hearing the whips and snarls from the taskmasters, Connor wondered where they all had come from. Why were they being forced to work this way?

Finally, the herds thinned. When the last group passed, Tonic patted him on the shoulder and said, "Ready?"

"No," Connor said.

They stood and stepped out of the obsidian hollow to find themselves surrounded by five taskmasters who stepped out from behind columns. Their chests were bare. They wore heavy black pants that shone metallically and just ended above taloned feet gripping the rough stone like eagles gripping a perch. All held uncoiled whips ready to snap.

"Well, well, well," one of them, a beast of a shadow with a face covered in scars, said. "What have we here?"

THE FOREMAN

The taskmasters' hands tensed on their whips. Tonic clenched his staff in both his hands. Connor wished he hadn't lost his staff and found himself jealous of Mouse's dagger sheathed on her belt. His knees trembled.

"Dunno, Ragger," a taskmaster said to the one who'd spoken first. "Looks like a couple of Casters to me."

"Couple of half-casters," another chimed in, its voice a raspy hiss. "And a..." He trailed off as he glanced at Tonic.

"A deserter from the lines?" the fourth said.

"I'm no worker," Tonic snapped.

Ragger snapped his whip with a quick roll of his wrist. The end coiled around Tonic's staff at the middle, and with a hard jerk, Ragger yanked the weapon out of Tonic's hands. The pole clattered across the obsidian until it came to a wobbling rest at the base of a pillar. Tonic raised both his fists.

"Definitely ain't one of ours," one taskmaster laughed. "Got fight in him."

"I'll fight the lot of you," Tonic said. "Even if you're cowards enough to fight five on one."

"You talk big for such a sliver of shadow," the first taskmaster said.

"And you sound as ugly as you look," Tonic said.

Connor tried to mentally will Tonic to be quiet. There had to be a way out without fighting. Could they run?

"Oh, I like him," Ragger said with a dry grin. "Bet we could mold him into a proper taskmaster if we toughened him up." Then, the grin vanished. "'Cept you're trespassing," he said. "And we don't take well to trespassers."

"We're not trespassing," Mouse said. She'd drawn her dagger and gripped it in one fist. "We're here to see the Foreman."

Connor was stunned. Mouse's face clenched with determination, and she fidgeted on the balls of her feet as if about to spring. She would have looked fierce if she weren't so small.

"Are you now?" Ragger asked, dropping to one knee in almost a fatherly way. Somehow, the friendliness of his posture was more menacing than when he'd been standing. He clacked the talons on his toes against the obsidian. Connor had the distinct impression Ragger could eat Mouse. "And if I may ask, what is your business with it?"

Ragger calling the Foreman 'it' lingered at the back of Connor's mind as Mouse said, "We're here to make a deal."

"Well, now, that's something we can accommodate. We love deals here," Ragger said, rising to his feet. The other taskmasters laughed. With deft hands, Ragger coiled his whip and fixed it to a leather clasp on his waist. "Can't get enough of 'em, can we boys? Mines would be much emptier."

Ragger gestured down the winding cliff path to the edge of the lava lake. The heat swelled as the group descended, zigzagging back and forth from switchback to switchback. Pebbles clattered over the edge with every step. Connor's clothes were drenched and heavy with sweat, but now they steamed as the heat evaporated the liquid from the fabric. His cheeks hurt from squinting hard against the brilliance of the flames. The epicenter of the flows in the lake blazed a white-hot radiance beneath the smoke column. Would he catch fire before he reached the bottom? Thankfully, the path maintained enough distance to prevent this until it reached the Foreman's office. Connor wondered if the path was built to make those who walked upon it uncomfortable.

Up close, the Foreman's office was even more terrifying. The walls, which had appeared smooth from the bluff, jutted spikes like a hedgehog's quills, each with a tiny barb at its end. The wall had appeared uniform black from afar, but up close, the quills were denser in some spots than others, creating light spots and shadows. The subtle shading formed images: skulls and frenzied mouths bristling with teeth. Connor also made out images of a bull fighting a lion and a ram trampling a pair of scales.

The doors were pale white and towering, twelve feet high and twelve feet wide. The petrified wooden frame was carved into enormous bones. More curving bones arched over the doors like a huge ribcage. As Ragger approached, the two halves of the rib cage spread as if on their own, and Connor felt like they were about to enter the belly of some ravenous demon.

Connor strained to make out what lay inside the darkness, even as his mind shouted for him to run away as fast as he could. He fought the urge to flee. If he evaded the taskmasters, where would he go? Back to Gissu?

Connor looked at Mouse. She bit her lower lip, arms crossed over her stomach, hands shuffling up and down her biceps. She stared straight ahead. He couldn't abandon her. She was probably as scared as he was.

Tonic was different. If the damage the intense light was inflicting on his form was daunting him, Connor couldn't tell. He stood straight and firm. That's how I need to be, thought Connor. Tonic might be scared, but he's facing it bravely. Connor wished he'd asked the teen more about Leon's story. Maybe a story of courage could have helped him feel braver. Tonic's bravery in front of the taskmasters might be the reason they hadn't been attacked on the spot. At the same time, his mother's voice warned him not to be reckless.

He grit his teeth and stepped forward. Tonic and Mouse did the same.

The darkness inside was almost total at first due to the sharp contrast against the brightness of the lava. He made out dim shapes, but everything was indistinct. Even the lanterns glowing down the edges of the long vault barely lit the walls. They paused a few feet inside to let their eyes adjust.

Gradually, Connor's vision improved. The hall itself was wide and large. A heavy purple carpet ran down its center, blending into the purplish black of the obsidian floor. Against each wall, a line of chairs sat armrest to armrest, all unoccupied. The only break in them was in the middle of both walls where great, red double doors stood, both pairs shut. The corners of the room were so dark, Connor couldn't tell where one wall ended and another began.

A raised platform, upon which rose a huge and ornate throne made of the same pale white material as the doors with a matching bone-like design, stood at the far end of the hall. Something enormous sat on the throne. The talons of the taskmasters behind Connor thumped softly and erratically on the carpet as they stepped. He wondered if they were nervous too, and, if they were, what it said about the chances of three children.

When the shape on the throne spoke, its voice boomed throughout the hall.

"What is this rabble you bring," it said. "Why are you not minding the workers?"

Ragger jabbed a fat finger into the middle of Connor's back, prodding him forward.

"Trespassers," Ragger said. "Found them hiding at the edge of the pit."

"Each of you is charged with ten workers," the voice boomed. "Yet it takes five taskmasters to bring three trespassers?"

Ragger said nothing, but Connor heard the other taskmasters recede towards the door. Connor proceeded slowly, but Ragger's talons stopped clacking behind him. He felt the distance between him and the taskmaster grow with each step closer to the throne. He still couldn't quite make out what sat there, except it was far larger than any shadow he'd met. Was this the same thing he'd seen on the parapet? That had the shape of a man? What sat before them seemed almost shapeless. Or, like it was changing shape, its edges bulging and expanding. Connor wondered if this was the real reason for the room's darkness. It was what

Mouse had meant when she explained why the shadows loved umbrellas.

When Connor had crossed about half the hall's length, Ragger cleared his throat and said, "They're here to make a deal."

The thing on the throne stood, towering at least fifteen feet high. Connor gasped. The Foreman's shape changed rapidly, its muscles swelling and shrinking. Its face, stern and masculine, morphed into one strikingly feminine, then into another that was half masculine and half feminine. Great wings sprouted from its back, and sharp curving spikes burst from its shoulders before vanishing back into its mass. It spawned great antlers one moment, then a long, coiling tail with a scorpion's stinger at the end the next. It even took the shape of a pair of giant conjoined twins who merged at the ribs, both with grim bearded faces. The effect was dizzying, and Connor was already dizzy from the hunger, thirst, and heat.

"Have out with it then," the Foreman boomed.

Connor slid his thumb under the strap of his backpack. A soft vibration rumbled inside the bag as the cub started to purr. He couldn't say what Mouse had in mind when she said they wanted a deal, but he suspected the cub was central to it. Connor hoped Tonic would do the speaking, but Tonic looked at him as if to say, "This is your show." Connor forced himself further forward. A horrible sulfurous stench bloomed as he did, emanating not only from the lava outside but from the Foreman itself.

Connor's voice sounded tiny in the great hall's expanse as he said, "We want to find the Neverborn thief who stole our shadows."

The Foreman snorted, and one of its legs, if the masses of shadow it stood upon could be called legs, sprouted a giant hoof that pawed at the ground three times like a bull about to charge.

"I have no dealings with shadow thieves or the Neverborn," the Foreman snarled. "Even speaking with them is punishable. Do I want to end up working the lines?"

Connor felt the blood drain from his face.

"B-But—" he stammered as fear welled up in him. He forced himself to move his gaze from the beast ahead to Mouse. She stared back, her eyes wide. He couldn't fail her. She needed this even more than he did. So, he swallowed hard. "But someone as important as you hear a lot of things."

"I have many ears," the Foreman growled. "As many as I want."

"So, surely you've-" Connor began, but the Foreman cut him off.

"The Shadow Police also have many ears, and they're especially tuned to hearing things that don't want to be heard."

"But they're not here in this magnificent fortress," Connor said, almost choking on the word 'magnificent' since, when he said it, he actually meant 'terrifying.' "They wouldn't dare try."

The Foreman chuckled, a soft, evil chuckle full of menace and rancor. "You're here, aren't you?" he said. "Creeping in like mice through cracks. The Shadow Police are also mice, cockroaches, wiggling into every space, no matter how well you mortar."

Both times the Foreman said "mice," Connor was certain he saw the beast's eyes fall on Mouse. Did he know her name? Had he known they were coming? How?

"You could be a trio of their mice," the Foreman said. "You claim you seek a deal, yet you slink about like thieves. Maybe you hope to steal from me?"

"How—" Connor began.

"I have many ears, and I have been listening."

"Well, even if you had dealings with the thief, I would never tell," Connor said, rambling in his nervousness. "I couldn't tell. Especially not the Shadow Police. They're looking for me."

Connor snapped his mouth shut as Tonic and Mouse shot him a "shut the heck up" glance. Stupid, stupid, Connor thought.

"Then tell me why I shouldn't have Ragger bring you straight to them," the Foreman said, staring straight at Connor with horrible, hollow eyes. He flicked his gaze to Tonic and Mouse, and said, "And the rest of you for helping a wanted Caster?"

"Because we're here to make a deal," Mouse said.

"So you say," the Foreman said. "Enough of this banter. Out with it."

Connor took the bag off his shoulder and sat it on the floor in front of the Foreman. Kneeling, he unzipped the bag and pulled out the shadowcat cub with both hands. He half expected it to leap at him like it had in Blackwood, but this time it hung docile in his grip, still purring. It bent its neck and licked his hand.

"If you can tell us where to find our shadows or where to find the thief," Connor said, "this cub is yours."

The Foreman's shape seemed to shrink and settle into a form much like the statue of The Thinker on the cover of Connor's history book from Mr. Paxter's class.

"Interesting," the Foreman muttered. "It would be good to have an equal around here."

Mouse bit her lower lip. Tonic held his breath. The cub licked Connor's hand again and tried to reach his face with its jet-black tongue. Connor regretted offering it.

Then, the Foreman's form exploded into a flurry of transformations. It became a giant, then a buffalo, then a fat and coiled serpent before returning to something more or less human.

"I accept your deal," the Foreman said with a horrifying sneer, far more horrifying than anything Connor had seen on the face of the Shopkeeper. The Foreman flung his arm out to the doors on the left side of the hall. They burst open as if by the force of his will. The room beyond was almost empty. A bright light shone a spotlight into the room's center, illuminating a single chair.

On the chair stood Quiet. Around Quiet's neck hung a noose. Beside the chair stood a tall, thin shadow. Its features were sharp: pointed nose, jutting brow, narrow chin, and prominent cheekbones. It wore a black cloak that hung loosely from its shoulders over a tight black shirt and pants. While Connor barely remembered what he'd seen upon waking in the middle of the night, he knew exactly who he was looking at.

The Neverborn Thief.

THE CHOICE

Anger bloomed in Connor. Images of leaping onto the Neverborn Thief and pummeling him with fists and feet flooded him. He let the cub fall from his arms and charged.

He'd hardly made it three steps when something wrapped around his waist with a sharp pain and jerked him to a stop. He struggled vainly before giving up and looking down. A braided cord held him like a leash. Ragger's whip.

"Tut tut," Ragger said. "No fighting here."

"Give it back!" Connor shouted. "Give me my shadow back!"

The Neverborn Thief chuckled as Connor squirmed against his restraint.

"Give?" The Neverborn Thief said. "I was given nothing, so I give nothing."

"You're a monster," Connor shouted.

"Nonsense," The Neverborn Thief said with a wag of his finger. "Monsters do because they are. I do because I can."

Connor's rage blinded him again, and he threw himself against the whip with all his might. The leather grip gave no slack.

"And monsters don't reason," the Thief said. "But I can be reasonable. We can discuss this. Maybe even arrive at a deal."

"I'll never deal with you," Connor said, but his voice faltered. What he'd hoped would sound confident came out childish and petulant.

"Oh, but I think you will," The Neverborn Thief said, stepping closer. "I have your friend. Surely, this little shadow has worth to you?"

With the Thief so close, Connor wanted to renew his frenzy against the whip, but he forced himself to look at Quiet. Tears rolled down her cheeks.

"They found me in the Daggers," she said. "Looking for you."

She tried to drag her toe across the ground, but her foot found nothing but air. For a moment, she tottered on the chair's edge.

"It's not your fault," Connor said and he took a deep breath. He couldn't fight free from Ragger's pull. He needed to calm down, but ow could he be calm in the face of such an awful enemy, especially when he'd been tricked yet again? The worst part was that the Foreman's trickery was his fault. He should have negotiated and been more specific. He could have requested safety and asked the Foreman to help him subdue the thief. Would such demands have been accepted? It didn't matter. He had nothing more to offer.

The Neverborn Thief leaned towards Connor, so close that if Connor reached, he'd touch the shadow. Ragger would simply pull him back.

"I hear they call you Little Bit," the Thief said. "And you are. Such a little bit. I'm surprised you made it this far without crawling home to mommy. I remember how you screamed for her in the night, your pure, delicious terror and helplessness."

The Thief's goading stirred Connor's blood, but he couldn't let anger overtake him again. Instead, he peered at the Neverborn's face. Dark tattoos covered the Thief's face. Swirls of stars and flame surrounded tattoos of faces, and each face wore an expression of horror.

"You like my art?" the Thief asked. "The faces of those whose shadows I've stolen. I have a place on my back for you and your little

Mouse."

Connor had been so absorbed with the Thief he'd forgotten Mouse and Tonic. He glanced back. Both stood behind Ragger, and Connor thought that if they jumped on the taskmaster, he might lose his grip on the whip. They didn't move, however. Their expressions were filled with uncertainty. Fighting their out wasn't an option.

Connor asked, "What do you want?"

"The rest of your shadow, of course," The Neverborn Thief said. "For you to either give it willingly or to go home and eventually let it be mine in time. Do that, and I'll release your friend."

"Don't," Quiet said.

Connor wondered whether he could simply give up his shadow. Would it be so bad to be Shadowless? He would be with his mother, and she would love him, even if he couldn't appreciate it. Would that be better than letting Quiet hang?

A thought burst into Connor's mind.

"But you can't kill her," Connor said. "Shadows can't die like that."

"Smart boy. Absolutely right," the Thief said. "The chair and noose are theatrics. We can't all be as imposing as the Foreman. I so didn't want to disappoint."

The Thief gestured to Quiet and said, "But I can hang her. Again, and again. Crush her windpipe. Break her vertebrae. Have you wondered yet what might happen if I cut off one of her fingers? Or her whole arm below the elbow? Will it grow back? I can make her suffer a thousand times more than you ever could because she would never die... But if you give up this pesky chase, I'll not only let her go, I'll make sure she finds her mother. I'll even let Mouse go so she gets another chance to get her shadow back from me."

Something about the Thief's offer struck Connor as odd. He detected a note of need in the bargain. Was there a reason the Thief needed to get Connor's shadow? He didn't have time to consider this further, though, because Tonic said, "It's a trick!"

The Neverborn snarled at Tonic. "This is none of your concern. This is between me and Little Bit."

It is my concern," Tonic said. "I don't doubt Quiet told you about our deal with Connor." The Thief grimaced, and Tonic continued, now speaking to Connor, "If you accept his offer, then Quiet and

Mouse will have caused you to fail. They will have violated the deal. But if you refuse, you break your deal with them."

"That can't be," Connor said. "That's not right."

"Right is the letter of the law," the Thief said.

Connor's heart crashed in his chest, and his knees almost buckled. He was too young to face this. If he accepted the offer, who knew what torment Mouse and Quiet would suffer. At the same time, if the Thief kept the deal, they would get something they wanted. If he refused, he would be subject to torment himself, and they would get nothing. But maybe they could find a way to keep trying. At least then only he would bear the consequences of his choice.

Something nagged at him about all of this. It seemed too easy. If he refused, where would he be? He would be here, caught by Raggers, stuck between the Thief and the Foreman. Quiet would still be in the Thief's hands, and Mouse and Tonic would be helpless. If he accepted, he would go home, he would have more freedom. Connor remembered what Mosley said. Even Shadowless, he would still have time. He would be even stronger in the Shadowlands. Was it possible the Thief assumed he wouldn't know this? Also, if Mouse got her shadow back, she wouldn't have to return to the Shadowlands and face the penalty for breaking the deal. It would only be Quiet who suffered.

He looked at Mouse, then Tonic, then Quiet. He let his gaze linger on Quiet, before he said to them all, "You need to trust me."

Tonic nodded to Connor. Of all of them, he stood to neither gain nor lose from the deal, and Connor was grateful for it. Quiet stared at him hurtfully. Mouse looked at the ground and said softly, "I do."

That was enough for Connor. He wished Quiet would agree, but part of him was still angry at her for her betrayal in The Judge's chamber. As Connor faced the Thief, a thought occurred to him.

"Tell me your name," Connor said.

The Neverborn Thief hissed at Connor, his whole body leaning into the sound. His features quivered with rage.

"I'm Neverborn," the Neverborn growled. "I have no name, nor do I give any."

Connor didn't know why the Thief reacted in such a way, but part of him felt glad to have gotten under his tattooed skin. He had to take advantage of the Thief's loss of composure. Maybe it would help him bargain. He puffed out his chest a bit and raised his chin. "What do you propose?"

"You die," the Thief spat. "And I take what will be mine soon enough, anyway."

Connor wanted to smile at this, but he kept his face smooth. He even forced a bit of a frown and wrinkled his brow in what he hoped looked like fear or worry. The Thief's anger had gotten the better of him, but Connor couldn't let him spell out that side of the bargain any further.

"And what do I get in return?" Connor asked.

"I release this pathetic girl," the Thief said, waving a dismissive hand to Quiet. "And I will see Mouse has her half shadow."

Connor was surprised the Thief seemed willing to give up Mouse's shadow, but supposed the Thief figured one sure bet was better than two unsure ones. Either way, Connor knew he couldn't let the Thief think too carefully about what he'd offered.

"And you'll see to their safety?"

"I can't," the Neverborn Thief said. "They'll pay for betraying you."

"Then swear you will not harm them," Connor said.

"So be it," the Thief nodded with what seemed like reluctance.

"And Tonic?" Connor asked.

"I'll walk him to Gissu myself, fending off every shadowcat along the way if he wishes," the Thief said with an impatient smile. Then the smile vanished. "Do we have a deal? Or must we renegotiate?"

"Little—" Mouse started, but he didn't listen. He couldn't risk the Thief realizing his mistake. As he said, "We have a deal," it was as if the faces in the Thief's tattoos came to life, their eyes widening further, their mouths working the word "No!" over and over. It was too late, though. He'd already said it. What did he miss?

The Thief snapped his wrist so his finger pointed straight at the chair upon which Quiet stood. Connor sent one last look to Mouse, whose mouth was wide open with shock or disbelief or distress. He didn't trust the Thief to keep his word, so he said, "Your end first."

"Very well," the Thief said.

He waved a shooing hand at Quiet who slowly reached up and removed the noose from her neck. When she was down, she ran straight to Tonic and threw her arms around him. Tonic knelt and returned the embrace, whispering reassurances in her ear.

"And Mouse?" Connor said.

"What about Mouse?" the Thief said.

"You said you would see that she has half of her shadow."

The Thief turned and gazed at Mouse for a few seconds.

"And I see she still has her half-shadow," the Thief said.

Connor felt his mouth fall open. How had he been so stupid?

"I-I-I'm sorry," Connor stammered to Mouse as the Thief broke into nasty laughter. The Thief then looked to the Foreman, who stood in the middle of his great, dark hall, peering in with interest. The Thief pointed to Mouse and Quiet and said, "These two deal breakers are yours."

Devastation filled Connor's heart. So that was how one ended up working the lines in the Daggers. Not only had he failed to get Mouse her shadow, but now she'd suffer the whips of the taskmasters. How long could she withstand their punishment? If Mouse died again, she'd surely become Shadowless. Despite everything, all the times when he'd felt deceived, weak, and powerless, Connor felt more helpless than ever.

His one consolation was that the Thief's terms only said he had to die, and the Thief would get what would have been his. He didn't say Connor couldn't come back. And if Connor took his shadow back, then his shadow was not something that would have been the Thief's. He tried to hold onto this hope, but it was almost impossible. Despair filled his heart as he eyed the noose. He began his slow walk to the chair, his mind filled with Mosley's hanging and the cruel, thunderous drum beaten by the crowd's feet. Mouse, Quiet, Tonic, Raggers, and the Foreman watched in silence, but Connor heard the intensifying rhythm echoing in his head. He could almost feel the stamp of the crowd's feet through the floor with each step he took.

You're not going to die, Connor told himself. It's going to hurt, and you're going to go home. And you're going to come straight back. He wished his head would swim and blur the way it had in the cell, but somehow his mind was clear as ever, full of the laughing and jeering faces of Mosley's crowd. Connor felt warmth spread as he wet himself for the second time in the Shadowlands.

Connor mounted the chair as the Thief stepped up beside it. No wickedness could match the Thief's grin as Connor pulled the noose over his head. The tattoos on the Thief's face twisted and writhed as if they too were witnesses.

The Thief took Connor's left hand and pulled it behind his back. For the first time in a while, Connor couldn't actually feel a shadow touching him. It was as if his hand moved of its own accord. The other hand followed, and a cord wrapped around his wrists, binding them tightly.

Connor took as deep a breath as he could muster the instant before the Thief kicked the chair away. Connor felt his body fall, the noose snap tight on his throat.

Immediately, his head felt too full of blood. Pressure built in his face and temples. His neck screamed with pain as the rope dug in, cutting off both air and circulation. His whole body leapt to life, thrashing and bucking in the air. Connor's vision was blotted out in patches, and his chest heaved to gasp for air, though any air he drew would only prolong matters. His feet arched backward; his knees bent wildly as if trying to kick the middle of his back.

Then, the fight left all his muscles at once. They fell limp around him, dangling. His head felt like a black cloud buzzing with bees, their droning growing louder until it overwhelmed all else.

Then, a strange pulling sensation. He was moving, going somewhere new, where the World of Light awaited.

THE NOOSE

Something was wrong. Of course, everything happening was wrong, but now he was in total darkness, and something was wrong in an even more horrible way. The rope bit into Connor's neck all over again. His hands were still bound behind his back. His head still felt stuffed full, and his lungs cried for air but they got none. The drone of bees returned.

He was still being hung. His body thrashed. What was happening?

Connor's foot kicked something hard, unyielding, and flat. He slammed his foot onto it, tilting sideways. He thrust his other foot out, and it too found something hard and stable on the other side. The pressure on his neck loosened a bit. He straightened his knees, his legs splayed. The bees swarmed.

He managed a gasp, and bolts of pain shot down his esophagus. The noose was still tight, but the air calmed his head. His neck hurt so badly.

192

Hot blood ran to his chest from the rope. He took another breath, then another. He still couldn't see. Where was he? His breathing slowed as he drew through his nose. Ammonia, vinegar, and bleach flooded his nostrils. Cleaning supplies. The janitor's closet. He was in the janitor's closet, and the light was off.

Connor jerked his wrists against the binding. He sawed his wrists back and forth, pulling harder with each pass. Each motion worked more freedom even as the cord bit into his skin. One hand tore free, and the motion sent him toppling. He flailed his arms for balance. He couldn't bear for the noose to tighten again. His temples throbbed. His throat throbbed. The bees faded.

Connor slid his fingers under the noose, working the knot with his other hand. His throat smarted as his knuckle rubbed the raw flesh. The noose slipped over his head, still dangling from the ceiling against his cheek. Connor wanted to drop down. He didn't know what he would land on. The janitor's closet had merged with Mouse's closet in the Shadowlands, and he was afraid of falling into the mess. He reached for the unscrewed bulb. It was still there. He twisted it until it flickered on.

If the janitor's closet had been as destroyed in the real world, someone had done one heck of a clean-up. One foot was planted on the desk, the other on the shelf holding the cleansers. The rolling chair was overturned beneath him. Carefully, he lowered himself down. Blood dripped from his hand to the floor, onto something written in what also appeared to be blood.

The message read, "Welcome Home."

Connor's body chilled. He felt he was in a kind of danger he'd never imagined he'd be in. The Neverborn Thief must have come into the real world while he hung in the Shadowlands, and somehow hung him here, too. Connor threw his gaze at every shadow in the room. Was the thief still here? Would he try to finish the job? No shadows moved other than his, which was more incomplete than ever.

Each heartbeat drew fresh pain from Connor's injured neck. He hadn't considered that the Thief would attack him in the real world. Of course, he should have realized it was possible; after all, the Thief had stolen his shadow from his bedroom. He wasn't safe anytime or anywhere. He might be safer in the Shadowlands.

Connor glanced up at the bulb. Should he go straight back? Where would he reappear? Quiet's hall in Gissu? On the riverbank? Looking at the noose, he knew without a doubt he was not ready to go back. Whether he returned to Gissu or Blackwood, he had no idea where to go once he got back, except to help Mouse and Quiet, which meant returning to the Daggers to face the Taskmasters and the Foreman.

"I'd think carefully about what you do next," a voice said from under the desk.

Connor jumped. For a moment, he was certain the voice belonged to the Thief, but it was pinched, nasal, and feminine. The shadow under the desk bulged, and Sergeant Dandrich popped out.

"You've been doing dangerous things," she said.

Connor's spine tingled, and his palms grew sweaty. Was Dandrich here to arrest him? She'd helped him at the gates of Gissu, but she hadn't been friendly about it.

"What do you want?" Connor said.

"To help you, of course," Dandrich said.

"How do I know you're not like The Judge and Captain Sallow?" Connor said. "How can I trust anyone from the Shadowlands?"

"I can't say I know everything you've been through," Dandrich said, "but I was arguing with The Judge to get you out when you went home."

Connor noticed Dandrich said "went home" rather than "escaped," and he took it as a good sign. Still, he'd been betrayed and tricked too many times.

"You didn't do a very good job of it," Connor said bitterly. "And you sure haven't done much to help me get my shadow back."

"I know, and I'm sorry," Dandrich said, looking at the floor. "You have to understand there's little I can do. Shadow Law is restrictive, especially for officers. Even backroom deals are as binding as actual law. That's why I helped you at the gates; I could step right in."

"You could have been nicer about it," Connor said.

Dandrich sighed. "No, I couldn't," she said. "The truth is, I'm not exactly allowed to help you. There was a time when I could have gone straight to the Daggers to arrest the Thie—"

"Wait," Connor said, his face growing hot. "You knew where the Thief was? And you let us walk in there?"

"I had no choice," Dandrich said. "Things are getting worse in the Shadowlands. Shadow Theft is one of the highest crimes in our world, but more and more rules are being put into place to obstruct intervention."

"Why? If it's such a bad crime?"

"The Shadower," Dandrich said.

"What do you mean?"

Dandrich reached to the shelf and pulled a rag from a box labeled "clean" in black marker. She dabbed at the blood on Connor's neck. The wound stung, but Connor tried not to pull away. Between his neck and wrists and the cuts on his face... Connor's thoughts paused. He reached up to his cheek. The cuts on his face from Blackwood's branches were gone. They hadn't healed; they were gone.

"When the Shadower first began making deals with the police, they seemed good," Dandrich said. "He'd trade information about criminals for what he called 'small favors' to be paid later. We made more arrests than we'd ever had, recovered countless shadows. It's how I became a sergeant. I had more leads than time to track 'em down."

Sergeant Dandrich paused and fidgeted with her badge.

"Then," she continued. "The leads stopped, and new rules started. They came from the top; the Shadower began to collect its debts. I could get arrested for telling you this, but he controls Captain Sallow, the other captains, and the judges. The Shadower gave us enough information to arrest practically all the thieves in the Shadowlands—except for his. Now, he uses his influence to make sure they're safe."

"What does he want?" Connor asked.

"I can't say for sure," Dandrich said, "but I believe he's amassing an army. We've been losing contact with villages and towns to the North, but a few reports have made it through. Nothing connects to the Shadower directly, but they say whole settlements have been enslaved."

"Can we stop him?"

Dandrich chuckled.

"You're a brave kid," Dandrich said. "But I'm afraid these are happenings far beyond your age and abilities. Worry about recovering your shadow. I'm only telling you this, so you understand why it's so hard for me to help."

"But if we don't do something, who will?" Connor said.

"The Thirteen only know," Dandrich said with a shake of her head. "Those with enough power to try are in the Shadower's pocket. And as for the rest, sadly, most shadows are more concerned with trading a rubber ball for a new pair of shoelaces."

"I hate the Shadowlands," Connor said. "It's an awful place."

Dandrich winced. "I hate to hear you say that. It's always been a hard place, but there's good in it. Beauty. Families and friends. There's even happiness, though it's getting harder to find. Moreover, I've spent a little more time in your world than most because of my duties," she said. "And from what I've seen, things happening in the Shadowlands are reflected in things happening in the Light. To truly stop these things, one would need to take the darkness out of people altogether. And that's something even the Thirteen couldn't manage."

Dandrich crumpled the rag she'd been cleaning Connor with and stuffed it into the trashcan with the wads of paper towels and candy bar wrappers. Connor's skin was still stained with blood, because the sergeant didn't have any water, but it looked a little better. Though he was grateful for the kindness, a troubling thought came to him.

"Why me?" Connor said. "Why are you helping me? Why haven't you helped Mouse? Or the Pale Boy? What makes me so special?"

A strange look passed over Dandrich's face. The look bothered Connor. It was the look his mother got when he asked her a question she didn't want to answer.

"I can't answer that as well as I would like," Dandrich said. "Certain things prevent it, but I can tell you this: I'm here right now because a terrible crime has been committed. One I couldn't stand by and allow."

"Which crime?" Connor asked.

"Your hanging," Dandrich said.

"But I made a deal," Connor started, but Dandrich waved her hands.

"Your hanging in the Shadowlands was legal," Dandrich said. "But your hanging here broke our most powerful law. No shadow is ever allowed to take the life of a Caster in the World of Light."

"Why not?" Connor said.

"You think we want the World of Light coming down on us?" Dandrich asked. "Few Casters find our world. Some know of it, but there are more who we don't want to know. They would come in search of power, and they're the type who most easily fall in league with those like the Shadower."

"What about Journeyman?" Connor asked. "And The Judge was a Caster?"

"Journeyman trades half his shadow to get there," Dandrich said. "Not only does he risk becoming Shadowless if he stays in the Shadowlands too long, but every time he enters it, he takes back more of the shadow with him. Eventually, everything will be darkness and confusion for him. He probably didn't tell you that part. People like him think what they want is worth the cost, but they don't like to admit the price."

Connor knew what she said made sense. Would he ever be the same as before his shadow had been stolen? He thought about his conversation with the Pale Boy. Even if he got his shadow back, Connor wondered whether he'd be able to play Life and Monopoly. Could he care about games when he knew how things could be?

"What do I do?" Connor asked.

"I can't promise to catch the thief in time," Dandrich said. "But he'll be drawn to you if you return. I don't know why he hates you enough to try this, but he'll want to finish the job."

"Could it be because I asked him his name?"

Dandrich nodded vigorously. "Some of the Neverborn embrace the fact they don't have names and all the problems that come with them, but most hate any reminder of how lost they feel."

"Why do names matter so much?"

"A name isn't a word people call you by," Dandrich said. "It is a symbol of your identity. We grow into or against our names. One way or another, they come to fit us, come to fit who we are. No matter how long you go by a nickname, if I were to call you by your real name, it would be hard for you not to react."

Dandrich fell silent for a moment. Then, she said, "I know I haven't fully answered your question. I'll say this: the Shadowlands alters who you are, and your name can help it happen. Right now, though, none of it matters. You need rest. Eat. Sleep. Get stronger."

"But then what?" Connor asked.

"I suspect you'll have to figure out how to trick the Thief."

Connor didn't like that thought at all. He'd tried to trick the Thief in the Foreman's office, and it had been a disaster.

"Can't you help me at all?"

Dandrich looked down again. At first, he thought she was looking at the floor, but then Connor realized her eyes were fixed on her badge. There were tears in them. Slowly, Dandrich reached up to her chest and slid the badge off her uniform. Then, she reached over to the trash can and let it fall from her fingers. Unlike the bloody rag which still poked out of the refuse it had been stuffed under, the badge seemed to melt into the shadows of the can and vanish.

Dandrich said, "Do you know where you'll come back?"

Connor stared at the trash for a moment, processing what had happened. Though he could be mistaken, it seemed quite clear Dandrich had just resigned from the Shadow Police.

"The bank of the river in Blackwood, I think."

"The Shadowrun," Dandrich said. "I'll meet you there. I'll bring supplies. Be there tomorrow at midday."

"Thank you, Serg—" Connor began, but Dandrich held up her hand.

"Just Dandrich now," she said. "And when we're alone, you can call me Renee."

Dandrich looked abruptly at the door and disappeared like a puff of smoke. The knob rattled and turned, and the door cracked open.

THE NURSE'S OFFICE

"Who's in there?" said a voice from the other side of the door. Connor searched, but there was nowhere to hide. He was about to cram himself under the desk when the door swung open. Mr. Paxter stood on the other side.

"It's me, Little B—" Connor broke off as he realized he'd almost given his shadow nickname. "Connor. Connor Brighton."

"Connor? What on earth are you—?" Mr. Paxter asked, but then his eyes widened so much they about popped from their sockets. "My God!" Mr. Paxter's eyes flicked to the noose and exclaimed, "What did you try to do?"

"Nothing!" Connor protested, waving his hands as if the motion explained his innocence.

Mr. Paxter dropped to one knee. He tilted Connor's neck back and examined the boy's throat. "Who did this?"

Connor didn't know what to say. How could he explain? No adult would ever believe his story, so he said, "You wouldn't believe me."

Mr. Paxter's face grew solemn. His mouth pressed into a flat line. Then, he said, "Let's get you cleaned up. Afterwards, you will explain."

The impulse to shrink back or run through the nearest exit surged in Connor. His muscles twitched as Mr. Paxter reached for Connor's wrist, but the teacher stopped when he saw the injuries there. He rose, placed a hand on Connor's back, and eased him forward. Connor didn't resist, but he wanted to. It was night, judging by the light in the hall. What was Mr. Paxter doing here so late?

Connor voiced his question as Mr. Paxter escorted him past the principal's office.

"Working late," Mr. Paxter said. "I was on my way out and thought I heard voices."

Most of the hallway lights were out, but one light flickered as Mr. Paxter led Connor past the Principal's office to the nurse's office on the other side of the hallway. Connor vaguely remembered the thrill of sneaking past the secretary at recess. He'd thought he was so clever. Now, he doubted he'd be thrilled about anything again.

With a jingle, Mr. Paxter fished a set of keys from his pocket and selected one. He unlocked the nurse's office, opened the door, and shuffled Connor inside. For a moment, Connor thought it strange Mr. Paxter had that key, but the teacher also coached the school basketball team and likely needed to open the office if the nurse was gone for the day.

Mr. Paxter was about to sit Connor down on the cot, but then he dragged a small metal chair from the corner. Connor looked down at himself. He was filthy from head to toe. His clothes were saturated with soot and grime, and his skin was smeared gray everywhere but the bright red of his injuries.

Drawers opened and jars clinked as Mr. Paxter quickly gathered supplies: cotton swabs, paper towels, gauze pads, band-aids, alcohol, and Neosporin. He turned on the faucet of the little sink and wet one of the paper towels. Slowly, he cleaned Connor's neck, dabbing the blood with the wet towel, then using cotton balls soaked in alcohol to clean the spots where the rope had broken the skin. Each pat stung and burned, but how could he cry about a little sting after everything he'd been through?

As Mr. Paxter knelt to get a better angle, Connor thought it strange to have two people, his teacher and Sergeant Dandrich, take care of him almost identically. However, Mr. Paxter was much more thorough because he had more than a rag to work with. He concluded by taping wraps of gauze around Connor's neck and wrists. It reminded Connor of how his father used to clean him up whenever he hurt himself. Connor wished for his father. If anyone knew what to do, it would be him.

The teacher said nothing during the whole process, but when he finished, he asked, "So, what happened?"

"I told you," Connor said. "You won't believe me."

Mr. Paxter let go of Connor and stood. He nodded and shook his head as if talking to himself about something. His lips even moved, though he didn't say anything.

Finally, he looked Connor square in the eyes and said, "What you're doing is dangerous."

Connor felt his jaw drop. Did Mr. Paxter know? Sergeant Dandrich had said nearly the exact same thing.

"What do you mean?" Connor said.

"Where you've been is no place for kids."

"And where have I been?" Connor said.

"The Shadowlands. I knew something was wrong with your shadow, I knew it." Part of Connor couldn't believe how lucky it was that an adult, his teacher, knew about the Shadowlands. The other part couldn't conjure a positive reason Mr. Paxter would know.

As if reading Connor's thoughts, Mr. Paxter asked, "How do I know about the Shadowlands? I've known since I was little. Before I was born, I had a twin brother I absorbed in the womb. His body became part of mine, so he never cast his shadow."

"But that doesn't mean he didn't have one," Connor said.

A somber smile turned Mr. Paxter's lips.

"Indeed. You can imagine how terrified I was when his shadow first came to me in the middle of the night when I was five. I thought he was a ghost or a monster. In a way, as I found later, I was somewhat right on both accounts. I tried to tell my parents the things he told me about the Shadowlands, but they didn't believe me. They convinced me he was an imaginary friend and the things he told me were fantastic ideas I'd dreamt up."

Mr. Paxter paused and scratched under his chin.

"As I got older, my 'imaginary friend' didn't go away, and I began to think I was crazy. I spent my teenage years getting more and more lost, especially since my twin's stories, the things he told me about the Shadowlands, got uglier and uglier. At first, he'd told me about colorful umbrellas and awnings, about shadow parades and Nightglass towers and whole deserts of rust. Then, he told me about stalking monsters and executions and murders. I was only about sixteen, but I thought: how could my mind invent such horrors? Even worse, he seemed to enjoy them."

"When I was in college, I tried to explain it to a woman I was in love with, but she also thought I was crazy. Drifted away from me. She gave other reasons, but I knew the truth. When she left, I was devastated. To be perfectly honest, I planned to kill myself. I say this because it's what I remembered when I found you and the noose.

"One night, I sat at the top of my stairs as depressed as a person can be. Gradually, the world around me seemed to melt away, and I found myself in the Shadowlands sitting on a mound of melted metal beside a great river. I searched for my brother for three days but never found him. But the shadows there confirmed everything I'd been told was true and more. I tried to convince myself it was all a hallucination, but something inside me knew what I'd experienced was real. I wasn't crazy, and even if I couldn't tell anyone about it, knowing the truth was enough. I haven't heard from my brother since."

When Mr. Paxter fell silent, Connor knew there was a question he had to ask.

"Is there any way you can help him?"

Mr. Paxter nodded.

"I can allow him to become my shadow."

"Why don't you?" Connor asked.

"His darkness would become a part of me. The things he described were sometimes so horrible. It was bad enough when I thought I was conjuring them. I don't want to imagine thinking those things." The teacher paused a moment and then added, "It may not seem this way, but I suspect you're lucky you found your way to the Shadowlands.

With your shadow stolen, you might have fallen into apathy and despair without knowing why."

"I don't feel very lucky," Connor said, sharper than he intended. However, he also remembered Mouse hadn't met the Shadow Police at all the way he had. Why was Dandrich helping him and not her?

"Do you know anything about the Shadow Police?" Connor asked. "They came to me right after my shadow was stolen, but I don't think they come to everyone."

"I can't really say," Mr. Paxter said. "But I imagine they're no different from real police. Only so many of them to go around, always more crimes than officers. If they came, you're either lucky, or they had some reason to pay attention to you."

Connor realized there was something more important to ask.

"When you went to the Shadowlands you still had your shadow, right?"

"Yes."

"How did you get back?"

Mr. Paxter frowned. "That's a story I'm not going to tell you."

Something about his frown gave Connor chills.

The teacher brushed his hands off on his pants. "We've been here long enough," Mr. Paxter said. "Past time I take you home. Your mother must be worried to death."

Connor opened his mouth to protest, but a profound tiredness flooded his bones. Maybe Dandrich was right; he needed rest. If he was too weak when he returned to the Shadowlands, he might die and return too soon, or he might not have the strength to do what was needed. Whatever that was.

Mr. Paxter patted Connor on the back and ushered him from the nurse's office, through the hall to the front doors of the school, and into the parking lot.

A VISITOR THAT ONE NIGHT

The drive home in Mr. Paxter's emerald-green sedan was quiet. Connor's thoughts scattered like a flock of birds whenever he tried to grab hold of them. He gazed out the window as familiar houses and gas stations passed. He'd seen them countless times as his mother drove him to and from school, and now, exhausted as he was, they seemed little more than shadows in darkness. They looked unreal, like something trying hard to be real.

As the car turned onto his street, however, he didn't feel ready to see his mom, especially with the marks on his neck and wrists. His wounds would confirm her worst fears; he hadn't run away and hid out at a friend's house. He hadn't hunkered down in a safe place in childish rebellion. He'd been journeying through a strange town full of nasty people, a forest full of wild animals, and a quarry... everyone he met betrayed him, or he'd been forced to betray them. He didn't ever want his mom to meet the Foreman or the Thief.

Connor asked Mr. Paxter to stop a couple of houses away from his house.

"What do I tell her?" he asked. "My mom, I mean."

"The truth," Mr. Paxter said. "The truth has power in the World of Light the same way lies have power in the Shadowlands."

"But I need to go back," Connor said. "She'll never let me."

Mr. Paxter nodded. "The truth is the only thing that might convince her," he said. "And it would be wrong to tell her anything different after what she's been through."

"Can you come with me?" Connor asked.

"I'll walk you to the door," Mr. Paxter said, "but it isn't my place to interfere."

"No," Connor said. "Can you come with me to the Shadowlands?"

Mr. Paxter shook his head. "I got there by accident the first time," he said. "I can't and won't replicate those circumstances."

Connor understood, but he didn't like it.

Mr. Paxter exited the car, and the click of his door shutting caused the bottom to drop out of Connor's stomach. Until that moment, facing his mother seemed like it might get postponed.

Mr. Paxter walked Connor to the door and rang the bell. Connor's heart rate accelerated. Maybe she wasn't home. Maybe she was at the police station or out looking for him. The garage was closed, so he didn't know if the car was there.

Rapid footsteps echoed within the house just before the deadbolt was thrown. The doorknob twisted so quickly that Connor barely had time to breathe before the light from inside poured onto him, blocked only by his mother's silhouette.

She cried out and dropped to both knees in front of him, drawing him tight. "My boy," she sobbed. "My sweet boy."

Connor burst into massive heaving sobs, too. He returned the embrace. The wetness of her tears smeared his cheeks, yet he felt none of her warmth. He might as well have been embracing a fire hydrant. Connor sobbed even harder. What he wouldn't give to feel his mother's arms. Everything in the Shadowlands was worth the hope of holding his mother properly.

Connor couldn't say how many minutes passed before their sobs subsided. His mother's cheek shifted against him as she regarded Mr. Paxter.

"I know you," she said, letting go of Connor and standing.

Mr. Paxter shook her hand. "I'm Mr. Paxter," he said. "Connor's history teacher. I met you and your husband a couple of years ago at a parent-teacher open house."

"Of course," Connor's mother said, letting go of Mr. Paxter's hand to wipe the tears from her eyes. "Where was he? How did you find him?"

"At the school," Mr. Paxter said. "I was heading home when I heard him in the janitor's closet."

Connor's mother looked at her son, and she gasped as she registered his bandages. "Oh my god," she said. "What happened?" She shuffled Connor behind her and glared at Mr. Paxter. "What did you do?" she said.

Mr. Paxter held his hands up. "Nothing, I assure you, other than clean his injuries and put on the bandages," he said. "He was like that when I found him."

"It's true, Mom," Connor said. "I'll explain everything."

Connor's mother eyed Mr. Paxter. Connor felt bad for the teacher, who had done nothing but help him. He shouldn't be treated like he'd done something wrong. Connor knew this feeling all too well from standing before The Judge.

"I swear," Connor said. "Mr. Paxter's been as nice as can be."

Connor's mother looked down at him again and said, "Go inside and sit at the kitchen table. Don't move a muscle until I get there. I'm going to talk to Mr. Paxter, and then you're going to do some explaining as I call the police and tell them I've found you."

Connor nodded and slipped straight to the kitchen. It wasn't long before he heard the door close and his mother strode in. She crossed to the cabinets and grabbed a glass, then made her way to the fridge where she poured orange juice. Then, she brought the glass to the table, slid it in front of Connor, and planted herself in the chair beside him.

"Where on earth have you been? Do you know how worried—?" She broke off and took a deep breath. She clasped her hands on the table and said softly, "What happened?"

Connor stared at the wobbling surface of the juice. Then, he began,

"It started with the nightmare I had the other day…"

Connor told his story: waking up with the Thief in his room, the Shadow Police, the Pale Boy, the closet, the two bullies in the Iron Desert, the shadowcats, Journeyman, Gissu, Mouse, Quiet, Tonic, The Judge, Mosley, the Shopkeeper, Blackwood, and the Daggers. He did his best not to leave anything out, even recounting as best he could the story of Basket and the Flower Petal. His story stretched on as night deepened around them. His mother listened in near silence, occasionally grunting or muttering "hm." Connor couldn't remember ever speaking so long in his life as he poured the story out. When he reached being hung both in the Shadowlands and the janitor's closet, and Mr. Paxter finding him, he fell quiet.

His mother regarded him for a long time. Then, she looked away, staring at something in the kitchen near the stove. Finally, she turned back to Connor and said, "Well."

The word hung in the air before vanishing like steam off a pot.

"Well," she said again.

Connor fidgeted in his seat. He slid the glass of orange juice a little across the table. Then, careful not to sound rude, sarcastic, or impatient, he asked, "Well, what?"

Connor's mother furrowed her brow and said, "Quite a story. As unbelievable as stories come." She paused and tapped her fingers on the table. "But you believe it. Your teacher said I should believe you. But I must say, I find his involvement rather suspicious. I'm going to mention it to the police."

"Mr. Paxter's been awesome," Connor said.

His mother met Connor's eyes with the type of earnestness that compels one to listen. "Please understand that adults might seem one way and turn out and be completely different to what you expected."

"Like Journeyman?" Connor asked.

Connor's mother faltered for a moment, as if hesitant to compare the real world to the story Connor had told, but she said, "Yes, like Journeyman. But Connor, someone tried to hang you—in the real world. Someone real did it."

"The Thief…" Connor said.

"I know what you said," his mother said, "But what if Mr. Paxter did this to you and you didn't know it? It's an awfully big coincidence he happened to be there."

"Then why would he be so nice?" Connor said. "Why wouldn't he try to kill me again?"

His mother thought about this. Connor felt glad she was actually discussing the situation.

"It's not easy to take a life," his mother said. "Especially a boy's. Maybe he couldn't bring himself to try again. He could be headed back to the school to clean up the evidence. I should call the police right now. Maybe they can catch him."

Connor's mother rose and turned to the phone, but Connor grabbed her wrist. He couldn't say for certain why he trusted Mr. Paxter, but he did.

"Mom, please," Connor said. "Don't make trouble for Mr. Paxter."

She threw her free hand up, and tears burst into her eyes.

"What am I supposed to do?" she exclaimed. "I have to do something!"

"There's more," Connor said. He gulped. He hadn't told her the most important part. "I have to go back."

"Back where?" his mom snapped.

"The Shadowlands," Connor said. "Otherwise, I lose my shadow."

"I don't care!" she shouted. "You will not go back there even if there is such a place. You're not going anywhere ever again! I can't—"

Connor's mind raced as he searched for what to say. Could he go back there after seeing how upset his mother was?

"Mom," Connor said. "I have to. You remember the Pale Boy, the one with the Bible salesman?

"How could I forget?" his mother asked. "I know they were involved in you running away in the first place."

Connor wanted to insist he hadn't run away, but he also knew it would move the conversation away from the point.

"Did you speak with the Pale Boy at all?"

"Elias," his mother said. "His name was Elias. His father called him Eli."

"Okay, Eli," Connor said. "Didn't Eli seem strange to you? Somehow wrong?"

His mother sighed again. Then, she told Connor about what happened after he'd gone to the Shadowlands for the first time.

Apparently, she'd spoken with the salesman for some time before deciding to send him on his way. Then, she'd discovered Eli alone in Connor's room with Connor gone. She'd wanted to call the police immediately, but the salesman explained there was indeed something wrong with his son. He'd said his son had always struggled very badly socially, but that his son had concocted a story about his shadow being stolen. A coping mechanism, the father had said. It was easier for Eli to accept his struggles if he blamed it on something else.

"I don't know why," his mother said. "Something about what he said struck me as reasonable. I didn't believe him, but I found myself accepting it anyway. It was so obvious they were involved with your disappearance, but—"

Connor took his mother's hand as her eyes welled with tears. The turmoil on her face was unbearable.

"The Shadowlands protects itself," Connor said. "I don't know how it works, but it makes people not want to believe it exists."

"I let him and his son walk right out of here," she said.

"I don't think it's your fault," Connor said. "I think you would have believed anything he told you. Why do you think you didn't call the police the entire time I was gone?"

"I don't know," she said. "I was afraid it would make it real. I was embarrassed I'd lost you. I didn't think I could handle the stress."

Connor squeezed his mother's fingers. "Are those really reasons you'd let your son stay missing?"

His mother gently withdrew her hands from his and brushed the tears from his cheek. "When did you grow up so fast?" she whispered. "It feels like I've missed so much of you growing up. I'm so sorry, Connor. I promise things will change.

"You didn't miss anything," Connor said. "I grew up a lot these last couple of days."

His mother drew him into a hug and whispered, "Either way, things are still going to change."

Then, his mother pulled away and walked to the phone.

"But Mom—" Connor said.

"I have to tell the police you've been found. They shouldn't be looking for you anymore, regardless of where you've been. They'll need to ask you questions."

"Do you believe me?" Connor asked.

His mother hesitated. "We'll talk later," she said. "First, we need to talk to the police."

"And Mr. Paxter?" Connor said.

"I'll tell them he found you at the school and brought you home. You'd been hiding in the woods behind the school. I must tell them something. If he hasn't done anything wrong, there shouldn't be much trouble."

Connor understood. Like so many things now, he didn't like it, but he understood. No matter what, there were more pressing problems. He glanced at the clock—past 10. The meeting at the Shadowrun was just fourteen hours away. He had to convince his mother to let him return, and this time, he needed to be better prepared.

Before the police arrived, Connor and his mother discussed how to handle them. She decided it would be best if Connor were in bed with a single lamp on when they arrived. With less light in the room and a blanket over his torso, they might not notice Connor's injuries and be hesitant to disturb him. Connor would wear a long-sleeved turtleneck to hide his wrist and neck as best they could. As much as it pained her to say so, his mother thought it best to go with his initial story of running away as their explanation. It was simple and believable, though Connor felt weird having his mother lie to the police. It seemed like something that should only happen in the Shadowlands.

It went more smoothly than they could have hoped.

Connor hardly had to say a word. Two officers arrived, and though he overheard them asking his mother a few questions at the outset, he also heard frequent interruptions from their radios. Apparently, something else important happened to distract the officers, and even when they asked questions, they only seemed to listen to part of the answer before jumping to their next question. Connor suspected this somehow had to be the influence of the Shadowlands at work.

Perhaps the biggest surprise was that only one officer even entered Connor's room, at which point Connor stirred, feigning grogginess, and sat half up. He gave a half-hearted, "Hello, officers," at which point the radio squelched about some sort of pursuit. The officer returned to his partner, and a couple minutes later, Connor heard the front door open and his mother promise to bring him to the station to file a full report.

When they left, his mother told him to get ready for bed. He took a long bath. As hot as the water was, it barely felt warm to him. Nonetheless, the warmth cheered him up a little. He considered playing with his toys in the tub. He hadn't played in the bath for some time, having favored showers for the last couple of years, but he'd feel too guilty sloshing his boats and action figures while Quiet and Mouse were in the hands of the Foreman. Would they ever find anything to smile and laugh about? Connor understood now why his mother couldn't immerse herself in board games and video games.

Connor tired of the tub, his skin wrinkled and pruney. He drained the water and dried himself before pulling on the pajamas he'd brought into the bathroom. As he brushed his teeth, however, he worried about going to bed. If he fell asleep, wouldn't he be vulnerable? Twice now, the Neverborn had come after him in the World of Light. Dandrich said it was unforgivable, so the Thief might be wary to do so a third time.

Another thought occurred to Connor: if the Shadow Police wanted Connor for escaping, why didn't they come arrest him? Were they too unwilling to forcibly take him out of the World of Light?

Connor grabbed the box of gauze and the white medical tape and returned to his room, where his mother waited by his bedside. She'd brought in a chair, put a throw pillow on it, and now sat with a book in hand. It wasn't one of the novels Connor was used to seeing her read, and it certainly wasn't one of the bedtime stories she used to read to help him sleep. This was a plain black book with a red ribbon hanging from it as a bookmark.

Connor slipped under the covers and sat up in bed. His mother smiled. He tried to memorize that smile as long as it lasted on her face. When he returned to the Shadowlands, he probably wouldn't see a smile so warm and kind again. After staring at him for a few seconds, she re-wrapped his injuries, sat back, and patted the book she held.

"I want you to know, I believe you," she said. "As crazy as it is, I believe you."

Ironically, Connor could hardly believe her. What had changed? What did it mean? He didn't assume she was okay with him heading back into danger, but it was a start. His mother continued. "I need you to know why. Until tonight, I wasn't sure if I should tell you this. I wasn't even sure part of it had happened until I heard your story and took out this journal."

Her eyes moistened with fresh tears.

"I wrote in this every night after your father died. It kept my thoughts straight. I was so confused, and it was so hard to take care of you alone."

"I know," Connor said. "I'm sorry."

"It's okay," his mother said. "It's not your fault. It's your father's fault."

Connor's spine stiffened. He said, "He died in a car accident. He lost control of the car and swerved into the other lane."

The tears rolled down his mother's cheek.

"He did... but he was driving drunk. He'd had a bad day at work. He thought he was going to get fired. It scared him to tell me, so he went to a bar and drank to delay coming home."

Connor frowned. This didn't fit his image of his father. His father was good, not the type who drove drunk. Only careless people drove drunk. His father had said so himself.

After sniffling to hold back her tears and wiping her cheeks, his mother continued. "There's more. The other car. A mother was driving, and a little boy, two years old, was in the back seat. There was something wrong with his car seat, and he died."

Connor's head spun as his entire understanding of his father shattered, replaced with something ugly and horrible. It was bad enough he faced horrors in the Shadowlands. How could such things exist in his home? In his father?

"No," Connor shouted, throwing the covers off and jumping to his feet. "It's not true."

"It is true," his mother insisted. "I had planned to tell you when you were older."

"Then why tell me now?" Connor demanded. "Why tell me at all?"

"You deserve the truth," his mother said. "Especially after all the lies you told me you heard in the Shadowlands. I know it had to be hard for you to tell me the truth about where you've been, just as it's hard for me to tell you the truth about your father. He was a good man, but he made a terrible, terrible mistake."

His mother paused and cleared her throat.

"There's more," she said.

Connor fumed. How dare she tell him such awful things and then add more? He'd almost felt happy entering his bedroom, and if he failed in his quest, it might well be the last time he ever felt that way. She should have let that last.

"Sit back down," his mother said.

Connor did, though his body trembled with agitation.

"It's why I got out this journal," his mother said. "I had to make sure I hadn't invented the memory."

Connor cocked his head. Her uncertainty intrigued him.

"What memory?"

His mother sighed. Connor thought he'd heard his mother sigh enough for a lifetime.

"A week after he died," his mother said. "The day after the funeral. I couldn't sleep. I was tossing and turning and crying. I didn't know how I would go on." She stopped again. Clearly, she didn't know how to go on.

"What happened?"

"I thought… maybe it was a dream, maybe I'd fallen asleep. But he came to me. Sprouted right out from the darkness behind a chair. He was all black. I could hardly make him out at all, but I knew it was him. That's why I thought it must be a dream. It felt like a dream, where it seemed real, but you know it's not. Well, this time it felt unreal, but I somehow knew it was."

She furrowed her brow. She didn't think she made sense, yet Connor knew what she meant.

"He told me he was lost, kept saying over and over that he was lost, that he loved you and me, that he was sorry, and that he was lost. I have pages and pages of it in the journal. I wrote as much as I could remember as soon as he was gone, and he was gone so suddenly."

Connor felt hot tears under his eyes. His mother had never let him see her so distraught.

"But I had to have imagined it. There was no other explanation," she said. "At least I thought. But when you told me about the Shadow Police sprouting out of the shadows in your room, the memory returned."

His mother took Connor by both hands. "I believe you. I don't know how or why this is happening, but I think you were in the place where your father came from."

She paused, then said, "Don't go back."

"I have to," Connor said.

"I know," his mother said.

She looked away, then began singing. Normally, Connor would have protested. He was way too old to be sung to, but after everything he'd been through in the Shadowlands, there was something appealing about pretending he was a little kid for a minute. It looked like his mom felt the same, because fresh tears ran from her eyes as the melody flowed:

Hush little boy, now don't you fret,
Mommy isn't finished watching over you, yet.
As you slumber, as you snore,
Mommy's sitting outside your bedroom door.
Sleep my baby, don't lose a wink,
Mommy's always a little closer than you think.
In your nightmares and in your dreams,
Mommy's always closer than she seems.
There's going to come a day when you're far away,
Mommy won't be able to watch you play.
And even though she won't be near,
Mommy's going to be in your heart my dear.

NUMBERS ON A CLOCK

Connor's mother sang until he drifted off. As he slipped into a slumber, he couldn't help feeling relieved to be falling asleep. His mind needed a break. There was too much to process. Thought by thought, he slipped into a soft blackness.

Of course, everyone knows the passage of time changes in sleep, but to the sleeping boy, it seemed he'd hardly fallen into slumber when he dreamed of Mouse. At first, he dreamt of her home and parents. Though he had no idea what Mouse's parents looked like, he saw a smiling warm couple with dirty blond hair like their daughter. He dreamed they were hiking in the mountains, smiling and laughing all the way, her father picking her up and helping her over the rocks until they stopped at a trickling brook to watch a deer drink, the water cool and refreshing on its lips, soothing its parched throat.

And then, he was the deer; the thirst he'd felt in the Shadowlands returning tenfold. He slurped greedily at the water. Despite being nearly tasteless, it was the most amazing thing he'd ever tasted, and he could feel his sides expanding and contracting in desperate breaths as he fought to breathe around mouthfuls of water. No matter how much he gulped down, it wasn't enough to slake the drought he felt within. A heat spread through his entire body, burning him up like a fever. He clattered his hooves on the shoreline rocks and plunged his head into the chilly flow to cool himself.

When he raised his head from the current, he looked up at Mouse and her family and the forest. Only, they weren't in the forest anymore. They were in the Daggers, where the searing heat caused the water to sizzle into steam in the soft hair of his face. He lurched forward to plunge his head into the water again, stopping short as he realized the flow was no longer water, but lava. His fur burst into flames around his ears, and fire streaked his vision. Through them, he saw Mouse burst into tears, her face soot black with grime, as the taskmasters whipped her back.

"Work or watch us flay the skin right off that animal," Ragger shouted, as he brought his whip down upon her. Mouse cried out in pain. Her shirt tore down her spine, and the skin between her shoulder blades broke open as her parents watched, helpless.

He opened his mouth to scream but only managed to make a lonely mewling sound. The flames engulfed his body, leaving his hair blackened, as brittle cinders trailed off into dark smoke. He tried to leap forward, to interpose himself between Mouse and the next blow of the whip, but he was chained to the rocks. A tight clasp around his neck kept his head down. He was no longer a deer, but himself on all fours; the falling ash was accumulating around him. It passed his elbows and reached his hips. Something hot within still glowed red; a glow reflecting devilishly in the eyes of the taskmasters. Their grins spread wide, rust dripping from their fangs to their withered lips. He was desperate to wake, watching blow after blow fall until the ash deepened over his eyes and covered his head. After that, the only thing he saw was a red glow.

Then he realized the red glow was light beaming against his closed eyelids.

Connor opened his eyes. It was daylight. Sweat drenched him. The chair beside his bed sat empty; the journal upon it was closed, the bookmark hanging out, no page marked.

He sat up. Something felt strange. Of course, everything felt strange since the shadow thief first appeared, but this was different. His mind was still in a sleep haze, and the tension from his dream still lingered in all his muscles, but the light felt wrong.

"Mom?" he said.

There was no answer. He was surprised she hadn't been there when he woke, but she was the adult in the house and probably had things to take care of.

Connor rose out of bed and got dressed. As he brushed his teeth, he examined his neck in the medicine box mirror. The wounds were mostly scabbed. He ran his finger down one of them, tracing the pebbled surface. Had the worst already happened?

Wiping a bit of toothpaste from his cheek with his sleeve, he padded down the hall towards the kitchen. The house was so bright he had to squint, probably due to both his time in the Shadowlands and sleepy-headedness. He needed to wake up and mentally prepare.

He walked into the kitchen and immediately froze, and his blood ran cold. His mother had obviously heard him get up, because she was frying eggs over the stove. She had set the table, and a glass of orange juice awaited him. Neither the breakfast nor his mother jarred Connor, though. It was the clock on the microwave over the stove.

It read 12:30.

He was supposed to meet Dandrich at noon, and he'd neither set an alarm nor told his mother to wake him. Part of him wanted to tell his mother what was happening, but he couldn't spare a moment, and he'd lose more than a moment if he had to discuss things with her. He turned and ran toward his room, pausing only to grab his sneakers beside the door and his jacket from the coat hook.

When he passed through his door, he froze. His gaze jumped from his shelves to his closet to his chest of drawers, his desk, then his shelves again. The memory of Shade Row came to mind, specifically the tables hawking broken bits of toys. He had little time to think it over, so he darted to his dresser. From the bottom drawer—full of assorted toys— he pulled out a Ziploc bag full of green, plastic army men. He grabbed a handful of the army men and thrust them into his pocket. He snagged a couple of bouncy balls, a pack of playing cards, and a digital watch with a T-Rex printed on the face.

He pulled on his jacket, slipped on his sneakers, and reached for the closet doorknob. As he did so, his eyes caught the teddy bear on his shelf, still out of place where Officer Bell had left it. He grabbed it, then threw himself into the closet. The bulb was still unscrewed, so all he had to do was shut the door and pull the chain.

When he opened the door, he was in Blackwood by the Shadowrun.

The coal-red sun was directly overhead. Its light caught falling ash, making the flakes glow a slight red like sparks drifting up from a campfire. It was the brightest he'd ever seen the forest, which wasn't saying much. Unfortunately, he saw no one on the riverbank in either direction. There was no sign of Dandrich. He would have no help. How could he have overslept so badly? What was he going to do?

Clutching the teddy bear to his chest, Connor paced in a panicked circle. The trees loomed over his head like angry giants waving fists of branches about in the wind. The river roared like a lion with endless breath. The ash cascading down from the sky seemed like an impenetrable blanket threatening to smother him. The boy turned around. Perhaps it was the stuffed animal in his fingers, but he'd never felt like such a helpless child.

Connor stuffed the little teddy bear into his jacket pocket and took another deep breath, slow and through his nose. Even if Dandrich had been there, the chase of the Thief might end up with a boy facing the Thief alone, anyway. No matter who came to help, he could not rely on them to solve his problem for him. He had to be prepared to do it himself. If he could accept that, any help he did get would make what he did easier. No matter what, he didn't have the time to wait for someone who might not come again.

Connor adjusted his belt, made sure everything was secure in his pockets, and turned in the direction of the Daggers.

As he took his first step from the shore, he stumbled over something, nearly careening face-first onto the bank. When he recovered his balance, he sought what tripped him up and found a small backpack with a note pinned to it. The note read:

Little Bit —

I can't wait any longer. They know I'm helping you, and they're not happy about it. I knew this was the spot because Casters leave a trace when they come and go from the Shadowlands. Others might soon find this place, if they haven't already. In the bag, you'll find supplies. Guard them well. They are precious here. The stunlight only has three charges, so use it only in great need.

Connor opened the bag, disappointed as he went through its contents. There was an orange, two slices of bread, a cookie, a bottle of water, a bundle of black cloth, and a flashlight. That was all he was going to get? He kicked at the ground by the river's edge.

Then, he took a deep breath and a second look at what he had. Food and water. Not shadow food nor blackwater. Real food. This was the first time he'd seen real food in the Shadowlands. The bright skin of the orange almost glowed, and Connor considered that real food must not be easy or cheap to come by here. Moreover, it would keep his strength up, especially if he saved it for when he needed it. The Thief would expect him to be famished and exhausted if and when they met. It could be an advantage, and he needed any advantage he could get.

The black cloth... well, Connor wasn't sure what to do with it. The fabric was little more than a thin blanket with a mottled color containing dark blues, purples, and browns shifting with the light. It seemed like simple cloth, though he figured it might come in handy if he had to sleep somewhere.

On the other hand, the weight of the flashlight told Connor it was more than a flashlight. Was it the weapon Dandrich referred to in the note? It was shaped like a flashlight and had a bulb on one end. The switch, however, was protected by a plastic casing that had to be flipped up before the thing could be turned on. It made sense for a shadow weapon to look like a light. What better way to fight shadows? He wanted to test it out, but if he only had three charges, doing so would be a terrible waste.

Connor arranged the weapon, cloth, and food back into the pack, stuffed the teddy bear on top, and then slipped the bag over his shoulder. The bag wasn't heavy, but its weight still brought a sense of security. Perhaps most important of all, the presence of the bag and its contents told him that some adult shadows meant what they said.

Connor set off through the trees, watching for shadowcat nests and anything else potentially dangerous like the fly-trap grove. If he didn't get back to the Daggers to begin with, nothing else would matter. Still, it troubled him, and he didn't know if he'd be able to do anything at all for Quiet and Mouse; the entire trip could be a waste.

No, Connor thought. Not a waste. Even if I can't help, I owe it to Mouse and Quiet to get to them and try. He only hoped he wouldn't have to watch them be whipped.

As Connor drew near the edge of the Daggers, he slowed and began moving from tree to tree. The glow brightened between the trees, and soon he could see the base of the outer pillars. It did not surprise him he didn't see any guards. No one would expect him to come back. They likely doubted he could do any actual harm even if he did. And they would probably be right.

When he was about thirty yards from Blackwood's edge, he stopped dead in his tracks. For a moment, he didn't know why. His feet refused to move an inch further.

Then, his mind registered the unmistakable sound of a low growl behind him. A shadowcat.

Turning, Connor unslung his bag and pulled out the stunlight. He didn't want to use it so soon, but he heard another growl rumble off to his right. These two shadowcats were most likely the cub's parents. He hadn't forgotten Journeyman's story. It would be too much of a coincidence to stumble on more Shadowcats so quickly after returning since they were so territorial. They must have finally made it across the river and been watching the place where he'd awoken, waiting for a fresh scent.

Connor glanced back at the Daggers. If he could beat them there, would they follow? Not only were there taskmasters wielding whips, but most likely the bright glow of the lava robbed them of their natural advantage. Unfortunately, he suspected they were far too close for him to beat in an outright run.

Nervous pins prickling up his spine, Connor spotted the first black shape slinking between two petrified trees. Was the other still off to his right? Or had it worked its way behind him?

Connor pointed his weapon at the approaching cat and flipped the plastic casing off the switch. The cat froze, one of its paws raised in mid-step. The cat's tail, which had extended straight back, suddenly relaxed and wavered back and forth. Connor's father had told him once that when cats waved their tails, they were uncertain.

The shadowcat recognized the weapon.

The cat sat on its hind quarters, raised one of its paws to its mouth, and began to wash its face. Connor had no idea what to think. As dangerous as the shadowcat was, he saw it as a big, cute cat at the moment. He half expected it to roll onto its back and expose its belly. A new rumble emitted from the creature. It seemed to be purring.

Then, Connor's blood went cold. He spun and barely registered the other shadowcat charging towards him before he pressed the weapon's switch. The light it emitted was dazzling. Connor had never experienced anything so bright. His eyes seared with pain. His vision flashed into a green mess. He spun again and pointed the weapon to where he thought the other cat had been, back-stepping fast until he tripped over a tree root. As he crashed onto his butt, he kept the weapon extended, his finger on the switch.

His vision gradually returned as he waited in breathless anticipation for an attack.

Finally, he made out the shadowcats. The one he'd flashed lay motionless on its side. The other had moved next to it, wobbling as it tilted its head down and licked the cheek of the downed beast, mewling softly. Had he killed the still cat?

The other shadowcat crouched and growled at Connor, causing him to take several slow steps towards the Daggers. Then, it turned back to its mate and continued licking its face and neck. Its mate twitched its legs. At least he knew the weapon worked, and it didn't kill. He continued his careful shuffle towards the quarry, not taking his eyes off the animals until they were indistinguishable from the surrounding shadows.

When he reached the edge of the trees and the ominous, fiery glow surrounding the obsidian teeth, a mixture of relief and dread swirled through his core; relief at leaving the Blackwood and the shadowcats, dread at entering the quarry where the Foreman and his taskmasters waited. He also worried the shadowcats might follow him into the Daggers, and he couldn't think of anything worse than being caught between the taskmasters and a pair of vengeful shadowcats.

He made his way into the stone maze until he spotted the lava stream. He listened for the echoes of picks and hammers. His ears were more accustomed to the quarry acoustics, and it was easier to head towards a sound than to avoid it.

As he moved towards the mine track, he half-expected Tonic to come up behind him like before. His hope dimmed the further he went. He didn't like going alone, but at least this time, he didn't need to get to the complex. He preferred to avoid another meeting with the Foreman, even with the weapon. Would it be effective against something so monstrous? Tonic had said the Foreman and the taskmasters were something older than shadows.

He shoved those thoughts aside as he came upon the first group of workers spread in a line. Each worker chipped at an obsidian column while a taskmaster paced up and down with a whip in hand. Connor didn't see Ragger. He felt in his gut that Ragger would oversee Quiet and Mouse's line.

The workers tended to their work with grim and sad faces. Even though they were shadows, Connor could see the accumulated grime caking their skin. Several of them had nasty gashes on their cheeks and foreheads, most likely from the whips. Connor wept merely looking at them.

A couple of hours and three more work lines later, he peeked his head from a sheltered spot between a cluster of columns. Quiet raised a pick as big as her over her head. For several minutes, Connor watched her grind and hack away at the obsidian. Bits and chunks flew past her face and peppered her, while Ragger stood easily within sight. Could he approach her without exposing himself? A thought occurred to him.

He unslung his bag and pulled out the piece of cloth, which he held against the obsidian. Because of its mottled hues, the fabric practically disappeared against the stone. Connor wrapped the cloth over his body and dropped onto his belly. He wouldn't be invisible, but he would be hard to see by someone who wasn't looking for him. If he worked his way to the other side of the column where Quiet was working and they were careful, they might be able to speak.

He wiggled his way over the jagged ground. Three times he stopped and pulled the cloth over his head as Ragger passed among the columns. Each time, he held his breath until he risked a peek. He pulled himself up behind Quiet's dagger and wrapped himself in the obsidian cloth.

"Quiet," he whispered.

A loud clatter followed a startled squeak from the other side of the pillar.

"Hey," Ragger snarled. Connor feared he'd been discovered until the voice snapped, "Hoist that pick. Get back to work!"

A whip cracked, and Quiet cried out. Connor winced. A second crack snapped, and Quiet burst into tears even as the chink from her pick rang out.

Connor waited several moments. Should he speak again and risk causing Quiet more pain? He had no choice.

"Quiet," he whispered. "It's me, Connor."

Quiet's pick struck stone again. She didn't answer. His choice had put her there, and his whisper caused her to drop the pick. How could he make it better? He needed to say something else, but what? He had no idea how to free or help her.

Instead, he said, "Where's Mouse?"

"Dead," Quiet said. "Dead and gone."

Connor's heart twinged with pain. Of course, Quiet didn't mean Mouse was "dead" dead, but rather she'd returned to the World of Light. At least he hoped that was what she meant. It also meant she was most likely Shadowless.

"What happened?" Connor asked.

"What do you think?" Quiet said, too loud for Connor's liking. The anger in her voice was clear. "She was weak. From hunger. From thirst. From the pain you put her through."

Grief made Connor want to give up and return home, but he couldn't. He had to push on. If he succeeded, even if he couldn't help Mouse, at least there would be value to his choice.

"I want to help," Connor said.

"You can't," Quiet said. "I betrayed the deal. I must carry out my sentence."

Connor didn't want to know, but he couldn't help but ask. "How long?"

"Ten years," Quiet snapped. "I'll never find my mommy now."

The whip snapped again, and Connor pulled the cloth over his face.

"Who you talking to?" Ragger bellowed.

Connor's heart thudded. He felt Ragger's looming presence behind Quiet. All she had to do was point him out. To Connor's relief, she said, "Myself, sir."

"Keep it quiet," the taskmaster shouted, giving her another lash. White hot anger swelled in Connor's chest. Part of him wanted to blast Ragger with the flashlight to make him pay for striking Quiet. However, it would do little good, especially since there could be more taskmasters nearby.

After a couple of minutes, Connor said, "What can I do to make this right?"

"Nothing," Quiet said. "Nothing will make it right. But I'll help you."

"Why?" Connor asked.

"Because you can still help Mouse," Quiet said. "If you can get to the Thief before he takes her shadow to the Shadower."

"Why do you care so much about Mouse?" Connor asked.

Quiet remained silent as she hacked away at the stone. Finally, she said, "Mouse is my grandniece. My mother was her grandmother's sister. I've been watching over Mouse her whole life from under her bed, the corners of her room, the cracked closet door…"

"Your grandniece?"

Quiet paused, and Connor's mind reeled. Though he tried to remind himself that Quiet was a lot older than she looked, this was hard to believe.

"I was there the night her shadow was stolen," Quiet said. "I came to check on her while the Thief was in the act. I'm the one who interrupted him."

"You saved her then."

"No, I failed her," Quiet said. "If I'd come seconds sooner, I could have prevented everything, but I'd been looking for word of my mother. If I hadn't been so selfish…"

Quiet trailed off. Connor didn't know what to say. Surely, Quiet knew the Thief was to blame.

After another moment of silence, Quiet said, "You can get your shadow back and show the thief he can be beaten."

"How?" Connor said.

"He's in Hallowdell," Quiet whispered. "I heard him talking with the Foreman. He's gone to wait for your shadow and complete his deal with the Shadower."

Quiet whispered directions and swore it wasn't far and would be easy to find. Apparently, Hallowdell was where the miners lived, including Quiet now.

"What if I wait until your shift ends?" Connor said. "Maybe I can try to free you."

"You don't have time," she said. "I'll be here for hours. And Tonic will be waiting for me, anyway. He'll help me through."

Connor's ears perked up. Maybe he'd be able to find Tonic and get help.

"But, Connor," Quiet said. "Be careful. I think the Thief meant for me to overhear him."

"Well," Connor said, thinking of the weapon, "If he did, I have a surprise for him."

"There's something else," Quiet said.

"What?" Connor asked.

"There's going to be an eclipse," Quiet said. "He will be at his most powerful."

Connor didn't have to ask what Quiet meant. The Foreman and his terrifying shapeshifting had been limited to his fortress. The eclipse would throw the whole Shadowlands into darkness. The blood drained from his face as he imagined the Thief taking on many hideous forms: giant bats and spiders, creatures swarming with tentacles and teeth.

"I can't win," Connor muttered.

"Don't give up," Quiet said. "Remember: your shadow doesn't want to be stolen."

Rocks clattered behind Connor. He turned and gasped. Raggers loomed, whip in hand.

"Thought I smelled something familiar," the creature growled.

Connor tried to back away but pushed against a pillar. The camouflage shroud fell away. Raggers clenched his fist around the handle of the whip.

"Wouldn't have imagined you foolish enough to come back after the deal you got," Raggers said, his taloned feet gripping the rough obsidian, "But I can't say I've ever had much imagination."

Connor's whole body wanted to freeze in terror, but he had to act.

He had to escape. "Didn't expect you to," he said. "Doesn't take imagination to serve like you do."

He tried to sound confident like Tonic had, remembering how the boy's bravado had earned him respect from the taskmasters, but his voice trembled.

As if reading Connor's mind, Raggers said, "Your friend isn't here to protect you."

"No, but I am," Quiet said, stepping around the pillar. Quiet flung her pickaxe at Ragger, her whole body swinging with the throw.

Ragger's hand shot up and swatted the tool out of the air as Connor dashed between pillars, still clutching the camouflage blanket as it flapped behind him.

He heard the taskmaster snarl at Quiet, "That's gonna cost you once I'm done with this one." Connor stumbled as a whiplash snapped above his head, ripping out a few of his hairs. Connor veered behind the closest pillar and kept running, each step slamming into the shifting stones. Every footfall threatened to twist his ankles, and a fall would mean the end.

Connor wove from pillar to pillar, trying to keep the daggers between himself and the taskmaster as his pursuer clamored behind him.

His mind raced. He had the stunlight, but it only had two charges left. Who knew how fast the taskmaster would recover or for how long he would pursue Connor once he gets back to his feet? The last thing he needed was for this beast to show up as he faced the Thief. No, he had to stop Ragger for good, but it was difficult to think clearly while concentrating on his footing and staying out of reach of the whip. He didn't know where he could escape except Blackwood, and he had no idea which paths would take him there. Meanwhile, every step could be his last. Sweat drenched his whole body, and the world blurred. He would never make it. He'd be cornered. It was only a matter of time.

Ahead, Connor heard the clink of picks and the grate of shovels. As he broke between a pair of fat pillars, he spotted a line of workers pounding away at the obsidian with two taskmasters walking down the row, their attention fixed on the prisoners.

Connor charged straight towards the back of the nearest beast, as Raggers burst with a roar between the two spikes he had crossed. The taskmaster in front of him turned, and its eyes widened as it saw him charging. Connor dove, his head thrusting between the monster's legs as Ragger's whip whistled through the air. The thong lashed around the taskmaster's thigh. Ragger, frenzied as he was, was already jerking back on it. As Connor crashed to the ground, the taskmaster toppled sideways with a furious howl.

Despite flares of pain in his knees and elbows from hitting the rocks, Connor lurched back to his feet and dashed on. The downed taskmaster howled in rage. The beast landed on top of the whip, and Ragger jerked at the cord. Connor kept running, his heart and legs pumping, his limbs aching with every move, his breath tearing in and out of his chest. Behind him, Ragger and the taskmaster barked at each other like wild dogs. This was his chance.

Heat bloomed across Connor's face as he dashed over a ridge. His heart fell into his belly. Ahead, a lava stream far wider than he could jump blocked the path. He raced towards it, the heat intensifying so fast, Connor felt like he was in an oven. When he knew he couldn't get any closer, he flung himself behind a pillar. Raggers hadn't crested the ridge yet, but if Connor didn't do something now, he never would.

Connor took the flashlight weapon in hand, unslung Dandrich's pack, and flung the bag towards the lava. It landed on the rocks about halfway there. As it stopped moving, he heard gravel tumble off the ridge. There was no escape now. His palms grew so slick with sweat, and his fingers trembled so badly; he was certain the smooth weapon would tumble from his grip.

The fear grew as Raggers, almost gleeful with rage, bellowed. "Olly olly oxen free!"

Connor's breath raced in panic. It was too loud. He fought to slow it, breathing in through his nose and out through his mouth. He pulled the camouflage blanket over himself. Raggers would look for it, but Connor hoped he'd spot the bag first.

On the other side of the pillar, more rocks tumbled as Raggers descended the slope.

"Nowhere to run, Little Bit," the beast said. "Come out now, and I'll spare you the whipping." Then, Raggers chuckled a terrible chuckle. "I lie," he said. "Nothing will spare you the whipping."

As if to prove his point, Raggers lashed the whip into the air three times, each time snapping a little closer to where Connor stood. There were a couple more pillars nearby, but there weren't many places he could be hiding. Raggers knew it. If the plan didn't work, it would be seconds before he was caught.

"I tire of this game," Raggers hissed, his voice now very close. Was the taskmaster coming to the pillar or heading for the bag? Connor didn't know, and he didn't dare peek out. "Every moment I look for you is a moment I'm not punishing your little friend. These are moments I'll have to pay for, and if I pay for them, you'll pay for them."

Connor adjusted the blanket enough so he could peer through a sliver of an opening. As he did, Raggers passed the edge of the pillar. Connor held his breath. The taskmaster's gaze locked onto the bag. He hulked forward, each step knocking about the loose rocks covering the ground near the lava stream. Raggers stopped a few feet from the bag and turned, his gaze slithering about.

Connor flung down his cover and stepped from the pillar.

"Ever have your picture taken?" he asked.

Ragger swung his arm back, the whip falling behind him, ready to strike.

Connor thrust the flashlight forward and closed his eyes.

"Say cheese." Connor pushed the button.

Ragger didn't collapse like the shadowcat, but he shrieked as loud as anything Connor had ever heard. He flung his arms over his eyes. Connor's ears rang so loudly it hurt, but he charged forward and threw himself into the taskmaster with all his weight. His shoulder struck the middle of Ragger's chest. The blinded beast staggered backward, its taloned feet backpedaling until its heel caught in a gap between two rocks. The beast toppled. Its head and shoulders crashed onto the lava stream.

Ragger's mouth flung open as if he were about to shriek again, but only a jet of flame burst from his jaws. The flame engulfed the beast's body in a roaring inferno that was taller than Connor.

And then Ragger was gone. There was no more flame, no ash, no smoldering body. It was as if the taskmaster had never existed.

"That shot's a keeper," Connor said to himself, dropping his hands to his knees and letting all his fear out in a series of massive gasps. He burst into tears, staring at the spot where Ragger had burned. He'd won.

However, he couldn't savor the victory. Ragger had stirred up the other taskmasters at the line beyond the ridge. Connor could hear them bellowing.

Connor bent down and snatched the pack. The cloth was almost hot enough to burn his fingers. The sweat steamed off his skin. Without another glance, he retrieved his camouflage blanket and threw it over his shoulders. He limped away from the lava stream as fast as his aching body would allow. He did not stop until the temperature dropped enough for him to break into a fit of violent shivering. He didn't know if he'd destroyed Ragger for good, but he'd beaten the taskmaster. If he could beat the taskmaster, then maybe he could beat the Thief.

The hope was a bitter pill, however. Connor suspected the Thief would be far, far harder to beat.

SOMEWHERE HE DIDN'T WANT TO SEE AGAIN

Escaping the quarry was easy despite how it bustled. An alarm had spread, and the obsidian teeth were alive with searching beasts. However, only Ragger had known about the camouflage blanket, so Connor avoided the main paths and curled up in crooks and crannies at every sound. Outside the quarry, the cool air was a blessing, and he let the wind—free of ash—draw the sweat off his skin. He couldn't remember cold ever feeling so good.

The smoldering sun and the opalescent moon approached convergence. Connor dreaded facing the Thief under the eclipse. After a short trek along the edge of the Daggers, he reached the Hallowdell road. The landscape opened up as the quarry receded behind him. He'd half expected to emerge back into Blackwood, but here it was flat and sprawling. The road itself was much like the Nightglass road, paved with obsidian and lined with lanterns, though the lanterns were less frequent here.

A tall shape, far taller than him, with four legs and an oblong head, caught his eye. It appeared tied to a post, and at its feet, a figure sat cross-legged. Connor tensed and sought a place to hide, but the figure, a shadow, rose.

Connor clasped the flash weapon and took a hesitant step forward. They'd closed the distance halfway towards each other when Connor burst into a run.

"Tonic!"

Tonic thrust out his hand and clasped Connor by the forearm. Connor did the same to the teen. The teen didn't smile, but he gave a firm nod before he released Connor's arm.

"You should get your shadow back," Tonic said.

"I had to see if I could help Quiet," Connor said. "And find out about Mouse."

Tonic smiled. "You really are a friend, then."

Connor returned the smile. "You need friends in a place like this more than anything. I don't think anyone could survive here alone."

"Then maybe you finally understand why I help," Tonic said.

Connor did. "Sorry, I doubted you."

Tonic waved the comment away and asked, "Do you have a plan?"

"No," Connor said. "But Quiet said the Thief is waiting in Hallowdell. I brought stuff to trade, and I have a weapon."

Connor held up the flashlight device. Tonic's eyes widened, and he whistled.

"Only the Shadow Police are allowed to have those. You've got friends in high places."

"Just one," Connor said. "But I don't think she can help me anymore."

"Still, that'll catch the Thief off guard."

"But I still don't know how to get my shadow back," Connor said. "This will only stun him. I think I killed Ragger in the lava, but I doubt there's lava in Hallowdell."

Tonic took a shocked step back, regarding Connor with a raised eyebrow. "Wait," he said. "You killed a taskmaster?"

Connor nodded.

Tonic laughed and slapped Connor on the back. "I'll be," he said.

"You keep on like this, and they'll be telling stories about you. Little Bit and the Whip."

"Figure out my myth later. When you do, though, please change my name," Connor said.

Tonic grinned. "But there's got to be some sort of record that'll trace it back to the real you."

"I think I'd rather be forgotten," Connor said.

"The Shadowlands never forgets," Tonic said. "There's a record of everything. The most rundown shanty or the most broken-down shop still needs a record… heck, even my horse—"

Connor frowned. A wild idea struck him—a long shot, but something more than just a thought. He glanced past Tonic to the object he'd noticed on his approach. It was his horse.

It wasn't just an idea anymore.

It felt like the beginning of a plan.

"I think I know where to start," he said, walking around the teen towards the animal. As he drew closer, the shadow horse appeared different from a regular horse. A mane of spikes ran around its neck like a collar and a similar bristle jutted out around its tail. "We're going to need your horse."

"Where do you need to go?" Tonic asked.

"Somewhere I never wanted to go again."

* * *

The walk from Gissu to the Daggers had taken hours, despite them travelling in a straight line. On horseback, even steering around Blackwood, the ride seemed to eat up the distance. The landscape blurred by as the horse tore across the ground, and Connor explained his idea.

"About time someone gave that shadow a taste of his own brew."

"I hope we can pull it off," Connor said.

"It's a crazy plan, but it's bold, and Light. Boy, do I like something bold!" Tonic said. He dug his heels into the horse's ribs to spur it faster and whooped. "Right now, Leon's got nothing on me."

They rode the horse hard to the back gate of Gissu where Tonic jerked back on the reins. The horse reared, lifting its front legs off the ground as it skidded to a stop. The lurch nearly threw Connor off, but he held tight, knowing his plan depended on them seeming urgent. The gates were closed, but two guards stood inside, appearing taken aback by the ferocity of the riders' approach.

"Open the gate," Tonic bellowed. "Urgent business for the Shadow Police."

The guards looked at each other. Both were burly, and each clutched long iron rods.

"Out with it then," one guard snapped. "If you're one of the Shadow Police, I'm a beam of sunlight."

"Caught this boy lurking around the walls," Tonic said, thrusting a thumb over his shoulder to Connor. "Word is, The Judge wants him for escaping."

"Best hand him to us then," the guard said.

"Think you can get him to the station faster than my horse?" Tonic replied. "Think I'm going to give up my bounty to you slivers of shadow?"

The guard frowned and looked at the other. The other shadow shrugged, so the first shadow reached for the gate lever.

"You come back this way," the guard said. "Better have something for us, or it'll be you going in front of The Judge."

"I know what oils the locks here." Tonic sneered.

The guard rolled his neck and pulled the lever. Tonic spurred the horse forward when the gate was barely open enough for them to ride through. As the guards diminished behind them, Connor chanced a glance back. The gates were already closed.

"Well, we're in," he said. "Don't think it's going to be so easy for us to get back out."

"Leave it to me," Tonic said.

Tonic navigated straight to Shade Row. Several shadows looked at them curiously as they passed, leaving Connor to suspect horses weren't at all common here, but no one tried to stop them. Given what he'd seen already, likely none of them cared.

When they were a couple of stalls down from the Shopkeeper's store, Tonic brought the animal to a stop, and they dismounted.

"Keep low," Tonic said. "If he sees you, we're shadowcat bait."

Connor nodded and dropped to all fours. He crawled to the front of the Shopkeeper's store and pressed against the wall. All he had to do was stay underneath the window and get close to the door. Meanwhile, Tonic walked his horse straight to the storefront and tied it to the leg of an empty table. Then, the teen disappeared inside.

Connor kept his crouch and thought about his breathing, keeping it slow and even. He could feel his pulse race, and his hands shook a little. He'd been certain he'd never enter the Shopkeeper's store again. Now he planned to rob it. Who knew what sort of penalties they'd face if they failed? He could end up on the gallows himself, listening to the thundering feet.

A minute later, Tonic returned to the door, talking to someone inside.

"An excellent animal, really," he was saying. "As good as any you'll find this side of the Midnight Mountains."

"I'll be the judge of that," the Shopkeeper's voice answered.

Tonic passed through the door and stopped beside his horse. The Shopkeeper stepped into the doorway and hitched his thumbs in the waist of his pants. He was barely a yard from where Connor waited, holding his breath.

"A good size," the Shopkeeper said. "Haunches look strong. You've been feeding it well."

"I spend more time feeding it than me," Tonic said.

"It shows," the Shopkeeper said with a sneer. He left the doorway and stepped up to inspect the horse more closely. This was Connor's chance.

Connor crept through the open door, keeping his head low as he ducked through the doorway. He crawled under the table holding the shadowcat pelts and veered towards the counter. He peered underneath, looking for the box of debts.

The box was not there.

Sweat beaded on Connor's forehead. He felt his palms and armpits grow slick. Where was it? He felt behind several objects to the back wall of the counter, but still found nothing. He cursed and glanced around the shop. His eyes fell upon the door behind which Journeyman and the Shopkeeper had their argument. It was cracked open.

Connor crawled back around the counter and to the door. He peered through the opening into what looked like a combination of storeroom and office. It was lit by several small lanterns and candles whose flames cast ghostly shadows from all the shelved objects. As Connor crawled inside, the door hinges creaked. Connor glanced back over his shoulder through the front door to where the Shopkeeper appeared to be inspecting the horse's quills.

Inside the back room, Connor rose. Metal shelves held jars full of insects, animal parts suspended in fluid, and many items from the World of Light—knives and paperweights, each dangling a small tag. Curiosity burned in Connor to know what these things were, but he approached the desk, which stood against one wall. There, on a tattered blotter rested the box of promises.

Connor picked up the box and pulled out its contents. He shuffled through the papers, skipping to the bottom of the stack. He smiled. His hunch had been correct. The final note was written in a different hand than all the rest. It read, "Roderick Howe. No memory of the past and a deed to a shop in Shade Row. Two hundred shadows."

Connor raised his eyebrows.

There wasn't time to think about it. He slipped the Shopkeeper's promise into his pocket and returned the rest of the receipts into the box. Then, he picked up the box and a candle, walked straight to the front door of the shop, and stopped behind the Shopkeeper.

Tonic smiled when he saw Connor, knowing they had what they came for. The Shopkeeper saw Tonic's smile and froze in the middle of inspecting the horse's teeth. The Shopkeeper turned. His eyes widened as he registered who was behind him. Even if everything went wrong, the look of discomfort on the Shopkeeper's face made the endeavor worthwhile.

"Little Bit," the Shopkeeper said. "Never thought to see you again."

The Shopkeeper tried to take a step back, but his back pushed against the horse, which stamped its hooves anxiously. Fear slipped across the Shopkeeper's features. Clearly, he didn't like to be caught cornered, even if his ambusher was a little boy.

"Never wanted to see you again," Connor said. "But here we are." Then, before the Shopkeeper could open his mouth to respond, Connor added, "Roderick."

The Shopkeeper's face lightened several shades, and his eyes about burst from his skull. He quickly collected himself and his face dropped into a grim mask that almost resembled the menace Connor had seen in their last encounter. Almost.

"What's it to ya?" the Shopkeeper said, a tremor in his voice.

"Not much," Connor said.

The Shopkeeper reached towards Connor, but Tonic stepped between them. The horse shuddered with an apprehensive whinny as the Shopkeeper's hand brushed against Tonic's chest.

"You give me my box, boy," the Shopkeeper said, drawing his hand back, trying to maneuver away from the horse. The horse jittered on its hooves, keeping right against the shadow's back. Connor noticed Tonic had undone the horse's tie. "You've no right to it."

"Seems I have every right," Connor said. He moved the candle closer to the promise box and opened the lid. "And right now, I'm thinking how easily I could turn this candle flame onto all these promises. Thinking, I'd like to see your face as you watch them burn."

"I'd be ruined," the Shopkeeper said. "What do you want?"

Connor smiled. He didn't know if he managed the same humorless smile the Shopkeeper was so fond of, but he did his best.

"You know the Thief," Connor said. "And I need to know where he keeps my shadow."

"Won't do you any good," the Shopkeeper said, his face etched with desperation. "You won't be able to get it back, and he'll come looking for me if I tell you. The Shadower will come looking for me."

"Then you should keep better company, Roderick," Connor said. He dipped the candle into the box, the flame catching the edge of one of the promises. The paper shriveled and blackened at the edge, a little wisp of smoke rising.

The Shopkeeper looked frantically over his shoulder. Several shadows had gathered and watched with greedy interest.

"Stop using my name," the Shopkeeper said.

"I'll stop when you tell me what I need to know," Connor said.

Then, the Shopkeeper seemed to deflate. Any bit of menace and defiance fled him, and as large as he was, he looked like little more than a scared little boy.

"Inside," the Shopkeeper said. "The Thief keeps the shadows he steals inside himself."

Connor and Tonic frowned. This was not good news, and though he normally wouldn't trust a thing the Shopkeeper said, he knew the shadow was telling the truth.

"How do I get it out?" Connor asked.

"Short of either ripping the Thief to pieces and combing through his innards or reaching straight down his throat," the Shopkeeper said, "I don't know. I really don't know."

Connor nodded, then dipped the candle flame back into the box of promises.

"No!" the Shopkeeper bellowed, lurching forward.

Tonic shoved the off-balance shadow hard, knocking the Shopkeeper against the horse. The horse reared up on its hind legs and its fore hoof came down on the Shopkeeper's shoulder. The shadow tumbled forward, crashing against the side of the shop.

"No, no, no," the Shopkeeper cried as the flames rose from the promise box.

"This box is an evil thing," Connor said, setting it on the ground as it grew hotter. "And I don't think I should let you have an evil thing like this anymore."

"The Judge will hang you for this," the Shopkeeper whispered.

"Been there, done that," Connor said. "And I wonder if I'd be so sure. If I had to guess, I have a feeling his name was in the box, too."

The Shopkeeper covered his face with his hands and sobbed.

Tonic nudged Connor. "It's time to go. The police will be here any minute."

Connor nodded. "One more thing." He stepped into the shop and snatched a shadow dagger off a display table before stepping back outside. "Let's go," he said to Tonic. "I've got a Thief to gut."

Tonic mounted the horse and then pulled Connor up behind him. Then, he spurred the animal towards the gate of Shade Row, leaving the quivering shopkeeper in the shadow of his store.

"How are we going to get out of here?" Connor asked as the blurring shops gave way to blurring shacks. The gate loomed ahead, and the same two guards were still at their posts. Tonic snapped the reins and dug in his heels. Their mount lurched into a full gallop, its hooves thundering. The guards raised their heads at the sound.

"Stop!" one guard shouted, bracing itself and raising its staff

Tonic jerked the reins right before they reached the guards, and the horse once again reared up, flailing its hooves onto the nearest guard. The blows struck without mercy, throwing the guard backward against the wall. The other guard leapt back, even as Tonic lunged sideways on the horse and took hold of the gate release lever. The guard raised his staff overhead, but Tonic squeezed the steed's flanks with his knees, and the horse gave a trained kick back with both legs, catching the guard dead in the chest as the gate churned open.

Then, with a cowboy-like, "Heehaw," Tonic kicked the horse on, and out of Gissu it sped.

CHAPTER 26

THE ROAD TO HOLLOWDELL

The swath of land to the East of Gissu was little more than an open plain, like one might see in pictures of Kansas or Oklahoma. Occasional shadow plants and thickets dotted the distance, as did the occasional shack. It differed from the emptiness of the iron desert. Something about the desert seemed like it should be empty. This area felt like everyone simply chose not to live there.

Tonic followed the road to a fork. One path continued straight on, while the other veered north towards the Daggers. The animal eased to a stop. Tonic helped Connor down and then dismounted. The teen paced frantically, clearly still worked up from the action.

"Guarantee they'll be telling stories about that," Tonic said. "Bet you no one's done something like that in Gissu for a hundred years. Most fun I can remember having."

"The fun is yet to come," Connor said. He'd spent the entire ride both elated and shocked that they'd succeeded.

"For you," Tonic said, scratching the inside of his elbows. "I've got to get back to the Daggers and wait for Quiet."

For a moment, Connor thought Tonic was joking, but the teen's eyes dropped to his shoes.

Connor's heart fell. "We still have time," he said.

"I know," Tonic said, shuffling his feet and rubbing the back of his neck. "But I have to wait there for her. I told her I'd always be waiting."

"A deal?" Connor said.

"A promise," Tonic said. "And I've stretched it enough for our adventure already."

Connor wanted to protest; he sure could use the teen's help to figure out how to use what they'd learned from the Shopkeeper—in a way, the task seemed more impossible than ever—but there was no way he could ask Tonic to turn his back on Quiet any longer. Instead, Connor said, "Thank you for everything."

"No thanks needed," Tonic said. "Do understand that when I tell Quiet about what we did, I'm going to make myself seem more heroic than I already was."

Connor chuckled, and the two shook hands.

"Hallowdell is a few miles down the road. Shouldn't take you more than a couple of hours," Tonic said. Then he added, "Try not to cut across the farms. Farmers don't take kindly to trespassers."

Tonic climbed back on his horse and trotted up the road to the Daggers. Connor turned and headed on. Despite being alone, Connor did feel a bit more hopeful. He and Tonic had won a real victory. It could be the start of a streak. It had to be.

After a while, the empty plains changed. In the distance, Connor saw long, intentional rows of trees and what appeared to be fields of crops divided by meandering fences. Occasional buildings that resembled classic farmhouses, barns, and grain towers loomed. They were silhouettes, but they could have come from a postcard of Iowa or Kansas taken at dusk. Indeed, if Connor didn't know those buildings would be as slipshod as what he'd seen in Gissu, he wouldn't have been able to distinguish them from the farms of the World of Light. He even heard a sound reminiscent of the calls of cattle. He was tempted to veer off the road to look at the farms themselves, but Connor didn't want to ignore Tonic's warning.

A strange chittering sound drew Connor's gaze to a fence alongside the road. On top of one post sat a pair of black rats, the shadows of rats really. They stared at Connor, chattering to each other as if discussing him. They reminded him of the rats in the story of Luza and Ereb.

A twinge panged his heart as Mouse's face came to mind, the way she'd looked when she'd told the story on the bank of the Shadowrun. He remembered the way she'd slipped her hand in his as they talked. Had Mouse ever seen the shadowfarms? He wished she could see them now. These farms couldn't be much different from how Luza's farm would have looked. If shadows didn't die, the rats watching him now could even have been the same rats.

Connor felt himself drawn towards the little animals. In the story, Luza had talked with the rats and found it futile. He said, "Did you eat Luza's vines? Did you see the Great Flare?"

The rats darted off the post and into the field. As they departed, he ached for everything he'd put Mouse through. She liked love stories, she had said. He wouldn't have said he loved Mouse; he didn't know how one loved a girl yet, but weren't all stories when one person sacrificed themselves to save another just a love story?

New determination surged through him. He wouldn't fail her again. He would reach the Thief and take their shadows back no matter what the cost. For Mouse.

Connor pressed on, gazing into the fields he passed, watching for more rats among the posts and beyond. Only some farms were fenced in, but all were edged with black tufts of grass skirting right up to the road. Connor paused and broke off a blade. It was brittle and stiff, and it shattered more than tore. Petrified, Connor thought. How could so many things in the shadowlands be so ancient they'd turned to stone?

After a good while, the rattle of a shambling cart approached, not from further down the road, but from behind. Connor ducked and scurried off the road, not wanting to meet anyone who might be coming from the quarry. He dropped flat among the thickets of brittle grass and pulled the obsidian blanket over him. It didn't match the landscape as well as it did in the quarry, but someone would need to look directly at him to spot him.

He waited for the cart to trundle past. Even in the dim light of the shadow day, Connor could make out the pepper-haired man walking between the two poles of the rickshaw.

Journeyman.

A mixture of emotions flooded Connor—anger, fear, even a bit of hope. Journeyman had both fended off the shadowcats and betrayed him in The Judge's chamber. Which version was the real him? Which one was he now

Journeyman stopped. He lowered his poles and adjusted his belt before stepping around the side of the cart and pulling his flask off the seat. He drank deep, glancing down the road back to the quarry. He turned and gazed towards his destination, not once looking out into the fields. Was this intentional? Connor hardly dared to breathe until Journeyman recapped his flask, took up the poles, and continued.

As the cart resumed its wobbling path, however, something fell from its side with a soft thunk. Journeyman either didn't notice or pretended not to.

Connor waited. Part of him wanted to follow Journeyman. The possibility that he would lead him to the Thief was worth not losing sight of him. At the same time, Connor wanted to know what had fallen.

It was a little black bundle.

Was it a trap? What if it contained something horrible? Its fall couldn't have been an accident. No way Journeyman didn't notice it, and even now, he didn't look back.

Connor crawled on his hands and knees, keeping as low as possible. The sharp edges of the petrified grass bit his palms, not quite breaking the skin, but poking and prodding uncomfortably. When he reached the road, Connor recognized the bundle as being Tonic's backpack. A note was pinned on the outside: "We're even."

As he took hold of the bag, Connor knew what was inside the moment he touched the bulky and soft backpack. It rumbled under his fingertips. The shadowcat cub.

Connor opened the bag. The cub cracked its eyes as soon as its head cleared the cloth. Glassy eyes, the irises purplish black of obsidian. The cub came to life, wriggling the rest of the way out of the bag with its eyes fixed on Connor. It purred loudly. Free of its constraints, the cub strutted back and forth several times. Then, it ambled up and rubbed against his leg, friendly as any housecat. Connor smiled as he knelt and scooped the purring cat into his arms. It licked his face with a rough, black tongue.

Part of Connor wanted to catch up with Journeyman and ask for more help, but the note made clear Journeyman's stance. They were even. If he were to approach Journeyman again, he wouldn't be able to trust him. The man would do anything to help his son, even at someone else's expense. As much as he hated to admit it, Connor understood. Journeyman's story was also a love story, and not all love stories were happy.

Connor regarded the shadowcat in his arms for several moments, letting the creature lick the ash off his face. Part of him wanted to keep the cub, but he wouldn't feel right trading anything living for his own gain again. How would it be any different from the way Journeyman betrayed him? Connor suspected trading the cub was what Journeyman expected Connor to do, and that alone made him not want to.

Connor also remembered the cub's parents in Blackwood, and how he'd stunned one of them with the flashlight when they'd tracked him down. The other had tended to the one he'd stunned. He couldn't say how smart the shadowcats were, but they cared about each other. He set the cat down in the grass.

"Go," he said. "Shoo."

The shadowcat rubbed up against first Connor's left leg, then his right, purring louder.

"Go back to your parents," Connor said, waving his hands.

The cat ignored his words and actions.

"GO!" He took a swinging kick at the cat, intentionally missing it.

The cat crouched and flattened its ears. It didn't hiss or growl, but it eyed him. Connor kicked two more times, the last time coming so close to the cub's face, it must have felt the wind of his shoe. Slinking low, it crept away, looking back several times at Connor. A cloud of dirt kicked up around it, and it disappeared among the shadows of the grass.

Connor set out after Journeyman, the cart now a moving speck. He kind of hated driving the cat away. Its affection had been comforting. Unfortunately, it had a place where it belonged, the same as he had a place where he belonged—at home with a whole shadow and his family intact.

Connor paused. That he and his mother were a family intact had never occurred to him before. Since his father's death, he'd seen his family as broken, as missing a member it could not be a family without. Now, he realized his family was still whole, just different. The thought brought a little warmth to him, and he smiled as he refocused his attention on catching up with Journeyman. He moved as quickly as he dared, at first jogging along the road itself, then veering off in a trotting crouch into the grass as the cart loomed. It was easy to outpace the lumbering rickshaw, though the sharp grass was taking its toll. By the time he'd drawn within thirty yards of the cart, scratches smarted all over his palms and knees, a couple of which seeped tiny amounts of blood. He hoped they would reach the end of the road soon.

HOLLOWDELL

Connor had no idea of knowing how long he crawled behind Journeyman. Every motion drew a wince until his hands and knees became a fine mess of dirt and blood. Eventually, the petrified grass thinned and gave way to empty dirt. Arising from that dirt down the road stood the outskirts of Hallowdell.

The town was smaller than Gissu, and as unimpressive as Gissu had been, Hallowdell was even less. There was no lantern-hung wall. The buildings all stood low and squat. Connor couldn't make them out well yet, but he imagined them every bit as unkempt and ramshackle as he'd seen in Gissu. He couldn't imagine the miners who lived here had much to work with, and they were probably too tired and beaten to fix things up.

The relief of his trek almost being over was short-lived, because it meant facing the Thief—somethinghe still hadn't formed a plan for.

He had the flashlight, but it wouldn't be enough simply to stun the Thief. He had a shadow blade, but he'd never even thought of using a knife as a weapon outside of action movie fantasies.

What he needed was help, but he had none and had no idea how to get it. Tonic and Quiet might as well have been on the moon. Dandrich? Who knew where she could be, or how he'd find her before he needed to act. Connor wished Mouse was with him, even if she didn't know what to do. Together, at least, they might have figured it out. How could he win by himself? He'd beaten the Shopkeeper, but the Shopkeeper had something to lose. Connor was not so sure the same could be said about the Thief. Despite not being able to find a source of hope, Connor found himself, somewhere, somehow, believing he would come up with some solution. Hope was a funny thing.

Journeyman wheeled his cart between the first two buildings on the outskirts, and Connor pressed himself against one. These buildings were not made of metal like in Gissu, but of beams fashioned from petrified wood, some with branches or nubs still jutting off from them. They were all lashed together with flimsy ropes and twine.

Also, unlike Gissu, there was no sign of a hub like Shade Row. Instead, various stalls stood randomly scattered between houses. Most were empty, but a handful displayed various bits of shadow food and little knick-knacks or articles of clothing with haggard vendors behind them. A couple of shopkeepers stood outside tiny stores, but these stores either didn't have awnings or their awnings were simple grays and badly tattered. Connor fingered the toys he'd stuffed into his pockets before he'd left his house. He'd hoped to trade them for something useful, but now he suspected there was nothing useful to be found. One passing shadow gazed hungrily at him, causing him to quicken his step.

The streets were almost deserted, too. A few shadows lay slumped on the sides of the road or sat against buildings. Most gazed vacantly, too exhausted and emaciated to do more. Connor saw through the doorless fronts of the buildings where more residents curled up on the floors of their homes, tossing and turning. Connor felt renewed pity for them. Their lives had to be awful. Did no one stand up for them?

A strange thought occurred to him: he didn't understand how the

Shadowlands worked. While the Shadow Police enforced some laws, and The Judge practiced a form of justice, where did those laws and notions of justice come from? Everyone seemed so miserable, it was hard to imagine they wouldn't fight it. The great leaders from his history class—Lincoln, Jefferson, Ghandi, and Martin Luther King Jr.—all rallied thousands, sometimes even millions, to protect their rights. Even in his school, the students sometimes rebelled against unfair treatment. And if the students didn't, the parents did. Why did no one stand up for anyone here? Shadows like Quiet and Tonic helped each other, but how come no one tried to help everyone?

The thought was swept away as Connor realized Journeyman was disappearing down a side street. He hurried to catch up, darting from place to place to keep out of sight, knowing it might be his only chance to find what he sought. He skirted the edge of a disheveled shack onto the road Journeyman had taken. The gray-haired man headed towards a slightly larger house at the end of the street. For the first time, Connor noticed Journeyman seemed to struggle under the weight of the rickshaw, grunting as he went. An especially large sack rested in the cart's bed. What was Journeyman hauling?

Connor kept his distance, peeking through the slats of broken-down crates, over heaps of sacks filled with who knows what, and around the sides of rusted barrels, though Journeyman had yet to look back. In fact, he glanced around so little, Connor knew it had to be on purpose. Not once had he taken his eyes off the road. Surely, he would have chanced a couple of random turns of the head.

However, Connor grew certain of Journeyman's destination. The house ahead looked a little sturdier than the those surrounding it. This particular house's heads had bright silver rivets dotting the joints of the petrified wood beams, and also sported a wide, heavy-looking door. Indeed, as Journeyman drew up to it and set down the poles of his cart, he had to throw his entire weight against the door to slide it open. Then, he re-hoisted the poles and drew the cart inside. The rickshaw barely cleared the entryway as one of its wheels caught a moment on the frame before Journeyman wriggled it loose. With a loud clang that rang through the whole street, the door closed.

Connor's head hurt, and his throat was dry. A strange panic flooded him. He wanted to turn and run, feeling far too young for this. How did adults do this "being brave" thing? It might actually be easier to become Shadowless.

A sharp twist in Connor's stomach disrupted his despair. He remembered the food and water Dandrich had given him, and he ducked into the first building without a door. Inside, he found himself upon a gaunt shadow lying on its side on the floor.

"Shhh," Connor said.

The shadow groaned, and its eyelids fluttered. Connor thought it was a man but couldn't tell for sure because its face was so sunken. Its body was thinner than anyone he had ever seen. Its clothes were a terrible tatter of fabric. It sat up as Connor stepped far enough into the home to be out of sight from the road.

"Who are you?" the shadow said.

"Little Bit," Connor said, then quickly added, "I can't be seen."

The shadow didn't offer any introduction, and Connor didn't feel like pressing it. Hoping the shadow was too weak to do anything, Connor squatted and unslung his bag. He felt better knowing Dandrich's flashlight was right there if he needed it, but he doubted he would. He pulled out the orange and peeled it, pocketing the rinds so as not to make a mess in someone else's home, as shabby as it was. Then, he dug into the sticky pulp, every bite a delight he'd never known possible.

The shadow's eyes opened wide. Connor immediately felt guilty about the juice running down his chin. He peered inside the bag.

"'Would you like some cookie?" he asked, pulling out the bit of cookie.

The shadow shook its head. "Can't eat Caster food."

Connor's heart filled with pity for the form before him.

"Is there anything I can do to help?"

The shadow regarded Connor, blinking a few times with slow, drowsy eyelids. Then, it drew a deep breath and, with what seemed like all the strength it could muster, said, "If you see my brother in the Light, tell him I'm sorry."

Connor doubted he could do any such thing, but he asked, "What's his name?"

The shadow furrowed his brow. "I— I don't remember."

"What was your name?" Connor asked.

"I don't remember." The shadow closed its eyes and fell silent, breathing sharply.

Tears welled in Connor's eyes. Nothing should live like this. He wished he could help every shadow here, learn who they were, and make apologies so they would find their way out of the Shadowlands. But he was only a kid. This was all so far beyond him that it was overwhelming to even think about.

Connor finished eating in silence.

After devouring the orange, he pulled the flashlight out of the pack and slung the bag over his shoulders. As he stepped through the door, he stopped in the fading light and turned back. He stuffed his hands into his pockets and pulled out the plastic army men, which he laid in a pile in front of the shadow.

"Trade them," Connor said. "If I can figure out how, I'll tell your brother you're sorry."

The shadow opened its eyes and ran its gaze over the toys. It sat up, a strain flooding its features as if the act took the whole of its strength. Likely, it did. The shadow reached out and picked up one of the army men. It was a bazooka man, its weapon poised on its shoulder. The bazooka men had always been Connor's favorite because they dispatched the imaginary tanks he pitted them against in the garden.

"I cannot accept," the shadow said.

"Please," Connor said. "Everyone here seems so sad. If I can help you…"

The shadow straightened slightly. "Then, you must accept something in return," it said, now looking Connor over with a curious gleam in its eyes. Hope, Connor realized. He had no idea what the shadow would trade the toys for, but he knew it was going to make a difference.

"I can't," Connor said. "You don't have much to offer."

The shadow nodded. "A story, then."

Connor looked out the door. Out of sight, Journeyman was conducting whatever business he had to conduct with the Thief.

"I don't have time," Connor said.

The slightest of smiles curled one side of the shadow's lips.

"You have the look of someone who's been chasing something for days," he said. "And judging by what's left of your shadow, I know what that is. A few more minutes will not change anything."

Connor didn't want to wait, but something in his gut told him he should. So, he gave a helpless shrug.

"Have you ever heard the story of Rake and the Needlestones?"

Connor shook his head.

The nameless shadow began, its voice hardly more than a whisper:

"Rake was a farmhand who made a living clearing the fields of shadow farmers. Drifted from village to village, a restless spirit, unable to settle. His parents had been farmers in the World of Light, but a fever took him at the age of nineteen. He'd lived his entire life loving his parents' farm more than anything. Every farm in the Shadowlands felt gray in comparison.

"At the same time, the smell of the earth, the feel of soil on his skin, and the wind sweeping across the fields was all he'd ever cared for, so he could never drive himself to seek another life. He would arrive in a new town at the start of the planting season and stay until its end.

"As he worked, he worked with a heavy heart, always hanging his head, never quite looking at what he was doing because it made him sad to linger too long on the fields. Through his labor and the fact that most farmers feed their hired help well, he'd grown robust and developed a reputation across the Shadowlands for his speed and dedication.

"One day, a farmer named Velch outside a village named The Skirts approached Rake with a bid to clear his fields of stones. Rake named his usual rate, but Velch insisted on doubling it. Glad for the windfall that, if carefully saved, would ensure he stayed fed for the next winter, Rake accepted and rode in the farmer's cart out to the fields.

"When they arrived, rather than a hoe, plow, or shovel, Velch brought Rake to a sledgehammer leaning against the plot gate and indicated Rake should heft it.

"This isn't what I need," said Rake. "This will shatter the stones and leave the soil coarse."

"Ah, but I must confess, I didn't tell you everything," said the farmer. "I was swindled. The seller, a man from the next farm, told me a story of woe and claimed to be in dire need of money lest he lose his lands altogether, and I bought this parcel thinking it would be a great help in increasing my trade. We'd lived adjacent as long as I didn't ask the proper questions. When I got to the field, I found a field riddled with needlestone rather than fallow ground. So, now the field is mine, and I staked a great deal on it.”

“Immediately, Rake understood the high wages. He'd cleared an occasional sprout of needlestone before. Dense as lead and hard as iron, it bristled with hundreds of sharp quills that left one aching for days if it broke the skin. Most workers wouldn't touch the stuff. Even the best-kept fields sometimes had a cluster jutting out from among the crops.

“As he looked out upon the field, Rake realized what looked like overgrown blades of grass and bristly weeds was more needlestone than he'd ever seen.

“This is bad work,” Rake said. “Even at twice my normal rate, it is not enough.”

“Please,” the farmer said. “No one else will do it. You have a reputation; I don't know anyone else who could do it.”

“Appreciative of the bit of praise and remembering how sometimes his parents had fallen on hard times, Rake sympathized with the farmer and agreed to help.

“The farmer shook his hands with both of his in great sweeping motions and thanked him profusely before taking his leave so Rake could begin his work.

“For sixteen days, Rake battled the field, swinging the sledge and shattering needlestone clusters. His arms ached from the effort of wielding the tool alone. Though his body was covered by clothing, flying shards of the nasty rock left his face and neck covered in scratches and throbbing without mercy, forcing him to squint and breathe through his mouth.

“For the first ten days, he worked from sunup to sun down, stopping only to eat and drink, but by the eleventh day, he'd used so much strength and his body hurt so much, he needed the strength of night, even if it meant more scratches and scrapes because he could barely see his work. On the sixteenth day, he worked without cessation for the full cycle of day and night, obliterating the last cluster of needlestone, then clearing the debris from the whole of the field with an indefatigable exertion enough to stun the most seasoned farmhand.

“Utterly spent, but with the field prepared for the plow, and covered head to toe in mud and dirt, Rake shambled to the farmhouse to collect his pay.

"When he arrived, however, he found Velch was not alone, but among a small crowd—all his regular hired hands as well as another farmer and all of his hands. Rake was not surprised when Velch refused to pay him and threatened to have him beaten if he did not leave and never come back.

"If he were well rested, Rake might have been able to take on three or four of the farmhands, as strong as he was, but not the sixteen he saw before him. And now, he was so exhausted, he wouldn't have been able to raise his hands in fists if he'd wanted to fight back.

"So, without a word, he turned and left.

"He took a week to recover from the cruel demands he'd subjected his body to. Then, he set forth away from the village until he found a deep wood, where he prowled among the trees and their roots until he found a nest of shadow vipers whose poison would leave one writhing in agony for a month. He set down a line of burlap sacks, and one by one caught sixteen shadow vipers, one for each of the farmers and their hands. Then, when night fell the following day, he crept back to the farms.

"With the stealth and speed of a shadowcat, he slid one of the burlap sacks into each of the beds of the sleeping farmers and their hands, moving from one house to the next. Some awoke to the screams of their fellows before they too found themselves bitten by the venomous snakes, the serpents quite angry about being snatched up and kept in a sack for a full day.

"Their cries still echoed as he disappeared across the wilderness beyond the farms.

"For his part, Rake never worked a field again. They say he took up residence in the city of Vissa and made candles and lanterns for a hundred years. One day, however, he disappeared altogether and has not been heard of since."

The shadow fell silent and looked at Connor curiously. Then he asked, "Do you know why I told you this story?"

Connor thought for a moment. "Because even when outnumbered, Rake still found a way to win?"

"No," the shadow said with a shake of its head. "Rake did not win. His work was his only connection to who he was, and his entire reputation was built through it. He lost everything."

Connor furrowed his brow.

The shadow continued, "Those who seek their shadows are split between desiring justice and revenge. So, too, was Rake. He chose the latter, and it cost him everything that mattered. What will you choose?"

Connor didn't have an answer. He thought about the pleasure he'd taken in breaking the Shopkeeper. He knew what he did was right; the Shopkeeper needed to be brought down. But should he have felt so good about it? Connor wondered how he would feel when he confronted the Thief. Alongside his fears and apprehensions, he could feel the burning anger to get revenge for his hanging, for the pain Mouse and Quiet felt at the hands of the taskmasters. Shouldn't he want revenge? The Thief was a monster, feeding on creating misery for others. Weren't revenge and justice the same thing in a time like this?

The shadow lay back, clutching the bazooka man to his chest. All strength seemed to leave him. He didn't fall asleep, but aside from his open eyes, the only sign he was alive was a soft rattle in his breath.

Connor felt like he should say something, but he doubted the shadow would respond. Knowing he'd lingered long enough, he took one last look at the still form and then ducked back into the street towards the house Journeyman had entered.

ECLIPSE

The house stood directly ahead. It had no windows, so Connor had no fear of being seen. Instead, he stopped in the middle of the street and stared at the building, which was so small compared to the terrifying bone work and iron of the Foreman's office, and Hallowdell itself seemed far less threatening than the stares and bustle of Gissu. There were no lava flows or gallows or shadowcats, yet he found this house more menacing than anything he'd faced so far.

Overhead, the sun and moon were beginning to overlap, and Connor's eyes, which had grown sensitive to the poor light of the Shadowlands, picked up on a new shade of darkness overtaking everything. Soon, the moon would block the sun and blanket the whole of the Shadowlands under the eclipse. Connor remembered how the Foreman changed shapes and grew in his hall. He shuddered to imagine facing the Thief in the same form, especially in the small building ahead.

Additionally, shadows were straggling onto the streets. Their skeletal forms stumbled out of the open doorways, shielding their eyes against the dim sun. They ambled about, wandering in circles or pacing back and forth with anxious energy. Several cast frequent glances at the sky, waiting for the sun to disappear. Connor knew he should be off the streets before that happened.

Without further hesitation, Connor stepped toward the house. He wouldn't be able to open the doors himself—Journeyman had barely been able to. Instead, Connor checked out the building's sides, crossing from left to right. No windows, no cracks or missing slats.

Frustrated, Connor took a few steps back. Had he come this far to fail, simply because he couldn't get in? He rolled his eyes, and they passed over the roof. There, they stopped.

The house had a chimney, and beside that sat a single skylight propped open. Immediately, he re-examined the sides of the building for places to climb. The walls were smooth except for the vertical bars of the frame. Why did this one have to be so much better constructed? Could he shimmy up one of the corner posts? It would make noise.

He examined the neighboring buildings. The one on the right was too low to get on top of the house, even if the patchwork roof hadn't looked about to cave in. On the other side, though, that house's roof reached high enough. It was flat, so Connor couldn't see if it would hold his weight, but the space between the buildings was narrow, so he could jump.

He made his way over to the house made of petrified trees, where jutting nubs of branches offered perfect grips. He found a hold and scrambled up to the roof as easily as climbing a tree. Thankfully, the roof supported his weight.

However, from the new height, the space between the buildings looked much larger. The tiny alley was narrow, but piled chunks of petrified wood and sharp pieces of metal cluttered the gap below. If he fell... Connor's courage ebbed.

He shook his head as he perched on the roof's edge. Failure wasn't an option. If he fell and hurt himself or worse … he would return to the World of Light, probably without a shadow. He was going to make it.

Connor bent his knees, and held his arms out to keep his balance. Then, he jumped.

For a split second, as his body crossed the gulf between the buildings, he was convinced he was already falling. His chest seized, his heart and lungs frozen within. He was about to crash into a rusty metal spike standing out from the rest. An image flashed through his mind of himself stuck upon it, its gnarly point jutting through him.

His foot landed on the new roof. For a moment, the rest of his body didn't follow. He wobbled precariously on the edge, his arms waving through the air, his head lolling forward and back. Images of death flashed through his mind faster than ever.

His body steadied. Not only had he made it, but he barely made a sound. He dropped to his hands and knees and crawled to the skylight.

Below, the room was dimly lit by a small, flickering fire. It surprised Connor that there was light at all, but he figured it was for the benefit of Journeyman. He saw neither the Thief nor Journeyman, but the rickshaw poles stood out in the glow. There was silence within.

As his eyes adjusted to the darkness, the rickshaw's carriage took form out of the surrounding shadows. It was directly below the skylight. He could drop right into it. The cart had been emptied of whatever had burdened it, so the landing wouldn't be difficult. A bit of luck, Connor thought.

Without waiting, he lowered his legs through the skylight. As he did, he felt exposed and vulnerable, so he let himself slip down.

A little too quickly.

When his feet hit the rickshaw, the rickshaw tilted on its wheels and dumped Connor to the floor with a crash. He landed on his stomach.

There was a soft laugh, and The Neverborn Thief's nasty voice said, "Well, well, well. Not a bad entrance, even for such a rough landing. You've come to give me what's mine?"

Connor pushed up with his palms and thrust himself to his feet. He pulled the flashlight-weapon from his pocket and spun, stopping when he saw the Thief leaning against the fireplace. He flickered in the glow, the tattoos coming in and out of focus, each of the faces wide-eyed with concern and fear. He wore a heavy black cloak, concealing his body. Connor aimed the flashlight at the Thief, who casually raised his hands as if to joke, "Don't shoot."

"Now, now, now," the Thief said. "Let's not be too hasty here."

"Give it back," Connor shouted.

"Shouldn't we discuss this first?" the Thief asked, wearing a mean smile. "We've got lots to talk about."

"No, we don't." Connor didn't want to get trapped in a negotiation. He didn't want to make the same mistake as before. The Thief was clever. "Give it back right now."

The Thief gazed at Connor, and Connor saw his wary glances at the weapon. The Thief had to have something in store for him. He was too confident.

"Want to hear my counterproposal?" The Neverborn Thief sneered. "To negotiate? It would be only fair to do so."

"There's nothing fair here," Connor said. "Not about this place. Not about you. You took what's mine, and I want it back."

"I took your shadow fairly," the Thief scowled. "You hardly even knew you had it, and you sure didn't care to use it."

The Neverborn Thief rolled his shoulders, and in the motion, his cloak fell, revealing his full figure etched with tattoos like the ones on his face. "Look at you," the Thief said. "At your indignation. Wanting back what you took for granted. If I had a body, I'd do anything to protect it. Would you have fought for your shadow if I hadn't taken it? You Casters only care about what you have when it's gone."

"There's nothing right about stealing," Connor said.

The Thief smirked. "I don't know much about the Caster world, but I love your story of Robin Hood. Stole from those who didn't deserve what they had and gave it to those who did. Am I any different? Have you earned the right to say what is right? Did you earn your shadow?"

"Earned or not," Connor said, "it's mine, and I want it back."

He knew he was right. There was nothing the Thief could say to change his mind.

The Thief crooked an eyebrow. "At what cost?"

Connor paused. What cost could there be? He shook his head. He couldn't let the Thief break his confidence.

"Would you take your shadow back," the Thief said, "if it brought your mother misery?"

Connor laughed. He saw what the Thief was doing. He wanted him to feel guilty about what he'd put his mother through by coming into the Shadowlands.

"Better she be unhappy now and have her son her whole life than me becoming Shadowless."

The Thief nodded and waved his hand as if he expected the answer.

"But what about your father? Should he suffer for your selfishness?"

A cold feeling struck Connor. His body vibrated with alarm like a struck bell. "My father?" he asked, his voice sounding small as it escaped his lips.

The Neverborn Thief's wicked grin spread wide, revealing sharpened shadows of teeth, every tooth a fang. The tattoos all hung their mouths open with terror. The Thief motioned to the darkness behind Connor. Connor turned. There, Journeyman stood, and beside him stood a figure covered in a heavy, black cloth. Journeyman pulled the cloth away, leaving Connor breathless.

There, beside Journeyman, stood the shadow of his father.

The light filtering through the skylight suddenly failed, and the room plunged into a deep darkness as the moon completed its eclipse of the sun. Even the fire seemed too dim. Tears sprang to Connor's eyes. A sob caught in his throat.

His father. He'd not seen his father for so long, and he was every bit as emaciated and disheveled as any shadow in Hallowdell. Still, Connor could not fail to recognize those eyes, those lips, that nose, those cheeks.

"Daddy," Connor blurted out, the trapped sob escaping at the same time. "Dad!"

He lurched toward his father's arms, but Journeyman stepped between them, holding up one hand.

"Ah-ah-ah," the Thief said from behind Connor. "You don't touch the goods, yet."

Connor stared at his father. His father hadn't tried to move, barely glanced his way, before his gaze fell back to the floor. Connor didn't understand. How could Dad not rush forward and sweep him into his embrace? How could anything, even the Thief, stop him from doing so?

"Dad?" Connor asked.

His father looked past him. Connor looked back over his shoulder as the Thief gave a nod.

"I'm sorry, son," his dad said. The firelight glistened on his wet cheeks.

"Sorry?" Connor said. "You're here! I never thought I'd see you again!"

Connor's tears flowed. His chest heaved. It never occurred to him that he might find his father in this place. It was a miracle. Yet, something was wrong. His father wasn't overjoyed. His father was here. What was happening?

"you are you going to tell him, or should I?" the Thief asked. Connor didn't need to look back to imagine the horrible smile contorting the Thief's face.

Connor's father finally met his son's eyes.

"I don't understand," Connor said.

His father sighed. "I'm the reason you're here," he said.

"What? What do you mean?" Connor asked. It couldn't be. There was no way.

"What did your mother tell you about how I died?"

Cold slithered up Connor's spine and a knot formed in his belly.

"She told me the truth," Connor said.

Connor's father nodded. "I… I made a deal," he said. "I promised the Thief your shadow."

Connor's jaw dropped.

"What? Why?" said he asked. "How could you?"

"The boy…," his father said. "The boy I killed. The Thief promised he'd help me apologize so I could find my way to the light."

White-hot anger and oily betrayal flooded Connor, twisting through his body. "No! How could you?"

"You don't know what it's like to have done what I did," his father said. "He was a little boy, a baby boy like you once were. Let him have your shadow so I can make things right."

Connor's lips quivered. A week before, if anyone had asked him who he would have trusted the most in the world, the answer would have been his parents. But now… How could a parent do such a thing?

Surely, you couldn't make something right by hurting someone else. That was why he'd let the cub go. That was why he'd told his mother the truth. What his father asked embodied everything wrong with the Shadowlands, the whole stinking place.

The Thief stepped up beside Connor. The firelight shifted over his body, and as he turned sideways, Connor glimpsed Mouse's face tattooed on his lower back. While the other faces looked horrified and scared, rage twisted Mouse's face. So, she had lost her shadow, Connor thought. She was beyond his help. Despair filled Connor's heart. Quiet was lost to the work lines at the quarry. Mouse had lost her shadow, and his father...

"You can't think solely of yourself," the Thief said. "If you give me your shadow, I'll help your father find the boy he killed. And I'll help Journeyman get what he needs for his son. You'll be fine. You'll be Shadowless, but is that so bad? You'll miss it at first, but soon, it won't matter to you at all. Not an enormous price to pay to know you made others happy. That you made your father happy."

Connor wanted to shout back at the Thief, to refuse, but how could he refuse his father? Wouldn't he give anything for his father? Shouldn't a son give anything for his father?

Connor's father said nothing, but he leaned forward where he stood, his face pleading, desperate. There was so much pain there. It hurt Connor to see his father in such pain. He couldn't imagine the burden the man must feel to have taken the life of a child. Looking at him tore Connor in two. He opened his mouth. He was going to say yes. To agree. For his father.

Then, for the first time since he'd come through the skylight, he looked at Journeyman. Really looked at him. What he saw in the man's face shut the boy's mouth.

The gray-haired man's eyes, smoldering with more than the flickering orange light of the small fire, were fixed on Connor's father. The muscles of their sockets quivered; his upper lip trembled. His hands were balled into tight fists at his sides. The hatred Journeyman bore for Connor's father was unmistakable.

Connor understood. Journeyman would do anything for his son: hurt, betray, maybe even kill. But he would never ask his son to do the same for him. Journeyman was willing to do what he did because of his absolute love for his son, while Connor's father was acting out of love for himself. It was the most horrible thing he had ever realized in his life.

"No," Connor whispered, his eyes still locked on Journeyman. He wanted to look at his father, was desperate to, but he couldn't do it. He didn't know if he could ever do it again.

"I don't think—" the Thief began, but Connor cut him off.

"I said no," he growled. "And now I'll take what's mine."

The Neverborn Thief stepped back, turning to face Connor. "I was afraid of that," he said.

The Thief's body bulged, as if huge bubbles of shadow were rising to his skin. He bent over with the effort as strange shapes emerged from his lower back and shoulders.

There was one spot, however, that didn't change at all. Or at least it didn't seem to transform with the rest. It was the tattoo of Mouse. The anger melted from her features. She gazed at the door and smiled.

A tremendous shudder rocked the entire house an instant before the door flung wide open. A glowing figure stepped into the entry, enormous with brightness. The entire room rippled as a wave of light slammed the Thief's body back into a mere sliver of its original form. The tattooed faces all burst into expressions of joy.

It was Mouse.

Chapter 29

THE SHADOW FARMS

"**G**ive our shadows back!" Mouse shouted.

The Thief hissed, his body thrusting forward with the force of the eruption. The faces all over his body twisted and fought against their restriction. For a moment, Mouse's tattoo bulged on his back as if trying to pull itself from his skin. However, though Mouse's Shadowless radiance had initially diminished the Thief, his body was already returning to its regular size. The bubbling resumed. Connor cursed the eclipse, knowing the Thief wouldn't have recovered so quickly if he weren't drawing power from it.

Mouse threw her shoulders back and tilted up her chin with confidence as she raised an accusatory finger at The Neverborn Thief.

"My name is Lily," she said. "And you are a cheat and a liar. We will have what belongs to us."

Enormous claws sprouted from the Thief's fingers, and he swatted at the air between him and Mouse. Connor winced, forcing himself not to turn away, even as Mouse stepped closer to their enemy. Was she crazy? He could take her face off.

Instead, Mouse laughed. "Have you forgotten your deal in the quarry?" she said. "You agreed not to hurt me, and you didn't say for how long. You can't do a thing to me unless you'd like to smash rocks for a long, long time."

Connor couldn't help letting out a whooping cheer, even as The Neverborn Thief howled in rage. Mouse had done what he couldn't: trapped the Thief with his words. He crouched and snarled as if he were about to leap at Mouse like an attacking cat. For a split second, Connor was certain the Thief would attack, regardless of the consequences, but then their enemy bolted out the door.

"Come on," Connor said to Mouse, but she didn't move. She remained frozen in place. The strength and confidence she'd exuded seconds earlier seemed to have vanished. In fact, despite still blazing with light, her figure seemed shrunken and deflated.

"Where?" she asked. "Why? Why does it matter?"

For a moment, Connor didn't understand what was wrong with her, but then he remembered what Mosley had said. Being without a shadow forced one to fight to care. And right now, Mouse was losing that fight. It must have taken all she had to get there. Unfortunately, Connor knew he didn't have time to snap her out of it if he didn't want the Thief to get away.

"Go," Journeyman said, pointing out the door.

"But Mouse—" Connor started.

"I'll look after her," Journeyman said. "And your father."

Connor started at the mention of his father. Somehow, he'd almost forgotten he was there. He looked at his dad and found the man he'd once known, once looked up to with every part of his heart, sitting crumpled on the floor. As diminished as Mouse looked in her Shadowless despair, it was nothing compared to how broken his father now was. A great pity overtook him.

"I can't leave them," Connor said.

Journeyman placed a hand on Connor's shoulder. "Yes," he said. "You can."

Connor looked out the door. What stood beyond was an enemy he didn't know he could catch up to again, let alone beat. Here, in this house, there was something of a family. What if he belonged here? What if that was why he could never quite seem to win?

"Your shadow is almost gone," Journeyman said. "When the eclipse ends, and it will end soon, your shadow will lose the last of its strength, and it will belong to the Thief."

So that was it. And that was enough.

Connor took one last look at Mouse. She met his eyes, her gaze floating and confused. Her brow furrowed. She didn't recognize him.

"Ereb?" she said.

"Yes, Luza," Connor said. "I'm going to get the rats out of the corn."

With a grim smile, Connor bolted into the streets of Hallowdell.

He'd only taken a few steps when he realized he didn't know where to run. Shadows filled the streets now in clumps, shoulder to shoulder thick in some places. Where could he look? How was he going to find the Thief among so many?

He tried to scan the faces of the crowd. They all stood still, gazing up into the sky, their forms swelling and bulging with the strength the unnatural night offered them. All of them held rapt smiles on their faces.

All but one.

A shadow stood in the doorway of a small shack, staring at Connor. Although it looked much stronger than it had before, he knew it was the shadow he'd seen lying on the floor of its home, the one who'd asked about his brother and told him the story of Rake. The shadow held up the plastic army man and then pointed at a gap between two of the houses and nodded.

Connor bolted for the gap, grunting a hurried thanks as he passed the shadow and ducked between the two shacks. On the other side, he crossed a street straight into the alley beyond without so much as a glance to either side. He hoped the Thief's priority was distance rather than finding a place to hide.

When the alley ended, Connor left the edge of Hallowdell, his feet pounding the dirt of the open fields. It was so dark beyond, he could see nothing outside the town even as he ran. Was the Thief jetting towards the farms? For all he knew, his target could have dropped into the grass to wait for Connor to sprint by. Connor had no choice but to keep running and hope good luck guided his judgment.

A blazing flash exploded from the ground one hundred yards ahead. In the instant before his vision blotched out, Connor caught a fleeting glimpse of two silhouettes against the strobe. The Neverborn Thief had to be one, so despite being blind, Connor kept his legs pumping. His feet thudded on tufts of petrified grass.

He had almost caught up by the time his vision returned, and though the darkness hung thick over the fields, he made out the motion of the two figures picking themselves up.

"You'll pay for this," Connor heard the Thief say, the rage-wrought voice unmistakable in the gloom.

"Probably," the second shadow said. "But it won't be you I answer to."

Even as he ran, he recognized the thin figure and pinched voice.

Connor skidded to a stop ten feet from where the Thief and Dandrich squared off against each other. Each circled the other on wobbly legs like two exhausted boxers. Dandrich held a baton in each hand. The Neverborn Thief's fingers had sprouted three-inch claws, but both staggered their steps and heaved their breaths. Apparently, both suffered the effects of the flash. With the darkness of the eclipse so deep, the light must have been devastating to both.

"Your kind will ruin us all," Dandrich said.

The Neverborn Thief laughed. "You've made the wrong enemies," he said. "The Shadower won't forget your meddling."

"Nor will he forget your failure," Dandrich said.

"I don't fail."

Suddenly, the Thief grew enormous. His height more than doubled, his arms growing massive and muscular. A huge scorpion tail with a blade as long as a sword for a stinger sprouted from the base of his spine. Dandrich, too, transformed, her height shooting up, her once gaunt arms becoming as thick as steel girders in a blink.

The Thief advanced with furious speed. Hissing and spitting with each swing, his clawed hands bore down on Dandrich as she beat his attacks aside with her batons. She retreated under the onslaught, her hands a blur as she knocked aside blow after blow. Connor drew his weapon, desperate to help, but he knew the flash would blind them both. If the Thief kept attacking, it would be all too possible for one of the vicious hits to land. Dandrich's back leg buckled as if her foot landed wrong, and she dropped onto one knee. She crossed her batons over her head where they caught both the Thief's blows in their intersection. For a split second, Connor was certain the rods would break. Her arms seemed to give under the impact.

Then, the former officer thrust forward and upward. The Neverborn Thief's arms flew up and out, and Dandrich drove her baton into his chest with all her weight behind it. The strike lurched the Thief's body up as if he were about to fly through the air.

Connor opened his mouth to cheer, but as he did, his lungs sucked a deep breath of fear. Despite how hard The Neverborn Thief had been struck, the scorpion tail bolted forward and then downward, arcing over Dandrich's head and inward. The blade pierced the officer between the shoulder blades. It burst from between her ribs before yanking her up into the air over the Thief's head.

With a snap, the tail launched Dandrich towards Connor. She crashed to the ground two feet from him. She sputtered and gasped, coughing up wet black liquid onto the dirt. Connor could only imagine it was blood.

The Neverborn Thief faced Connor, his tail snapping back into a striking position. Connor brandished his weapon but didn't have time to pop the cover off the switch before the Thief turned and ran, leaving Connor dumbfounded. If the Thief could beat Dandrich, he could tear Connor apart. He wanted nothing more than to turn and run back to Hallowdell, back to Gissu, all the way back to where his closet had left him on the Nightglass road. He didn't have a chance. What was he thinking?

But the Thief had run. Ran away. There had to be something he knew about Connor that he himself didn't. There had to be a chance.

Dandrich's voice, rasping and deathly, snapped him into action.

"Bring him down," she said, and then she fell still. Whether dead or spent, Connor had no idea. Nor did he wait to figure it out. He took off running after his enemy.

It was difficult to see The Neverborn Thief as he tore over the crisp grass. Connor drew his breath in long, even gasps as he followed. Remembering his days playing soccer, he knew it was more important to adopt an endurance pace rather than sprinting to catch up. If he ran full out, he'd find himself exhausted and breathless when the Thief slowed. If there even was a limit to the Thief's strength… Maybe it would run out when the eclipse ended, but if Journeyman was to be believed, it would be too late.

The wind pulled the sweat off Connor's face. He felt exhilarated as he hopped a low fence marking a division between fields. To his right, he heard a hollow lowing, and with a glance, he spotted several dark shapes milling about in the field, the shadows of cattle.

Ahead, rose a house surrounded by a thicket of trees. The Thief veered towards it, charging straight towards a hedge ringing the house's yard.

A sudden shout echoed through the darkness, followed by a loud crack. The Thief dove behind the bushes, but Connor kept running, seeing his chance to catch up. A second bang came, and a clot of dirt burst from the ground in front of him, pelting his face with stinging pebbles. His feet went out from under him, and he pitched forward, sliding through the sharp grass.

Connor had never heard a gunshot before, but he knew what the bang had been.

He was being shot at.

There was a flash from the front of the house as a third shot fired, tearing into the field a few feet to Connor's left.

"I'll shoot you both," a voice called into the night from the darkened eave of the farmhouse. "You get yourselves gone and don't you dream of touching my cattle!"

Hunched behind the bushes only twenty feet from Connor, the Thief looked back at him and laughed.

"So close," he said. "You could practically reach out and touch me."

Another shot fired, but this time there was no blast of dirt. Connor suspected the farmer fired into the air. It was almost maddening to be so close to the Thief and pinned down. For a moment, he wondered why the Thief was laughing, then realized a Caster made a much easier target than a shadow. He considered pulling out the obsidian blanket to camouflage himself and crawl toward the Thief, but there was no way he could confront the Thief with the farmer shooting at them.

"I don't want your cattle," Connor shouted towards the farmer with all the volume he could muster while lying down. "I'm trying to catch a Thief."

"I don't care if you're one of the Thirteen after the Eater of Light," the farmer shouted. "You have ten seconds to get yourself off my land before I put a dozen bullets in you."

The Thief stood and smiled. "That's our cue," he said. "Let the game resume." And then he was off.

Connor scrambled to his feet and into another run. He tossed several glances towards the passing farmhouse, but couldn't see the farmer in the darkness, nor were any other shots fired.

The house now behind him, Connor kept on the Thief's trail, the distance closing. He ran and ran and ran. How long could The Neverborn Thief keep going? Connor had spent a lot of summers and afternoons running for sports, but the eclipse tipped the advantage in the Thief's favor. A distinct burn invaded his calves. His chest felt like it couldn't expand large enough to hold the breath he needed.

When he sprang over the next fence, Connor's foot caught on the top bar, nearly sending him falling flat on his face. He pinwheeled his arms. His feet shuffled desperately to keep under the forward weight of his momentum. The effort to keep from falling seemed to tax his muscles in those few seconds far beyond the running. One thing became clear: though he was hardly fifteen feet away, he would be spent by the time he caught up with the Thief.

Then Connor saw something different about the open field ahead. A wide, winding trail of darkness weaved through it, curving into their path like a road. But not a road, he realized. A river. The Shadowrun.

The Neverborn Thief shifted his path parallel to the water, and Connor changed his path to intercept. Because his path was diagonal, the distance closed rapidly. As he fell back into step behind the Thief, they were only a couple of feet apart. Connor could almost reach out and grab hold of the shadow's swinging arms.

Further down the Shadowrun, the river widened abruptly, then disappeared as if into nothingness. A churning sound welled into the surrounding night. The air itself grew damp and misty. Connor didn't have to see it to know they were headed towards a waterfall.

When they reached the cliff, there would be nowhere for The Neverborn Thief to run except over the edge. Connor knew he had him. There was nowhere else the chase could go.

Then, the Thief did the unthinkable.

Without so much as breaking stride, he leapt off the cliff's edge into the open air.

Connor's right foot plunged over the edge. His left foot followed; his body surrounded by sudden space. For a split second, it seemed as if he were suspended motionless in the air as his jump reached its crest. He didn't know what lay below. Water? Rocks? Would he splash down or be smashed apart?

Everything blurred as he plunged toward darkness. He barely had time to look down and realize all he could see was blackness before disappearing below the surface of the fall pool. Connor's entire body was jolted by the impact and sudden embrace of the cold blackwater.

The turbulence of the waterfall in the depths of the basin spun Connor about as he thrashed his arms and kicked his feet. His eyes were open, but he saw nothing. Froth and bubbles burst against his cheeks and hands.

Then, air poured over his face as his head broke the surface. He treaded water, trying to get his bearings, scanning the water for the shore and The Neverborn Thief. He spotted them both as the Thief swam to the basin's edge.

As Connor started swimming, he was slowed because he still clutched Dandrich's flashlight. He had forgotten he'd been holding it. Now he gripped it so tightly, it might as well have been part of his hand. Would it still work after being submerged?

The Neverborn Thief reached the shallows and crawled onto the muddy basin shore. He turned onto his back once he'd dragged himself from the water. When Connor found his feet hitting the ground, he advanced with his flashlight aimed at the Thief, the cover off the trigger, his finger poised to press.

"Running is over," Connor said, his chest heaving, water streaming down his face from his hair, his clothes drenched and heavy. Despite his exhaustion, an exhilarated strength surged through him. This was it. He was about to end it.

"Not bad for such a Little Bit," the Thief said, pulling himself to his feet. The Thief, too, was breathless. "A fun little chase, but what now?"

Connor gestured with Dandrich's flashlight.

"Indeed," the Thief said. "An effective weapon. Lay me right out on this shore if it still works. It'll hurt, sure, but it won't kill me. It won't make me give you anything."

Connor's courage faltered. He still had no idea how he could force The Neverborn Thief to do anything. How could he get the shadow out? Connor thought about the shadow blade tucked in his bag, but having seen the Thief and Dandrich fight, he knew the knife would be worthless. He needed to think. He needed time to think, but he didn't have any.

The Thief nodded. "I bet you never figured out what to do once you caught me. You had your little weapon, your little surprise Mouse, but nothing can stop the Neverborn from getting what they want. Your quest was failed from the start."

Connor's hand wobbled around the flashlight as his heart crashed in his chest. Was the Thief right? Was there nothing he could do? What if the only choice was to make a deal? Could he make a deal with someone so openly evil and hateful? Dandrich had said he had to trick him, but not only did Connor have no clue how he'd do it, but something at the back of his mind told him it wouldn't be right to do so. He wasn't sure how it mattered against someone like The Neverborn Thief, but if he won through deception, he'd be exactly like any other shadow.

"And did you stop and think," the Thief continued, his form starting to bulge and bubble all over again. "What I could do to you? I can't kill you, but I can torment you until you die and return to the World of Light."

A hideous, gloating chuckle escaped the Thief's lips as he stepped towards Connor, a chuckle so evil it seemed to suck the little light left in the Shadowlands into the darkness. The Neverborn Thief's form exploded in size to ten times that of a giant. The behemoth let out a bellow. Its mouth opened wide and swooped down toward Connor.

Everything in him told him to dive to the side, but in a flash, Connor knew exactly what he must do. Utter darkness enveloped him like nothing he'd ever experienced.

THE HEART OF NEVERBORN

D rip.
Drip.
Drip.

Blackness all around. Drops fell into unseen pools, plinking and echoing. Somewhere far off, metal groaned, a sound like a dump truck bed tilting. Somewhere nearby, a soft, breathy sobbing. A damp smell hung in the cold, still air. Connor shivered. Something in his head spun.

The ground beneath him was cold, hard, and damp; wet stone, or at least it felt like wet stone. He groped blindly for the flashlight weapon, his fingers immersing into shallow puddles, his palms pressing contoured rock.

Where am I? Connor wondered. *Inside the Thief?*

If he was inside the Thief's mouth or belly, wouldn't things be soft

271

and squishy and probably smelly, like Connor imagined his own insides to be?

The drips continued.

The sobs continued. Who was sobbing? Who was in here with him?

"Hello?" Connor said. He tried to whisper, but his voice echoed all around, amplifying it.

The sobbing ceased. No answer came. Only more drips.

At the same time, all was not total darkness, and the spinning in his head seemed to slow. Blotches of faint light scattered across the ground. Puddles, he realized. They glowed a dim, cool blue. Though not as bright, their light reminded him of the Venus flytrap pool he and Mouse had stumbled upon in Blackwood. His body tensed, and he rose to his feet.

Whatever had been sobbing cried out. There was a splash of puddles as it moved away from Connor.

"I'm not going to hurt you," Connor whispered.

A soft whimper followed, and though Connor squinted, he still couldn't make out its source. However, his eyes adjusted, and the walls of the surrounding space took form. They gave off less light than the puddles, but they, too, were wet, and so also glowed faintly.

He was in some sort of cave, a cul-de-sac encased in stone. A tunnel vanished into the darkness on one side. Stubby stalactites and stalagmites extended in clusters from the ceiling and floor, respectively. It was from them that the drips fell. The water trickled in from unseen cracks. From the center of the clusters, rusted chains hung nearly to the floor. The whimpering thing was tethered to one of those chains.

A shadow…

Connor still couldn't make it out well, but judging by its size, it had to be rather young. Or, he thought, remembering Quiet, at least it had entered the Shadowlands rather young. It sat with its knees drawn to its chest, its arms locked around its legs, its face upright. He suspected its face had been buried in the arms before he'd spoken.

"Who are you?" Connor asked.

The shadow sniffled. One of its arms fell away from its legs, and it wiped its eyes with the back of its hand.

"We don't know," the shadow said. "We didn't think of it too much until we found ourselves here."

Connor cocked his head at how strangely the shadow spoke. He'd seen movies and read stories where kings and queens referred to themselves as "we," but he'd never heard someone talk that way. Perhaps this shadow had been chained here so long, it had gone crazy. He could see that happening to anyone who spent any length of time anywhere in the Shadowlands, let alone a place as dismal as this.

"Do you have a name?" Connor asked.

"I think of myself as Alexander," the shadow said. "It was the first name our mother thought to call us by."

Something about the way the shadow said "our mother" nagged at Connor and so did the name, but he dismissed the thoughts. He needed to know where he was and how to get out. And whether he was in any immediate danger.

"Is there anyone else here?"

"Sometimes," the shadow said, rocking back and forth. "Sometimes chained, sometimes not. We weren't alone long before you came, and he is always here somewhere, even when he doesn't seem to be."

Connor immediately knew "he" must mean the Thief. If so, he knew what the shadow meant when he said, "our mother." His mother once told him different names she and his father had considered. Alexander had been one of them.

Connor stepped closer and inspected the shadow's face in the dim light. He tried to see himself in the dark features, but it didn't exactly look like the self he saw in the mirror. It seemed like those eyes and cheeks were hung with heavy weight. Every curve held a burden. Every muscle trembled with strain. Did he simply never really look closely? Was this what other people saw when they looked at him?

Was this what his mom saw when they sat together at breakfast?

Was this what he saw on his mom's face every day?

Connor reached out and placed a hand on the shadow's shoulder. It was cold and damp. The tremors he saw in its face were even stronger in its frame.

"You're me, aren't you?" Connor asked.

"Not you," the shadow said. "Just a part, the part that the Thief managed to get away with. Not even enough to be a whole."

The shadow broke down in fresh tears, burying its face in its arms. Connor fell to his knees in front of it, wrapping his hands around its back and pulling it close.

"Don't cry," Connor said. "We're here together."

"Can't help it," the shadow bawled. "Our father is dead, and he betrayed us. Everyone betrays us. And if they don't betray us, they fail at helping us. Dandrich is dead. Quiet is a prisoner. Mouse is gone. Our mother can't protect us, can't even spend time with us. You never even really knew I existed. And now we're trapped here until he sells us off."

Connor didn't know what to say. It brought tears to his eyes to hear out loud the very things that nearly drove him to despair so many times on his journey. The hope and exhilaration he'd felt while pursuing the Thief fled, and he wept.

His arms around his shadow, around himself, Connor felt the same dread he'd felt when he stepped onto the chair under the noose in the Foreman's office. It was most likely the same fear Mosley felt when he mounted his gallows.

Somewhere far off, metal on metal cried again.

The sound jarred something in Connor's mind. Mosley. Mosley had said shadows were the dark parts of the one who cast them. His shadow would be no different, focused on the horrible things. What about the good? What about how close he and his mother had been after he'd told her the truth? What about how Dandrich had been willing to sacrifice herself for what was right? What about how he felt about Mouse, and how much she'd inspired him to be strong?

Connor understood how he couldn't be complete without his shadow. Without him, his shadow could only fall into despair; it needed the hope he brought to see things clearly. On the other hand, without an awareness of how things could go wrong, how could he ever make the right choices without hurting himself or others?

"We'll get through this," Connor whispered. "We're going to get out of here."

Shoulders still trembling, his shadow raised his head and met Connor's gaze. Then, its eyes flicked to the chain. The chain itself was thick with rust, and though Connor wasn't sure where the impulse came from, he grasped the chain in both hands and twisted. It broke clean through almost effortlessly. Particles of the dust flaked onto his fingers. His shadow's eyes widened, and the smallest smile crept onto its lips.

"Now, let's see about getting out of here." Connor rose to his feet and looked around the cave, his eyes falling on the tunnel. "Speaking of getting out, where the heck are we?"

His shadow reached a hand up, and Connor took it, pulling Alexander to his feet. Connor felt a bit odd thinking about his shadow with another name, but it was easier to understand than the fact he was pulling himself up.

"Him," Alexander said. "We're inside him. In his mind, in the place where he keeps the shadows he steals."

Connor didn't like that answer at all. It wasn't surprising; he'd let the Thief swallow him because, in the moment before it happened, he'd realized it to be the only way to get inside the Thief. But getting out of The Neverborn Thief's mind sounded harder than escaping his stomach.

"Will this tunnel lead us out?"

"Don't know," Alexander said. "I assumed it leads deeper."

"Joy," Connor said. He stepped towards the tunnel, his shadow falling in step behind him. The motion seemed so completely natural Connor felt like himself for the first time since it all began.

Ahead, the path vanished into darkness, but as he squinted, a brighter glow at the other end revealed a bend at the edge of sight.

Connor crept forward, stepping as softly as he could. But every scrape of the soles of his shoes on the damp, dirty ground echoed. He'd hardly taken ten steps before there was no doubt that, if something lay ahead, there would be no sneaking up on it. Of course, the Thief already knew he was there. The thought was freeing. Connor had been crouched and tentative, but now he stood straight and simply walked.

His shadow was another matter. Ten steps behind him, Alexander hadn't budged an inch.

"Come on," Connor said. "We don't have much time."

"We don't have enough time, you mean," Alexander said.

Connor rolled his eyes. Part of him wondered whether this was what it was like for his mother when he didn't want to do something.

"You know, you're kind of a drag," Connor said.

"And that's surprising?" his shadow said. "You've been dragging me around your whole life."

Connor groaned. He didn't have time for his shadow's resentment. "Apologies later." He strode back to his shadow and pulled him by the hand. His shadow complied without complaint.

When they reached the bend, Connor saw the source of the light. Ahead, the tunnel widened like the body of a snake with a large mouse in it, and on the left side of the bulge, there was a window partially blocked by chains and cobwebs that seemed to have grown from the cavern wall. Grown inside the Thief, Connor reminded himself. He couldn't forget where he was. Perhaps the dark, winding cavern around him was meant to make him afraid of the dark, afraid of being lost.

The pair approached the window, but even as they did, the cave wall changed. Threads of stone grew from the window's frame, weaving and crisscrossing. Connor barely had time to toss a glimpse into it before it had sewn itself shut.

Through the window, lay a room. The walls were striped yellow and green. A large crib stood in the center. There was a large forest green chair beside the crib and a banner on the wall over it. Connor couldn't read the banner's bold letters. There seemed to be something wrong with them, and the opening had closed before he could process what. Connor grabbed at the seam where the gap had been and tried to squeeze his fingers into it, but the threads that had closed it were actually made of stone. His fingers wouldn't penetrate even a fraction of an inch. Connor cursed.

His shadow tugged at his hand, and when Connor turned, Alexander was pointing at the wall on the other side. Another window had opened, and this one wasn't closing. Connor stepped up to it.

He was looking into the interior of a car. It was dark through the windshield, with only headlights illuminating a misty night that glinted off the orange reflectors on the road lines. Stores and restaurants rushed by on either side, and the dials on the dash glowed a ghostly white. Connor pressed to the window, and he gasped as he recognized the profile of his father. Tears rolled down his flushed cheek. He bit his lower lip. A blues song trailed out of the tinny speakers.

Connor yelled at the windowpane. His father's eyes flicked from the road, and his head turned to the side as if he heard.

The front of the car veered over the yellow line. Two bright lights flared ahead, directly in his father's path. Connor yelled again, pointing at the road, but his father's head turned even further as if searching for the source of the sound. The blaze of the headlights filled the entire window with pure white. Then the window was gone, and total darkness returned. Connor's eyes filled with green blotches from the light's intensity.

What had happened? Had he seen the car accident that had killed his father and the boy? Had it somehow happened because he'd distracted his father? What if his father had heard him? What if that was why he lost control of the car?

Connor shook his head and rubbed his eyes as if to wipe away both the thoughts and the smudges in his vision. As his eyes began to register the dim light of the tunnel again, he told himself it was impossible he'd caused the crash. The accident had already happened; things didn't work that way. The guilt he'd felt had to be what the Thief wanted him to feel. It was the only explanation.

At the same time, Connor remembered what his mom had said; his father had been afraid he was going to lose his job. If he'd lost his job, he wouldn't have been able to take care of Connor. Was that what had upset him so much? If so, could it really have been his fault?

Connor's vision noticed his shadow, and he realized he couldn't let himself think such thoughts. Those were his shadow's thoughts. His shadow let out a desperate sob and kicked the ground with its heel. Connor needed to press on, and now he felt he was better armed. Apparently, the Thief could show him things to disturb him, and he needed to prepare himself for what else he might see.

Connor took a deep breath and took his shadow by the arm. His steps seemed to slosh… He set his foot down in a depression that soaked his shoe and sock. The cave had grown brighter, and the entire floor was covered in a thin pool of glowing water.

A black cloud was mixing into the glowing liquid, like spilled ink. A strange, metallic smell wafted in on a cool, damp breeze, and it sent a shiver through his body. Was it the wind or the Thief's breath?

A distant cough drifted in on the shoulders of the draft. Connor cocked his head and waited without breathing. A moment later, the cough came again, weak but thick, the way his own coughs had sounded when he'd had pneumonia a few years before. What was it this time?

As Connor started into the tunnel to investigate further, cold and wet invaded his ankles. The water had risen over the tops of his shoes. Though still glowing, the water was now a murky black throughout. An inch-deep surge flowed over the surface, followed by another a few feet apart. From down the tunnel, a slow churn almost like waves echoed. There was no mistaking it. The water was rising.

Connor picked up his pace. Within ten yards, the water was up to his calves. The tunnel ahead wound out of sight. The churning grew steadily louder. By the time he reached the next bend, the water was up to his knees, and all he could see down the path was more water and another bend. What if the water kept getting deeper before he reached the exit? At this rate, it would only be a couple of minutes before he was submerged, trapped in the subterranean passage like a drowning earthworm.

Connor pumped his legs hard against the deepening water, each step taking more effort until he slowed to a jog with the water up to his waist, his hips thrusting against the resisting liquid.

It was then he realized he'd let go of his shadow. He turned and saw Alexander standing about twenty yards back, his hands thrust into his pockets, his head down. What was he waiting for? The shadow dropped to his knees. Connor yelped. What would happen if his shadow drowned?

He took a step back, but as he did, a loud rush came from around the next bend. Connor looked over his shoulder. A wall of water as high as himself rushed down the passage. It crashed into him moments later, knocking him off his feet and sending him spinning against the wall of the cavern. His head struck stone.

He sat up in bed with a jolt. His blanket, which had been pulled up over his shoulder, fell to his waist. Sweat drenched him. His head pounded more fiercely than he'd ever felt. His body throbbed and ached with every twitch of his muscles. He was terribly sick, and his thoughts were muddled.

Images of the cavern passed through his mind, mingling with a blur of himself in school earlier that day; or had it been a couple days? He couldn't be sure. He saw himself staggering down the hallway towards the nurse's office. In his confusion, he'd reached out for the nearest doorknob and twisted. The room he opened was dark, but he could make out mops and brooms and buckets and cleaners even as his legs went out from under him and he collapsed. He remembered himself sitting on the floor across from a young Pale Boy, reaching for the spinner on the Game of Life, the strength going out of his arm as he gripped the plastic piece, his body falling over the board, the Pale Boy crying out in shock.

He was terribly sick, and his thoughts were muddled. One thought, however, stood out from the rest.

Where was his mom?

Weak as he was, he dragged his legs off the side of the bed. He poured himself to the floor, like the sweat pouring down his back and forehead. Shivering viciously from the fever, he pulled the blanket off his bed and wrapped it over his shoulders. He trudged towards the bedroom door. The hallway passed in a blur, and he crossed the living room into the kitchen, hardly aware of anything.

His mother flitted about the kitchen like a bird arranging its nest. She washed a dish and then scurried over to the trashcan to toss a crumpled paper towel. She paused to grab her coffee mug and bring it to her lips only to cough and sputter at the first sip. Dark patches encircled her eyes, which appeared sunken like two marbles sitting in little bowls. She coughed again as she pulled a curler from her hair and continued buttoning up her blouse.

On the kitchen table sat a plate holding a half-eaten bagel—a disorder of papers covered every other inch. As Connor shambled closer, he realized they were bills, some stamped "Past Due" or "Second Notice" in red. A racking spasm of coughs doubled his mother over. When she finished, she looked up and met his eyes.

"Hey baby," she said, her voice harsh and raspy from whatever cluttered her chest. "I'm sorry, but I've got to go to work. Double shift today. I've missed too many days caring for you, and if I don't go back now, they'll fire me. And if I don't work a double, I won't make the mortgage. I've got all your meals labeled in the fridge for you. Ms. Crowley next door will stop by at lunchtime and dinnertime to make sure you're fed."

"But Mom," Connor said, his voice almost sounding foreign, it was so dry and thin. "I'm sick."

"I know, dear," his mom said. "But if I don't go today, I don't know how we're gonna make it. I already don't know how we're gonna make it, how I can keep going."

His mother coughed again, hard. She tried to cover her mouth with her hand, but it was too late to stop a blast of spittle and phlegm from spraying Connor's face.

"This isn't right," he said, wiping his face.

"I know it's not, sweetie," she said, drawing him into an embrace. "I know it's not."

Connor reached to hug back, but realized he felt nothing of her embrace. This isn't right, he thought again, and then again; but the last time, it was different. No. This wasn't right. This wasn't the way things were. Even in his mother's clutch, he could see the ground. Only a sliver of his shadow remained.

He pushed his mother back forcefully, a sudden anger swelling within him. Her eyes were full of hurt. How dare the Thief make him see this?

"But, baby…"

"No," Connor said. "I'm not here. I'm in the Thief."

And with that, his home was gone. He was standing in a new room. In front of him stood a crib, once a dark, brown wood, but now covered in dust so thick it looked like the fuzz on a wool sweater. There was a short, flat-topped dresser to his left with a strange foam pad on top, and to his right was a plush rocking chair so long unused, Connor couldn't tell where the fabric ended, and the dust began. There was a door, but it was shut. There was no seam between it and the frame.

A banner hung over the crib: "Welcome Home."

Connor stared at the banner for several moments until it dawned on him.

This was The Neverborn Thief's bedroom. Or rather, what the Thief wished had been its bedroom. He was Neverborn. All he wanted was a room like this, to have been born into the light. Pity filled Connor's heart. He thought of his bedroom—of how much he had, even if he often thought he had so little.

A small sob from behind him turned him around. There sat his shadow, again with its knees drawn to its eyes. However, his shadow looked insubstantial, faint, almost transparent—much the same way Tonic had in the brilliant light of the lava pool at the quarry. His shadow's time was almost up.

Connor's mind raced. What could he do to help? Was there some way he could strengthen it? Could he rejoin it to himself? That was the likely answer, but he had no idea how to go about it. He'd already touched his shadow multiple times.

He considered how he'd gotten to this room from the false version of his kitchen. He'd simply willed it. If he pictured his shadow as his own again, would it work? The more he thought about it, the more certain he became.

Half to himself, he said to his shadow, "Alexander, can I rejoin with you? Can I make it happen just by thinking it?"

His shadow sniffled and looked up. Then, he nodded.

"We're inside the Thief's mind," his shadow said. "Thoughts are the only thing with power here."

Connor pressed his lips together. He had what he needed. He closed his eyes and tried to clear his mind to focus, but something in him hesitated.

Could it be so easy? Why would the Thief put him right next to his shadow? Why would he show him the things he had if those very things would teach him how to win his shadow back? It was possible the Thief couldn't control these things. Maybe he'd underestimated Connor's ability to figure it out.

The image of Mosley's hanging came to mind. Aside from his robbery in the darkness of his bedroom, it was the only time he'd seen a shadow actually taken. There was more to the hanging than a simple public spectacle. What if it was necessary? What if the whole shadow had to be taken at once? What if that was why The Neverborn Thief had allowed Quiet to overhear him at the quarry? What if he needed Connor to come?

It all became clear as he remembered hanging. When he'd negotiated with the Thief, the Thief had offered to give back Mouse's shadow. The Neverborn Thief had played it off as a trick, but if Connor had been smarter in making the deal, he might have been able to force it. What if doing so had helped The Neverborn Thief as well?

Of course, Connor knew that would mean they'd been wrong about how one lost their shadow to begin with. But even that made sense to him. Everyone thought the shadow simply became weaker with each return to the World of Light until it eventually vanished. But who was ever there the moment the shadow was taken? The only witness would be the victim, if they even saw it happen at all. In fact, Connor realized, most people probably didn't interrupt the theft like he had.

He looked his shadow square in its eyes and said, "You're a trap."

An enormous sob burst from his shadow.

"Yes," his shadow said, then began repeating that single word, rocking back and forth, burying its face in its arms.

Fresh anger welled inside Connor. How could his shadow try to betray him? How could he not have told him the truth the moment they'd met in the cavern? If he had known, he would have left his shadow. He drew his leg back to give his shadow a hard kick but faltered. Doing so would solve nothing.

Instead, Connor tilted his head back and called out, "You're failing. You hear me? There's nothing you can do to make me join back with my shadow."

Silence answered.

"Damn you," Connor shouted, and kicked the leg of the crib. A puff of dust rose from the frame, and his eyes fell to a spot on the crib's mattress. It was a strange spot, far less dusty than the rest. It was almost as if something had sat there until only recently.

Connor didn't have time to think about it, however. A strange new sob came to his ears. For an instant, he assumed it came from his shadow before realizing it came from the walls, the ceiling, and the floor all at once. It was from The Neverborn Thief.

A drip fell onto the back of Connor's hand. He glanced down. A thick and viscous black stain sat on his skin. He lifted it to his nose. It smelled coppery.

He looked up to where it had fallen from. A spot spread across the ceiling. More drips bulged their way through, and a similar spot appeared at the top of one wall. Black liquid now ran down the faded yellow and green wallpaper as stains multiplied. Soon, the walls all streamed with the fluid, pouring from the ceiling to the floor, the pools spreading everywhere.

A chunk of ceiling fell, heavy with the weight of the liquid. One wall began to disintegrate, leaving an empty void of blackness that gushed forth, blasting everything in its path. Entire walls came down.

The ceiling collapsed.

THE GAME ENDS

Just as everything rushed at Connor, intending to both crush and engulf him, he was no longer there. Instead, he stood on the rocks at the edge of the fall pool. The Thief stood in front of him, back to normal size. Connor's backpack sat at his feet, and the flashlight was in the mud between the stones. He picked up the weapon and aimed it at the Neverborn Thief, who wore a dazed expression.

"It's over," Connor said.

"Never," the Thief said. "I'll eat you again and again until you give up your shadow."

"Not going to happen," Connor said. "I know how the place in your mind works. I know how to escape it."

"You think that matters? I'll never give back your shadow. And if you still have it when the Shadower's agent arrives, he'll simply take it from you. The Shadower never fails to get what he wants."

"I don't think that will be very good for you," Connor said.

"Maybe not, but eternity will end before I stop trying," the Thief said. "And there's nothing you can do to make me stop."

As Connor lowered the flashlight, a most peculiar sensation crept up his spine. A slow, rumbling vibration, much like the distant thunder of the falls, filled his body. He watched as the Thief's eyes suddenly flicked from Connor to something behind him. He didn't want to take his eyes off the the Thief, but for some reason, he had to look back.

There, creeping up out of the darkness, were three shadowcats.

The ones on the left and right were large and adult. The one in the center was a fraction of their size. It was the cub and its parents.

Connor smiled as the Thief took a step back. The faces tattooed on the Thief's body cheered silently, their mouths breaking into wide grins that mouthed unheard words of glee and justice. The two adult shadowcats arced off to the sides as if to come at the Thief from both directions. They hissed and snarled viciously. They dragged their claws through the grass.

The cub stepped up beside Connor. Its ears lay back, its body low. It wrapped its tail affectionately around his leg.

Surprise enveloped the Thief's face.

"I think they might find a way to convince you," Connor said. He reached down and scratched the cub's head. For a moment, its growl shifted into a purr. It rubbed against his knee before dropping into an attack crouch.

The Neverborn Thief retreated further, his feet sloshing in the water. His balance wobbled as the rocks shifted beneath him. For a moment, it looked as if he would topple. When he did, Connor knew the cats would be on him.

As he saw that very thing about to unfold in his mind—the cats drawing back to lurch forward like arrows on bowstrings, the Thief's feet sliding out from under him—Connor heard himself calling, "Wait!"

He didn't know if the cats would listen. He didn't even know for sure that his own voice was calling out. He'd not put the slightest bit of thought into what he said. yet he knew it was the right thing to say.

The Neverborn Thief crashed into the water and came up sputtering. He waved his arms, warding off the potential attack, but the cats stayed poised, ready to strike in an instant. They didn't look back at Connor, but their tails waved rapidly, confused. The Thief raised his head from the water. His face contorted in all manner of puzzlement. Connor himself was a little confused.

What he wasn't confused about was this: letting The Neverborn Thief, awful as he was, get torn apart by the shadowcats wouldn't be right. It would give Connor some measure of justice, and it might even get his shadow back, but what would he be losing in the process? He remembered the story the shadow in Hallowdell told him. He would be Rake taking revenge. There could be no questioning how much the Thief would suffer under the claws and teeth of the shadowcats, and Connor didn't want that on his conscience. Only benevolence could take something back in a world so full of fear and betrayal. He found himself thinking of the nursery in the Thief's mind, to the strange, clean spot in the crib where something had once sat.

And now, Connor knew what—or at least what kind of thing—may have sat there.

He tossed aside the flashlight, knelt, and unzipped his bag. He reached in and groped around until his fingers closed around something soft and fuzzy.

He straightened and walked towards the Thief, the teddy bear clutched in both hands. It had been his bear his entire life. His mom had told him he'd slept with it in his crib since he was a toddler.

"I want you to have this," Connor said. "I think you're missing something like it."

The Neverborn Thief's eyes widened like they'd fallen upon the seven cities of gold. "Why?"

"Because I want to make a deal," Connor said. "I'm going to give you what you want."

The Neverborn Thief raised a confused eyebrow, his eyes still locked on the bear. The faces all over the Thief opened their mouths, equally confused. They, too, watched the stuffed animal with avid expectation.

"You're going to give me your shadow?" the Thief said.

"No," Connor said. "I'm going to give you what you really want."

The bear passed from Connor's hands to the Thief's.

"I always wanted something like this." The Thief turned the bear over in his hands. "Was promised."

"By whom?"

"The Shadower," the Neverborn Thief whispered. "He said I can have one once I've given him the shadows he needs."

Connor crouched beside the Thief and rested a hand on his shoulder. The tattooed faces all softened and began to weep.

"The Shadower thought he knew what you wanted," Connor said. "But I'm going to give you what you really want."

"And what is that?" the Thief whispered.

Silence hung in the air as the first ray of sunlight broke free from the interfering moon. The light shined directly upon them, sparkling off the lake and bringing even the dull color out of the petrified grass.

Connor drew a deep breath. "Neverborn Thief," he said, "I give you your name. I name you Connor Brighton's Shadow."

The Neverborn Thief's mouth dropped open as if he were about to scream. Then the corners of his mouth spread upward—not into a hideous grin, but an expression of pure joy. Tears leapt from the Thief's eyes as he tilted his head back and let the light of the sun bathe his face in its glow.

A great wind rushed about the shore, swirling around them. The Thief's tattooed faces came to life in a new way. His skin bulged and stretched like when he'd transformed, but this time it was different. It wasn't The Neverborn Thief changing, but the tattoos. Their cheeks rounded and protruded. Their lips etched into deep lines, then parted into smiles. Soon, dozens of heads sprouted up and down the Thief's body, pulling and twisting against whatever confined them. An arm popped out, then another and another. The Thief wept silently, his face frozen in an expression of ecstasy as full torsos writhed from his body.

Moments later, a crowd of about thirty shadows stood around the Thief. They parted as one stepped to the front. Though he'd never seen her in this form, Connor knew the shadow belonged to Mouse.

"Thank you," she said, running up to Connor and throwing her arms around him. She kissed him on both his cheeks as she held him tight. "Thank you, thank you, thank you. Nothing can say how much this means, how much your sacrifice means."

For a split second, Connor wondered what she meant by sacrifice, but deep down, he already knew. As innocent as he was at his core, innocent enough to be moved by a simple stuffed animal, the Thief was a twisted soul carrying awful burdens from all the things he'd done, all the hate and anger that had enveloped him his entire existence. It would be as Mr. Paxter said about why he wouldn't take on his twin's shadow. But unlike Mr. Paxter, Connor wasn't afraid to take on such a burden. He would manage somehow. No matter what, seeing the gratitude on the faces of the shadows told him he'd done the right thing. True sacrifice could only come at the expense of the self, not another. That was where his father had been wrong.

Mouse released Connor from her embrace. "There's only one thing left to do," she said. "And then we can all go home."

She pointed to The Neverborn Thief.

Connor strode straight up to him.

"I never imagined..." the Thief started, but Connor shook his head.

"I know," Connor said, then threw his arms around the Thief. In his mind's eye, he imagined the shadow before him as his own. He didn't simply picture it; he let himself know it in his heart. The cold wind kicked up anew, but a strange heat erupted between Connor and the Thief. A bright light seemed to radiate around them, like a protective shell.

Then it was gone.

And so, too, was The Neverborn Thief.

In the renewed light of the sun, Connor could see his full shadow stretching away from his body.

AND WHAT FOLLOWED

The strange feeling that something was missing disappeared. Connor became acutely aware of the coolness of the wind and the faint warmth that came from the shadow sun. The rumble of the waterfall swelled in his ears. The oily scent of the blackwater flooded his nostrils. He could taste its mist coating his tongue and the insides of his mouth. As the shadowcat cub rubbed against his leg, he was both fully aware of the strength of the vibrations of its purr and the soft heat its body radiated.

The cluster of shadows he'd freed chattered excitedly. Several stepped towards Connor. A couple of them bowed. Others shook his hand or patted him on the back. They offered a frenzy of thanks, disappearing one by one as they did.

It all passed in a blur as Connor tried to process what had happened. He'd done it. He'd defeated the Thief and completed his shadow. In the process, he'd freed all the shadows the Thief had recently stolen. The only real triumphs Connor had ever known were winning a board game, a soccer game, or getting a good grade. None of that compared to how he felt now. He was growing, and for some reason, he felt a sort of radiance surrounding himself, much like Mouse when she'd appeared so bright while interrupting the confrontation in the house in Hallowdell.

Mouse's shadow was the second-to-last of the shadows to come up and thank him. She drew him into another embrace. As they held each other, she whispered, "I'll find you. In the World of Light, I'll find you."

While in his friend's arms, Connor realized two things. First, they were both weeping. He could feel Mouse's warm, wet tears pressing against his cheek. He could also feel her embrace in a way he never had before. Though he'd always known he was touching a shadow by the way they forced his body to move, his skin to compress, he'd never truly felt it. Now, he felt the warmth of Mouse's shadow's body against his, and it was wonderful.

"I guess this makes us a lot like Luza and Ereb," Connor said.

"Yes," she whispered, burrowing her face into his neck. "Yes, it does."

Suddenly, Connor's arms passed through Mouse and he embraced nothing. She and the other shadows he freed were gone except for one. His own shadow remained. It looked upon him with a profound sadness, its eyes trembling, its lips quivering. Connor had been so swept up in the exchange with the Thief he'd almost forgotten what he'd been fighting for. A terrible guilt struck him as he realized he didn't have room for two shadows.

"How could you abandon me?" his shadow said. "How can you leave me in this place?"

Connor ran his fingers through his hair and looked down at his feet. "I'm sorry," he said. "I didn't realize this would happen."

"Of course, it's what would happen," his shadow said. "If you'd taken a moment to think about the consequences..."

His shadow's words hurt. Yet again, he'd failed to think things all the way through. It was his greatest weakness. Then a thought occurred to Connor.

"But you've already taken on your name, Alexander," he said. "I think in some ways, I'd already lost you. I've grown so much in the last week that a lot of my fears, the fears you've always carried, aren't really my fears anymore. They're yours. And now it's your turn to outgrow them."

"But I'm going to be so alone. First Dad left, then Mother got too busy, and now you..."

Connor shook his head. "I don't think this has to be where we part," he said. "You will always carry parts of me with you, and if a part of me is in the Shadowlands, I don't know for sure why, I think that means I'll always be able to come here."

His shadow perked up. "You'll visit me? You won't leave me here?"

"Of course, I will."

Even as he spoke, a profound tiredness swept over Connor. His vision dimmed a bit, and his eyelids grew heavy. His breath came in deep draughts and sighs, and his muscles dragged him down to the ground.

His mind screamed against the feeling. He couldn't fall asleep. Not yet. He needed to go back to Hallowdell and find his father. There was so much he needed to say to him, so many things to tell him. There was no way he wanted their last meeting to be their goodbye.

Connor tried to drag himself to his feet, but his muscles refused to cooperate. Instead, he completely slumped to the ground. The shadowcat cub nestled its warm, purring body against him and began to lick his cheek. The adults lay on either side, bookending him with their breathing torsos. Connor knew he wouldn't be able to fight the exhaustion. No matter how hard he tried to keep them open, his eyelids drooped lower and lower. The last thing he saw before they closed was the shadow sun reflecting off the pool to the roar of the waterfall.

When Connor awoke, he was in bed. He lurched upright. How had he gotten back? Wasn't it supposed to be difficult to leave the Shadowlands with your whole shadow? The questions raced for a moment, but he was so warm and comfortable under his covers that none of it seemed important. There would be time to worry about questions later. The sun, bright and in a clear sky, poured through his window onto the form of his sleeping mother in the chair beside his bed. Her journal rested on the bedside table beside her.

"Mom?" he whispered.

Her eyelids fluttered, then half opened. She smiled at Connor when she saw his face. She raised one finger to her lips and said, "Shh."

She got up from the chair and lay in the bed beside him, wrapping her arm over him and kissing him on the cheek. She rested her head on the pillow next to his and began to sing softly. Connor knew there was no need to say anything. He wanted to tell her about what had happened but now was not the time. He also knew there were parts he'd keep to himself. She carried enough burdens, after all.

Instead, Connor simply closed his eyes and enjoyed the fact that he could feel the full warmth and comfort of his mother's love. Slowly, he fell back asleep.

Sometime later, the phone rang. Groggily, his mother shuffled her way to the kitchen phone. She was only gone a couple of moments before she returned.

"It's for you," she said with a funny smile. "A girl. Says her name is Lily."

THANKS

First and foremost, I must thank Joe Mynhardt and Crystal Lake Publishing for giving The Shadowlands the chance to appear in a second edition. Though I have work out through other presses, Crystal Lake included, I was heartbroken when I learned Neverborn's original publisher, Olive Ridley Press, was going to be shuttering its doors. I'm eternally grateful to Tim McWhorter for giving this dark adventure a chance in the world and the work he did in promoting it. Now, Neverborn is set to reach readers again, albeit it with a slightly older Connor and a slightly darker Shadowlands.

Next, I must thank my children Gillian and Elliott. The main reason I wrote the original draft of this book was in the hopes they might grow up enjoying it. It's really exciting to me to have a manuscript that might bring a little bit of joy into my children's lives.

Thanks, too, to my wife, Amber. She's always been my first and best reader, and she was the first reader of *The Neverborn Thief* back in its early days. Her feedback and opinions are always crucial in developing my work, and there are many parts of the final draft that I owe to her insights.

An additional thanks goes to my friend Chris Pell and his daughter Faith. Faith was the first target audience test reader for this book, and I found her feedback and observations to be immensely useful.

Of course, I also have to thank the rest of my family—Mom, Dad, Tiffany, Uncle Andy—they've all supported my work in different ways, reading drafts and parts of drafts, offering encouragement. Sometimes, even just asking about news can make a big difference in a writer's motivation.

Beyond that, I also need to thank the various friends who have helped along the way. Blaine, Jon, MJ, Andrew, Will, Angel, Tyler, Alex, Rick, Earl, Christian, Kris, Dana, Curt, Matt, Kevin, Michael, James, Travis, and everyone else whose names are flitting by me right now and not getting caught.

ABOUT THE AUTHOR

Andrew Najberg is a Tennessee author, teacher, husband, and father who wrote *The Mobius Door* (Wicked House Publishing, 2023), Gollitok (Wicked House Publishing, 2023), *The Neverborn Thief* (Olive-Ridley Press, 2024), *In Those Fading Stars* (Crystal Lake Publishing, 2024), *Try Not to Die in the Shadowlands* (Vincere Press, 2024), *Paradise Falls* (Wicked House Publishing, 2025), and *Extinction Dream* (Wicked House Publishing). He is also the author of the collections of poems *The Goats Have Taken Over the Barracks* (Finishing Line Press, 2021) and *Fighting Fermi* (Walnut Street Press, 2024).

Currently, he teaches for the University of Tennessee at Chattanooga where he has been a full-time member of the English department for seventeen years, teaching creative writing, rhetoric and composition, and Japanese literature. In his spare time, he loves to read, draw, play board games and video games with his kids, and watch horror and science-fiction movies. When he can, he tends his vegetable garden as best he can and dreams of travelling abroad with his family. He is working on two additional novels and plans for a potential sequel to *The Neverborn Thief*.

Readers…

Thank you for reading *The Neverborn Thief*. We hope you enjoyed this novel. If you have a moment, please review *The Neverborn Thief* at the store where you bought it.

Help other readers by telling them why you enjoyed this book. No need to write an in-depth discussion. Even a single sentence will be greatly appreciated. Reviews go a long way to helping a book sell, and is great for an author's career. It'll also help us to continue publishing quality books.

Thank you again for taking the time to journey with Crystal Lake's Crystal Cove Press.

You will find links to all our social media platforms on our Linktree page: https://linktr.ee/CrystalCovePress.

MISSION STATEMENT

Since its founding in August 2012, Crystal Lake has quickly become one of the world's leading publishers of Dark Fiction and Horror books. In 2023, Crystal Lake officially transitioned into an entertainment company, joining several other divisions, genres, and imprints, including Torrid Waters, Crystal Lake Comics, Crystal Lake Games, Crystal Lake Kids, and many more.

While we strive to present only the highest quality fiction and entertainment, we also endeavour to support authors along their writing journey. We offer our time and experience in non-fiction projects, as well as author mentoring and services, at competitive prices.

With several Bram Stoker Award wins and many other wins and nominations (including the HWA's Specialty Press Award), Crystal Lake Publishing puts integrity, honor, and respect at the forefront of our publishing operations. We strive for each book and outreach program we spearhead to not only entertain and touch or comment on issues that affect our readers, but also to strengthen and support the Dark Fiction field and its authors.

Not only do we find and publish authors we believe are destined for greatness, but we strive to work with men and women who endeavour to be decent human beings who care more for others than themselves, while still being hard working, driven, and passionate artists and storytellers.

Crystal Lake Publishing is and will always be a beacon of what passion and dedication, combined with overwhelming teamwork and respect, can accomplish. We endeavour to know each and every one of our readers, while building personal relationships with our authors, reviewers, bloggers, podcasters, bookstores, and libraries.

We will be as trustworthy, forthright, and transparent as any business can be, while also keeping most of the headaches away from our authors, since it's our job to solve the problems so they can stay in a creative mind. Which of course also means paying our authors.

We do not just publish books, we present to you worlds within your world, doors within your mind, from talented authors who sacrifice so much for a moment of your time. There are some amazing small presses out there, and through collaboration and open forums we will continue to support other presses in the goal of helping authors and showing the world what quality small presses are capable of accomplishing. No one wins when a small press goes down, so we will always be there to support hardworking, legitimate presses and their authors.

We don't see Crystal Lake as the best press out there, but we will always strive to be the best, strive to be the most interactive and grateful, and even blessed press around. No matter what happens over time, we will also take our mission very seriously while appreciating where we are and enjoying the journey.

What do we offer our authors that they can't do for themselves through self-publishing?

We are big supporters of self-publishing (especially hybrid publishing), if done with care, patience, and planning. However, not every author has the time or inclination to do market research, advertise, and set up book launch strategies. Although a lot of authors are successful in doing it all, strong small presses will always be there for the authors who just want to do what they do best: write.

What we offer is experience, industry knowledge, contacts and trust built up over years. And due to our strong brand and trusting fanbase, every Crystal Lake Publishing book comes with weight of respect. In time our fans begin to trust our judgment and will try a new author purely based on our support of said author.

With each launch we strive to fine-tune our approach, learn from our mistakes, and increase our reach. We continue to assure our authors that we're here for them and that we'll carry the weight of the launch and dealing with third parties while they focus on their strengths—be it writing, interviews, blogs, signings, etc.

We also offer several mentoring packages to authors that include knowledge and skills they can use in both traditional and self-publishing endeavours.

We look forward to launching many new careers.

This is what we believe in. What we stand for. This will be our legacy.

Welcome to Crystal Lake Publishing—Where Stories Come Alive!

THANK YOU
FOR
PURCHASING
THIS BOOK

www.ingramcontent.com/pod-product-compliance
Lightning Source LLC
Chambersburg PA
CBHW070442300726
48975CB00007B/2011